PRAISE FOR GLENN MEADE'S NOVELS

BRANDENBURG

"THIS THRILLER DELIVERS THE GOODS—TEN-
SION, ACTION, PLOT TWISTS—UNTIL THE SMOKE
CLEARS ON THE LAST PAGE."

—Booklist

"AN OUTSTANDING PREMISE... [MEADE] SPINS
OUT THIS INVOLVING YARN WITH SKILL AND
CLARITY."

—Publishers Weekly

"ONE OF THE BEST THRILLERS I'VE READ THIS
YEAR. IT HAS ALL THE SIGNS OF A BEST-SELLER.
FIRST CLASS PLOT, CREDIBLE CHARACTERS AND
DIALOGUE, AND EXOTIC SETTINGS—DEFINITELY
A WINNER."

—Ted Allbeury, author of *The Long Run*

"TERRIFIC ENTERTAINMENT, A PAGE-TURNER IN
THE BEST TRADITION OF THRILLERS. IT'S ALSO
UNSETTLINGLY PLAUSIBLE."

—Campbell Armstrong, author of *Jigsaw*

More . . .

SNOW WOLF

*St. Martin's Paperbacks titles
by Glenn Meade*

SNOW WOLF
BRANDENBURG

BRANDENBURG

GLENN MEADE

St. Martin's Paperbacks

Originally published by Hodder & Stoughton in Great Britain.

BRANDENBURG

Library of Congress Catalog Card Number: 96-54630

ISBN: 0-312-96525-7

Printed in the United States of America

St. Martin's Press hardcover edition/June 1997
St. Martin's Paperbacks edition/May 1998

10 9 8 7 6 5 4 3 2 1

To my parents, Tom and Carmel

ACKNOWLEDGMENTS

To all those in Europe and South America who gave their assistance in the researching of this book, my sincere thanks. In particular, I would like to acknowledge the following:

In Berlin: the staff of the Berlin Document Center, U.S. Mission, especially Director David Marwell and Dr. Richard Campbell who allowed me access to their original files; Axel Wiglinsky, Acting Director, Reichstag Security; Dr. Bose and Hans-Christopa Bonfert of the Berlin *Senatsverwaltung für Inneres* (Administrative Council for the Interior); the Berlin *Landsamt für Verfassungsschutz* (Office for the Protection of the Constitution); the staff of the *Wehrmacht Auskunftselle* (WASt.).

In Vienna: the administration staff of the Vienna Central Cemetery.

In Strasbourg: Jean-Paul Chauvet.

In Paraguay: Carlos Da Rosa.

Also, I would like to thank Janet Donohue, and Professor Jim Jackson, of Trinity College, Dublin.

There are others, in Europe and South America, who gave their assistance but who wish to remain anonymous; to them, my gratitude. At Hodder and Stoughton, my thanks go to my editor, George Lucas, for his professionalism, boundless enthusiasm, and commitment to this book. And to Bill Massey for his very insightful and invaluable advice.

"So we beat on, boats against the current, borne back ceaselessly into the past."

F. Scott Fitzgerald,
The Great Gatsby

PROLOGUE

Northeastern Chaco, Paraguay. November 21

Darkness had long descended as the tall, silver-haired man sat in the cane chair on the veranda. He wore a fresh white shirt open at the neck beneath his pale, linen jacket; his light cotton pants were pressed.

Beyond the wooden veranda, the rain fell in heavy sheets. A light was on overhead, moths buzzing around the shade. The man's silver hair shone under the light, and his tanned, handsome features looked sallow.

A boy served him iced lemon tea from a teak tray. He watched as the boy added two spoonfuls of sugar to the glass, then he turned his face to the nearby verge of the jungle. He saw the dark mass of the lush green forest beyond the downpour, the thick stems of bamboo and the fragrant mango trees.

He stared out at the torrential downpour, at the tangle of jade-green jungle plants, obscure in the gardens beyond the sheet of water.

Footsteps echoed on the wooden floorboards in the hallway and he saw Kruger appear moments later, smoking a cigarette. The security chief wore a gray sweater, the sleeves pulled up to reveal the thick black hair of his muscular arms. He sat in the cane chair opposite, a paper in his hand.

The silver-haired man turned to the servant boy and said, smiling, "Leave us, please, Emilio."

The man's voice was gentle and polite, and the nut-brown face of the young boy smiled back at him. "Sí, Señor."

He lifted the sweet lemon tea to his lips, sipped the refreshing liquid. Then he looked at Kruger, the man's stocky frame creaking the cane chair. An insect crawled across the table. Kruger flicked it away.

"A fax from Meyer," he said, waving the paper, "confirming for the twenty-fifth."

"So everything is going according to schedule?"

"Everything," Kruger said. "We meet Meyer in Asunción. Tsarkin has arranged for a suite in the Excelsior."

"Good," the silver-haired man nodded.

"And we leave here on the sixth. That's also confirmed. As is the stopover in Mexico City with Halder."

The elderly man nodded again. He was speaking softly, but his voice was compelling and Kruger listened respectfully.

"Before we leave, I want everything in this house destroyed. Everything we are not taking must be burned. Nothing must be left. As if we had never existed. You will see to it, Hans."

Kruger inflected his head in reply.

"Thank you, Hans."

The security chief stood and left quickly, his footsteps echoing on the wooden floorboards.

The silver-haired man remained seated, watched as Kruger crossed the veranda, stepped inside the house.

Alone now, he stared up at the rain forest beyond the sheeting wall of water. He hesitated, then slowly removed his wallet from the inside pocket of his linen jacket and took out a photograph. The grainy print showed a blond young woman and a dark-haired man.

He stared at the photograph for quite some time, meditatively. Then he slipped it once again into his wallet and took another sip of tea.

PART ONE

CHAPTER 1

It was Sally Thornton's last night in Strasbourg; she wanted to sleep with him.

It was raining hard as they came out of the restaurant near the opera, and when Joe Volkmann hailed them a taxi to take them back to his apartment, she knew she was going to stay the night. Men didn't ask a girl back for a drink and then send her home in a taxi. Especially not on a rain-soaked night. At least not the men she'd known. And liked.

She wore an emerald-green blouse that hugged her slim figure and matched her eyes. Her skirt was grayish green and tight, and her legs were sheathed in darker gray-patterned stockings. She knew she had a shape that most women would kill for. Generous, firm breasts and slim hips. But she wasn't quick to give her sexual favors. Nor was she looking for a long-term relationship (but she wouldn't turn one down if it came her way). But she simply wanted to like a man she took to bed. Though she knew little about Joe Volkmann, she liked him very much.

Sally had been in the intelligence services for five years since Oxford, and she had just finished a six-week temporary posting at DSE—*Direction de Sécurité Européene*—which had been created eighteen months ago by the European Union. The intent had been to form a European equivalent of the FBI in the U.S., or Britain's MI5, with investigation and enforcement powers that crossed national frontiers. In practice, DSE didn't quite live up to that intent. Despite the European Union, nationalism had not withered away. And there were other, more immediate problems. Still, her time in Strasbourg had been fascinating. But now it was time to go home, a week's leave in London before her posting to New York.

During the six weeks at DSE, Joe Volkmann had been her teacher and mentor. He had been friendly and warm, intense at work, yet reticent personally. He kept his distance, and she appreciated this. She had had an experience or two when work and personal lives had mixed disastrously. So today when he offered to help her pack, she was a little surprised, but she knew the offer was genuine and not a come-on.

He'd spent the afternoon in the apartment she'd sublet in Petite France, helping her fill the wooden packing crates with the Denon stereo equipment and the small items of antique furniture she'd bought. When she suggested a meal to repay him, he countered with tickets to the opera and dinner afterward.

The opera was *The Magic Flute*, music she loved. As she watched him throughout the performance, she saw that he listened to it attentively. And though he smiled at her a lot, and the evening had a romantic flavor, he didn't try to make a pass or to put his hand up her skirt or rub her up. That kind of activity was a specialty of the Italians if you ventured near their offices on the fourth floor.

Despite his reticence, he was far from cold. She got the feeling that he didn't push things; so the man was a challenge. That was one of the reasons she wanted him now.

His apartment on the Quai Ernest was on the first floor, and the balcony entrance overlooked a tiny, paved courtyard. It was a small, two-bedroom affair, and he kept it pretty neat for a guy. There was a TV in a corner, as well as a Linn hi-fi. There were also several hardcover books and paperbacks, and lots of CDs. Most of these were classical, but she saw some jazz and rock, and there were modern composers too, like Henze and Schnitke. Names she'd heard of, but whose music was unfamiliar to her. On shelves above the hi-fi there were photographs in frames, and more books.

He let her spend some time browsing. Then he said, "I like to see what other people read, too. It says a lot about them."

"Yes, doesn't it?" she agreed. "And their music."

"And their music." He moved past her and switched on the hi-fi. Choosing a disc, he inserted it into the CD player. Edith Piaf, Sally soon noted with approval. "What would you like to drink, Sally?"

She went to sit on the couch and crossed her long legs. She saw him look at them briefly, and she smiled to herself and said, "How about scotch?"

"A girl after my own heart," he smiled.

"With ice, and a splash of water," she added, echoing his smile.

She watched him go into the kitchen. He was tall, dark-haired, and well-built—not handsome in a conventional way, but he was attractive. And he looked more French than British. He was thirty-seven, though he looked younger. And he had something, only Sally Thornton couldn't figure out what. Something in the intensity—which carried over from his work, she couldn't help but notice. Something in the sensitive brown eyes, the same eyes she had seen in the woman in one of the photographs on the shelf.

He looked like the kind of guy who could protect a woman. . . . But then, all the men she worked with looked like that—trained soldiers and intelligence officers and hard-nosed narcotics specialists masquerading as police-men. And besides, she could look after herself, thank you very much.

She figured maybe what it was. Here was a man she could trust. He was a hard man, but he didn't come on hard. Certainly where she was concerned, his forcefulness was the last thing she had to think about. And his smile gave him away . . . he was vulnerable, she was convinced, under the detached, distant exterior.

He came back into the room carrying her glass and a darker version of the same for himself. He handed her the glass and sat across the couch from her. He had taken off his tie, and his shirt was open at the neck. She thought he looked more relaxed than she had ever seen him before.

As he sipped his scotch, he let his eyes fall on her and she was conscious of his stare—and of his gentle, unthreatening smile. In the background, Edith Piaf was singing *"Je ne regrette rien."* The rain beat on the window and she returned Volkmann's gaze.

"You're going to miss me, Joe?"

"Sure. There's a lot to miss."

"Then why are you smiling?"

"Because they're going to love you in New York."

"Who? The people at the embassy?"

"Those, too. But I mean the Americans. The men will
be beating down your door, Sally."

"Why, thank you for the compliment." She smiled,
pleased. "You'll come visit me sometimes?"

"If you like."

She smiled again, swirled her glass, and he went silent
for a time, thinking. After a long silence, he said, "You're
better off over there, Sally. Things are going bad in Europe,
and I think they'll get worse before they turn better." Then
he glanced at his watch. "Do you mind?" he asked. Before
she could answer, he walked over to the hi-fi and turned it
down. Then he switched on the TV. "The late news," he
said by way of explanation. "It's a professional vice."

"Go ahead," she sighed with a rueful grin. "It's my
profession, too. And my vice."

The news was indeed discouraging. The economic downturn was in its third year. Unemployment was over twenty
percent. Business failures kept mounting—solid companies,
companies you'd have thought would never fail. And in
Germany, where the East was never successfully integrated,
the downturn was worse than in the other nations of the
EU. Angry mobs rampaged through the streets. Except that
the images were in color, the scenes were very like those
seventy years before. And they both recognized that.

Joe rose and turned off the set. "You're better off in the
States, Sally," he repeated.

She didn't speak.

"But I'm sorry I waited this long to get to know you."

"Yes," she said. "Me too." Then she asked, "It's not
starting over, is it?"

They both knew what "it" was.

"I don't think history repeats itself. Christ," he added,
"I hope not. Especially not in Germany."

"Come visit me. Do that, please." She took a long sip
from her glass. "Meanwhile, Joe, I want you to tell me
about yourself."

"Where can I start?" he smiled, visibly relieved to be
on a more cheerful subject.

She shrugged. "Anywhere. I've worked closely with you
for six weeks and I hardly know a thing about you. How
long have you been in DSE?"

"Eighteen months."

"You like working in Europe?"

"Sure." And then, remembering the subject they'd just left, he added, "The problems are fascinating here. I like solving problems, don't you? That's one reason I'm in the profession. I'm easily bored."

She nodded assent.

"And before that?"

"SIS."

She uncrossed her legs and stretched them. He let his eyes fall on them appreciatively. "Were you ever married, Joe?"

He shrugged and sipped his scotch. "Divorced. No kids."

"And your folks?"

She glanced up at the photographs on the shelf. There were two of a couple and a young boy, one taken outside a pretty stone cottage and another on a beach. The boy was obviously Volkmann, about fourteen, and the couple were surely his parents. There was another of the boy and his father, a distinguished but sickly looking man in a heavy overcoat. They were standing near the cottage; the beach was down a long slope below. Yet another photograph showed just the mother. She was sitting at a piano in some great hall, a striking-looking woman, with great dignity and tremendous reserve—like her son. She was smiling. Sally guessed that Joe got his smile from her, as well as the eyes.

Then it came to her. "She's *that* Volkmann, isn't she? The pianist? Is she your mother? She hasn't played in years. Whatever happened to her?"

"Yes, she's *that* Volkmann. And yes, she's my mother. And yes, she doesn't play any longer. Arthritis crippled her hands. But she still does some teaching."

"And the photo was taken at Carnegie Hall, wasn't it?"

"You have a good eye," he said.

"I remember things." She smiled, then inclined her head toward the photo of Joe's mother. "She was a magnificent pianist. I loved her Schubert."

"I have all the recordings. Maybe I'll play some for you later."

"Yes, do," she said, then went on. "And your father?"

"He died six months ago."

"I'm sorry."

"Yeah, thanks," he said, almost inaudibly. "He was a good man."

"I don't think you took after him," she said, staring at the other photo. "He looks a bit otherworldly."

"You could say that," Joe chuckled. "He was an academic . . . a college professor. I've chosen a more active life."

"And you chose not to follow your mother, too?"

"No talent," he sighed.

"But you wish . . . ?" she asked softly.

"Sometimes I have regrets," he agreed. Then he changed the subject, leaning slightly toward her. "And you, Sally, do you like the active life? Are you looking forward to New York?"

"I don't know if you could call what I do active," she answered. "But yes, I like the States. God knows, Joe, we have nothing to hide from the Americans, or they from us. It's just liaison. But it's a good posting, and the expenses are great. Still, it's a bit of a waste having me there. The ambassador learns more in a week over lunch than our people do in a year."

He looked hard at her. "I got a call from Dick Wolsey in London the other day." There was heavy concern in his voice. "He claims the Germans and the French are trying to pull out of this operation."

"You mean out of DSE?"

He nodded and took a long swallow of scotch.

"They'd be crazy to do that. If they do, all of DSE will come tumbling down, and bang goes security cooperation."

"Did you hear any rumors?"

Sally shrugged and played with the top button of her blouse. "We've all heard the rumors, Joe. Wolsey will have heard them too—that it's all a waste of taxpayers' money. Everybody's in trouble financially. You see the same news that I do." She gestured toward the television set. "The Germans, the French, us. As long as the stock market makes dying noises, they have the frights. And when nations get the frights, watch out, it's each for themself."

"Did you hear Ferguson say if he's heard any rumors?"

Joe asked. Ferguson was head of the British section of DSE.

Sally Thornton smiled. "I hardly talk to the man. He's so bloody stuffy."

Volkmann laughed. "What about Peters?" Peters was Ferguson's Number Two.

"All Peters tells me is that I have good legs and he'd like to take me to bed." She paused, saw Volkmann glance at her legs again. "And that you're a terrific intelligence officer." She looked at him. "Do we have to talk about work?"

"Not at all."

She saw him notice her legs again, and she said, "Can I ask you a very personal question, Joe?"

"How personal?"

"Why didn't you ever come onto me?"

He let his eyes catch hers. "I like you, Sally. A lot. But I don't like to rush things. And I don't like to mix bed and work. My life is messy enough already."

"You're a very sensitive man, Joe Volkmann. Did you know that?"

His gaze remained on her, but he didn't say anything.

"Would you like to take me to bed?"

When Volkmann smiled, she smiled back and put down her glass. "My plane leaves at three," she said. "And yours?"

"Two-thirty," he said. He was flying over to London tomorrow to visit his mother in Surrey.

Sally was sleeping quietly beside him, nestled against him, but Volkmann was still awake, his back propped against a bunched-up pillow. . . .

They walked along the deserted Cornish beach together. It was November; the beach grasses were yellowed and dry. Waves swept up the sand, rattling the larger pebbles as they receded.

He had come down from the weapons course in Scotland for the weekend. The sun was shining and the sky pale and blue—one of those perfect days in autumn when the air is crisp and clear and it feels good to breathe. His father, frailer than ever, was wrapped in the tattered old tweed

*overcoat that always looked a size too big for him. They
sat on a driftwood log and the old man looked at him with
watery brown eyes.*

"Mama tells me they're sending you to Berlin."

*He saw the dark look on his father's face. Berlin brought
back bad memories.*

"It's a good posting, Papa. And with luck, I'll get home
once a month, so it won't be so bad."

"Is it dangerous?"

He smiled. "No, Papa. Not dangerous. It's intelligence
gathering mostly. Nothing for you to worry about. They're
not going to send me over the Wall with gun and camera."

"Mama said you went there last month."

"For three days, just to see the operation. I think they
were trying to find out if I really wanted the posting."

"And did you?"

He shrugged. "It's a change from Century House."

"And Anna?"

"She'll join me in a couple of months."

"What's it like now?"

"Berlin? Exciting. Full of energy. A little like New York,
but on a smaller scale. Good restaurants and lots of night-
life, if that's where your interests lie. Very international.
Very cosmopolitan. Not like the old days . . . not like sixty
years ago."

*He saw the old man look away toward the waves, his
face drawn as if troubled by some private thought. Joseph
Volkmann recognized the look, recognized the pain. The old
man stood, glanced at his watch, cut off the pain before it
took hold. He had had plenty of practice doing that.*

"Your mama will have lunch ready. We better not keep
her waiting."

"Papa."

*His father looked down at him, and Joseph Volkmann
was aware of the pink circle of rutted flesh on the frail
man's temple, the wound indelible and permanent. The
ones inside were not visible, but they were no less permanent.*

He said quietly, staring at the scar, "It's all in the past,
Papa. A long time ago. But sometimes I want you to talk
about it. Maybe it would help."

His father shook his head. "Believe me, Joseph, talking about it does not help. I tried to talk for twenty years and learned that it's much better to forget." The brown eyes looked down at him. "You'll learn that as you grow older, Joseph. Bury ghosts if you can. Don't let them live. Now come, let's not keep Mama waiting."

He watched as the old man moved away, the bony, hunched body lost in the heavy tweed overcoat.

He stood and followed his father.

The boy, Joe's father, was fourteen. The girls, the boy's sisters, were eight and ten. Drunken SS guards made them stand in front of a shallow pit, half-filled with the already murdered. While the boy watched, the guards stripped and raped the girls, then shot them and threw them into the pit. After that, they forced the boy to kneel down; an SS captain shot him in the face, and then they threw him on top of his sisters. The boy was terribly wounded. But the captain had been too drunk to aim properly. The boy waited, lying among the dead. Waited while the guards tossed dirt on top of the bodies. Waited until it was dark and the guards were gone.

CHAPTER 2

Asunción, Paraguay. November 23

Rudi Hernandez waited while the girl checked in at the desk, watching her figure appreciatively as he smoked a cigarette. The airport was busy, crowded with midday passengers, but his eyes were fixed firmly on the girl, wishing she were not his cousin.

He told himself, *Hey, remember who she is.*

But he couldn't help it, enjoying the view of the girl's long, silky, suntanned legs and the perfectly shaped hips and thighs that filled out the creamy-white summer skirt. Her blond hair was cut short, and it complemented her pretty face, her fine cheekbones.

The view was exquisite, and he smiled to himself. It was the Latin in him. He liked women. And he especially liked Erica.

It wasn't just her looks, of course. She was smart, very smart, a damned good journalist for one so young—twenty-five, five years younger than he was. *Maybe she's even a better journalist than I am*, he reflected. *I'm a reporter. That's it. I find stories. But she can write! She'll do books someday, just you watch*, he thought, proud of her.

But it wasn't just that she was smart. She was also a very fine person, both sensible and sensitive—wise beyond her years.

Why does she have to be my cousin? he sighed inwardly. If it weren't for their blood ties, he knew he'd have rushed over to her, torn up her tickets and taken her in his arms.

She turned and smiled at him, her business complete as she gathered up passport and tickets and picked up her carry luggage from the desk. She crossed to where he stood as he ground out his cigarette on the marble floor.

He smiled back. "Everything okay?"

Erica nodded. "I board in twenty-five minutes. We have time for a coffee." Her hand found his arm; her eyes were glistening. "I'll miss you, Rudi. It's a long way—and a long time—between visits."

"Yeah, I know. I'll miss you too, Erica."

He took her carry luggage and led her across the concourse to the small restaurant lounge. He found a vacant table and ordered two coffees and two brandies. As they chatted about little things, his mind went back to the day they had spent in the mountains, up in the rain forest near the border with Brazil, the day they had taken the guided tour. Magnificent country, a splendid day. And she was so relaxed, so easy to be with. *And my cousin. Damn!*

When the waiter brought their drinks, Erica took a sip of brandy and caught his eyes.

"I'm worried about you, Rudi. I'm worried about the story."

So am I, Rudi thought. *But I can't tell you that.*

One good thing about her departure was that it took his mind—at least momentarily—off of the story. It was a big one, all his reporter's instincts pointed that way. And it had many complex strands—leading only God knew where. Perhaps it would turn out to be the biggest story he'd worked on. And it was dangerous . . . one man was already dead, murdered. The bad thing about her departure—the *other* bad thing—was that he would have loved for Erica to work alongside of him. Her brains would have come in handy.

"I want you to promise me you'll be careful," she went on. "Promise me that?"

He smiled easily, letting his gaze rest on hers. "I'm always careful. You know that."

"Bullshit." She smiled ruefully, with a shake of her head.

With her fair skin and light hair, she looked so different from the South American women, the dark-skinned women in the *barrios*, and the contrast had turned heads. The Indian woman selling flowers on Calle Estrella had asked to touch her blond hair, saying it would bring her luck. "She is beautiful," the old woman had smiled as she stroked Erica's hair and looked at Rudi. "She will bring us both luck. Believe me."

And when the Latin men stared at her, he knew what they were thinking, and he didn't blame them.

He saw her look of concern.

"There's not much of a story, Erica. Not yet. Maybe it will turn into something big—"

"You know it will," she interrupted. "You know it and I know it. My thumbs are tingling, Rudi. When my thumbs tingle," she smiled, "well, believe them."

"That may be. I do trust your thumbs," he grinned. "But so far, I don't have much. Really very little." He shrugged. "Only what Rodriguez has told me. And the photographs."

"But the photos connect Rodriguez with that man Tsarkin—a very wealthy man. And my old school friend Dieter Winter." There was an ironic edge to her voice when she mentioned the last name. "And through them, the story leads to Europe. It's not local, Rudi, whatever it is. The lines go far." Her eyes clouded for a moment. "It's probably drugs," she said . . . which was what she had said the first time he told her about Rodriguez. "But it could be something else, too."

"We'll see," he said quietly, catching her thoughtful mood.

He remembered Rodriguez'-brown body, lying on the cold metal table in the mortuary of the city hospital, the feeling of nausea when the attendant pulled back the white sheet and he had stared at the man's pulped, bloodied flesh. He suppressed the shudder of fear he felt inside and leaned closer, breathing in the sweet scent of her perfume as though it were a refuge.

"But," Rudi said, "so far, we have no idea of where the lines go. I don't have any further leads. So far, Erica, there's no story. Just suggestions. Hints."

"And a dead man."

"And a dead man," he agreed.

"So you'll be careful." She looked hard at him, her face filled with concern.

"I promise."

Erica sipped her brandy, held the glass tensely in both hands. "What about the men who killed Rodriguez?"

"What about them?"

"Won't they come looking for you? Won't they be afraid you'll tell the police?"

Hernandez smiled, seeing her fear, trying to sound unafraid, trying to reassure her. "No chance. For one thing, they don't know me, they've never seen me. They don't know I exist."

"But what happens once the story breaks?"

Rudi took a sip of coffee; it was bitter, and growing cold. He grimaced, pushed the cup aside. "Look, I'm a reporter. We'll have to burn that bridge when we cross it . . . if there's a story," he added. "And besides, I have one or two friends—*policía*—who'll protect me if I need protection. You remember Sanchez."

She nodded. Sanchez was a detective captain in the *policía*. "Too bad he and I didn't meet."

"A good man," Rudi said. "Next time . . ."

Meanwhile, the girl saw him reach into his pocket, take out a bunch of keys. He played with them idly.

Rudi Hernandez was a handsome man. His brown hair, cut in a boyish fringe, made him look younger than his years. He smiled easily, as if life were constantly fun, constantly amusing. Even the noticeable scar that ran jaggedly across his right cheek was not unbecoming. It gave him an almost dashing, swashbuckling appearance. He toyed with the keys, watching her watch them, slipping them between his fingers.

He smiled at her. "Like I told you last night, everything solid I have on these people is in a safe place. So don't worry, Erica, I'll be okay."

She smiled back. Her hand moved to touch his, and he slipped the keys back in his pocket.

"Be sure you are," she said. "You're a good man, Rudi, and I care about you. I want you to be here the next time I come."

A loudspeaker announced her flight.

He walked with her to the departure gate, carrying her hand luggage. As they stopped at the security gate, he handed across her bag. "Give my love to everyone."

"I will."

She moved up to him to kiss his cheek. "*Auf Wiedersehen*, Rudi."

"*Auf Wiedersehen*, Erica. Have a pleasant flight."

He watched her pass the security gate. On the other side,

she turned and waved. He waved back before she disappeared from view.

He heard the public-address system crackle to life again, a shrill, metallic voice filling the terminal.

"Señor Rudi Hernandez, please come to the information desk. Señor Rudi Hernandez to the information desk, please."

The girl at the desk handed him the message. A telephone number was written on the slip of paper. There was no name. He found a telephone booth and dialed the number. After four rings, there was an answer.

"*Sí?*" a male voice said.

"This is Rudi Hernandez. Someone at this number left me a message to call."

"Yes, Señor Hernandez, one moment please." It was more like three minutes before a second voice came on the wire. This one Rudi recognized.

"Rudi, my friend." It was Captain Vellares Sanchez. "I only have a moment."

"So what's happening?" Rudi asked quickly, not wasting time on a greeting. They were close friends; they didn't need to oil the social gears.

"This is off the record, my friend, but one good turn deserves another." There was a pause, and then he went on. "Do you remember the man you suggested I keep my eye on?"

"Tsarkin?"

"Nicolas Tsarkin, yes, that man."

"What about him?"

"I'm up on Calle Iguazu. Number Twenty-three." That was Tsarkin's address, in the city's wealthiest suburb. "Perhaps you'd like to join me."

"So what's happening?" Rudi asked again, with swiftly growing excitement. He had been there, parked across the street, watching. Watching because Rodriguez had told him to. Watching and taking photographs of the big house with the white walls where the old man Tsarkin lived, the old man Rodriguez had told him to watch.

"Tsarkin's dead, Rudi," Sanchez said. "Suicide."

"Santa Maria," Rudi said. "I'll be right up. Give me twenty minutes."

"I'll see you here, Rudi."

Jesus, Hernandez thought. *First Rodriguez, now Tsarkin. Both dead.*

CHAPTER 3

A high wall surrounded the perimeter of the property, but Hernandez could see the expansive, sun-washed lawns as he drove up toward the hill, the house itself barely visible beyond the pepper and palm trees that lined the long driveway beyond the walls.

House was not the word: the property was a large estate. The house itself stood on a hill overlooking the city, large, two stories high, the bland, gray-painted exterior imposing but not inviting attention.

He noticed that the wrought-iron front gates were open, was about to drive the rusting old red Buick through when he saw the young *policía* step forward from behind the cover of the wall, hands dug into the leather belt that held his holstered pistol.

He was very young, in his early twenties, fresh-faced, and his uniform fit him badly. He stepped forward and raised his hand for Hernandez to stop. Hernandez hit the brakes abruptly and leaned out of the window, flashed his Press identity card as he smiled, tried to look friendly.

As the young *policía* checked the identity card, stone-faced, Hernandez said, "Nicolas Tsarkin. Old guy. Suicide. I'm here to cover the story for *La Tarde*."

The *policía* nodded. "Yes, Señor Hernandez. I was expecting you. Captain Sanchez left word."

Hernandez looked up at the house in the distance. "Is Vellares up there now?"

"*Sí*, Señor, he is waiting for you." He gestured through the open gate, and Hernandez passed through.

The old guy, Tsarkin, had had money. Lots of it, for sure.

The manicured lawns stretched down from the house for over a hundred meters. Hernandez could make out the house beneath the red, pan-tiled roof. He glanced to the left and right as he drove up the asphalt driveway; beyond the pepper trees there were yellow and pink hibiscus in bloom.

The gardens were something else. Mango trees, peach

trees, a couple of coconut palms, their fronds heavy and limp in the breezeless, hot afternoon air. They were the best-kept gardens he had seen in Asunción.

He kept the old Buick at a slow pace all the way up, taking in the place, remembering how he had wondered what it would look like beyond the white walls that led up from the road below, something telling him there was more to be learned here in this house than what Rodriguez had told him.

Halfway up the hill, the Buick's engine started to groan, racking the old rusted chassis.

Shit!

The big old American Buick was ready for the scrap heap. Twelve years old, a hundred and fifty thousand kilometers on the second engine. It had been a trusty friend for a long time, but he needed a new car badly. He took a little pressure off the accelerator. The car stopped groaning, then started up again after another twenty meters. He was coming around the bend now, seeing the house clearly and unobstructed for the first time: big and expensive-looking.

Thirty meters from where the asphalt driveway became gravel, the Buick gave out, the engine not responding to his foot as he pumped the accelerator hard, the car barely coasting along now, the road still a little uphill. He swung the wheel to the left and pulled over onto the grass verge, slammed the steering wheel with his fist.

Shit! again.

Hernandez switched off the ignition and looked up at the entrance. There was a stern-looking uniformed cop standing beside a blue-and-white car parked on the gravel driveway. Then he saw the big front door of the house open and the familiar bulk of Vellares Sanchez moving out into the sunlight, the hint of a smile on his face.

Hernandez climbed out of the car and waved. Sanchez waved back. Hernandez closed the car door and walked up toward the house.

Vellares Sanchez was forty, a large man who always looked like he needed a good night's sleep, with his dark, hooded eyelids. His thinning black hair was combed across his head in wisps. The white linen suit he wore was crumpled and ill-fitting. Everything about him looked in disarray. But Hernandez knew that the detective's disordered appearance was part of his act. Behind his hooded, sleepy eyes was a sharp, probing intelligence. Rudi Hernandez early on learned not to underestimate Vellares Sanchez.

He was a man of few words but of great warmth. And as Hernandez approached, he held out his hand. His grip was firm, his look curious. But before he got to what was obviously on his mind, he nodded to Hernandez' car.

"What's wrong with that heap of junk?" he asked, smiling.

Hernandez gave him an answering smile. "The choke's been acting up. Floods the engine. It'll be okay once the sun dries it out."

Sanchez listened with only half an ear, examining the young man standing before him. Hernandez was tall, brown-haired, pale-skinned, and handsome. The hair was short, and he was clean-shaven. He wore his clothes loosely, like a lecturer from the *Universidad*. He could have passed for a college teacher were it not for the jagged scar that ran across his right cheek.

They had known each other for ten years. Rudi was a fine reporter, with excellent connections—he knew everyone—and dogged energy. He dug until there was nothing left to dig. Hernandez broke more than one case before the *policía* did. But he was also a good man, and kind. There was a girl he kept in the *barrio*, not for sex—she wasn't his mistress—but because she didn't have everything in the head like other people did, and because she needed help. He gave it without asking for medals.

Hernandez was looking at him now with twinkling eyes, a smile on his face, but something else too. Excitement? Fear? Sanchez took a pack of cigarettes from his pocket and offered one to Hernandez. He lit them both and looked at the young man.

"So, Rudi," he said, "a few days ago you tell me to keep an eye on this man. Now he's dead. Do you have any thoughts?"

Hernandez looked around at the lush gardens, then back at the house. The smile grew broader. "Two thoughts," he said. "You can't take it with you, and money can't buy happiness."

"It sure as hell can't buy good health, my friend," said Sanchez, drawing on his cigarette, coughing.

"That why the old man killed himself, because he was sick?"

"He was sick for sure. But whether or not he killed himself because of that . . . well, we'll have to wait and see. But—" he poked a thick finger in Hernandez' direction— "I'm still waiting. What did you know about Señor Tsarkin that made you curious about him? You said he was connected with your friend Rodriguez, the smuggler. So what was the connection?" He paused. "Except that they are both dead."

"Well, there's a start," Hernandez said under his breath. Then louder, "I don't know, Vellares. I'm working on it. But I'll need some time . . . and some space."

"Right," Sanchez answered. "But you'll let me know when you've got something to tell me?"

"As always," Hernandez answered.

The two men had long ago worked out a modus operandi. There were times when they worked closely together and times when each had to keep a professional distance. This was one of those times. Sanchez also understood that he'd be the first to know when Hernandez had found whatever it was that sent him sniffing around this very rich and now very dead German.

Hernandez reached into the back pocket of his corduroy pants and pulled out a wirebound notepad, searched in his pockets for something to write with. "You mind if I take some notes?"

Sanchez shook his head. "Of course not. Only, my men from the forensic department haven't finished yet."

Hernandez nodded. "How long will they be?"

"They're almost finished."

"You got a pen I could borrow?"

"You still borrowing pens? Reporters are supposed to carry pens."

"I keep losing them. Holes in my pockets," said Hernandez, shrugging a smile.

Sanchez handed a pen to Hernandez. "It was the same

ten years ago, in the courts. How many pens you owe me now? Holes in your head, amigo.''

Sanchez went to turn. "Come inside. When the men finish, you can take a look around.'' There was enthusiasm in his voice now as he ground out his cigarette with the heel of his shoe. "You ought to see the place. This old guy had money to burn.''

"Tell me . . .'' said Hernandez, and followed Sanchez inside.

Hernandez looked around the house in wonder and amazement, but pretending more surprise than he felt, because this was how he imagined a rich man like Tsarkin might live.

The crystal chandelier in the hallway, the sweeping staircase, the dining room with the silver candlesticks and the hand-carved chairs of solid oak, the kitchen that was bigger than his whole apartment. There was a Jacuzzi with gold-plated taps, and a tennis court on the back lawn.

The servants' quarters were near the outdoor swimming pool. There were four servants, Sanchez told him, and three gardeners. They had all left for the afternoon, after Sanchez' men had questioned them.

Sanchez kept the study on the ground floor until last. The forensic men were finishing as they came into the hallway from the kitchen. Sanchez caught one of the men by the arm and took him aside to talk in private. When they had finished, Sanchez crossed back to where Hernandez stood, examining an oil painting of a sleek jaguar in a jungle setting. The painting was unsigned, but not bad. A good amateur, Sanchez thought.

"Well?'' Hernandez asked.

"Suicide,'' said Sanchez. "No question. Another problem less for me to worry about. We have a little time before they remove the body. You want to see Tsarkin?''

Hernandez nodded and Sanchez led the way.

The door into the study was open, the room large, like all the others. The first thing Hernandez noticed was the painting in a gilded frame swung back on hinges to reveal a safe in the wall, its gray metal door ajar. There were books on shelves along three walls. Hernandez looked around the room but couldn't see the body. His eyes went back to the safe just as Sanchez pointed toward the window.

"He's over there, behind the desk."

Hernandez crossed to the big polished desk and looked over, saw the trousered legs of the man first, then the pools of blood on the gray carpet. The man's head was covered with a bloodied white handkerchief. Hernandez suppressed the nausea he felt in the pit of his stomach and knelt down for a closer look.

"It's not pleasant. He shot himself through the mouth," Sanchez said.

Hernandez nodded. The handkerchief was soaked through in sticky, congealing blood. As he pulled back the material, he felt the congealing blood come unstuck from the dead man's face. He nearly vomited.

The face itself was almost unrecognizable above the mouth, the shattered jaw set in a final, contorted grimace, as if the dead man had feared the last moment before the gun had exploded and the bullet penetrated the roof of the mouth, shattering the cranium. The old man's wrinkled claw of a hand was raised and crooked, as if he were waving a grotesque good-bye.

Hernandez let the bloodied handkerchief fall back into place and stood up, seeing the gun then, big and frightening on the gray carpet a yard away.

Sanchez looked across at him. "You okay?"

Hernandez swallowed. "Sure."

"It must have been quick. No pain. Not the worst way to go, amigo."

Hernandez nodded.

"How much do you know about him?" Sanchez asked, walking over to sit in a comfortable leather chair beside the coffee table.

"Not much. No family. Retired businessman. Owned a number of businesses, import-export mainly. German, immigrated after the war. Made very little impact in this country, despite his wealth. Except for that, you'd hardly know he was here."

"You know about what I do about this man, Rudi," Sanchez observed. "He was a cipher. No religion, no charities, no notable vices. He just made money. Interesting."

"Do you know how old he was?" Rudi asked, notebook open, pad ready.

"Late seventies. I'm not sure exactly." Sanchez drew on his cigarette, coughed out smoke. "He had a long life. Hope I'm as lucky."

Hernandez said, "You mentioned he might have been ill?"

Sanchez flicked ash into a crystal ashtray. "One of the servants said he was in and out of the hospital for the past six months. Also, he had an appointment at a private hospital this morning. He was pretty sick. Cancer, the servant said. He'd lost weight. He didn't look too good." Sanchez glanced over at the corpse. "He looks a lot worse now. I'm having one of my men contact the hospital he attended. The San Ignatio."

Hernandez glanced at the body again, felt the sickness return. He turned, moved a couple of paces toward the open wall safe.

"Anything in there?"

Sanchez shook his head. "Nothing." He gestured to the fireplace with his cigarette. "Lots of ashes in the grate. Looks like he burned a lot of papers."

Hernandez stepped toward the fireplace. It had been his one hope, finding something, *anything*, but the old man must have been prepared, been sure before death to burn everything.

"Not a sliver of paper left. Nothing but ashes." Sanchez stared absent-mindedly at the grate. "I wonder what the old man had to hide?"

"I wonder?" echoed Hernandez.

Sanchez looked up, stared at him for a moment before looking away again. "Anyway, it's all over now. And it's a wrap." He looked away, pushed himself slowly up from the chair with effort. He took the handkerchief from his pocket and dabbed his brow. "This heat kills me. You want a beer? The refrigerator is full. Imported beers, too. German, Dutch, you name it."

"A beer sounds good."

Sanchez moved away. "I'll be back in five minutes."

Hernandez nodded. The detective turned and went out the door.

*   *   *

Hernandez stood there in the middle of the study, trying to think. His eyes went from the bloodied body to the wall safe, then to the fire grate. Why? Why had the old man killed himself? Because of his cancer? Or because of the people Rodriguez had told him about? Or maybe they had killed the old man too, made it look like suicide.

He crossed to the big, blackened fireplace and stood in front of it, stared down. He took a tong quietly from the stand of utensils beside the fireplace and raked the ashes. It was just as Sanchez had said. Not a sliver of paper. Only soot and ashes. What had they been, these papers?

He replaced the tong and moved toward the open safe in the wall, careful to tread softly, listening at the same time for Sanchez's return. He peered into the safe; it was empty, as Sanchez had said. He crossed quietly to behind the desk, tried not to look down at the body near his feet.

Blood covered the desk's blotting pad and polished surface. Hernandez felt queasy again. He swallowed hard, mopped his sweating brow with the back of his shirtsleeve.

There were three drawers on the left side of the desk. He tried the top one first. It was unlocked and slid out quietly. Inside were a pair of scissors, a letter opener, and some plain white sheets of bond paper.

He flicked through the sheets of paper. All blank. He slid the drawer shut and tried the next one. It was empty, unused, the smell of the applewood rising up to meet his nostrils. He slid back the second drawer and tried the last. More blank bond paper, some rubber bands, a box of staples. He closed the drawer and looked down at the drying blood that seemed to be everywhere, at the rigid corpse, at the one hand raised in the air as if waving good-bye. *So long, Señor Tsarkin.*

The old man had been careful. Very careful. Perhaps elsewhere he kept some information. Something that would point a way, open a door for Hernandez so that he might know what was happening. Gaining access to the house or study again would be difficult, perhaps impossible. This was his one opportunity. He stepped back toward the rows of shelves lining the walls.

There were books on Paraguayan history, a biography of

Lopez, gardening books, heavy tomes on import-export regulations. The rest were expensively bound novels. Hernandez plucked one from the shelf. It was in Spanish, its pages virgin, unread. He replaced the book and riffled through some more. The same. No thumb marks, the smell of paper strong. The old guy hadn't been a reader. They were for show, except perhaps the business books, part of an image that went with the property.

As he replaced the last book, the telephone rang.

Hernandez froze at the shrill noise disturbing the quiet of the study. It rang a couple of times, Hernandez listening to hear if Sanchez was returning, but nothing, no sound apart from the telephone. He crossed to the desk quickly and lifted the receiver.

"*Sí?*"

"Señor Tsarkin please." The man's voice on the line sounded prissy. Hernandez thought he heard music playing faintly in the background, Ravel's *Bolero*. He glanced down at the body of the old man on the floor, thinking for a moment. If it was a relative, it wasn't his business to break the news.

"What is it?" Hernandez asked more loudly.

"Señor Tsarkin! I did not recognize your voice."

Hernandez was about to interrupt, but the man spoke first. "This is the reservations manager at the Excelsior Hotel. I am telephoning to confirm that everything is in order. The executive suite you requested for Friday evening is Suite One-twenty. I am at your service and hope everything will prove satisfactory for your guests."

Hernandez said it automatically, feeling his pulse quicken. "Yes, I'm sure it will." He turned his head sharply toward the study door, thought he heard footsteps off in the distance. Sanchez returning?

"There is a slight problem, however, Señor," the man went on, his voice now more stilted, formal. "We have some regular guests flying into Asunción late tomorrow night. They require several suites, and we are heavily booked. You said you would require the suite only from seven until nine o'clock. If it is possible, I would like to confirm this so that our expected guests may be accommodated.'' There was a pause. "Could you confirm this, Señor?"

"Yes. Until nine.'' Hernandez swallowed, hearing his heartbeat quicken, hearing the footsteps outside become louder.

"Excellent!'' said the man. "Thank you, Señor. *Buenas tardes.*''

"*Buenas tardes.*''

Hernandez replaced the receiver and looked down at the body of Nicolas Tsarkin. Maybe not so *buenas.* When he looked up again, Sanchez was standing in the doorway, two cans of beer in his hands.

"Who was that?'' Sanchez asked as he came into the room.

"No one,'' Hernandez said with a dismissive shrug. "Some business associate of Tsarkin's.''

Sanchez looked at him for a moment, then offered a can of beer, watching as Hernandez pulled the ring of the chilled can.

Hernandez took a sip of the ice-cold German beer, the brand unknown to him. He looked over at Sanchez. "Good beer.''

Sanchez nodded. "And what specifically was the business about, Rudi?''

"An engagement he can't make now. Nothing important.''

"Right,'' Sanchez said with an intensely skeptical look. "You should have let me take that call.''

"All's fair,'' Hernandez laughed, "in love and journalism.''

"Sometimes I wish I didn't like you,'' Sanchez said. "Then I could put you in the very dark and very deep cell that you deserve.''

He raised the can to his lips and swallowed. The heat was terrible, not a whisper of wind blowing in through the open study window. There were tiny beads of sweat running down his face. He wiped his forehead with the back of his hand.

"Are you finished here?'' he asked.

"I guess so.''

"Drink your beer, then we'll see what we can do with

that car of yours. If I were a proper cop I'd have you in prison for driving a car like that.''

Hernandez smiled. He finished the beer in one long swallow, then tucked his notebook into his trouser pocket and slipped the pen in after it.

Sanchez said, ''The pen's mine, amigo.''

Hernandez smiled and handed it back. *''Gracias.''*

Sanchez put down the empty can and nodded toward the door. ''Come, let's get out of here. Dead bodies give me the creeps.''

Hernandez took one last look at the old man's corpse. Then he turned and followed Sanchez outside.

Hernandez drove back to the city through the dusty, hot streets and parked his car in the office lot of *La Tarde*, the old engine running smoothly now. He promised himself he would get it fixed just as soon as he had time.

He climbed the stairs to the newsroom and greeted his colleagues before going to his desk and switching on his computer. It took him only fifteen minutes to write up a filler on the old man's suicide, the bare facts, the name, the address, and the background information, remembering it all, no need for the notebook on the desk in front of him.

It was almost four in the afternoon when he filed his copy with the news editor, time for him to finish work. He flicked open his notebook, saw again what he had written there once he had left Tsarkin's house: *Friday, 7:00 to 9:00 P.M., Suite One-twenty. Excelsior Hotel.*

Two days away. The question was, what was happening? Why had Tsarkin booked a suite for only two hours? A meeting? It had to be a meeting.

If that was it, then what he needed was a plan, a plan to get in there, listen to what was being said. He tidied his desk, then went down to the lot and drove to the Excelsior Hotel on the Calle Chile.

The hotel lobby was busy. It was a plush palace of Oriental carpets and dark wood, the best hotel in the city. Hernandez took the lift to the first floor and found the suite with no problem, noting the nearby room numbers and the layout before going back down to the lobby and out to the parking area and the old red Buick, parked twenty meters from the hotel's fire-exit doors. Hernandez took note of the doors.

The day was still hot, and he kept the windows down on the way to his apartment, smoking as he drove, trying to work something out in his head, trying to come up with a plan. The key to it all was Tsarkin. Only now Tsarkin was dead.

When he stepped into his apartment twenty minutes later, he heard the gentle whirr of the air-conditioning unit by the window. He had forgotten to turn it off that morning. The room was cool, pleasant, and his body was very hot.

The apartment overlooked the city and had a sweeping view of the river south of Asunción. Rudi loved it. A bachelor's place, compact, one bedroom, a couch in the living room, where he had slept during Erica's stay. He went into the kitchen and poured himself a large scotch, added some cracked ice, then went to sit by the window, staring out absentmindedly at the river boats plying up and down the Rio Paraguay.

He glanced up at the photograph of his mother and father on the bookshelf in the corner of the living room. Why had his mother chosen to come to such a godforsaken city as Asunción? And yet it was home for him; he fit in more easily here than he ever had in his mother's homeland. There were many things he hated about this city, many things he loved. He hated the poverty, the corruption; he loved the girls, the sun, the easygoing *mestizos*.

He finished his scotch quickly, placed the glass on the table. He could still smell the scent of Erica's perfume lingering in the room.

He looked at the photograph on the bookshelf again, his father dark and handsome and smiling; his mother blond, pretty, but her Nordic face set in a harsh, strained smile. She should have smiled more. But then, she had never had much to smile about. That was the one thing the *mestizos* had done to his blood. Made him smile more.

He smiled now, thinking of the suite in the Excelsior Hotel, the plan coming into his head with such ease, so complete, that he picked up the telephone at once and began to call the number.

Perhaps the old Indian woman on the Calle Estrella had been right. Perhaps Erica would bring him luck.

He hoped so.

Because if not, then maybe he would end up dead too.

CHAPTER 4

Richmond, Surrey, England. November 24

There were no pedestrians in the quiet street of red-bricked Victorian houses, the small park it faced empty on this winter's day.

The black taxi drew up outside Number Twenty-one and Volkmann paid the driver and stepped out. It was cloudy and cold, the sky threatening snow as he went up the narrow front path. The garden was overgrown, dockweed and nettles climbing between the bare winter rosebushes.

As Volkmann unlocked the door and stepped inside, he heard the faint sound of music coming from the room at the back of the house and smiled. Cole Porter's "Night and Day."

He left his overnight bag by the door and passed the small parlor, its door open to reveal the silver-framed photographs on the mantelpiece and the walnut sideboard, the bric-a-brac his mother had collected over forty years.

In the kitchen, the big Aga range was fired, its metal throwing out a blanket of heat into the small room, the door at the end open, the music louder now as he stepped toward it.

She sat by the window of the music room, her gray head bent close to the Steinway piano. The silver-topped walking cane lay on top of the black, polished wood. She looked up as he peered around the door, smiled before removing her glasses.

"I was beginning to think you wouldn't come."

He smiled back warmly, crossed to where she waited and kissed her cheek.

"It's only two days, I'm afraid. I've got to be back by Saturday."

She touched his face with her palm. "No matter, it's good to see you, Joseph. How was your flight?"

"Delayed, two hours. Why don't we go into the kitchen? It's warmer there."

He handed her the silver-topped cane and helped her toward the door, holding her arm as she limped.

"I managed to get some tickets for the Barbican tonight. Think you could manage it?"

"Tonight? But that's splendid, Joseph."

"It's Per Carinni. He's doing the three Beethovens. A difficult program." He smiled down at the old woman. "And how's the patient?"

"Much better now that you are here. Let's have some tea, then you can tell me about Strasbourg."

It never changed; the house remained always as he remembered it each time he returned: the same familiar smells, the same peaceful quiet that enveloped him like a warm cocoon, and always music somewhere in the background. The radio was on, Bach playing softly.

They sat in the kitchen drinking tea. She had placed a plateful of cookies beside his cup but he left them untouched, the old guilt creeping in on him again, the thought of her alone in the big old house, shuffling around on the silver-topped cane.

She was seventy-two on her next birthday, and Volkmann remembered her as younger every time he returned. He glanced up at the photographs on the wall over the kitchen fireplace: his father and her, taken thirty years before, her dark hair falling about her face as she smiled out at the camera, himself a young boy sitting on her knee outside the cottage in Cornwall.

"Tell me about Strasbourg."

Volkmann put down the white china cup. "There's not much to tell. There's still a lot of work to be done. It's taken the best part of eighteen months to get things off the ground. And there's a lot of distrust about. The French don't trust the English, the English don't trust the French." He smiled at her. "And the Italians, of course, don't trust anybody. So much for mutual-security cooperation."

"What about Anna? Do you hear from her?"

"She telephones now and then. She met someone, a staff officer at the military college."

"Someone you knew?"

"No. He was four years behind me."

He stood up and placed a hand on her shoulder, smiled down at the wrinkled face.

"Come. I'd like to hear you play for me. We have some time before the concert. Then I'll call a taxi and have them pick us up at seven."

It was after one o'clock when the taxi, bearing them home after the concert, turned into the street. The snow had stopped and when they reached the park, the old woman told the driver to stop, they would walk the rest of the way, saying the exercise would do her good. Volkmann helped her out and gripped her arm, the snow soft underfoot, his mother ignoring his protests, saying she felt better, the evening had done her good.

The trees of the park were ghostly white as they passed the entrance, snow outlining their branches, the open spaces a gray expanse in the gloaming.

She wasn't limping now as they strolled toward the house. For someone of an artistic nature who had fallen ill, his father had once remarked, the doctor ought to prescribe a round of applause, not pills. Volkmann smiled in the darkness, remembering the remark.

She looked up at him. "Wasn't Carinni divine?"

They had reached the park entrance, and Volkmann looked down at her. "I've heard you play better."

She smiled. "You're a toady, Joseph. But you know the way to an old woman's heart."

She stopped to regain her breath, and he watched as she looked around at the snowy park landscape, then moved toward the entrance, stepping through the open gates. He stayed close behind her.

"This reminds me . . ." she said.

"Tell me."

"Of when I was a little girl. Of Christmas. There was always snow in winter in Budapest." She looked up at him and he could see her face dimly. "But that was all such a long time ago. Long before I met your father."

"Tell me again."

He had heard it all before, many times, her words like some comforting litany. The season of plenty in Budapest, and the anticipation of Christmas. When the blue flag was up on the frozen lake in Octagon Square, and the ice was thick enough for skaters, and the red candles flickered in the windows of warm houses, warm as an oven, the smell of burning oil lamps, great gray plumes of coal smoke rising in the cold air. Budapest long ago, the city of her childhood.

But she was silent. Volkmann looked down, saw her wipe tears from her eyes. He touched her arm gently.

"Come, you'll catch cold."

She turned her head then, looked out over the cold white park. Volkmann moved to grip her frail arm before the melancholy took hold. As he looked at her face, he remembered the young woman she had been on the beach in Cornwall all those years ago.

She looked up at him and he saw the grief in the wet brown eyes. "I miss him, Joseph. I miss him so."

Volkmann bent and took her wrinkled face fondly in both hands, kissed her forehead.

"We both do."

CHAPTER 5

Asunción. Friday, November 25

The giant Iberia 747 banked onto final approach and began its descent into Campo Grande airport.

Of all the passengers on board the packed flight to Paraguay's capital that late afternoon, none was probably as tired as the middle-aged man in the dark-blue suit who sat quietly in Row Twenty-three.

The flight he had endured earlier from Munich to Madrid had been tolerable, but the long haul from Madrid to Asunción had taken its toll and now his dehydrated body ached.

It was almost three months since he had last visited Paraguay. He hadn't enjoyed it then and it was unlikely he would enjoy it now. Mosquitoes. Heat. Temperamental natives. But this time his visit would be even briefer, twenty-four hours, and for that, he was grateful.

The man in the blue suit picked up the leather briefcase from the floor in front of him and clicked it open. He flicked carefully through the documents inside, checked that everything was in order.

A pretty stewardess moved down the aisle, a last-minute check on seat belts. The man glanced up, saw the slim hips sway rhythmically toward him. The girl paused, said something rapidly in Spanish as she pointed to the briefcase on his lap before moving on. The man in the blue suit clicked shut the case, tucked it neatly under the seat in front, and sat back.

Beyond the port window he glimpsed the sprawling, ragged suburbs of Asunción: the flat-roofed white- and yellow-plaster adobes and the tin-roofed shacks of the *barrios*. As the bowels of the big plane shuddered, he heard the whirr of the flaps extending and the dull thud of the undercarriage lowering into place.

Five minutes later, he saw the yellow lights of the runway rush up beneath him, and then the rumble of wheels on concrete as the giant aircraft touched down to a perfect landing.

*   *   *

The man—his name was Meyer—retrieved his suitcase from the carousel and passed unquestioned through customs twenty minutes later.

In the arrivals area, a tall, blond young man who stood out from the waiting crowd held a placard stiffly in front of him: *Pieter De Beers*. Meyer stepped forward and the young man took his suitcase and beckoned for him to follow.

A Mercedes stood parked nearby, its black bodywork muddied, and he saw the three men waiting inside. Schmidt sat impassively like a rock in front, and the two men reclined in the back.

Both wore immaculate business suits and both smiled when they saw Meyer.

One was young, in his middle thirties, and wore a light-gray suit. He was stockily built, and his dark hair glistened. Not handsome, but ruggedly attractive, and his broad face was deeply tanned from years in the sun.

The second man was in his early sixties, but looked younger. He was tall and lean and very handsome. His silver-gray hair was more silver than gray and was swept back off his face. He had the look of a self-assured diplomat. He wore a charcoal-gray business suit, a white shirt and a red-silk tie, and his gentle blue eyes radiated confidence and charisma. He raised a hand and smiled again as Meyer approached.

The blond young man put Meyer's suitcase in the trunk, and Schmidt got out to open the rear door for him.

When Meyer slid into the backseat, the two passengers shook his hand in turn.

"You had a good flight, Johannes?" the silver-haired man asked.

"Ja, danke." As he turned to the younger, dark-haired man, he said, "Any problems?"

Kruger glanced at him and shook his head. "No, but some bad news."

"Oh?" said Meyer, feeling uneasy now, wondering if it had anything to do with the project. It couldn't, he told himself. Everything was in order, he was absolutely certain.

"We'll talk about it on the way, Johannes," said Kruger as he leaned forward and tapped the driver on the shoulder.

"The hotel, Karl."

As the car started and pulled out from the curb, Meyer sat back, dabbing his forehead and silently cursing the heat, wondering what the bad news could be.

Rudi Hernandez was tired; he had been up until two that morning. Ricardo Torres had not arrived with the equipment he was loaning him until twelve-thirty, and it had taken him another hour to explain how to set it up.

"Make sure it comes back in one piece," Torres had said. "Otherwise, my boss kicks me out on my ass and I'm selling nuts outside the city zoo, *comprende*?"

Comprende.

The equipment was expensive. Torres had gone over the operation of the components with him, asking when he had finished, as he had when Hernandez had first telephoned him, "What you going to do with all this, amigo?"

Hernandez had smiled enigmatically and said, "Undercover work."

Torres had looked at him, one eyebrow raised archly. "Okay. But any damage, you pay, *sí*? Just remember that, Rudi."

Hernandez had said he would remember. There was no problem. He just needed to borrow the stuff for one night. He would return it intact.

He had gone to work early at *La Tarde*, finished at three and driven straight to the apartment. He already had everything organized, but went over it one more time so there would be no mistakes, no hitches.

There was a chance that the meeting at the Excelsior was simply a business conference. In which case he was going to a lot of trouble for nothing. On the other hand, he knew damn well he could be putting himself into serious danger. Rodriguez was very dead. And before he died, he had been very worried.

So, he thought, *if it's only a business meeting, then I have nothing to worry about. If it's something more interesting, then my plan had better work.*

If it didn't, he figured he was in big trouble, unless he could get out of the hotel fast. He remembered the fire exit on the first floor that led down to the rear of the hotel. A bolthole. He might need it.

He stood and went into the kitchen, poured himself a tepid Coke as he sat, then lit a cigarette, thinking about the plan, trying to see flaws. No real flaws, only risks, he decided.

He stubbed out the cigarette in the ashtray and stood up again, aware of his restless anxiety. From the bedroom he took the suitcase, already packed with the rest of the things he needed, then came back into the living room once again.

He laid the suitcase on the couch and flicked open the catches, checked that he hadn't overlooked anything, then turned his attention to the equipment Torres had loaned him, lying on the coffee table.

He took it piece by piece and placed it carefully in the suitcase among the clothes he had already placed there, making sure the equipment didn't rattle around, remembering that Torres had said it was sensitive. When he had finished, he checked through everything again, carefully shut the suitcase and thumbed the combination lock to another set of numbers.

He felt a shiver of fear go through him. He sucked in a deep breath, let it out slowly.

Relax, amigo. Stay calm. Otherwise you're dead even before you start.

He glanced at his watch. Five-thirty.

He just had time to change and then it would be time to go.

The black Mercedes moved slowly through the evening traffic toward the city. The glass partition between the driver and his passengers was closed, allowing the passengers their privacy.

Meyer looked out beyond the tinted windows at the lights coming on as dusk fell, at the smaller cars moving past on either side in the three-lane traffic, drawing him closer to the city, drawing him closer to his final meeting in this dreadful country.

A battered yellow pickup went slowly past the window, a cowboy-hatted Indian and his fat wife sitting in front, a crying child on her lap, windows rolled down, a radio blaring out Paraguayan harp music. In the back of the pickup, half a dozen restless, brown-faced scruffy children danced about like monkeys.

Dirty, idiotic Dagos. Meyer turned his head away in disgust. How had his people endured it here? He glanced at Kruger.

"The news you spoke of . . . ?"

"It's Tsarkin. He shot himself two days ago."

Meyer's eyebrows rose in surprise. "He's dead?"

Kruger nodded. "It was only a question of hours, anyway. Cancer. So he decided to take the quick way. He sent a letter to Franz Lieber before he did it. Said the pain was too much to bear. He wished us well, said he was sorry he couldn't make it."

Meyer nodded, understanding, vaguely remembering something Franz had told him concerning Tsarkin's health.

"A great loss," commented Meyer. And then a thought struck him, a terrible thought. "His papers?" His face showed concern as he looked at the silver-haired man seated opposite.

The silver-haired man smiled. "There is no need for alarm, Johannes. Tsarkin burned all his papers. Everything. Nothing can lead back to us. Nothing."

"Our people checked it out?"

This time it was Kruger who spoke. "Franz called at the house after the *policía* had left. There's absolutely nothing to worry about. He checked it out with the servants. The *policía* saw it as a straightforward case of suicide."

"He checked Tsarkin's study and belongings?"

"There were only some old photograph albums. He removed them."

"And Tsarkin's safe-deposit box?"

"He emptied it himself. Burned everything before he pulled the trigger." He looked across at Meyer. "I'm certain Franz has been thorough."

Meyer nodded and said, "And the arrangements for the meeting?"

"Tsarkin said the hotel was organized as usual, but Franz checked just to be certain. Everything is in order." Kruger paused. Then he smiled and said, "He was a cautious man, old Nicolas. As cautious in death as in life."

Kruger turned his face back toward the window. The silver-haired man reclined farther in his seat.

Meyer did the same, relieved.

Hernandez reached the Excelsior at five-fifty and parked the Buick twenty meters from the fire-escape doors that opened onto the parking lot.

He looked to make sure there was no one in the lot before he strolled over to the exit doors, placed his palms against the metal and pushed. The doors were locked by sprung bars that could be opened only from the inside. He had checked already to make sure they worked. They did. He probably wouldn't have to use them, but he wasn't taking any chances. Nothing must obstruct the doors from opening onto the parking lot.

A row of metal garbage bins stood nearby, twenty meters from the kitchen's rear entrance, but did not obstruct the exit. Satisfied, he crossed back to his car, removed his overnight suitcase and left the driver's door unlocked. He walked around to the hotel entrance. He was wearing dark-tinted glasses and a gray business suit.

As he walked over to the brightly lit lobby and headed straight for the reception desk, he saw a dark-suited man standing behind the counter, busy sorting through some papers.

The man looked up as Hernandez approached. "Señor?"

"I have a reservation for tonight. My name is Ferres."

"One moment, Señor." The man turned to the computer terminal beside him and tapped the keyboard with pudgy fingers. Without looking up, he said, "Señor Ferres. Room one hundred and four. The first floor." The man looked up, smiled a plastic smile. "Our last free room. You were lucky."

I hope so, Hernandez thought. He had telephoned the hotel the evening before last to make his reservation, explaining to the reservations clerk that he had stayed on the first floor before and had enjoyed the view, had a preference for it. He had waited expectantly while the man checked, breathed a sigh of relief when the man had said yes, but only a double. Hernandez had said he would pay for the double.

"Will Señor be settling his account in cash or by credit card?"

"Cash," said Hernandez. "And I would like to pay now. I intend leaving early tomorrow morning."

"Certainly."

"Also, I am having some friends call by shortly. I want a bottle of champagne and some canapés sent up to my room immediately."

"But of course, Señor. At once. I will see to it."

The bellhop carrying his suitcase led him to his room at the end of the corridor, five doors from Tsarkin's suite and on the opposite side of the corridor. Having the room on the first floor was imperative. And it had been the last one free, a good omen surely? The evening after telephoning the Excelsior, he had gone to the hotel once again to examine the corridor layout. The room he had been given was perfect, not too close, not too far away.

As Hernandez followed the bellhop into the room, the boy switched on the lights, placed the suitcase on the rack provided, waited for his tip. Hernandez obliged; the boy smiled, bade him good evening and withdrew.

Hernandez crossed to the window and stared out: lights coming on everywhere, darkness descending rapidly over the city. And there was real fear in him now. He checked his watch. Six o'clock. Whoever was going to use the room down the hall would be arriving soon. There was a sharp knock on the door.

He admitted the white-coated, smiling waiter, the food trolley he pushed laden with the champagne and canapés, watching him, the way he worked, listening to the chatter. The man made a fuss of arranging the trolley in the center of the room. Hernandez requested him to leave the champagne unopened.

"Of course, Señor." The waiter bowed and went to leave, but not leaving, a practiced art.

Hernandez peeled off some bills from the wad in his pocket. "That was excellent service. What is your name?"

"Mario, Señor. Mario Ricardes."

"Thank you, Mario." Hernandez handed the man the money, the waiter bowed and left.

Hernandez looked at the champagne and food. The story

was costing him a small fortune already. He hoped it was
worth it. The champagne was French and expensive, the
six sparkling glasses neatly arranged beside the bucket of
crushed ice. The canapés looked exquisite: neat, crisped
triangles of fresh bread with smoked salmon, anchovies,
various cheeses, meat pastes, arranged splendidly on a silver tray.

He went to sit on the bed, opened the suitcase and removed everything he needed, laid them neatly on the
spread.

He went to work quickly, setting everything out in its
place. When he was finished ten minutes later, he still sat
on the bed, lit a cigarette, then punched in the number to
call Suite One-twenty. There was no reply.

Whoever intended using the suite had thankfully not arrived early. Had someone answered, he would have pretended a wrong number and put down the phone.

Hernandez checked his watch again. Six-ten. He stubbed
out his cigarette in the crystal ashtray and stood up nervously.

It was time to go to the lobby.

It was a different hotel this trip, Meyer noted as the Mercedes drew up outside the Excelsior. But they had used the
hotel before, many times, he and Winter. But never together. The meetings to deliver the reports had alternated
between both men.

The hotels had been Tsarkin's idea; the location and
room would be different each time so there would be less
chance of electronic bugging or eavesdropping. Better than
the houses of Lieber or Tsarkin, where the prying eyes and
ears of servants and neighbors were a threat to security.

The house in the Chaco, of course, would have been
ideal, but it was too remote, and when the rains came, the
roads were often impassable. Hotels were better, less conspicuous. Businessmen and tourists came and went without
regard.

Schmidt and the driver stepped out of the Mercedes and
opened the doors, Kruger and Schmidt leading the way into
the lobby, Meyer walking beside the silver-haired man.

They waited while Kruger went to the reception desk,

carrying his briefcase. Meyer glanced around at the luxurious surroundings. The lobby was quiet. A couple of nice-looking girls sat in leather easy chairs nearby. A young man wearing a gray suit sat close by, reading a newspaper.

Meyer saw Kruger return from the desk. "Which room?" Meyer asked in German.

"One-twenty," Kruger replied.

They all followed Kruger to the lift.

Six-fifteen.

Hernandez had bought a newspaper and found a vacant chair in the lobby, facing the reception desk.

Background music played softly in the lobby, but he had a perfect vantage point, and if he concentrated hard, he could understand what was being said at the desk. He opened his newspaper, pretended to read, but kept his eyes on the entrance to the lobby from the street outside.

It was ten minutes later when Hernandez saw the men. His eyes flicked to the entrance instinctively as he heard them come into the lobby. Four men, all wearing business suits, all European-looking. Hernandez was suspicious immediately: the four men carried no luggage, and only two carried briefcases. They could have been simply returning from a business meeting in the city, but a gut feeling told him otherwise.

One of the men was obviously a bodyguard, a giant of a man, looking uncomfortable in his pale linen suit. He walked ahead of the group, big-chested, close-cropped blond hair. He had a swaggering, slow, awkward gait and looked like he was made of solid granite. Not the kind of man you tackled, unless you had an army behind you.

The second man was rugged, in his mid-thirties, with dark, shining hair. He carried a briefcase and looked like a company executive. The third was middle-aged, short, overweight, and wore a blue, crumpled business suit. He held his briefcase under his arm and he looked tired, as if he had endured a long journey.

But the fourth man was the one who stood out from the group. Tall, leanly built, his silver hair swept back off his handsome face.

The dark-haired man approached the reception desk

while the others waited nearby. Hernandez listened, trying to separate the faint, piped hotel music from the voices, but the man spoke quietly, very quietly.

"*Sí*, Señor . . ." came the reply from the desk clerk, and then a muttering of words in Spanish. The background music suddenly rose in pitch, almost drowning out the voices. *Shit. Speak louder, amigo. Louder.*

"All ready for you, Señor . . ." More babble. *Damn!* He hadn't heard the room number.

Hernandez went to stand, to move closer, but saw one of the men, the tired-looking one in the crumpled blue suit, glance over at the girls nearby, then at Hernandez. He shifted in his seat, looked down, pretending to look at his watch. He did not want the man to get a good look at his face. He was unfolding his newspaper when he heard the voice speak faintly, in German, in his mother's tongue, the language of his childhood, the man in the steel-blue suit, asking it softly of the dark-haired man, as he passed by Hernandez, moving toward the elevator.

"*Welche Nummer?*"

"*Ein hundert zwanzig.*"

Which number? A hundred and twenty. Hernandez felt a shiver of excitement.

These are the men.

He watched as they crossed to the elevator. The eldest of the men, the one with the silver hair, stood in the center of the group. He made a remark and the others smiled and laughed, but Hernandez couldn't hear what was said; the men were too far away.

The door opened and the men stepped in. Hernandez stood and watched the numbers over the elevator halt at floor one.

He waited for a minute before moving toward the second elevator, reached it seconds later as the doors opened. He felt a knot of fear in his stomach as he stepped inside and punched the button for the first floor.

When they stepped out on the first floor, Schmidt led them to the suite, inserted the key card and went in first, his big blond head touching the top of the door frame. He switched on the lights, checked the room, closed the curtains, his muscular bulk awkward but moving fast.

Kruger entered next, followed by the others. As Meyer closed the door behind him, Kruger was already unlocking the briefcase he carried. He took out the rectangular, hand-held electronic detector, held it chest-high, turned around in a circle, watching the small red indicator light at the tip of the device, listening for the alarm signal, but none came. None had ever come; it was only a precaution.

Kruger placed the device back in his briefcase and said, "All clear."

Schmidt took up a position in a chair by the locked door, sat down and folded his arms, two bulges evident on either side of his broad chest where, Meyer knew, the holstered pistol and the big, jagged-edged knife were strapped. The man was expert with either weapon, and intimidating all the more because of his perpetual silence. But his presence at these meetings always made Meyer feel secure. No one would tangle with Schmidt and live. One look at the man's frightening bulk told you so.

As the three men sat around the table at the end of the room, the gentle hum of the air-conditioner wafted in the air, but still, it was warm in the room, still humid.

Meyer dabbed his brow, flicked open his briefcase and removed his papers, placed them neatly in front of him, before looking up at the two men waiting silently for him to begin.

He said, "The report on Brandenburg first, I presume?"

The handsome, silver-haired man made a steeple of his slim, manicured fingers, and his gentle eyes sparkled as he nodded.

"If you would be so kind, Johannes. I know you must be tired, so let us proceed as quickly as possible."

Meyer nodded and dabbed the sweat from his brow again. Then he looked down at his papers and began to speak.

CHAPTER 6

Asunción.

Hernandez stood in front of the bathroom mirror. Gone was the gray business suit and the tinted glasses. The white shirt remained, but this time with a black tie. Instead of the suit, he wore a waiter's white service jacket, black trousers and black shoes he had bought the previous day in a small catering supplier on the Calle Palma. Without the glasses, his hair brushed down even more, he looked different, certainly different. He touched the scar on his right cheek. Nothing could be done about that.

If they were professionals, they would be careful to check the suite for listening devices. That was why he wanted to give them a little time. If his plan worked, he wouldn't be able to record all their conversation, but the men were going to be a while in the suite, so he should be able to hear most of it.

If the plan worked. . . .

He stepped out into the bedroom and took the single sheet of hotel-monogrammed notepaper from the bedroom's desk, checking the scribbled note he had written. *Champagne and canapés. Suite One-twenty.*

He knelt down beside the food trolley and raised the white linen cloth that hung over the edge. Underneath he saw the tiny microphone he had placed there earlier with the adhesive tape, checked again that it was secure.

Satisfied, he let the tablecloth fall back into place and then turned his attention to the second part of the equipment lying on the bed. It was a Japanese-made receiver-recorder, no bigger than a cigarette pack. He had checked the transmitter and it had worked properly, just as Torres had said it would.

The receiver was battery-operated, and Hernandez had inserted one of the two miniature tapes he had brought. Everything was ready to go. A spare two-hour tape lay on the bed, just in case it was needed. He stood up and checked his watch. Six-forty. The men had had fifteen minutes. Hernandez hoped it was enough time. He picked up the white waiter's towel and placed it over his left arm. He was ready.

For a couple of seconds, he hesitated, thinking of Rodriguez, the hideous, pulped flesh of the man's corpse, and a spasm of cold fear shot through him.

He forced the memory from his mind as he walked briskly to the door, opened it and peered out into the corridor.

Empty.

He pulled the trolley out behind him, checked to see that his room key card was safely in his trousers pocket, then closed the door after him.

He listened again in the corridor for any approaching sound.

Nothing.

Hernandez drew in a deep breath and let it out quickly, then started to push the trolley toward Suite One-twenty.

It took Meyer twelve minutes to read the report. He kept to the key points, careful to highlight his achievements, his personal contribution, his hard work, the attention to detail on which he prided himself. Now would come the questions. He looked up.

There was a smile on the handsome face of the silver-haired man seated opposite; he nodded his head agreeably.

They all heard the soft knock on the door, and their heads turned sharply. Meyer saw that Schmidt already had his pistol out and by his side. Another knock, louder this time, and Kruger stood up quickly from the table and crossed to the door, Schmidt calling out in Spanish, "Who is it?"

Kruger moved the big man aside and put his ear to the door. Everyone in the room heard the voice behind it reply.

"Room service, Señor."

Kruger nodded to Schmidt, and the big man stood back from the door, pistol at the ready.

Kruger opened the door a crack, but kept his shoulder firmly against it. He saw the room-service waiter standing there, a dumb smile on his face.

"We didn't order anything," Kruger said curtly. "You must have the wrong room."

"Really, Señor? Oh . . . I'm sorry. . . ."

The waiter looked at the slip of paper in his hand, then at the room number and said, "No, Señor . . . Suite One-twenty. Champagne and appetizers. Compliments of the hotel."

Kruger opened the door. He saw the champagne wedged in a silver bucket of crushed ice, the neatly arranged appetizers; then he looked back up at the waiter, gave the man a questioning stare.

The waiter showed him the order on hotel-engraved notepaper. "See, Señor . . . it's written here. Suite One-twenty. Champagne and canapés."

Kruger took the slip of paper, examined it carefully, then handed it back.

The waiter shrugged. "If you don't want it, Señor, I can take it back. It's no problem." He smiled affably. "It's a new complimentary service for our suite guests."

Kruger glanced again at the food trolley. He was thirsty and tired, and the suite was humid. The chilled champagne and the appetizers looked refreshingly tempting.

"Very well, you may come in."

Kruger stepped back, and the waiter wheeled the trolley slowly into the center of the room, close to the table where the others sat, several meters away.

As he began to undo the wire around the neck of the champagne, the man with the dark, greased hair said, "Leave it. We can attend to that ourselves."

The waiter nodded, a grateful look on his face. He patted the linen tablecloth, rearranged two of the glasses, coughed quietly.

Kruger took the hint, impatiently removed his wallet and handed the waiter a single note.

"Muchas gracias."

Kruger stared at him, noticed the scar on the young man's cheek. "Your name?"

"Ricardes, Señor. Mario Ricardes."

"See that we are not disturbed again, Mario."

"Yes, Señor. Of course, Señor. If there is anything else you wish, please do not hesitate to call room service."

Kruger nodded impatiently.

Hernandez turned toward the door, away from the silver-haired man, toward the big blond with one hand behind his back. He took one last look around the suite and tried hard not to make it obvious as he smiled.

"*Buenas tardes, Señores.*"

He had his hand on the door knob now as he bowed slightly, glimpsed the men at the table—the tired-looking man in the blue crumpled suit, then just a second's glance at the silver-haired man—before he closed the door after him, took three, four steps, then let out a long sigh.

Jesus. . . .

He walked quickly back toward his room.

The three men were seated at the table again.

Meyer felt relieved. The interruption by the waiter had proved a welcome hiatus. His throat was already dry from speaking in the humid room, and he was still feeling the effects of dehydration after the long flight. The iced champagne looked tempting, but it would have to wait. Meyer licked his parched lips. It was time to answer any questions.

The silver-haired man leaned forward, looked directly at him, his tone businesslike. "The shipment . . . ?"

Meyer nodded. "The cargo will be picked up from Genoa as arranged."

"And the Italian?"

"He will be eliminated, but I want to be certain we don't arouse suspicion concerning the cargo. It would be prudent to wait until Brandenburg becomes operational. Then he will be dealt with along with the others."

The silver-haired man nodded his agreement, then looked at Meyer intently.

"Those who have pledged their loyalty . . . we must be certain of them."

Meyer said firmly, "I have had their assurances confirmed. And their pedigree is without question."

Kruger shifted restlessly in his chair as he looked at Meyer. "And the Turk?"

"I foresee no problems."

Kruger said, "The girl in Berlin . . . you're absolutely certain we can rely on her?"

"She will not fail us, I assure you." Meyer glanced over at the elderly man. "There are no changes to the names on the list?"

The man shook his head firmly. ''They will all be killed.''

''Your travel arrangements?'' Meyer inquired. ''Everything has been organized?''

''We leave Paraguay on the sixth.''

Meyer looked at the two men. ''The schedule . . . perhaps I should go through it once more?''

Both men nodded.

Meyer ran a finger around the rim of his shirt collar. Even with the air-conditioning on, the heat was unbearably oppressive. Ninety-percent humidity at least. He found it stifling, wished the meeting would end. A matter of no more than ten minutes now, he was certain. Kruger would want to go over the key points again. He licked his dry lips, glanced over in the direction of the food trolley the waiter had brought, the neck of the champagne bottle visible in the ice bucket. He turned back to face Kruger.

''It's quite warm in here. Perhaps I might have a glass of water?''

Kruger nodded.

Meyer stood up and crossed to the side table where a carafe of water and several glasses sat on a tray. He poured himself a glass of the tepid liquid, glancing at the iced champagne on the trolley as he drank. God, he could do with some of that. And the appetizers looked so tempting. He had hardly eaten on the flight. The damned trolley was beginning to distract him. Meyer finished his glass of water and filled another. He would have to move the trolley out of the way, out of sight; it was beginning to bother him, the sight of that delicious, tempting food and the chilled champagne nestling in the ice bucket.

When he leaned across and gently pushed the trolley away, he was surprised that it moved so smoothly on its wheels. He saw it slide away rapidly, glide across the carpet and bump into the desk in the far corner, rocking the table lamp, almost knocking it over.

Meyer turned and saw Kruger glance up at him from his papers. Meyer returned to his seat, wishing the meeting would end.

*   *   *

Everything was going fine until Hernandez heard the click in the earphones.

He sat on the bed nervously smoking a cigarette. The Japanese tape recorder lay in front of him, the cores of the tape still turning smoothly. The men had been speaking in German; Hernandez heard the voices clearly as the machine recorded their conversation.

In his childhood, his mother had spoken to him in both Spanish and German, sometimes in Guarani, that curious, expressive mixture of Indian-Spanish that the ordinary Paraguayan preferred to speak. But German was second nature to him, the language his Paraguayan father had hated but his mother persisted in using.

And then he heard the *click* in the earphones.

The voices became muted, more distant, and then nothing, only a faint buzzing sound.

Hernandez swore out loud. He turned up the volume quickly, pressed the earphones closer. Nothing. Dead. Torres had said the equipment was good, sensitive, could pick up the buzz of a mosquito at ten meters. Well, either it was picking up the buzz of a mosquito right now or the microphone had worked itself loose or been damaged . . .

Or the men had found it.

Jesus Maria. Hernandez wondered whether to leave, just go, get out now. No, better to stay, because the men wouldn't know which room he was in, wouldn't know where the receiver was situated. And from the room, he could always call the *policía*.

Please, God, don't let them find the microphone.

Hernandez sat on the bed for another fifteen minutes, smoked two more cigarettes, listening to the faint buzzing in his ears. Then he heard a loud bang like a gunshot. Seconds later came the sudden sound of laughter in the earphones, the thin clink of glasses, the faint sound of voices.

"Prost."

"Prost."

"Prost."

A chorus of *prosts*.

Hernandez let out a loud sigh, began to relax, began to understand. The men were drinking the champagne. *Thank God*. They hadn't found the microphone.

*   *   *

The three men raised their glasses once more, in silence this time, the meeting concluded. Meyer looked at the silver-haired man, saw him sip the champagne. The man was pleased, very pleased, Meyer could tell. The meeting had gone well.

Finally Kruger put down his glass and said to Meyer, "We must take our leave of you. It's a long drive back north. The driver will take you to the safe house."

Meyer nodded. The silver-haired man placed his glass on the trolley and gripped Meyer's hand firmly in both of his, a warm handshake, Meyer feeling the pride, the pleasure, well up inside himself.

Kruger nodded to big Schmidt, who opened the door, stepped out into the corridor, eyes left, then right. He turned, nodded the all-clear.

Meyer and Kruger picked up their briefcases. The silver-haired man followed after Schmidt, then Meyer next, Kruger last, taking one last look around the room to make sure nothing had been left behind, before closing the door after him.

Schmidt led the way to the elevator.

Hernandez heard faintly the last words of the conversation in Suite One-twenty and then silence. *Damn Torres and his damned equipment.*

But at least he had something on tape. If only he knew what the men had been talking about.

He shivered inside, hearing the sentence in German again in his mind. *Sie werden alle umgebracht.* They will all be killed. Who were they going to kill? And Brandenburg? What was Brandenburg? And what was the list? The pedigree? And who was the Turk? Their words made no sense.

A chill coursed through Hernandez' body like an electric shock. Who were the men? Most likely dealers, big dealers from Europe. The ones who came over once or twice a year to renew narcotics contracts, to discuss prices. But there was something odd about the whole thing, something strange, a gut feeling he had that wouldn't go away. Two of the men spoke the accented German of immigrants, their vowels softened by the lisping Spanish. Only one spoke pure guttural German, the rough singsong German of Bavaria.

Hernandez shook his head, confused by it all.

"The driver will take you to the safe house," the voice had said. Where was the safe house? Right now it didn't matter; right now he wanted to leave the hotel as quickly as possible. But first he had to retrieve Torres' equipment from the suite. If he had time, maybe he could follow the men to the house they spoke of. But he doubted it. Unless he worked very quickly. He picked up the telephone and punched in the number.

"Room service," said the answering voice.

"Ah, room service! My colleagues in Suite One-twenty appear to have some difficulty in trying to contact you. They wish a food trolley removed from their suite. At once."

"Of course, Señor. *Pronto.* Suite One-twenty."

Hernandez replaced the receiver, threw off the waiter's jacket, dark trousers and tie, then dressed again hurriedly in the business suit and the blue-silk tie. There was no need for the dark glasses, he decided. He had everything inside the case within two minutes, ready to go, key card to the room in his pocket.

He saw the spare tape lying on the bed and stuffed it inside the pocket of his jacket. He was ready. He opened the door to his room a crack, listened and waited for the room-service waiter to appear.

As they came into the lobby, Kruger went ahead of the others and crossed to the reception desk. The man behind it looked up, flashed a white-toothed smile.

"Señor?"

"Suite One-twenty," said Kruger. "We are leaving now. The bill has been paid, I believe?"

The man consulted the computer. "That is correct, Señor. In cash, when the suite was booked. Everything was to your satisfaction?"

"Yes, thank you. My compliments to the hotel. The champagne and canapés were excellent. *Buenas tardes.*" Kruger went to turn but saw the receptionist stare strangely at him before quickly glancing down at his computer again. Kruger hesitated.

He saw the man look up again, a quizzical expression on his face. "Champagne? Canapés? We have no record of such an order, Señor."

Kruger swallowed. "I beg your pardon?"

The receptionist said mildly, "There is no record of such an order on our computer." He smiled. "Obviously a mistake."

Kruger said nervously, "The bottle of champagne and canapés delivered to our suite . . . you're saying they were *not* compliments of the hotel?"

The man smiled broadly, amicably, as if Kruger were joking. "No, Señor. Of course not. But I can check to be absolutely certain. Perhaps an order was sent to your suite by mistake. However, I doubt it."

Kruger turned visibly pale. The receptionist was already reaching for the telephone beside him, dialing a number. A moment later he spoke into the receiver, rapidly, but Kruger wasn't listening to the man's conversation. Something was niggling at him, worrying him. He was a cautious man, a man who never overlooked minor details, a man who checked and double-checked facts before coming to a conclusion. But this was odd. . . .

The man replaced the receiver and looked at Kruger. "Room service has no record of such an order sent to Suite One-twenty, Señor. It's most strange."

Kruger could feel the palms of his hands sweat. He glanced across at the others, waiting for him.

Kruger said rapidly. "The waiter . . . his name, I think, was Ricardes."

The man smiled again. "It was he I just spoke to."

"The young man was tall. A scar on his right cheek."

The receptionist scratched his head. "No. Ricardes is not tall. And a scar? No, certainly not. I don't understand, Señor."

But Kruger did. Kruger understood. His mind was racing. And he tried to focus his cold fury. He waved a dismissive hand at the man behind the desk. "A misunderstanding, obviously." Then he stepped back a pace, as though remembering something. "Excuse me, but I think I've left something in the suite."

The man smiled. "Of course, Señor. *Gracias*."

Kruger turned and crossed quickly to where Schmidt, the silver-haired man and Meyer waited, the three men staring at him now, sensing his disquiet, seeing the perplexed look on his face. Kruger looked palely at them.

"I think," he said in a voice as cold and icy as death, "I think we may have a problem."

Hernandez heard the room-service waiter pass by his door, saw the flash of the man's white coat and glimpsed his face. It was a different waiter this time. He waited until the man had knocked several times, and, receiving no reply, had taken a plastic key card from his pocket and inserted it in the door. As he stepped inside, Hernandez moved forward, closed his door, and crossed the hallway quickly.

He followed the waiter into the suite; the bemused man turned to look at him.

"Señor?"

Hernandez pretended to search through his pockets as he smiled. "I was just about to leave, but I think I have left my glasses in the bathroom. Would you be so kind as to fetch them for me?"

The waiter smiled. "Of course." He crossed to the bathroom, switched on the light and stepped inside.

Hernandez knelt down beside the trolley and fumbled for the tiny transmitter taped underneath.

In the lobby, Kruger wasted no time. He acted quickly. In such matters he had sole responsibility and now he exercised it. He gripped Meyer's arm and spoke rapidly, firmly, hardly pausing for breath.

"Take the chief and go outside to the car. Tell Karl he is to drive you both to Franz's place and wait there until you hear from me. Tell Johannes to stay with the second Mercedes and remain at the entrance to the lobby. Werner is to go to the rear of the hotel. If there's a fire exit, tell him to wait by it. Give Rotman and Werner a description of the waiter who came to our room. Tall, dark-haired, young, perhaps thirty. Scar on his right cheek. As soon as they see him, I want him killed. Tell them, Meyer. I want him killed.''

Kruger saw the silver-haired man look grimly at him, an uncharacteristic fury in his voice.

"I want him found, Hans." The man's voice almost shook. "No matter what it takes."

Kruger gave a sharp nod of his head. The silver-haired man went past, Meyer beside him, and strode quickly toward the exit.

Kruger beckoned to Schmidt. Both men walked rapidly toward the elevator.

"I'm sorry, Señor, I can't find your glasses. You're sure you left them in the bathroom?"

As the waiter came out of the bathroom, Hernandez smiled and stood up from the trolley. He held up the glasses in his hand, the microphone-receiver already in his pocket.

"How stupid of me. I must have dropped them . . . here they are. But thank you for your help."

The man smiled. "No problem, Señor."

Hernandez allowed the waiter to pass with the trolley. "I'll just check that I left nothing else behind."

"Of course, Señor." The man left, closing the door after him.

Hernandez looked quickly around the room. The men who had been here were professionals. They would have been careful not to leave anything behind. He checked nonetheless. Finding nothing, he stepped from the room, closed the door after him.

He crossed the corridor and went into his room. A minute later he had stepped outside again, dragging his suitcase after him. He closed the door, saw the elevator open.

As the two men stepped out, Hernandez froze. There was a split second of mutual recognition, a split second in which he felt his heart stop and saw the two men hesitate and stare at him—the dark-haired man and the big, rugged blond bodyguard from the suite. Then Hernandez saw the blond reach inside his jacket, the butt of a pistol appearing.

Jesus Maria!

Hernandez turned and ran back down the corridor toward the fire-exit doors.

"Halt!" There was a rush of feet behind him as the shout in German rang out.

Hernandez reached the doors and pushed through. He raced down the emergency stairwell, the suitcase banging against the walls, slowing him. He cursed its weight, hearing the racing footsteps behind him on the stairs.

"Alto! Alto!" The voice was shouting in Spanish now, but Hernandez—not stopping, ignoring the call, intent on reaching the safety of the car, taking two, three steps at a time—descended the stairwell rapidly. He reached the ground-floor exit ten seconds later, his chest heaving. As he pushed open the emergency doors and burst out into the darkness, he hesitated.

Jesus Maria again!

He heard the men racing down the stairwell behind him. If he didn't slow them quickly, he'd never reach the car. He scanned the area frantically, saw the row of metal garbage bins nearby. He thrust out his free arm wildly and grasped one of the metal lids, turned in the same movement, placed the lid on the ground and kicked, wedging the lid between the base of the metal doors and the concrete. He raced toward the car, not hesitating to look back.

Hernandez reached the Buick just as he heard the fists pounding madly on the doors behind him, the voice raised in frantic anger.

"Sind Sie da, Werner? WERNER!"

Fists beat on the metal like a roll of mad drums, but the wedge held. Hernandez flung the suitcase into the car and climbed in, the voice from behind the door louder now, desperate.

"WERNER! SCHNELL!"

Hernandez fumbled to insert the key in the ignition. The key found its mark and he switched on.

The engine spluttered and died.

Hernandez felt every drop of blood drain from his body. *"No! Please! Not now! Start, please start!"*

He turned the key again, pumped the accelerator, turning at the same time that he heard the deafening noise behind him, the grating sound of metal scraping on concrete as the garbage lid gave way and the two men burst out through the emergency doors.

Jesus Maria!

The Buick's engine suddenly exploded into life. Hernandez hit the accelerator hard and the car shot forward. As he swung out into the exit lane, he saw a figure come racing toward him out of the darkness.

A man. Thirty meters away. Hernandez saw him reach into his jacket, fumble for something.

Werner . . . the man must be Werner.

Hernandez pushed the accelerator right to the floor. As the Buick rocketed forward, he flicked on the headlights and switched to high beam, saw the man shield his face from the sudden glare as he raised a pistol in his right hand. It was only a split second, but it was enough. The man twisted to the left to avoid being hit, his body crashing into the hood of a nearby car, the glare of the headlights catching the look of terror on his face.

Hernandez swung the Buick between two parked cars and drove at high speed toward the Calle Chile.

It took Kruger and the men two frantic minutes to race to the front of the hotel, where the second Mercedes waited.

The driver was already gunning the engine, saying, "What's going on?"

Kruger was like a man possessed. He flung open the door and pulled the driver bodily from the car, climbed in and found the phone in the glove compartment. He punched in the number desperately.

As the number dialed out on the crackling line, Kruger cursed. He heard the click and the line was lifted at the other end.

"Sí?"

"Have we a clean line?" Kruger spoke rapidly.

"One moment." There was a long pause. "Go ahead."

"It's Kruger. I'm at the hotel. We have a problem. I think someone overheard us discussing Brandenburg."

There was another long pause at the other end.

Then the voice said, *"Jesus. . . ."*

CHAPTER 7

Asunción.

It was dark, and the man and the two girls sat around the poolside table of the big house in the wealthy suburb of Asunción, sipping drinks the manservant had brought. There were lights on under the swimming pool, giving the smooth water a turquoise color.

Franz Lieber looked across at the two beautiful young girls sitting opposite.

They were both half-caste *mestizos*, and very young and very ravishing, no more than sixteen, and they looked like twins. They were voluptuous, as only young girls can be, their bronzed, silky flesh protruding in all the right places. Cheap jewelry dangled from their wrists and necks, and their short, tight summer skirts displayed generous portions of their legs. Each had plump, firm-looking breasts and magnificent thighs.

Lieber smiled and said, "My friend will be here soon. In the meantime, relax, enjoy yourselves."

Lieber saw the girls smile. One of them leaned forward to sip her vodka, showing her plump breasts to Lieber deliberately. Only sixteen, thought Lieber, but already she knows how to use her body like a weapon. He was definitely going to enjoy these two.

The wiser of the two said, "Madame Rosa says you are very generous, *sí*?"

Lieber grinned. "I'm always generous to girls who please me."

The girl laughed and said, "Then I will please you very much." She looked at her friend and they both giggled. Lieber smiled back wolfishly. He was fifty, with thick gray hair swept back off his forehead. He was a big man, and big-boned. He also had big appetites; in food and drink, as his generous belly testified, and especially in women.

Tonight he and Hans were going to enjoy themselves, play some bedroom games with the girls. It was a favor Lieber extended to certain guests, a refreshing, stimulating end to an evening. He glanced at his watch. Hans would be here soon. They would have some cold drinks with the girls first and then go up to the bedroom. In the meantime, he would have some fun. . . .

He smiled at the girl who had not spoken. She was fresh, not long in the business, Lieber guessed.

"What's your name?"

"Maria."

"Come here, Maria."

The girl glanced at her friend. Her friend nodded and the girl stood up slowly, came around to stand in front of Lieber. She looked good enough to eat. . . .

Lieber rested his big hand on the girl's leg just above the knee and kneaded the soft flesh. He gave another wolfish grin. "Lift your dress, Maria."

The girl obeyed. She pulled up the tight black dress to reveal a pair of skimpy white panties and pouting thighs. Lieber could see the wisps of dark hair protrude from under the tight, flimsy cotton and the plump outline of her crotch. He let his hand ride slowly up the back of the girl's bronzed thigh, had just slipped his hand under the panties onto the girl's round, smooth left buttock when the mobile phone on the poolside table rang.

Scheisse!

Lieber held onto the girl's flesh and lifted the phone with his free hand.

"Sí?"

He heard the voice, recognized the urgency in it. He let his hand slide off the rounded skin, covered the telephone mouthpiece and turned sharply to look at the girl, then at the other.

"I need to talk in private," he said curtly. "Go inside and wait." He gestured to the open french doors behind him, light spilling from a sumptuously furnished room beyond.

The two girls hesitated.

"Now!" Lieber roared.

The girls jumped at the sound of his voice, speaking in whispers as they crossed quickly to the open french doors. Lieber waited until they were safely inside and out of listening range, then pressed the button on the scrambling device clipped to the phone.

"Go ahead," he said.

Lieber listened to Kruger's frantic voice.

When he had finished, all Lieber could say was *"Scheisse. . . ."*

Hernandez's eyes flicked to the rearview mirror as he drove toward the center of the city, not knowing where to go, what to do, only that he needed to hide.

He swung the Buick left onto the Calle Chile, past the illuminated pink dome of the Pantheon on the Plaza de Heros. The traffic was thin, and Hernandez wove swiftly in and out of the lanes. His heart pounded with fear as he watched to see whether the twin beams of a car's headlights would appear rapidly behind him. But none did. No one was following him. Not yet.

The red Buick was a problem. Its color made it easily identifiable, and the men had seen the car, no question. He needed somewhere to hide it, somewhere nearby. He swung right again, then left, toward it, the brightly lit Plaza Constitution, keeping watch in the rear mirror, but he knew he had had a head start, feeling a little better now as he drove past the Plaza, the route dipping down toward the river, where the streets became narrower and darker. Hernandez knew now where to go.

The warren-like riverside *barrio* of La Chacarita loomed ahead, a drowsy dark place of tin-and-cardboard shacks built on muddy river flats. He could smell the river now, the rotten smell of sulfur and silt and mud, the river low; and a familiar fishy odor swept into the car through the open window. When he reached the river's edge, he turned right, drove for three hundred meters and halted outside a shabby house of peeling white plaster.

Hernandez climbed out and pulled the suitcase after him. La Chacarita was for the poorest of the poor, a tough area that even the *policía* avoided. He locked the driver's door and checked the others before stepping up to the house and knocking softly on the door.

He glanced up and down the street. A couple of doors away, a group of old men sat chatting on the stone steps outside an old shanty dwelling. They glanced up but otherwise paid him no attention. Hernandez looked behind him, toward the river; there was a full moon, the river silvery, dotted with *camelotes*—floating clumps of matted waterweeds that looked like malignant bumps on the surface of the silver water.

Hernandez heard a scraping noise behind the door and turned back.

A girl's voice called out softly, "Who is there?"

"It's Rudi."

He heard the rattle of a metal bolt being slid, and a moment later the door opened. A young girl stood there in the dimly lit hallway. She wore a plain white-cotton dress, and her brown eyes sparkled at her visitor. There was a look of innocence on her beautiful brown face, a look that always brought out the tenderest feelings in Hernandez.

"How is my little girl?" Hernandez smiled.

She smiled back shyly, and her long brown hair fell about her shoulders as she looked down at the suitcase. There was a sudden expression of fear on her face.

"You are going away, Rudi?"

Hernandez shook his head, spoke urgently. "No, Graciella. But I need a place to stay until the morning."

She did not ask why, simply nodded and led him inside and closed the door. She took Hernandez by the hand into a small room off to the left, with a single ancient wooden bed set against a peeling wall, above the bed a tiny red light flickering below a picture of the Virgin, the room frugal, but spotlessly clean.

"You sleep in my room, Rudi?" The girl looked up into his eyes. Her body was full, would have been undeniably tempting to any man, but Hernandez shook his head.

"I'll sleep on the kitchen floor, Graciella." He smiled fondly at her and cupped her face in his hand. "Now, be a good girl and make me some *yerba mate*."

The girl nodded and smiled back at him. As his hand came away from her face, she took hold of it silently and led him toward the kitchen.

It took Franz Lieber five minutes to make the necessary phone calls. When he had finished, he sighed and looked reflectively at the turquoise water of the swimming pool, its pale, icy-blue calm as smooth as a sheet of glass. In contrast, there was a rage inside Lieber.

Jesus. . . .

Just when everything was going smoothly, just when everything was coming together, some snooping bastard goes and fucks it up. The man was dead once they found him, whoever he was, of that much Lieber was certain. There was no place in the city the man could hide.

How could anyone possibly have known about the meeting? Lieber ignored his drink and concentrated hard, searching for weak links, for flaws. But there were none, especially in South America, especially in Paraguay, not here, not on his territory. The only ones who had known about the meeting were top people, and they could all be trusted, of that Lieber was certain. So how?

He sighed heavily. The consequences of failure were too awesome to even contemplate. Years of planning destroyed, millions wasted. *Millions.* Lieber grimaced. He had invested heavily in this, in time and money, and now everything was in jeopardy.

The man would simply have to be found, no matter what resources it took. He had contacted the necessary people; the men would be out looking already. At least forty men scouring the city, watching the airport, the railway and bus stations, the main roads leaving the city. Lieber just hoped the man hadn't too much of a head start. The description Kruger had given him over the telephone had been vague—tall, young, maybe thirty, dark-haired, a noticeable scar on his right cheek—but the man's car, a big, ancient red American car, that was something. He had seen few of those in Asunción.

Lieber pushed himself up from the chair angrily. The Mercedes would be here soon. He would have to get rid of the girls.

"Noberto!"

The *mestizo* manservant appeared moments later, scurrying out from the house toward Lieber.

"*Sí, Señor?*"

Lieber gestured toward the house. "Take a car from the garage and drop the girls off at Rosa's." He produced his wallet and handed the servant a wad of notes. "Here, give them this. Tell them I don't need them tonight.''

"*Sí, Señor.*"

"Do it *now. Pronto!*"

Lieber stepped into the house, taking the phone with him, and went through to his study. The room looked out onto the driveway that led up to his property. He poured himself a generous measure of scotch and drank half of it in one swallow. As he went to stand by the window, the phone buzzed in his hand. It was Kruger.

Lieber switched on the scrambler and said, "I've got forty men out looking. Stinnes is doing the coordinating."

"The airport, the railway station?"

"All being covered. Including the main roads out of the city. The men have a description of the car and the man."

"The others should be with you any minute. We want this *Schwein*, no matter what it takes." There was a pause, then Kruger's voice said urgently, "You know the consequences for all of us if he isn't found . . ."

Lieber swallowed. "Don't worry, he'll be found. Contact Stinnes, he's waiting for your call."

The line clicked dead. As Lieber put the phone down by the window, he saw the headlights of a car sweep into the driveway and bear rapidly up the path. The Mercedes had arrived.

CHAPTER 8

The girl lay sleeping on a tattered mattress by the old blackened stove.

She was seventeen, and Hernandez loved her—not like he did his other women, but in a special way, a protective way. Graciella Campos had a mind that would have fit more comfortably into the body of a ten-year-old. In the *barrio*, she could have been trodden on, used, abused, this little flower.

When he had met her, the men were already queuing up to use her body for a handful of *guaranís* at a time. He had been writing an article on the orphans in the *barrio* when a woman had told him about Graciella. Could Hernandez help?

When he met the girl, he had been struck by her incredible beauty and innocence. Her grandfather guardian had died; she was penniless, and he had taken pity on her. He had offered to pay for a place for her outside the shantytown, this little delicate flower living in the dungpile of La Chacarita. But the child in the woman's body had refused, was scared outside of her natural habitat. The *barrio* was home to her despite the grinding poverty.

So Hernandez had become her guardian, given her what he could afford each week, gotten her a job on the cleaning staff at the cathedral near the Plaza. He'd arranged with the woman who introduced them to call on the girl every day, attend to anything she couldn't manage. But the girl somehow always managed.

The men no longer bothered her. A friend of his, a tough, honest man who worked on the small riverboats, acted as her guardian angel. Already the man had cut and bloodied the faces of several men who had not respected his protection.

The house Graciella lived in had three tiny rooms. They were in the largest, the room that served as a kitchen, a room the girl had proudly decorated in a simple, clean way. Whenever Hernandez came by, he always made sure he brought her something—a plant, some candy, a cheap trinket—to please her, to see the smiling brown eyes look up at him with innocent gratitude. But not tonight.

It was after 3:00 A.M. now, and Hernandez sat restlessly at the rickety old kitchen table. The girl had refused to leave his side and sleep in her tiny bedroom, wanting to be near her protector. But Hernandez was not tired. Too much was going through his mind. The girl had proudly made them a supper before she had fallen asleep on the mattress on the floor.

The tape machine lay on the table and he had the earphones on. He had listened to the tape so many times in the last seven hours that he knew the words the way an actor knows his script, every word engraved in his memory, every inflection noted. The girl had been mildly intrigued. When she had seen Hernandez with the tape machine, she had smiled and said, "Music, Rudi?"

Hernandez smiled back and shook his head. "No, something more important than music, Graciella." The girl hadn't comprehended and had turned back to her cooking. It would have been pointless trying to explain; she would never have understood.

Now he looked again at the tape. What was on there wasn't much, certainly not as much as he had hoped for, but it was something, something to go on. But what?

He rewound the tape, pressed the "play" button.

"The shipment. . . . ?"

"The cargo will be picked up from Genoa as arranged."

"And the Italian?"

"He will be eliminated, but I want to be certain we don't arouse suspicion concerning the cargo. It would be prudent to wait until Brandenburg becomes operational. Then he will be dealt with along with the others."

Pause.

"Those who have pledged their loyalty . . . we must be certain of them."

"I have had their assurances confirmed. And their pedigree is without question."

"And the Turk?"

"I foresee no problems."

"The girl in Berlin ... you're absolutely certain we can rely on her?"

"She will not fail us, I assure you." Pause. *"There are no changes to the names on the list?"*

"They will all be killed."

"Your travel arrangements ... Everything has been organized?"

"We leave Paraguay on the sixth."

"The schedule ... perhaps I should go through it once more?"

He pressed the pause button, sighed.

What was the shipment the men talked of? The white powder Rodriguez mentioned? And the men, who were they? Buyers from Frankfurt? The men who came to South America to negotiate contracts? Or were they? Hernandez sensed that something did not fit into place. Something was strange about the older man, the one with the silver hair, but he didn't know what.

A shiver rippled down his spine. He replayed the last part of the conversation again.

"We must take our leave of you. It's a long drive back north. The driver will take you to the safe house."

He waited for a moment, then pressed the stop button.

He made up his mind then that he would phone Sanchez, tell him everything he knew, ask his advice. But already the men would be changing their plans, surely? Hernandez shook his head. In a way, he had risked so much for so little: voices on a tape, discussing something he could not comprehend.

He glanced at his watch. Three-ten. Sanchez wouldn't be on duty until eight, maybe nine, in the morning. Hernandez cursed silently. He wanted Sanchez to hear the tape. Perhaps he could help decipher it.

He looked down at the angelic face of the sleeping girl and felt a twinge of guilt. The men wouldn't find him in La Chacarita, he felt certain of that. But no matter how remote that possibility, he was putting her in unnecessary danger.

And if the men were out looking for him, he could not allow her to become involved. He would leave after sleeping for a couple of hours, move into the throng of early morning traffic on the Plaza. It would be safer than to drive across the city toward his apartment.

Hernandez sighed and looked down at the tape machine. He pressed the eject button, and the tape popped out. He held it between his fingers. Perhaps it would be better to put it in his safe place until he could speak with Sanchez. Because that way, he would have nothing incriminating on him if the men found him.

The spare, unused tape lay on the table where he had left it.

Hernandez stood. The girl stirred, turned over, continued her sound sleep. He would leave the car, it would be safer here. It wasn't far to walk to the station where he kept the rented locker. He could take the side streets and be back in twenty minutes once the tape had been safely hidden. He stepped quietly into the hallway, slipped back the bolt of the front door and took the spare key from the nail behind the door where the girl always left it.

The man was tired.

He had scoured the streets of Asunción all night and now it was after three o'clock. There was a year's pay for the man who found the car or the driver, and the thought of all that money was the only thing keeping him awake. The description of the man he was looking for had been vague; really, he needed a photograph. But the car was a help. It was easier to find a car than a face, and an old red American model shouldn't be difficult. But so far, he hadn't had any luck. None of the other men either; he had passed them in their cars as they scoured the city. He wondered what was going on.

He had met Model and Kaindel at a coffee stand near the Plaza Constitution. They didn't know either. Only that the man or the car had to be found, on Franz Lieber's orders. The money was proof enough that this was important.

The man rubbed his aching eyes and turned his car onto the Plaza. The dark streets of La Chacarita loomed beyond. Not the kind of place you ventured into unless you wanted to risk your life or catch something from a cheap whore. Even the thieves here were legendary for their quickness. They joked about it in Asunción: make sure that if you're driving in La Chacarita and you have to give hand signals, that you're not wearing a wristwatch.

The man grinned to himself. He had the car phone beside him to call for help, a forty-five automatic pistol in the glove compartment, and a knife under his seat. Any dago hassled him and he'd blow a hole in the bastard the size of a fist.

He drove across the brightly lit Plaza and the car rolled gently downhill into La Chacarita. . . .

It took Hernandez ten minutes to walk to the old railway station through the maze of narrow back streets. He wasn't afraid; many people knew him in the *barrio*. The streets were deserted and he walked slowly.

Fifty meters from the old porticoed station entrance, he froze. Parked across the street facing the entrance, visible under a flickering street light, were two cars, a dark Mercedes and a white Ford. Two men stood beside the Mercedes, smoking, talking. Hernandez swallowed. Such a sight would not have troubled him normally, but there was something odd about the scene. No trains were due for another four hours at least. Why would men like these wait outside the station at this hour? Both men wore suits, looked European. Like the men at the hotel. Like businessmen. Hernandez stepped into the shadows.

He looked toward the entrance, caught a glimpse of two more men standing idly by. One was young and blond and wore a leather jacket and open-necked shirt; the second was middle-aged, burly and casually dressed. These did not look like businessmen, but they were waiting for him, Hernandez felt certain. Covering the station should he try to leave the city.

Damn!

He took a deep breath. What he had done at the hotel must have set off alarm bells.

Relax. Take it easy.

But what if there were more men inside the station? How then could he get safely to the luggage box?

He waited in the shadows for several more minutes until a thought struck him. He smiled. Perhaps there was a way. He turned quickly and walked back the way he had come.

*   *   *

Hernandez reached the rear of the station minutes later. A double wooden gate served as a rear entrance, a small peephole visible. This was the entrance the railway workers used.

He entered through the judas gate and stepped into a small yard. As he went through, he saw a station worker in uniform sitting in a tiny, glass-fronted office reading a magazine. The man stared up at him for a moment, then continued reading. People living in the *barrio* took this shortcut all the time.

A minute later, he was on the nearest platform. An ancient diesel engine stood silently up against the buffers, the smell of grease and oil thick in the humid air. The area where Hernandez stood was deserted, but he could see the platforms nearest the station entrance clearly, perhaps sixty meters away.

There were Indians and peasants sleeping nearby. An old man selling water and pistachios slept at his stand, his head down, nestled in his arms. Women in their colored shawls, waited with their husbands and sleeping children for the early morning trains. But no men in business suits, no burly looking men like those at the hotel. The locker area wasn't far, tucked away behind the shuttered concession stands, thirty meters from where he stood.

His eyes searched the distant crowd again, but he could see nothing unusual, no men like the ones he had seen outside. Still, it would be prudent to be careful. Hernandez hesitated, saw a railway official sleeping soundly on a nearby wooden bench. His uniform jacket lay on the back of the bench. Hernandez crossed to where the man lay, saw that no one was watching, took the jacket, tugged it on and continued walking.

When he reached the locker, he inserted the key.

"Señor . . ."

Hernandez heard the voice behind him and froze. He turned his head slowly, felt the instant fear. He saw the elderly man standing there.

"Por favor, Señor . . ."

The man's face was dark mahogany, his skin deeply wrinkled from sun and hard work. He carried an old battered suitcase. An unlit cigarette hung from his lips. He smiled at Hernandez and pointed to the cigarette.

It took Hernandez a moment to understand. Then he fumbled with shaking hands in his pockets, gave the old man the cheap plastic lighter and said, "Keep it. I have another."

"*Muchas gracias, Señor.*"

The man turned and shambled away. Hernandez exhaled. Quickly, he opened the locker door, placed the tape on top of the envelope containing the photographs and locked the door again. He replaced the keys in his pocket, crossed back to where the sleeping official lay and returned the jacket. Then he walked back toward the rear exit.

The man had decided to drive down to the river and work his way back up, zigzagging through the warren of dark, narrow streets. At the water's edge he stopped, wrinkling his nose at the smell of sulfur and rotting fish that drifted into the warm interior. He wondered whether to turn left or right. He decided to turn right. He had the doors locked, and the automatic pistol was out now, on the seat beside him.

He had gone almost three hundred meters, driving slowly, eyes scouring the waterfront and the tiny alleyways that ran between the shanty homes, when he glimpsed the flash of red. He slowed instinctively. An old red Buick, its rear badge unmistakable, its chassis rusting, stood parked in front of a house with white peeling walls. His hand automatically reached for the gun as he pulled into the curb. He smiled and grabbed for the phone on the seat instead and punched in the number quickly.

The line clicked. A voice said, "*Sí?*"

The man said, "It's Dortmund . . . I think I've found the car."

Hernandez walked slowly back along the river, taking his time.

La Chacarita was a deserted place of shadows at this early hour. The tape was in a safe place; he would tell Sanchez about it tomorrow, tell the man everything he knew, hope that he could help him. Leaving the tape in the locker had been a wise decision, he reflected. Even if the men caught him, he could bide his time, perhaps do a deal if he was forced to. If he had the tape on him and they caught him, then surely he was dead. What the voices on the tape said must be important. The presence of the men at the station testified to that.

He was too nervous and excited to sleep. He stopped by the river and lit a cigarette, thinking, knowing that something was happening, something really big, something that was worth killing for, remembering the faces of the men on the first floor as they came out of the elevator, knowing with certainty that they would have killed him. He would tell Sanchez all this; it was too dangerous for him to pursue this alone now. The men at the hotel were powerful; how else had they sent people to look for him? If the railway station was covered, then so was the airport, perhaps even the main roads. Hernandez shivered. His only hope now was Sanchez.

The big detective would want to know why he had not come to him immediately, why he had withheld information from him that day at Tsarkin's house. But Hernandez would worry about all that later.

He looked at his watch in the light of the moon. He had been away for almost half an hour. It was time to get back to Graciella's place and try somehow to get some sleep. He flicked away the lighted cigarette, watched as it cartwheeled into the silvery water, then turned and started to walk back toward the house.

As he approached he saw that the front door was open.

He froze.

He had closed the door after him, he was certain. Or had he? His mind was in such turmoil. Perhaps he had not? *Jesus, anyone could have come in and . . .*

Hernandez heard the *click* and wheeled around instantly, felt the blood draining from him, saw the two men armed with pistols lunge toward him, their faces a blur because already there was a rough hand over his mouth, stifling his cry, another gripping his hair, jerking his head back as other rough hands pushed him into the house. As the door burst in, he was propelled forward with an almighty force, into the kitchen now, lights blazing in the tiny room, crowded with men . . .

Hernandez felt a sharp punch in his side, the hand still on his mouth, stifling his scream. The faces around him were a blur as more blows rained down, pulped his face, bruised his body until he could hardly stand, blood on his lips, its salty taste in his mouth. Rough hands pushing him back against the wall, two quick, sharp blows to his kidneys making him want to throw up.

Two big men held Graciella, her tiny body like a rag doll's between them. A white towel gagged her mouth and there was blood on her pretty face, terror in her innocent eyes. The recording equipment lay on the kitchen table still. Two men stood over it, two of the men he had seen at the hotel: the dark-haired one who had opened the door to him, and the older, silver-haired man, handsome, maybe sixty. Both stared at Hernandez with contempt.

The dark-haired man stepped quickly forward, glared into Hernandez's eyes. The hand that covered Hernandez's mouth came away for an instant and the man's fist smashed into Hernandez's face. There was the sharp crack of bone breaking and he reeled back in pain, the bridge of his nose shattered, his scream muffled by the hand again over his mouth; then another blow struck him, across the back of the head, blows raining down on him again. Someone gripped his hair and jerked his head up so that he was staring into the face of the young, dark-haired man.

The eyes were steel-gray and cold. He spoke quietly, threateningly, but with urgency in his voice.

"You will answer my questions. If you lie, the girl dies. If you tell the truth, she lives. You understand?"

The man jerked his hand toward Graciella. The two men holding her yanked her head back savagely by the hair until the whites of her eyes showed. Hernandez heard her muffled cries of pain. One of the men ripped her dress, her small brown breasts exposed. The second took a big silver knife from behind his back, pressed the tip of the blade against the girl's left nipple.

The dark-haired man said again, "You understand?"

Hernandez wanted to vomit. He nodded quickly.

The man stared into his face. "How did you know we

were at the Excelsior? Answer quickly now.''

The hand on Hernandez's mouth came away.

Hernandez said weakly, his breath coming in gasps, "I was at Tsarkin's house the day he killed himself . . . covering the story for *La Tarde* . . . a call came . . . from the Excelsior Hotel . . . I answered the telephone . . ."

The eyes of the dark-haired man lit up, understanding. He suddenly wrenched at Hernandez's pockets, ripped out the wallet and examined the contents. He plucked out the Press identity card, scrutinized the photograph, then handed it to the silver-haired man, who stood nearby watching, the one in charge, before he nodded silently for Hernandez to go on.

Hernandez's voice came in short, staccato gasps, thick with fear, as he told him about Rodriguez. What he had been told about the men. About the equipment. About his plan. The dark-haired man turned pale. He turned to look at the older man, whose face was even paler, eyes glaring over at Hernandez.

The dark-haired man turned back, nodded toward the table and said sharply, "The tape. We checked it, it's blank . . ." His tone demanded an explanation.

Hernandez sucked in air. His body on fire with pain; the blows had almost crippled him.

"Answer!" the man screamed.

"The microphone . . . there was a problem with it . . ." Hernandez began quickly, but the man suddenly cut him short with a sharp wave of his hand, as if he knew, a sadistic smile on his face now, his hand coming up to seize Hernandez's jaws in a painful pincer grip. Hernandez wanted to scream: *No, the real tape is in a safe place, I can take you to it. We can deal.* But the man spoke quickly.

"Rodriguez . . . what he told you . . . who else did he tell?"

Hernandez tried to shake his head. The man's grip still held him. "He told no one else . . . Only me."

"You are certain? I want the truth."

"Yes."

"And did you tell anyone else?" There was an urgency in the man's voice now. His grip tightened.

"No. No one."

Pause. "Tell me . . . why did you leave this house?"

"To get some air. I . . . I couldn't sleep."

"Where did you go?"

"I . . . walked along the river."

The man's eyes searched Hernandez's face, searched for the truth. "The cargo Rodriguez told you about . . . what do you think it was? Answer truthfully now. The girl's life depends on it."

Hernandez looked at him through bruised and bloodied eyes. "White powder. You're shipping cocaine." Saying it and not caring, knowing now that he was dead no matter what he said, knowing that Graciella was dead, only hoping for the child it would be quick, without pain. . . .

The man released his grip. Hernandez begged, "Please . . . the girl . . . knows nothing. She's only a child."

The dark-haired man was smiling now, laughing as if something had amused him. He turned toward the older man with the silver hair. The man nodded.

The dark-haired man turned back. He stared into Hernandez's eyes.

"You dumb, stupid dago fuck!"

Then he turned and clicked his fingers. It happened quickly. The man holding the knife in front of Graciella raised his hand. The blade flashed. Hernandez was about to scream, but a hand came over his mouth again. He watched in horror as the knife came down, sliced through the girl's soft brown flesh, slit her throat from the valley between her breasts to the navel of her stomach. Hernandez saw with horror as the blood spurted out in a fountain, the whites of the child's dying eyes looking to heaven, her body suddenly limp, engulfed in blood. Hernandez felt the vomit rise in his stomach.

And then the big, blond bodyguard he had seen in the hotel stepped forward out of nowhere.

Hernandez saw the flash of another blade as the man drew a jagged knife from under his coat. Hernandez tried vainly to scream, but the hand trapped the cry in his throat, other hands pinning him hard against the wall.

Then it was as if everything was happening in slow motion. Hernandez watched in mute horror as the jagged metal arced and dug savagely into his chest. He felt a searing pain as the blade plunged into flesh like a hammer blow, felt the flow of hot blood as the sharpness sliced down through his gut. Through the fogging mist of pain engulfing him, he was faintly aware of the dark-haired man stepping back, the hands that held him releasing their grip, and he slid back against the wall, slid down into the dark, growing pools of his own blood.

PART TWO

CHAPTER 9

Strasbourg, France. Thursday, December 1

A log fire blazed in one corner of the restaurant, and the walls had been freshly painted in warm brown colors, giving the place a cozy atmosphere.

From where they sat by the window, Volkmann could see the spire of the old cathedral rise into the gray afternoon sky, the patchwork of the red- and brown-slated rooftops of the medieval center of old Strasbourg stretching in serried, jagged rows as far as the eye could see. A cold wind blew across the Place Gutenberg, and needles of fine rain clawed at the window.

You could usually set your watch by Ferguson's appointments, but almost half an hour had gone by and they had ordered and there was still no sign of him.

The head of British DSE hated German food, which was why when they were having their weekly informal meeting, Ferguson always chose a French restaurant.

Volkmann turned to stare beyond the window again, toward the bronzed statue of Johann Gutenberg. The cold Place was almost bereft of pedestrians despite the nearness of Christmas. In the window of a nearby shop, a fat, red-faced little salesman was standing on a chair, struggling to hang coils of silvered decorations among the shop's seasonal window display.

Tom Peters sat opposite, sipping from a glass of Bordeaux. Ferguson's right-hand man and the Section's number two, Peters was a stocky Welshman of medium height, his graying sandy hair swept back off his ruddy face.

He looked across at Volkmann and said, "There was an article in *Le Monde* only last week. Some hack reckoned that within another few months, it'll be like the bad old days of the Great Depression." Peters nodded toward the struggling salesman across the street. "For that poor man's sake, I hope all the work is worth it."

Volkmann smiled and drank the red, fruity wine Peters had poured for him. "Did Ferguson say what it was he wanted to talk about?"

They were in a secluded corner of the restaurant on a slightly raised dais, away from the other diners. Peters sipped his wine appreciatively, then grimaced and looked out balefully at the view.

"Something to do with the bloody Germans."

The worries Volkmann had discussed with Sally Thornton seemed to be coming to pass. DSE was not working. On the face of it, the organization seemed to be dying of boredom, but he knew the problems went much deeper than that.

Meanwhile, Krull wasn't at his desk in the German Section and hadn't been seen for days. Even the people in the French and Italian Sections seemed to be spending more time than usual lingering over coffee. The only lively presence was in his own department, the British, and that of the Dutch. Both Sections were busily working at their desks as if nothing were amiss, incorrigible bureaucrats that they were.

Ferguson arrived moments later. A tall, gaunt man, pasty-faced, pushing sixty, he dressed like an English squire in Donegal tweeds, checkered shirt, and woolen tie knotted thickly. He took a seat at the table, apologizing.

"I see you've started without me." Ferguson glanced at the open wine bottle, smiled briefly and accepted a glass from Peters.

"Have you ordered? Then I suppose I had better do the same."

Ferguson ordered the fillet of sole with lemon sauce. He sipped his wine and sat back, glancing out the window at the pigeons swirling around the Gutenberg statue like limp, gray rags. When he turned back, he spoke quietly.

"I had a meeting with Hollrich, that's what delayed me. He's been in Bonn for the past week."

"Anything that concerns us?" Peters asked.

"It's the people in Berlin and Bonn," Ferguson replied. "They're talking about money problems, fiscal cutbacks. Considering the circumstances prevailing just now, it's as good an excuse as any. They may want to scale down their involvement in security cooperation. Concentrate on the problems closer to home."

"They would, wouldn't they?" Peters remarked.

Ferguson swirled the rich, fruity wine before swallowing again. He grimaced slightly as he looked back at Peters and Volkmann. "Hollrich says it's mainly money. That the mandarins in Bonn are whining about the need to cut back on spending."

"The whole operation is run on a shoestring, for God's sake. You made that point to Hollrich, sir?" Peters said.

There was a silence at the table for several moments as the waiter brought their orders. Ferguson waited until the man had left before replying.

"It's not as simple as that, Tom," he said. He cut his fish with measured care. "Hollrich's chief concern just now is with the internal situation in Germany. The rest of Europe's problems hardly matter ... much less, of course, those of the rest of the world. And God knows, the problems in Germany are serious. You watch television, you've seen the protest marches and the riots. The chancellor is in trouble with a minority government. He's too weak to take any kind of forceful action.

"I know it increases the work load for everyone else, but there you have it. I wanted to inform you both of what's happening so you are aware of what's in the air but to carry on as if it's business as usual. I'm seeing Hollrich again on Monday. Naturally, I pressed the importance of staying within DSE. I told him to pass on that message to his superiors."

Volkmann asked, "Anything else?"

Ferguson hesitated and glanced out toward the square for a moment before turning back.

"There is something, actually. Something I want you to look into. A favor for Pauli Graf of the German Section." Ferguson paused. "It's a difficult time, and I don't want to rock any boats. However, something has come up that I think we should look into."

Volkmann said, "Which area?"

"He didn't go into details. But it looks to be some sort of smuggling thing. Perhaps narcotics. According to Graf, Hollrich wasn't remotely interested. He said they hadn't the time or the manpower."

Volkmann asked, "So what's the problem?"

"A girl in Frankfurt, an old acquaintance of Graf's, was

in South America recently. She talked with him. Told him
some things that may well be quite interesting to us."

"Us?" said Peters.

"DSE, obviously," replied Ferguson.

"Why can't Pauli Graf handle it himself?" Volkmann
asked.

"As I say, the Germans don't seem to want to touch this
girl's information." He spread his arms helplessly. "Who
can figure the Germans, especially now? Anyhow, Graf got
short shrift from Hollrich, and Graf himself is being posted
back to Berlin as of tomorrow. Apart from the manpower
constraints, he seemed to think his department wasn't really
interested because the crime—if there was a crime—took
place in South America, outside his jurisdiction." He
looked up. "That is of course arguable if, say, the smuggling of narcotics is involved. And then on top of that, the
girl failed to go through proper channels—a definite no-no
where Hollrich is concerned, good bureaucrat that he is.
She didn't take her information to the *Bundespolizei*, so he
won't touch her."

"Any particular reason why she didn't go to them?"

Ferguson shrugged. "None that I know of. After Pauli
told her he couldn't help her, she told him she wanted to
talk to one of our senior people. That she had information
concerning a smuggling operation into Europe. She wants
to talk to someone from DSE in person."

"Who do you want to handle it?" Peters asked.

"I had thought Joseph," Ferguson said. He looked back
at Volkmann. "You've got the language and the experience
in the field. You know your way around. It may be nothing,
of course, but then again, no harm in checking."

"Nothing more than that?" *There's precious little to go
on*, Volkmann thought. *It seems the point of all this is that
Ferguson is helping out his friend Pauli Graf. Which trans-
lates to me doing some work the Germans should be doing
themselves.*

Ferguson looked mildly irritated. "No. I've told you
everything I know."

Volkmann glanced over at the fat salesman across the
street. The man had finished his display and was peering
hopelessly out of the window.

"What about the girl?"

"Her name is Erica Kranz. Age twenty-five. Freelance journalist by profession." Ferguson took a slip of paper from his inside pocket, handed it across to Volkmann. "I've written out her address and phone number. I think you ought to pay her a visit, see what it's about."

"When do you want me to start?"

"You could drive up to Frankfurt tomorrow. But give the girl a call first."

"Who do I report to?"

"Me. And if I'm not around, you can contact Peters and he'll pass the message on. I've already requested information on the girl from Koller of the German Section. I should have the file delivered to you tonight. Sometimes I despise the Germans for their bureaucracy, but sometimes I thank God for it. They have files on everyone. At least you'll be prepared."

Volkmann glanced out the window. The fat salesman across the square was standing at the entrance to the shop, hands clasped behind his back, examining his work. The square was still empty of shoppers.

When Volkmann turned back, he saw Ferguson and Peters observing him. Ferguson's eyes flicked to the salesman. The head of British DSE frowned, then spread thick, hard butter evenly on a crisp white roll and poured himself another glass of wine.

"I think I read somewhere recently that during the Depression it was just the same—everyone who was still in business chasing after what few pennies were in circulation. A dreadful mess. But thank heavens we can leave such problems in the incapable hands of economists and politicians."

Ferguson smiled.

Peters glanced over at Volkmann and raised his eyebrows, but Volkmann smiled, sipped his wine, and said nothing.

The Orangerie Park, with its exotic birds, miniature lake and cascading waterfalls, its landscaped gardens and its pavilion built by Napoleon for the Empress Josephine, lies within a short walking distance of the offices of the DSE.

Unlike the imposing headquarters of Interpol in Lyon, the bland, modern offices of the *Direction de Sécurité Européene* in Strasbourg are little known. Situated near the Parliament building on the Avenue de l'Europe, the six-story building houses an amalgam of all the twelve European intelligence agencies and specialized police forces, whose representatives pool and act on matters of mutual security within the European Community.

Whereas the main target of Interpol is the international criminal, its actual powers remain limited. Its officers, drawn from the police forces, are confined to providing primarily an information service, processing and disseminating information within three main, clearly defined criminal categories: criminals who operate in more than one country; criminals who do not travel at all, but whose criminal activities affect other countries; and criminals who commit a crime in one country and flee to another. But since the nations of the world have varying degrees of difference in their respective criminal and legal procedures, Interpol's officers do not have power of arrest, despite popular portrayal to the contrary in books and films depicting agents moving freely from country to country, making arrests where they please. The organization therefore is limited to providing a clearinghouse for information on criminal activity, however effective.

The DSE has a function not dissimilar, but concerns itself with four main categories of criminal and terrorist activity, and only as they apply to European security and criminal matters. And unlike Interpol, its officers are drawn not only from the specialized police forces within Europe, but also from the intelligence services of member countries. Its officers also have powers of arrest, albeit these powers are strictly limited by protocol and to within the member states.

Category One covers terrorist activity, both indigenous terrorism and terrorists from countries outside Europe who may use Europe as a base or as a target. Category Two is concerned with smuggling in all its forms, but prime areas of interest are narcotics, arms, precious metals and gems. Category Three covers espionage as it relates to both national or community security, and industrial matters; Category Four covers fraud and counterfeiting.

Within DSE, each individual member state has its own Section in the Strasbourg headquarters, representing that country's state intelligence agency and police force. Each Section maintains a staff of no more than twelve senior officers and administrative personnel, and liaises with other national Sections in areas of mutual concern and interest where these areas overlap. Thus the principal raison d'être of DSE is to provide a cohesive, united agency to combat all four categories of criminal and terrorist activity and to maintain a comprehensive and shared computerized database on these activities.

Joseph Volkmann's office in the British Section was on the third floor, which also housed the Dutch Section. Below the window was a small square, called simply the Platz, empty on this cold December afternoon. He had arrived back from lunch at two and gone straight to work, sifting through the reports and filing his paperwork. There were the usual subjects: narcotics, smuggling, terrorism; intelligence reports ready to be acted on or filed away.

When he finished over two hours later, darkness had already fallen outside, lights coming on in the office buildings all around.

He took the slip of paper Ferguson had given him and dialed the girl's number in Frankfurt. When Erica Kranz answered, he told her he was a liaison officer with DSE, explained that Pauli Graf had asked someone to have a talk with her.

"Can you tell me what this is about, Frau Kranz?"

The girl's voice sounded uneasy, and Volkmann thought he detected a trace of fear in it. "I'd rather not discuss the matter over the telephone, Herr Volkmann. But it is important. Could we meet?"

"I could drive up to Frankfurt tomorrow morning. Pauli Graf gave us your address. Unless you want to meet somewhere else?"

There was a pause on the line, and then the girl's voice came back. "I would appreciate your coming here, Herr Volkmann. My apartment is on the top floor. Is midday okay?"

"Midday is fine. Good afternoon, Frau Kranz."

At five, Volkmann cleared away his desk, went down to

the parking lot and drove to his apartment. It was a modest place by Strasbourg's standards, a compact two-bedroom apartment in one of the old houses along the Quai Ernest, overlooking a small, paved courtyard.

It was after ten when Koller from the German Section appeared with the file, looking irritated. Volkmann offered the man a drink, but Koller refused and seemed put out at having to call at the apartment.

"Do you mind telling me why you want the girl's file?"

"Nothing special. Just routine."

Koller inquired no further. "Please see that the copy I've given you is returned."

When Koller had left, Volkmann ran a hot bath and poured himself a large scotch. After bathing, he lay on the bed and read Erica Kranz's file.

It made interesting reading.

Erica Kranz was born in Buenos Aires, Argentina, of German-born parents. She had one older sister, married to a Frenchman and living in Rennes. Her father had died in South America when she was three, and the girls had returned to Germany with their mother in the same year.

A graduate of Heidelberg University, majoring in journalism, she had dabbled at the university with the Greens and other ecological-political organizations, but she had no known political affiliations or activities at present. Single. Twenty-five. No known vices, no convictions. She worked as a freelance journalist and had frequent assignments from the popular German women's magazines.

All very straightforward, Volkmann thought. But then came a paragraph about the girl's father that sent chills through his soul.

Manfred Kranz had been a major in the Leibstandarte SS Division during the last war. He had once been wanted in connection with war crimes committed in France and Russia. Twenty male inhabitants of a small village in southern France called Ronchamp had been publicly executed during the German retreat. Manfred Kranz was the unit commander responsible. And in Russia, he had been implicated in the execution of two hundred prisoners of war during the German assault on Kiev. He had never been brought to trial, the Argentine authorities refusing to cooperate in his extradition.

Letting his mind wrap around all this, Volkmann crossed over to the bedroom window and stared out.

It had stopped raining and the clouds had long disappeared and darkness fallen. He could see the lights of Germany now, burning into the winter's night beyond the Rhine. He never took the trip across the border unless he had to. Ferguson knew he disliked dealing with the Germans. With few exceptions, he had avoided social contact with them even when he had worked in Berlin, that least German of cities.

He set the travel clock for seven, undressed slowly, turned off the light and lay in the bed. The paragraph about Manfred Kranz had disturbed him, and he tossed restlessly for some time before he finally fell asleep. He dreamed about his father.

CHAPTER 10

Volkmann found the apartment block with no difficulty, tucked away behind a cluster of red-bricked, prewar buildings near the Eiserner Steg on the south side of the river. It was modern, four stories high with a gray mansard roof. The girl was waiting for him in the open doorway when he came out of the elevator.

She was tall and full-figured, with dusky skin and pale-blue eyes. Her long legs were clad in tight blue jeans tucked into high leather boots, and she wore a loose black sweater. Her blond hair was tied up, emphasizing her high cheekbones. She wore hardly any makeup and her face looked tense. Volkmann introduced himself and showed her his identification before they went inside.

In the background, he heard a Schubert string quartet playing softly. The girl crossed to a mini hi-fi on a shelf by the window and lowered the volume.

"I was just going to make some coffee. Would you like some, Herr Volkmann?"

"A coffee would be fine."

"Please, make yourself comfortable."

Volkmann watched her as she went into the kitchen. Though her file said she was twenty-five, she looked a bit older. She would have passed for a model, or a female executive with one of the Frankfurt commercial banks.

The apartment was spotlessly clean and furnished in a modern style, large and airy, filled with potted plants and bookshelves and pale leather furniture. The bookshelves were full, and Volkmann noticed an open book lying on the couch. He picked it up and glanced idly at the cover. It was a book of poetry by Adrienne Rich.

When the girl returned with two cups of coffee, she sat opposite Volkmann on a white leather couch, her legs crossed. She picked up the book and glanced at the open pages before looking up at Volkmann. Her face appeared pale and drawn, and now that Volkmann looked closely, he saw that the blue eyes were red-ringed from crying.

As she placed the book beside her, she said softly, "Are you familiar with the work of Adrienne Rich, Herr Volkmann?"

He half smiled and shook his head. "No, I'm afraid not." Then he looked at her and said, "Perhaps you had better tell me what you told to Pauli Graf, Frau Kranz."

"You are German, Herr Volkmann?"

"British. Your people in the German Section of DSE weren't particularly interested in your case. Pauli Graf has been posted back to Berlin, and he passed you onto us unofficially." He looked at her face. "If it matters, I can ask your people again."

She shook her head. "No. I was just making an observation. Your accent, it's a little different, that's all."

She brushed a strand of blond hair from her face and looked away toward the window, then slowly back again.

"Until last week, I was in Asunción in Paraguay on a week's holiday. I stayed with my cousin, Rudi Hernandez." The girl bit her lip, hesitated before going on. "During my stay with him, I sensed that he was troubled by something. When I asked him what it was, he told me he was working on a story. Something the newspaper he works for as a journalist knows nothing about."

When the girl hesitated again, Volkmann asked, "What sort of story?"

"Rudi had learned from a pilot he knew in Asunción, a man named Rodriguez, that certain people were smuggling cargoes out of South America into Europe. A week before I arrived in Paraguay, this pilot, Rodriguez, telephoned Rudi and asked him to meet him. He told Rudi he had a favor to ask. He wanted Rudi to write a story, a newspaper article, but not to publish it, to hold it somewhere safe, with a lawyer perhaps. If Rodriguez was killed, Rudi was to publish the story."

The girl hesitated again before going on. "Rodriguez had worked for these people who did the smuggling. They had hired him and his aircraft to transport a number of cargoes. His business was smuggling, and he was used to dealing with such people. But now he was certain the men who had hired him had been watching him and wanted to kill him."

"Do you know what these cargoes were?"

The girl shook her head. "Rodriguez thought they were narcotics, but he wasn't sure. All he could say was that there had been several consignments, all delivered to Montevideo in Uruguay over a period of almost a year. The consignments were packed in sealed boxes. Rodriguez said he had been very well paid by these men. He also gave Rudi the name of the man who had hired him to do the work, Nicolas Tsarkin."

Volkmann gave her a questioning look.

"Rudi knew very little about him. Said he was a businessman, a German immigrant, no criminal connections that he could find."

Volkmann nodded. "Go on, Frau Kranz."

The girl sighed. "Two days after Rodriguez had delivered the last consignment for these people, he noticed that he was being watched. That's when he became afraid and contacted Rudi. He told him he thought he had become involved in something over his head, something very big, and that these men meant to kill him. So Rudi agreed to go along with Rodriguez' request and write the story. I think he thought he might be onto a good story, and that Rodriguez would allow him to publish it regardless. But three days later, Rodriguez' body was found in a street in Asunción. He had been killed by a car. There were no witnesses, and the car didn't stop. Rudi was certain that the people Rodriguez had worked for had murdered him. That is what had been troubling him."

"What made him so certain these men had committed murder?"

"The way Rodriguez had died. And Rodriguez had told Rudi the men he had worked for were very secretive. Their secrecy was almost obsessive. Rudi said they killed Rodriguez because they wanted no one to know what they were doing."

Volkmann hesitated, put down his cup. "Did Hernandez inform the police in Asunción about all of this?"

"No. He wanted solid evidence first. He wanted the names of the people involved, and he wanted to be sure of the cargoes, what they contained. And that what these people were doing was definitely illegal."

Volkmann looked at the girl for a moment, then turned

away toward the window. The sky was gray beyond. He hesitated, then turned back.

"Frau Kranz, I really don't see how this matter concerns DSE. You have no solid proof."

The girl was silent for a moment. "No, but Pauli Graf told me once that the department he belonged to concerned itself with many areas . . ."

"Yes, but South America isn't exactly our territory."

"There is something else that might interest you in all of this."

"Tell me."

"Before I left Asunción, Rudi had asked me to check up on something for him. He needed certain information. Four days ago, I telephoned Rudi's apartment to tell him of my progress. There was no reply. So I telephoned his office. A reporter at the newspaper, he told me . . ." The girl's voice trailed off, her head bowed. Volkmann could hear the Schubert quartet, muted, barely audible, the music filling the silence.

"Told you what?"

"He told me Rudi was dead. The police had found his body in a house in Asunción. The house of a young girl. They had both been murdered."

Erica Kranz took a handkerchief from the sleeve of her sweater, wiped her eyes.

Volkmann asked, "How do these murders concern DSE?"

She looked at Volkmann steadily. "Before Rodriguez was killed, he took Rudi to Tsarkin's house, a big estate on the outskirts of Asunción. They watched this house from a short distance away. Rudi wanted some photographs for the story. He had a telephoto lens fitted to the camera. Two men came out into the grounds of the property, walking together. Rodriguez pointed out Tsarkin. But what interested Rudi was not the man Rodriguez had pointed out, but the second man present, walking with him. You see, Rudi recognized him, had seen him before. In Europe, not in South America."

"I don't understand."

"Rudi had met this man five years before at a party at

Heidelberg University, where I was a student. His name was Dieter Winter.''

"Go on.''

"Rudi was staying with my family at the time, and I had brought him along to the party. Winter had a heated argument with Rudi that almost came to blows. Rudi remembered him vividly. He said it was the first time he had ever wanted to hit someone. He showed me one of the photographs he had taken of the men in the grounds of the house in Asunción. An old man and a young man strolling together. The old man was Tsarkin, Rudi told me. The young man could have been Dieter Winter, but I wasn't sure. He had been a student on the campus, but I hardly remembered him. So Rudi asked me to check up on him as soon as I returned home and to send him a photograph of Winter if I could get one, just to be certain.

"When I returned to Frankfurt, I discovered that Winter's name had been in the newspapers here in Germany. The police found his body in an alleyway in Berlin a week ago. He had been shot to death.''

The girl reached across for a large buff envelope that lay on the coffee table. She removed a newspaper clipping, handed it to Volkmann. It was no more than a couple of paragraphs and described the discovery of a man's body in an alleyway near the Zoo U-Bahn in Berlin. He had been shot five times at close range. There were no witnesses, and the man's identity was given as Dieter Winter. There was a request by the *Bundespolizei* for anyone to come forward with information.

Volkmann handed back the clipping. "This man Winter, what was so strange about him being in Paraguay?''

The girl shrugged. "It just seemed strange to Rudi that Winter should be there, so far from Germany. And the fact that he might have been involved with these people who killed Rodriguez.''

"Have you mentioned this matter to anyone else?''

"Only to Pauli Graf.''

"Why didn't you go to the police?''

"I had the feeling that Pauli seemed to think it a matter for your people. And besides, the *Bundespolizei* are really only interested in what happens on German territory. But your people, Pauli told me, don't only work in Europe.''

Volkmann put down his coffee. "What exactly do you want me to do, Frau Kranz?"

The girl looked at Volkmann intently. "I would like to know why Rudi died, and who killed him. I intend traveling to Paraguay again early next week. Rudi would have wanted someone to follow up his story. I'm a journalist, that is my profession. But my interest is also a personal one."

"You haven't answered my question."

The girl hesitated for a moment, as if struck by Volkmann's bluntness, then said, "You have contacts in the police and security services of other countries. Perhaps you could give me a letter of introduction, suggest someone I could talk with in Paraguay. Or even advise me."

"I advise you to leave it to the Paraguayan police. Use the proper channels and leave Pauli Graf out of it." Volkmann looked directly at the girl. "Tell the *Bundespolizei* what you told me. They'll pass it on to their own people in DSE if they think it's important enough."

There was a hint of impatience in the girl's reply. "That's what Pauli Graf told me. But that takes time and I'm leaving for Asunción the day after tomorrow." She looked at Volkmann steadily. "I would appreciate any help you could give me, Herr Volkmann, despite your advice. It would make things easier, I'm sure. Besides, as I said, the *Bundespolizei* don't normally concern themselves with a crime that happens on the other side of the world. But your people . . . Pauli Graf told me their interests are wider. But then, perhaps I have been mistaken."

The Schubert rose and fell faintly in the background as the girl continued to look at him expectantly. Suddenly she looked very young, and Volkmann saw the pain in her eyes. On the other hand, he had little appetite to tangle himself in German problems.

"To be honest, I'm not sure this is DSE's territory."

"I understand, Herr Volkmann. But thank you for listening."

Volkmann stood up. "When does your flight to Asunción leave?"

"Sunday next. From Frankfurt-Main."

"I'll check with my people. I can't promise anything, but if there's anything I can do to help, I'll telephone before you leave."

"Thank you, Herr Volkmann."

"Good morning, Frau Kranz."

Erica watched as Volkmann crossed the corridor to the elevator. She closed the door after her and went to stand by the window. The Rhine barges were having a bad day of it, the sturdy vessels tossing about in the gray swells. She saw Volkmann cross the street below and walk toward a parked car, his raincoat flapping about his legs.

There was something distant about the man, she considered. So different from Rudi, who had always smiled, and yet the same soft, brown eyes. And there was something else, too. She had sensed an almost palpable dislike in his manner toward her. A formality she found disturbing. And she had seen the tension in his eyes and around his mouth.

She watched as he walked away, then dismissed the thought from her mind as she went to wash the coffee cups.

It was after four when Volkmann arrived back in Strasbourg. Ferguson and Peters were both out and he wrote his report and delivered a copy to Ferguson's secretary, along with a copy of the girl's file.

She told him Ferguson was in Paris and wasn't expected back until later that evening. Volkmann sent a security fax to the *Bundespolizei Hauptquartier* in Berlin requesting information on Dieter Winter, giving what details he could about the man and requesting a photograph, if available.

Volkmann left the office two hours later, arriving at his apartment a little after six. At ten o'clock, Ferguson telephoned.

"I read your report. A little nebulous, but interesting."

"Any reply to the request I sent to the BP?"

"It arrived this evening. Along with a photograph."

"What did they say about Winter?"

"Graduated from Heidelberg five years ago, majoring in history. Involved in several right-wing groups during his student days, but no arrests. The BP has no idea of why he was killed. The area where it happened is a stamping ground for petty drug dealers. They tried that tack, however, and came up with nothing.''

''Had Winter any narcotic convictions?''

''None. But considering the area where the shooting happened, that's the angle the BP hinted at.''

''Nothing else?''

''The weapon used in the Berlin shooting is the bit that interests us. A Walther nine-millimeter, but South American-manufactured ammunition. The BP thinks it was the same weapon used in the killing of a German industrialist named Pieber in a Hanover restaurant a year ago. A British business colleague of Pieber's named Hargrove was wounded in the same attack and died a couple of days later.''

''What do you think, sir?''

''God only knows. It could be anything. Personally, I think you ought to take the trip along with the girl. This journalist in Asunción could have been onto something that might concern us. There are several bodies now. Someone had reason to kill. I'd be very interested in learning what that reason is.''

''You really think it's necessary?''

''Bearing in mind what she said, yes, I think so. We can always bill the expenses to the Germans if it ends up in their court. And besides, Hargrove was a British subject, after all.''

''So what do I tell her?''

''Just that we're probing. That Winter's death interests us. See Peters about tickets first thing tomorrow morning. I take it the girl won't have any objection?''

''I shouldn't think so.''

''Good. I'll make contact with the people in Asunción and send them a copy of her statement, translated, of course. Goodnight, Joseph.''

Volkmann heard the line click and put down the receiver. He sat on the bed, half undressed, before turning off the bedside light. His mind went over the meeting with Erica Kranz, the sighting of Winter in Paraguay and the shooting in Berlin, the murders in Asunción. How did they connect? Or did they connect? There were no answers, not yet, there couldn't be, only more questions; a pebble thrown into a pond, eddying in endless circles.

He had left the copy of the girl's file with his report. He recalled again the paragraph on the last page of her file, the information about her father's crimes. Though these happened a long time before the girl was born, and her father was dead before she had a chance to really know him, he still shivered now in the darkness, remembering that single paragraph.

CHAPTER 11

Asunción. Monday, December 5

The detective who welcomed Joseph Volkmann and Erica Kranz in the arrivals area that Monday morning wore a crumpled white suit that seemed a size too large for his stocky body. His dark eyes looked tired. Introducing himself as Captain Vellares Sanchez, he led them to an unmarked police car and drove toward the center of the city.

A shimmering wave of intense heat had hit them as they stepped from the terminal, the air dry and breezeless, hot enough to hurt their lungs. It was summer in Asunción, trees and flowers in bloom, eucalyptus and palm trees lining their route, palm fronds hanging limply in the scorching afternoon air.

Volkmann sat beside the girl in the rear, the windows rolled down but still the heat oppressive. The big detective mopped his face with a handkerchief as he drove. He barely spoke, except to inquire of his passengers if they had had a pleasant flight.

The city they drove through was a riot of color and noise, a mixture of old and new: nineteenth-century facades and yellow-bricked adobes and tin-and-wood shanties existing side by side with modern buildings and apartments. Ancient yellow trolley cars screeched noisily along the main avenues.

The detective's office was on the third floor of the *Comisaria Centrico*, the Central Police Station, on Calle Chile. It was a drab, hot place with peeling gray walls and ancient furniture. An old rusting filing cabinet stood in one corner, an electric fan whirred overhead.

A young recruit brought them strong, aromatic Paraguayan tea. *"Yerba mate,"* explained Sanchez. "You have been to Paraguay before, Señor Volkmann?"

"Never."

"The tea is an acquired taste. But as good as beer on a hot day."

Sanchez removed his jacket and loosened his tie, waited until the young recruit had left before he unlocked a drawer in his desk and produced two files. His own file and the one containing the report the *seguridad* had received from the people Volkmann worked for, translated into Spanish. He had read these yesterday morning over coffee, and had had two men from his department check out the information.

Now he smiled briefly at Erica, remembering Hernandez talking about her, appreciating her beauty. Striking. Long legs. Sexy. Like one of the girls you saw on the cover of the glossy, gossipy American magazines. A figure that would bring an instant reaction from men.

He put the thought from his mind as he opened the files and looked up at Volkmann. The man could have been a cop, but Sanchez knew he wasn't. Something more than a cop. The *seguridad* had telephoned him late the previous day, sent him a copy of the report they had been sent from Europe, asked him to cooperate, told him to let Volkmann see the necessary files, asked if he needed a translator.

Sanchez told them he didn't: he spoke English and this was an opportunity to get some practice. He wondered, not for the first time, why the two had traveled together, wondered what more there was to the deaths of Rodriguez and Hernandez.

He looked up. There was a map of Asunción City on his desk, a mark in red indelible pen to indicate the area where the bodies had been found. He turned the map around so they could see it, indicated the street where the house of the young girl stood, and spoke slowly.

"We found the bodies here on the morning of the twenty-sixth, in a house in the district of La Chacarita, near the Paraguay river, a short distance from the main railway station. Rudi's car we found parked outside the house. The keys of the car we found in the grass outside, as if someone had thrown them there."

When the detective paused, Volkmann asked, "Who does the house belong to?"

To the young woman whose body was found with Rudi Hernandez. Her name was Graciella Campos, age seventeen. But her mind, it was the mind of a child, you understand? She had no family alive. She rented the house."

Erica leaned forward, a look of pain in her blue eyes. "Did this girl know Rudi?"

"*Sí*. He gave her money. To pay for food and rent and clothes. It was a kindness, you understand. Not a payment for anything else. They were simply friends."

Erica Kranz's face was pale, not from the heat, but from hurting inside. She nodded, as did Volkmann.

Sanchez lowered his voice out of respect. "The girl and Rudi had both been killed with knives. A drunk old man who sometimes sleeps in an alley near the girl's house found the bodies. The girl usually gave him some hot tea in the mornings. When she didn't answer his knock, he tried the door. It was open. When he discovered the bodies, he told a local priest, who called the *policía*."

Volkmann asked, "How long had they been dead?"

"Not long. Maybe four, five hours."

Sanchez took several police photographs from the file and handed them across to Volkmann. He looked at Erica Kranz. "Forgive me. But I would prefer you did not look at these, Señorita. They are not pleasant."

There were five photographs, taken by forensics, all in vivid, horrific color. Volkmann examined them carefully. Two were of the body of Hernandez, two of the girl, one photograph of both bodies lying close together, faces up. The brown face of the girl looked pitiful in death. The savagery of her wounds shocked Volkmann. The knife had slit her stomach open from chest cavity to navel, exposing the internal organs, the viscera. The simple white frock she wore was ripped apart above the waist and drenched in blood.

He next studied the photograph of the body of Rudi Hernandez, tried not to allow his expression to change, for Erica's sake. The man had suffered much the same fate; the torso had been slit from chest to groin, his innards spilling out onto the bloodied floor.

Volkmann grimaced and handed the photographs back to Sanchez, who quickly replaced them in the file.

Volkmann asked, "Señor Sanchez, did the forensic people find anything?"

Sanchez looked at him blankly. The girl looked up suddenly, translating quickly into Spanish, *forense*. Sanchez remembered the word now, smiling at the girl, a brief sad smile, telling her he understood her grief.

"You speak Spanish very well, Señorita," Sanchez told her.

"I was born in Buenos Aires," Erica answered quietly.

Sanchez nodded. Hernandez had not told him that. He looked at Volkmann again.

"The forensic people believe that different knives were used to kill the victims. Both blades were hunting knives. The one used to kill Rudi had a very big blade. Perhaps a bowie knife, they think. But other than that, nothing much. No fingerprints. Some faint footprints, but nothing they think would really help. There were bruises on the arms and faces of both bodies that suggest several people helped in the murders. But whoever they were, they were careful not to leave anything behind. No prints, no real clues the forensic people could use. And a knife is not like a bullet. Sometimes it is more difficult to trace such a weapon. My men searched the area around the house and the *barrio* itself. Nothing was found. No discarded knives or bloodied clothes. Nothing."

Sanchez saw the girl wince as he spoke, wondered if he should be so explicit. He picked up the cup of steaming tea and sipped the green, aromatic liquid. His visitors had so far left theirs untouched; he should have ordered Cokes, he told himself; the *yerba mate* was sharp to the taste and steaming hot.

He paused to take a pack of cigarettes from his pocket, offered them to Volkmann and to the girl. When both refused, he lit one for himself and further loosened his tie as Erica leaned forward slightly. She spoke quietly, her voice strained.

"The place where the bodies were found. Did no one see or hear anything? Were there no witnesses? Surely someone must have heard something?"

Sanchez blew out smoke and shook his head. "The old man I spoke of saw and heard nothing. He had drunk a lot of *cana* the night before. I have spoken also to many people in the *barrio*, in La Chacarita. It is the same story. No one saw or heard anything. And believe me, they would have talked. The girl's death shocked them all. Some old men saw Rudi arrive at the house around seven-thirty in the evening before he died. They did not see him come out. And a man who sleeps down by the river says he woke and thought he heard a car drive along the waterfront very early in the morning, while it was still dark. What time, he was not sure. But he said he heard nothing unusual.'' He paused for a moment before going on. ''There is one small thing, however. It may be important.''

Sanchez hesitated again, then said, ''The day after Rudi and the young girl were murdered, *La Tarde* published a story about the deaths. There was a photograph of both on the front page. A night watchman at the central railway station on the Plaza Uruguaya came to see us. He said he saw a man who looked like Rudi come in the back of the station very early on the morning of the murders, maybe three o'clock. But he could not be certain. He was tired, had been on duty since the previous afternoon.'' Sanchez shrugged. ''Perhaps Rudi was at the station, perhaps not. Perhaps he meant to leave Asunción, take the girl and go someplace if he thought he was in some kind of danger. But the ticket office was closed then. Or maybe, if it *was* Rudi, he simply had something on his mind and went for a walk, to get some air.''

Sanchez looked directly at Volkmann. ''Of course, the report your people sent changes matters, I believe, when we consider what Rudi said he was doing, writing this story. Also, there are two other things that are important.''

The detective tapped his cigarette ash into a cracked glass ashtray on the desk in front of him. ''Number one, Rudi's Press card was missing. And also his wallet. Yet he still had money in his pocket. Not much. But enough. And a gold ring and a watch he wore were not taken.''

Volkmann sipped the bitter tea and looked at the detective. ''You're saying that whoever murdered Hernandez and the girl didn't intend to rob them?''

''*Sí.* I think we can forget about a simple robbery that went wrong. And the girl was not sexually assaulted. We must eliminate all the irrelevant motives. For this reason, I think your report to us suggests that Rudi and the girl may have been killed out of other motives. A robber would have taken all the money, the ring and the watch, unless he was disturbed at his work. I don't believe that happened. No one reported hearing any disturbance, and the bodies were not discovered until seven that morning. Also, the way the killing was done. It was not an ordinary murder. To kill like that, brutally, with knives, you must be someone crazy. You understand? So I don't think the motive was to rob. I think it was to kill.

"There is a clue to this. Rudi borrowed some equipment from a friend he knew, a man named Torres. He is a technician with an electronics company. Torres went to the newspaper office when Rudi had not returned this equipment to him. When they told him Rudi had been murdered, he came to us."

"What sort of equipment are we talking about?" Volkmann asked.

Sanchez drew on his cigarette, exhaled slowly. "Special electronic equipment that would allow a person to hear and record something spoken from a distance away. Japanese, and expensive. A small microphone-transmitter and a receiver that work on a very high radio frequency. I am sure you have heard of such equipment, Señor. The equipment was borrowed by Rudi the day before he was killed. We questioned Torres. He said he asked Rudi what he wanted the equipment for. Rudi said that it was for *trabajo clandestino . . .* undercover work."

Sanchez glanced at the girl, to make sure his words were correct, saw that she understood. He looked back at Volkmann as the man spoke.

"That was all Rudi told Torres?"

"*Sí.* No more. Not where he was going or why exactly he needed the equipment. Only that he would return it safely the next day. We have not found the equipment. It was not in the girl's house, or in Rudi's car or apartment. Perhaps it is still lying around somewhere, wherever Rudi used it, if he did use it. Or perhaps the people who murdered him have it, or have destroyed it."

Sanchez paused, looked at Volkmann, speaking softly. "I believe Rudi used the equipment the day or night before he was killed." He tapped a file in front of him. "There's one other thing. In the report your people sent us, it says that Rudi Hernandez was observing the home of a man named Nicolas Tsarkin. According to Rodriguez, Tsarkin was the man who originally hired him, no?''

"That's right," Erica Kranz answered.

"And that there is a connection to another dead man, Winter, in Germany?" the detective asked.

"That's right," she repeated.

"Interesting," he said. "Let me tell you a few other things. First, Rudi and I were friends. We helped each other out when we could. Sometimes a tip. Sometimes more than that. Second, not long before he was killed, Rudi gave me a tip. Keep an eye out on Señor Tsarkin, he said—though without going into the reason why. That was the way with his tips sometimes. But I was familiar enough with him to take what he said seriously."

"Did you find anything?" Volkmann asked.

"No, nothing." He paused dramatically. Then resumed, "Third, on November twenty-third, Señor Tsarkin put a gun in his mouth and blew his brains out. Another death. Interesting. Fourth, I called Rudi and asked him to join me at the scene of the suicide. I asked him then why he was interested in Tsarkin, but he wouldn't say. Perhaps he didn't know. But, fifth, there was a phone call at the Tsarkin home that he answered." Sanchez raised his eyes to heaven. "Holy Mother of God," he said, "I have half a dozen men on the scene who are capable of lifting a telephone receiver. But a reporter grabs it and takes the message, then stonewalls when I ask him about it. So, sixth, it is reasonable to assume that the phone message led to the tape equipment. But the people behind Señor Tsarkin, the ones who killed Rodriguez and Winter, as well as Rudi and Graciella, must have caught onto Rudi. And then they found him and killed him."

He waited for a moment to let all that sink in. "Now that I have your report, we are looking even more deeply into Señor Tsarkin, but nothing as yet has emerged."

Volkmann nodded and asked, "What can you tell us about Rodriguez?"

Sanchez sat back. "Noberto Rodriguez was a smuggler. His body was found two weeks ago in the city. Our forensic people said he had been killed by a car. The car drove away, did not stop. There were no witnesses. We thought it was an accident that someone did not report, a drunk driver perhaps. Or even a fellow criminal. But my men would have heard whispers in the underworld. In Rodriguez' case, they heard nothing. But now I know from your report that something else is possible . . . that these people he worked for killed him.''

''What kind of work did Rodriguez do?''

''He was a middleman who smuggled goods from the supplier to the purchaser. He chartered an old DC4 he owned. He flew cargoes mostly to the ports of Montevideo in Uruguay or Porto Alegre in Brazil, for shipping onto Europe and America.''

''Are we talking about narcotics?''

Sanchez nodded. ''*Sí*, narcotics of course. But also whatever made a good profit. Gold. Jewels. Leopard skins. Rodriguez was one of the best. Very, very good.'' Sanchez allowed himself a brief smile. ''So good we never catch him.''

Volkmann loosened his tie, the heat in the small room cloying even with the fan whirring away. ''Rodriguez' friends, people who knew him, people who might have worked with him, have you talked with them?''

''Rodriguez nearly always worked alone. And concerning the people he did work for, he told no one. To tell would mean death.'' Sanchez paused. ''However, there is a man he sometimes worked with, a man named Santander. A smuggler also. We are trying to find him, but so far we have had no luck.'' Sanchez shrugged. ''And even if we find Santander, he may know nothing. Rodriguez was not the type to discuss the people he did business with.''

''Have you talked with Rudi's colleagues at the newspaper, his friends?'' Erica asked. ''Perhaps he confided in one of them about his story.''

Sanchez nodded briefly. ''They knew nothing about any special story Rudi was working on. We also checked Rudi's desk and locker at *La Tarde*. Also his apartment. There was nothing in any of them that would suggest such a story. And no photographs like the ones mentioned in the report. Nothing that would help us.''

''Rudi said that anything he had, he kept in a safe place . . .''

Sanchez flicked a glance at Volkmann, then looked at Erica and nodded. "*Sí*, Señorita, I read that in the report I received. I must tell you that I had every bank in Asunción contacted yesterday. Rudi Hernandez had an account in one, but no deposit box. I am also having the banks outside Asunción checked just in case. But that will take time." He looked intently at her. "I have read the report Señor Volkmann's people sent, but I would like to ask you myself. Did Rudi say anything else concerning what information or evidence he had?"

"No."

"Did he suggest where this safe place might be?"

Erica Kranz shook her head. "All he said was that what he had was not much. But that it was in a safe place."

The detective nodded. "I will have a photograph of Rudi shown to the bank people my men spoke to, in case another name was used. Do you remember if Rudi said anything else? Anything, no matter how small, no matter how unimportant it seems to you?"

"No. I'm certain."

Sanchez tapped the file containing Volkmann's report. It was all there: Hernandez and Rodriguez observing the men at the Tsarkin house, what Rodriguez had told Hernandez, in the girl's words. It had helped, opened a door, even just a little.

He glanced at his watch and stubbed out his cigarette. There was a long silence. All the questions had been asked. There was nothing more to be said. Nothing until his men turned something up, if they were lucky. The heat in the small, drab room had become unbearable. He went to close the file, the meeting at an end, but hesitated and looked at Erica Kranz.

"Rudi's parents are dead, *sí*?"

She nodded.

"His belongings . . ." Sanchez said solemnly. "Rudi's things . . ."

He paused, saw the girl nod once more. She understood. He removed a set of keys from an envelope in the file and handed them across to her.

"These are the keys to Rudi's apartment," Sanchez explained. "In case there is anything from it you wish. Something personal, photographs perhaps. I have kept copies of the keys for myself.''

Erica accepted the keys. ''Thank you.''

Sanchez pushed himself from the chair and stood, picked up his jacket.

''And now, Señor, Señorita, I will take you to your hotel.'' He looked at the girl and said gently, ''Perhaps I might speak with Señor Volkmann in private first? I have some police business to discuss.''

Erica nodded and stepped out into the hallway. Sanchez watched her leave, then turned to Volkmann.

''The security police in my country, the *seguridad*, keep a file on certain citizens. Rudi Hernandez was a journalist. Journalists are, shall we say, a special case. Because of their work, you understand.''

Volkmann nodded, and Sanchez crossed to behind his desk, removed a file from a drawer, came back and handed it to Volkmann.

''This is a copy of the file. It's not much. Hernandez was not a troublemaker. There is nothing of much interest. But perhaps it may help you understand the man.''

Volkmann took the folder.

Sanchez said, ''About the man named Winter, my men are checking with the immigration people. I will let you know as soon as I have something.'' He pulled on his coat. ''The report your people sent. You have nothing more to add?''

Volkmann shook his head. ''You received a photograph of Winter?''

''*Sí*, I have it here.''

He removed a photograph from a file on his desk. A head-and-shoulders shot, enlarged. The man in the picture was young, blond, sharp-featured, thin-lipped. Sanchez stared at the photograph, then looked up.

''It is a difficult case, I think, Señor Volkmann. Strange. Most strange. And Rudi was a good man. I want to tell you I will do everything I can. We were friends for many years.''

''The bodies are still at the morgue?''

''No. The funerals were three days ago. Had I known Miss Kranz was coming, I would have delayed the burials.

But the forensic people had finished their work. And the police morgue is full. Tomorrow I will take her to the cemetery. She may wish to say a prayer."

"I'll tell her. Thank you."

"I will also take you to see the girl's house where the bodies were found. And we can talk with Mendoza, Rudi's editor, and with Torres, who loaned Rudi the equipment." The detective buttoned his coat. "And now I will take you to your hotel. Your people, they have made arrangements?"

"The Excelsior," said Volkmann.

Sanchez said, "It's a nice hotel."

CHAPTER 12

Asunción.

Volkmann and Erica checked into the hotel, and after dinner, he ordered a taxi to take them to Rudi Hernandez's apartment.

It was a bachelor's place: a bedroom, kitchen, living room, and a tiny bathroom. An old portable typewriter stood on a desk near the window, below a cluttered bookshelf and a portrait of an ancient railcar pulled by a wood-burning steam engine.

On one of the bookshelves there were half a dozen photographs in small silver frames. Hernandez's family, Volkmann guessed. One of a blond woman and a Latin man, the man smiling broadly, the woman's face serious, unsmiling. There was a silver-framed photograph of Erica taken in a Bavarian inn, looking much younger, her hair long, laughing out at the camera and holding a stein of beer, her arm around a young, handsome, smiling man.

Volkmann looked at her now. The long flight and the seven-hour time difference between Frankfurt and Asunción was taking its toll, and she was thinking, he guessed, of the last time she had been in the apartment. He saw her pick up the photograph from the shelf and stare down at the image silently.

"Rudi?" Volkmann asked.

She looked up and he saw the faint smudges under the blue eyes. "Yes."

She replaced the photograph and sat down quietly on the couch while Volkmann went to look around the apartment. The police had been untidy in their work; there were drawers open in the bedroom and clothes left in disarray. In the kitchen, all the cupboard doors were ajar.

When he came back into the living room, he found Erica staring silently out the window. The lights of the city twinkled beyond the glass, a clear view down to the Rio Paraguay, boats moving back and forth in the encroaching darkness.

As he moved closer, she turned and he saw tears running

down her cheeks. And then she was burying her face in his chest, her body racked by a fit of crying. He held her until the tears ebbed and she pulled away from him slowly.

"Forgive me. I . . . I kept remembering. The last night I was here with Rudi. And what the detective said today . . . about the way Rudi died."

"It's been a difficult day. How about I pour us both a drink?"

The vodka and tonic bottles were on the coffee table, a bowl of ice between them. There were small beads of perspiration on Erica Kranz's forehead and she had taken off her shoes.

"Tell me about Rudi," Volkmann said.

There was a look of pain on her face. "He was a good and kind man, and a good journalist. He loved life. Rudi was always quick to laugh no matter how black things were." She shrugged. "I really don't know what more to tell you."

There had not been much to read in the police file Sanchez had given Volkmann: two pages in English, translated especially—personal details, political affiliations, age, family background. But he wanted to hear the girl's story, wanted to know if there was more: hidden things, private things, things that all men keep to themselves, or share with a woman. Some small clue, something that would open a door for him.

He took a pack of cigarettes from his pocket, offered one to Erica, lit them both.

"Tell me about Rudi's background."

"You mean his family?"

"Yes, his family."

She stared down at her drink for a moment, then looked up. "Rudi's mother and mine were half sisters. After the war ended, they were brought as children to Argentina by my grandparents. Years later, Rudi's mother met a Paraguayan, a biologist who was studying at the university in Buenos Aires. When he graduated, they married and went to live in Asunción, where Rudi was born. He was their only child."

She toyed with her drink, looked up at the photographs

on the shelf. "Rudi was very much like his father. He always laughed. Rudi's mother was sterner. She was not a happy woman, I think."

Volkmann glanced up at the picture of the blond, pretty woman. Pretty, but not smiling. "Why?"

Erica brushed a strand of hair from her face, looked at him. "My mother told me a story once. She and her sister lived in Hamburg during the war, when they were children. One night the city was being destroyed with firebombs. It was the worst of the air raids. In the bomb shelters, people were praying and everyone was frightened. When a bomb fell nearby, the ground shook and the lights went out. People were crushed in the chaos. Rudi's mother was only a child and she was frightened. She ran out of the shelter, distraught. But what she was to see outside on the streets was even worse—burning buildings, corpses, the inferno of that terrible night. Childhood friends she had known, relatives, many were dead. She became withdrawn after that. She was a sensitive child, and the experience affected her terribly. Rudi used to say she relived that night every day of her life. She was always a sad person."

"How did Rudi's parents die?"

"My uncle often took his family with him when he worked on biological surveys. A light aircraft they were on crashed in the southern Amazon. Rudi was a passenger too, but he survived. They found him four days later, badly shocked and bleeding. His face was permanently scarred. For a long time afterward, he was devastated. He began to visit us more often in Germany because we were the only relatives he had left. But he couldn't live there, he said, even though he spoke the language. I think Rudi found the Germans too stern, too serious. The Paraguayans were his people."

Erica looked down at her empty glass. "May I have another drink?"

Volkmann poured another for each of them, spooned in the ice cubes. "Why did your family return to Germany?"

She sipped her drink, held the glass in both hands. "My mother had met my father and married him in Buenos Aires. He was a businessman, a German immigrant, and much older than she. But he died when I was three, so I don't remember him.'' Volkmann considered bringing up what he knew about her father, but decided against it. "My grandparents had died also, so I guess my mother felt a little lost.

"She sold my father's business and decided to return to Germany. She still had relatives there and thought that it was better for me to study there. After I graduated, she married again and moved to Hamburg. We drifted apart after that. The whole family did. But Rudi and I always wrote. He was like an older brother.''

Something about Erica made Volkmann want to reach over and touch her, comfort her, but he didn't know how she might react. Instead, he said, "I've been wondering about Dieter Winter. Did Rudi say what they talked about when they met in Heidelberg?''

Erica frowned. "I asked Rudi that same question. It was just small talk, he said. Winter was very drunk when they met, but he seemed intrigued by Rudi's background, by the fact that he was half German and from South America. That's another thing Rudi thought strange when he told me he had seen Winter in Asunción. At the party, Winter asked Rudi if he socialized among the German colony in Paraguay. Rudi said no, that they bored him. He preferred the easygoing Latins. He said Winter seemed to take the remark as a personal insult and became quite aggressive.''

"Is that what made Rudi dislike him?''

She shrugged. "He found him pompous and a loud-mouth. And Winter had said that if Rudi thought so little of Germans, he should go back where he belonged. Just like the immigrant workers in Germany, Winter said. Germany didn't need another *mischling*.''

She put down her glass. "That word. I'm sure you know it's not a nice word. It's used to describe someone who is only half German, a half-caste.''

Volkmann nodded.

The heat that came and lingered in the small apartment was stifling, despite the air-conditioning. Volkmann stood up, placed his empty glass on the table, looked down at Erica.

"Sanchez said he'd call tomorrow morning to take you to the cemetery to visit Rudi's grave.''

"Will you come too?"

"If you want."

The girl nodded. "Yes, I would prefer it. Thank you, Herr Volkmann."

"Call me Joe."

He gestured to the telephone nearby. "You think you could call a taxi to take us back to the hotel?"

Erica Kranz nodded.

Volkmann picked up the things from the coffee table and went back into the kitchen.

It was after eight when they returned to the Excelsior. There was a pre-Christmas party in progress in one of the hotel's ballrooms. In the lobby, tuxedoed men and beautiful, olive-skinned women in sleek dresses stood around an illuminated Christmas tree sipping drinks.

Erica looked tired in contrast, her mascara smudged. As the taxi had passed the offices of *La Tarde*, she had suddenly started crying. In the dim cab, Volkmann had reached across and held her hand, felt her lean into his shoulder, smelled the scent of her perfume, her blond hair brushing his cheek. She had stared out of the window, wiping her eyes but holding onto his hand until they had stepped from the taxi.

They took the elevator to the fifth floor and their adjoining rooms. Volkmann opened her door for her. "If you can't sleep or you want to talk, I'm in the next room."

"Thank you, Joe. You've been very kind. Please forgive me for crying, but it's been a hard day."

He waited until she had closed her door, then went into his own room. The air-conditioning was on, but the room was still humid. He undressed slowly and lay naked on the bed in the cloying darkness.

He could still smell the scent of her perfume as he closed his eyes and fell asleep.

The telephone rang in Volkmann's bedroom an hour later. He switched on the bedside lamp and picked up the receiver sleepily, hearing the stilted English, recognizing the voice.

"Sanchez here, Señor Volkmann. Did I wake you? My apologies . . . the jet-lag . . . I remembered just as I rang."

"What's the problem?"

"No problem. Something has turned up. The man you are interested in . . . the German."

"Winter."

"*Sí*, about him. And something else. Santander . . . the one who sometimes worked with Rodriguez. He was picked up by the local *policía* in San Ignacio late this afternoon. A place not far from the border with Argentina. He is being brought back to Asunción tonight. It would be best if you came to my office."

Volkmann said, "I'll phone for a taxi."

"No. Rest for now. My men have to check some things out first. I need a little time. I'll send a car to the hotel for you at midnight. Bring the girl if you wish."

"Midnight," repeated Volkmann.

"*Sí*. Rest, my friend," said Sanchez, and then the line clicked dead.

CHAPTER 13

Sanchez was seated behind his desk.

There were dark rings beneath his eyes, and his face looked swollen from lack of sleep. A coffeepot stood on a tray beside him, three cups poured, a half-smoked cigarette lying in the glass ashtray on the desk. Volkmann and Erica sat opposite him.

Despite his exhaustion, the detective was alert and interested, Volkmann wondering if it was because he and Hernandez had been friends or because Ferguson had pulled the right strings. It didn't matter; the man was with them, helping.

The small, drab office was cooler now, the fan still whirring away on top of the rusted filing cabinet. Sanchez opened a fresh file and stared down at its contents, several sheets of handwritten paper in Spanish.

"Winter visited Paraguay eight times in the last three years. Each time at intervals of approximately four months, each time for a stay of only two or three days. The reasons on his immigration papers say 'company business.' "

Sanchez glanced up, then back at the file. He had already explained to Volkmann that the details—Winter's date and place of birth registered on the immigration papers—matched with the information that Volkmann's people had sent in their report to the *seguridad*.

"On each immigration paper a hotel address was given for the period of his stay. On each occasion that he flew into Paraguay, he landed in Asunción. Four times from Miami, three times from Rio de Janeiro. All connecting flights these, from Europe. The other time was direct from Frankfurt. The last time Winter visited Paraguay was three months ago. Then he stayed at the Excelsior Hotel. Before that, at the Hotel Guarani. Before that, the Excelsior. Before that, two small hotels. But mostly the Excelsior or the Guarani. I have a list, you may see it if you wish."

Sanchez handed Volkmann a page and he examined the list.

When Volkmann looked up, he said, "You've checked with all of the hotels?"

Sanchez shook his head. "So far, only the Excelsior and the Guarani. The list I received from our immigration people only late in the evening. My men have still to check the others. It may take some time."

"The immigration papers Winter filled in before landing. Was there a company name given on any of them?"

"No. None."

"So who paid Winter's hotel bills?"

"In the two hotels we've checked so far, Winter paid. In cash. Always in cash. And in each case, he used a suite, not a room, although he was the only guest registered."

"What about telephone calls Winter might have made from his suite? Do the hotels you've checked keep a record?"

"Sí. They keep a record of all local and long-distance calls made by their guests, that is the law. But the hotels my men checked so far, the Excelsior and the Guarani, they have no record of any calls made by Winter. The only things on the bills were meals and drinks."

Sanchez picked up his coffee, sipped the black liquid, replaced the cup. Seeing the still-lit cigarette, he puffed on it once more before crushing it in the ashtray.

"No company name," said Volkmann. "No telephone calls. What about the car-rental firms? Have you checked with them?"

"I have a list of all the car-rental firms in the city. They will be checked as soon as my men have time." Sanchez consulted the file again. "The photograph your people sent of Winter. I had my people ask at the hotel if any of the staff remembered him. But of course no one did." Sanchez shrugged again. "Big hotels, lots of new faces every day. My men are still checking the last few hotels on the list, small places, but probably the same answers, I would guess."

Sanchez looked across at Volkmann. "On the night shift, I have fewer men. There are other things to be attended to. Things happening now. Murders, crimes, you understand. When they get some time free, they will check at the other hotels." He turned to Erica Kranz. "But at least we know

now that Rudi was not mistaken about seeing Winter in Paraguay."

Volkmann said, "But there's no record of Winter being in Paraguay at the time Rudi Hernandez claimed he saw him. And no connection with Nicolas Tsarkin?"

Sanchez shook his head. "No. But a man can cross a border in a remote place, or use a false passport. Or perhaps a record was not kept. This sometimes happens. I have also sent a request to all border posts, just in case the immigration paper was not returned to Asunción." He shrugged. "Officials in such remote places can be forgetful of their duties."

"You said that in both hotels you checked, Winter always hired a suite."

"*Sí*. Always." Sanchez consulted the file again. "On eight occasions."

"That suggests he meant to entertain, or impress. Or both."

"Perhaps. But we need more information." Sanchez shrugged. "And that may take a little time."

Erica Kranz leaned forward in her chair. "What about this other man? The man who sometimes worked with Rodriguez?"

"*Sí*, Miguel Santander."

"Have you questioned him?"

"*Sí*. Before you arrived. He had heard about Rodriguez's death. I told him we are now treating the case as murder. Santander thinks we consider him a suspect. I allowed him to think this. He says Rodriguez's death had nothing to do with him. He claims he has been near the southern border for the last two weeks. Up to no good, of course. But he cannot come up with a good alibi." Sanchez smiled briefly. "That suits us. That way, he is scared. And he has talked a little." He stood up wearily. "Maybe you ought to hear for yourself. He is downstairs in one of the interview rooms. Come, I will take you."

The interview room had the same gray, peeling walls as Sanchez's office. Apart from three chairs and an ancient wooden table, the room was bare of furniture.

When Sanchez led them in, Volkmann saw a thin-faced

man who looked to be about thirty seated at the table between two young, standing *policía*. The man was deeply
tanned, unshaven, his stubble making his dark face appear
even darker, his features more Indian than Spanish. His
grubby hands fidgeted nervously.

Sanchez gestured to the two *policía* to leave them.

When the men withdrew, Sanchez offered the two chairs
to Volkmann and Erica Kranz. The girl accepted; Volkmann remained standing.

"This is Miguel Santander," Sanchez said. "He speaks
a little English. Or if you prefer, I can translate."

Santander smiled weakly. "Please, I speak English. I like
to practice." His smile broadened, showing a row of
stained, uneven teeth as he looked at Volkmann and Erica.

Sanchez did the introductions, explaining only that his
two friends were interested in Rodriguez's death. He offered cigarettes to everyone, including Santander, took one
himself, lit them.

He said to Santander, "I want you to tell my friends here
what you told me. Slowly. So they can understand you.
Comprende?"

"*Sí.*" Santander looked at the man, then at the girl. He
glanced back at Sanchez. "From where do I begin?"

"From when Rodriguez asked you to help him."

Santander nodded and drew on his cigarette nervously as
he glanced continuously from Volkmann to Erica.

"One month ago, Rodriguez come to me." He began to
speak, his voice strained, staccato. "He say he need help.
He need to hire plane from friend of mine for some work
he is doing. His own plane is old, and he need part for an
engine generator. So until he get part, he need to hire other
plane."

Santander glanced at Sanchez, then back at Erica and
Volkmann, as if waiting to be told he was understood.
When no response came, he carried on. "This work of Rodriguez, sometimes it can be dangerous. For my friend who
owns the plane, I need to know it's going to be okay, that
there are no problems. No risk. Or perhaps only small risk.
Because if Rodriguez have trouble, my friend, his plane,
maybe it is taken by the *policía*. So I say to Rodriguez to

tell me about this work he is doing so I know if it is okay to hire him my friend's plane."

Santander looked at the faces around him and shrugged. "Rodriguez, he don't want to tell me anything at first. But he need plane, so he must tell me. Some people, they use him to fly cargo across the border. To Montevideo. Already he has done many trips. These people, always they want Rodriguez to work alone. No one else. And always he must fly at night."

Santander wiped his mouth with the back of his hand, then looked up at them again. "Each trip is always the same. No change. Rodriguez, he fly plane to quiet place up north in the Chaco. There is no runway in this place. Just field. A field in the jungle with lights. He land there and men are waiting. They put boxes on plane. Boxes made of wood and steel. He fly these boxes to Uruguay, to near Montevideo. He fly low, at night, so the radar don't see him. In a field near Montevideo, it is the same. No runway, just field with lights. When he land, men are waiting to take boxes off plane. Then Rodriguez, he do the same again, once maybe in two months. This happens over maybe one year." Santander shook his head. "And no problems. Never any problems."

Santander paused, scratched his stubble nervously. "I trust Rodriguez. To me, he never tell lies. He say to me there is nothing to worry about. The plane of your friend will be safe. He said he only had to do one last trip. And this last trip, it is a special cargo. Just one small box. Then he is finished working for these people." Santander paused again, looked up at Volkmann. "Rodriguez, I know he is good pilot. The best. So I say, okay, you got the plane. But before I get him the plane, he phone me and tell me he don't need it. He get the part for his engine generator."

Santander sat back, looked at Sanchez. "That is all I know. Rodriguez was a friend. Me, I would have no reason to kill him. I never kill person in my life." He glanced at Erica Kranz, then at Volkmann, a plaintive look on his face. "This, you must believe."

Sanchez said to Volkmann, "Do you have any questions for Señor Santander?"

Volkmann nodded and looked down as the man's dark, Indian eyes flicked nervously up at him.

"When was the last time you saw Rodriguez?"

"One month ago. When he ask me about the hire of plane of my friend."

"Not afterward?"

"No, I swear. He phone me in a bar two days after I meet him, to tell me he don't need to hire plane. I don't see or speak to him again."

"The name Rudi Hernandez. Did you ever hear Rodriguez mention that name?"

Santander thought for a moment, shook his head. "No, Señor."

"Hernandez. Rudi Hernandez. You're certain?"

"Certain. I never hear him say that name."

"Did Rodriguez mention the names of the people who hired him, the people he flew his plane to Montevideo for?"

Santander shook his head. "No names. Rodriguez never tell names. In such business, sometimes people you work for, they don't give you names. It is better that way, you understand?"

"The places Rodriguez picked up and dropped off the cargoes of boxes. You know where they are?"

"Rodriguez did not say exactly. Only that they were empty places, quiet places. Places with no towns, no villages. The place in the Chaco where he picked up the boxes, he did not say. When I ask Rodriguez, all he would say is that it is one of the old German *colonias*. There are many up north, Señor."

"The men who loaded and unloaded the boxes. Did Rodriguez say what they looked like? Did he ever describe any of them?"

Santander thought for a moment. "No. He say only that these men, they are good at their work. They work quick. Rodriguez only have to wait for ten, maybe fifteen minutes and boxes are loaded. The same in Montevideo." Santander thought for another moment. "But I think Rodriguez say that in the *colonia*, there was an old guy in charge."

"A German?"

Santander shrugged. "I guess."

"Did Rodriguez describe him?"

"No, Señor. He only say that he was old."

"How many men did the work of loading and unloading the plane?"

"I don't know, Señor. Rodriguez did not say."

"Did Rodriguez know what cargo was in the boxes he carried?"

Santander scratched his stubble again. "He did not tell me. I don't think he know. But these boxes are heavy, I think. Except the last one."

"Why do you think they are heavy?"

"Rodriguez say he need a lot of runway. A long field. To lift off. And also a lot of fuel in the tanks."

"He said nothing else?"

"No, Señor. I am certain. Nothing. I tell you everything." Santander looked up at Sanchez. "I tell the truth. Believe me."

Volkmann sighed, feeling the tiredness taking hold of him. There was no air-conditioning in the room, the humidity high. He paused before going on.

"How many boxes did Rodriguez carry on each flight, before the last one?"

"I don't know, Señor."

"Big boxes, small boxes?"

Santander shook his head, shrugged his shoulders. "Sorry, Señor . . ."

"These people Rodriguez worked for, how did they pay him?"

Santander shook his head again. "Rodriguez, he tell me nothing about that. But I think cash. After each trip. In such business, that is how it is done."

"How did Rodriguez meet them?"

"Rodriguez did not tell me."

"Is there anyone close to Rodriguez, someone maybe he might tell things to about his work? A woman, a friend maybe?"

"No, Señor. Rodriguez, he always keep things to himself. Even when he was drunk, he did not talk about his work. To nobody. I am certain. That way, there is no one to tell the *policía*."

"There is nothing else you remember? I want you to

think hard. Anything. No matter how small.''

"Nothing. I swear it." Santander made the sign of the cross.

Sanchez said, "If I discover you are lying to me, amigo . . ."

"As God is my judge. Rodriguez was a friend . . ."

Sanchez grimaced and stubbed out his cigarette, turned away and looked toward Volkmann. "You have any more questions, Señor?"

Volkmann shook his head.

The three of them were seated in Sanchez's office again. The detective had more coffee, fresh and hot, brought to them. It was after two, the room silent now except for the gentle whirr of the fan overhead.

Erica Kranz sipped her coffee thoughtfully. Volkmann turned to Sanchez.

"You think Santander is telling the truth?"

"*Sí*, I believe him. And he is not the type of man who kills. Just a petty smuggler. I think he told us everything he knew." Sanchez picked up the coffee cup. "What he said about the old man in the German colony, it helps a little. But there are many German colonies in Paraguay. People who came here before and after the last war. Immigrants."

Sanchez sipped the hot coffee, placed the cup on the desk. "What Santander said, it was not much, but it makes the picture just a little clearer."

Volkmann's thoughts, meanwhile, were elsewhere. After a time, he looked at the detective and asked, "The electronic equipment Hernandez borrowed. What distance could it work over?"

Sanchez shrugged. "Not far, maybe a kilometer."

"Hernandez could have been anywhere the night he was killed."

"I agree. The only clue I have as to where he was on the morning of his death is the word of the night watchman, the man who works at the railroad station and claims he saw him." Sanchez shrugged. "Who knows what Rudi was doing there, *if* he was there? Maybe he used the recording equipment there, but I don't know, I don't think so. The man at the station says the man he saw carried nothing and was in the station for perhaps only five minutes, maybe a little longer. But the equipment, Torres' equipment, you would have needed something to carry it in. A bag, a small suitcase perhaps.''

Volkmann looked at the detective. "Let's say Hernandez *was* at the station. Why does a man go to a railway station in the early hours of the morning? And why enter through a rear entrance?'' He was thinking aloud, but he asked the question, saw Sanchez frown.

"Perhaps it was the quickest way?'' Sanchez replied. "Rudi meant to buy a ticket on a train to someplace, leave Asunción? But the ticket office was closed at the time, until later in the morning.''

"Wouldn't he have known that?''

Sanchez nodded. "I understand. It leaves a question. If Rudi *did* go to the station and stayed for only a short time, it suggests perhaps that he had a purpose. But what purpose? I do not know the answer. Why do people go to a train station in the early hours of the morning? To catch a train, or to meet one, if there is one. But neither is possible in this case.''

Sanchez glanced at the girl. She looked up then, met his eyes for a moment before looking away again. She was listening to the conversation but not listening, preoccupied, her hands restless, a frown on her face, Sanchez thinking: she is still grieving, that one.

He looked at Volkmann. He was thinking too, weighing things up in his mind, going over words said.

Volkmann said finally, "What about the other hotels on the list?''

"My men have not called in yet. I will have the communications desk call them up.''

Sanchez stood, shuffled the pages of the file on his desk before closing the folder. Erica looked up at him, a strange expression on her face, her lips pursed, her brow furrowed in concentration. In her right hand she fingered the keys to Rudi Hernandez's apartment and car. He remembered that she had been toying with them while he spoke with Volkmann.

Now she spoke softly, in Spanish. "You asked why Rudi

might have been at the railway station. At the station . . . are there boxes, or lockers, . . . for luggage, for people to leave things?''

Sanchez raised an eyebrow. He looked down again at the bunch of keys in the girl's hand; she was holding one of them between thumb and forefinger. He answered her in Spanish.

''I believe so.''

The girl hesitated. ''Maybe Rudi had one of those boxes?''

Sanchez looked at her blankly.

Volkmann looked at them both, wondering what they were saying.

CHAPTER 14

Asunción. December 6, 3:45 A.M.

At the train station they had found the tape and the six photographs in the locker marked Number 39.

Each photograph was of the same two men. One was Dieter Winter, the other Nicolas Tsarkin. Winter's blond hair and thin, sharp features were unmistakable when compared to the head-and-shoulders shot Sanchez had received in the report Volkmann had given him yesterday afternoon. Tsarkin he knew from a photograph in one of the bedrooms of the old man's mansion. Sanchez had never seen the man's actual face; it had been blown away when Tsarkin committed suicide.

The pictures had been taken with a telephoto lens. The two men were walking on the grounds of Tsarkin's estate— the last place he had seen Rudi Hernandez alive, he had explained to Volkmann and Erica.

So, Sanchez thought, *confirmation of a connection between Winter and Tsarkin. This suggests larger connections, thin wisps of a web, lines beginning to join.*

If only the tape made sense . . .

They had listened to it eight times. Erica had translated the conversation for Sanchez, then transcribed it in Spanish, the detective reading the girl's writing slowly, questioning the inflection of words in the handwritten script—like Volkmann, curious, perplexed—reading the cryptic words over and over, asking Erica to translate again from the German, making sure the transcript was right, no nuance ignored, no word overlooked.

In the smoke-filled office now, Sanchez looked across at Volkmann and said, "You want to hear the tape again?"

Volkmann nodded, said yes, he wanted to hear the tape again. Sanchez pressed the "play" button on the cassette player lying on his desk before lighting another cigarette and sitting back.

Volkmann listened, hearing the deep, guttural voices fill the silence of the room once more, almost knowing the words from memory now, but wanting to hear them again.

"The shipment . . . ?"

"The cargo will be picked up from Genoa as arranged."

"And the Italian?"

"He will be eliminated, but I want to be certain we don't arouse suspicion concerning the cargo. It would be prudent to wait until Brandenburg becomes operational. Then he will be dealt with along with the others."

Pause.

"Those who have pledged their loyalty . . . we must be certain of them."

"I have had their assurances confirmed. And their pedigree is without question."

"And the Turk?"

"I foresee no problems."

"The girl in Berlin . . . you're absolutely certain we can rely on her?"

"She will not fail us, I assure you." Pause. *"There are no changes to the names on the list?"*

"They will all be killed."

"Your travel arrangements . . . Everything has been organized?"

"We leave Paraguay on the sixth."

"The schedule . . . perhaps I should go through it once more?"

There was a long pause on the tape until Volkmann heard a voice speak again.

"It's quite warm in here. Perhaps I might have a glass of water?"

They heard the clink of glass a few moments later, the sound of water poured, the long silence, then the *click* on the tape, followed by a faint buzzing noise.

Sanchez leaned across and pressed the "Forward" button. There was another long period of silence on the tape, only a muted, buzzing noise, until the sound of voices came again, but this time very faintly, the words fuzzy, crackling, barely audible.

"Prost."

"Prost."

"Prost."

Another pause, then very faintly, *"We must take our*

*leave of you. It's a long drive back north. The driver will
take you to the safe house."*

Silence.

Sanchez waited for a while to make sure the conversation
had finished, hearing what he thought on the tape was the
faint sound of a door being closed; then he leaned across
and switched off the machine.

Volkmann looked down at the scribbled notes he had
already written on the fresh page of his notebook, his own
shorthand of the taped conversation. Sanchez asked what
the word Brandenburg meant. Erica explained that it was
the name of a city west of Berlin, and was also the name
of a German province that had once contained part of the
state of Berlin. The famous Brandenburg Gate that stood
near the Reichstag, the old German Parliament building,
had once been the original entrance to the territory.

Hearing the answer, Sanchez nodded but scratched his
head, a confused look on his face; the explanation did not
help.

Finally, after a long, thoughtful silence, he spoke. "Brandenburg," he said slowly, "is not a place. It is obviously
a code for something else."

Volkmann nodded, agreeing. He had come to the same
conclusion.

"But for what?" Erica asked.

"Exactly. For what? For drug movements?" Sanchez
looked at each of them. "Possibly. We'll have to dig
deeper, won't we?" His shoulders drooped with exhaustion
and helplessness.

"And what is the list?" Volkmann added. *"They will
all be killed"?* he quoted. "Who? Where? How many? And
who are the Italian, the Turk, and the girl in Berlin?"

Volkmann tried to concentrate on the tape. Three different speakers, he decided, listening carefully.

*"Your travel arrangements . . . Everything has been or-
ganized?"*

"We leave Paraguay on the sixth."

The sixth. Today.

Volkmann asked Sanchez to rewind the tape on those
lines. He listened again to the faint voice that had spoken
the reply, the same voice, Volkmann felt certain, that had

later said, *"We must take our leave of you. It's a long drive back north . . ."* North, where was north? They had discussed that line also, he and Sanchez. North in Paraguay meant a vast area of jungle and swamp and scrub land called the Chaco. Sanchez had pointed to it on the nicotine-stained map on the wall.

North could even mean over the border . . . Brazil . . . Bolivia. Or simply a suburb far north of the city. Anywhere.

Volkmann looked across at Sanchez and asked, "What about Nicolas Tsarkin? He can't be a complete cipher . . ."

Sanchez had the file open on his desk, the coroner's report, the letter from the oncologist at the San Ignatio hospital. He had explained it all briefly to Volkmann and the girl; now he glanced at the file again.

"All I know at this time is what I have in the report I filed after investigating the suicide. The man was eighty-two, a retired businessman, a naturalized citizen of this country for many years, and a former director of many companies. On November twenty-third, in the San Ignatio hospital, he was given only days to live by the doctors who attended him. He had stomach cancer. The bleeding had become very bad. The doctors who treated him at the hospital were not surprised when they learned the old man had shot himself. He was in pain, and very weak, despite drugs to help him."

"You're certain it was suicide?"

Sanchez nodded. He yawned, put a hand to his mouth, blinked several times. "There was no question. He was alone in the room at the time. And considering his poor health, there was no need to probe much into his affairs. But now it is a different matter. After I received your report the other day, I asked one of my people to find out more about Señor Tsarkin. I will have the relevant files in the office of immigration checked as soon as the office opens this morning. My man is also checking Tsarkin's house to see if there are any papers he might have kept. Anything that might help us."

Volkmann looked at the detective. "You said there was a safe open in the study where you found the body. And embers in the fireplace."

"*Sí.* But this sometimes happens when people kill themselves. Private letters, personal things, they destroy them beforehand.'' Sanchez shrugged. ''Especially if they have something to hide. In Tsarkin's case, we know now that is most likely true. One of my men is also checking the calls made to and from Tsarkin's house recently, especially on the twenty-third. I mentioned that there was a call Rudi Hernandez answered. Perhaps we can find out who made it.''

It was still dark beyond the office window. Sanchez could hardly keep his eyes open, the smoking helping to keep him awake. He should have finished work at five the previous day. But as with so much police work, he could never plan a day with certainty. He had telephoned his wife, told her he would be late, how late he didn't know, yet somehow knowing that this one would drag on.

''How long before you get the information on Tsarkin's background?'' Volkmann asked.

Sanchez looked up and shrugged. ''The office of immigration records does not open until ten o'clock. Then we can check Tsarkin's past. When he came to Paraguay, and from where. But it may be a slow and difficult task, perhaps taking several days. Also, I will have Tsarkin's servants questioned again as soon as I can get another man. Perhaps they know some things about their dead employer. Business acquaintances. Friends. People he socialized with.''

Sanchez looked at his watch. Almost four o'clock. He, too, remembered the words on the tape, the words the girl had transcribed.

''We leave Paraguay on the sixth.''

He pushed himself achingly up from the chair and stretched his arms. The smoky air in the office stung his eyes, yet he stubbed out his cigarette and lit another. He slowly shook his head. ''A question. In the hotels Winter stayed at, he always hired a suite. You asked a question. Why does one person need to hire a suite?'' He paused. ''To impress someone? A business contact, or a woman perhaps?'' He paused again. ''A suite, it is also big enough to hold a meeting, *sí*?''

Sanchez raised his eyebrows questioningly. He looked at Volkmann and Erica.

''A hotel would also be a suitable place for someone to

hire a room and try to listen to what was being said in another room nearby, would it not?'' He looked down, plucked the list of hotels from the relevant file and shrugged heavily. ''Perhaps it is worth investigating. Just now, it is all I can think of.''

Volkmann said tiredly, ''It's possible. But which hotel? Asunción's a big city.''

Sanchez briefly examined the list. ''The hotel Winter stayed in most often, your hotel, the Excelsior. Perhaps if we tried there first? Then the Hotel Guarani.''

The receptionist insisted on calling the night-duty manager first.

The man appeared minutes later, tall and immaculately dressed in a dark suit, crisp white shirt and gray silk tie.

Sanchez showed his identity card and stated his request. The manager offered no resistance, led them politely to his office around the corner from the lobby. The room was small, but uncluttered.

He pulled up chairs for all of them and asked Sanchez, ''The date again?''

''November twenty-fifth.''

The manager crossed to one of the filing cabinets and rummaged through a drawer. He finally removed several thick wads of registration cards held together with rubber bands, brought them over to the desk and sat down.

''Is there a particular name you wish to check on?''

''Hernandez. Señor Rudi Hernandez. He may have been a guest here.''

''Information regarding guests is kept on computer. However, the original registration cards are maintained in alphabetical order, so it should not be difficult to find.''

The manager riffled through the first block of cards he picked, flicking through them expertly. ''Hernandez . . . Hernandez . . . yes.'' He looked up at them. ''One Hernandez, but the first name is—'' he consulted the card again ''—Morites. Morites Hernandez.''

Sanchez held out his hand; the manager passed him the registration. A commercial traveler, the card declared, from São Paulo.

Sanchez glanced at Erica's handbag and asked in English, "Señorita, do you have any correspondence from Rudi with you?"

Erica hesitated for a moment. She glanced at Volkmann, then looked back at Sanchez and said, "In my room . . . I have a letter in my suitcase."

"Would you be so kind as to bring it to me, please?"

Erica Kranz nodded silently and left. When she returned five minutes later, she handed the letter to Sanchez, unfolding the pages first, the manager looking on curiously as Sanchez compared the handwriting on the registration to the handwritten letter he placed beside it on the desk.

The writing sloped in different ways; the writing on the registration cramped, secretive; the writing on the letter Rudi had sent to Erica large, stylish, the letters fat, generous.

Sanchez looked up. "No. Not the Hernandez we are looking for."

The manager appeared slightly relieved. Sanchez said, "November twenty-fifth. How many people stayed at the hotel?"

The manager looked from Sanchez to Volkmann and Erica, this time switching to perfect English. "It was a busy night, I remember. We were full. There was a convention, and several functions—"

"How many people?" asked Sanchez.

"Perhaps three hundred guests."

When Sanchez sighed, the manager shrugged. "I'm sorry I haven't been able to help you."

Sanchez looked determinedly at the man. "We will need to check all of these cards."

The man stared at him in disbelief. "*All*, Señor?"

"*Sí*. All. And I will need a list, a computer list, of all the guests who stayed here on November twenty-fifth. Their names. Their passport numbers if they were foreigners. Who made their reservations. Who paid their bills." Sanchez paused. "Your computer. It has all this information?"

The manager nodded, dumbly.

"Then please see to it at once," said Sanchez.

"Señor, you realize the hour? I have other duties to attend to. Perhaps when the day staff arrives—"

Sanchez interrupted sharply. "I need this information now. It cannot wait. So please do as I ask. Otherwise I will be forced to contact your superior." His voice softened a little. "I would be grateful for your cooperation, Señor."

CHAPTER 15

Asunción. 5:55 A.M.

It had taken them almost an hour to find the hotel registration card.

It was Volkmann who found it, the three of them sitting around the desk, a pile of cards and a page from Hernandez's letter in front of each of them. The signature on the card was in a different name, Roberto Ferres, but the style was unmistakably the same: the sloped and dotted letters, the amplitude of the script, matching Hernandez's writing exactly.

Once Volkmann had found the card, Sanchez had requested a list of guests staying on the first and second floors. Now information lay in front of him, as yet unexamined, several reams of folded computer printout sheets. Sanchez held the registration card in his hand as he looked up at the harried manager.

"The room that Señor Ferres hired on the first floor. The bill was paid in advance?" The information was on the registration card, but Sanchez asked just the same. There was an amount included in the bill for a bottle of champagne and canapés. That had puzzled him.

"Yes, in cash," the manager replied, glancing at the card in Sanchez's hand.

"Was the room key returned?"

"There is no need for our guests to return keys. The locks are opened with plastic disposable key cards. For security, the numbers are changed by computer each time a new guest checks in and a new plastic key card is issued. Each guest has his own individual code."

Sanchez nodded.

"You wish to see the room where this gentleman stayed?" the manager asked. "I believe it is unoccupied at present."

"Perhaps later." Sanchez knew it was pointless. By now, the room would have been cleaned a dozen times. He looked at his watch. Six-fifteen.

Sanchez asked, "If there had been a disturbance in Señor

Hernandez's ... Señor Ferres's ... room, would it have been reported?''

The manager looked slightly alarmed. "What kind of disturbance?"

Sanchez shrugged. "A fight. A disagreement. Excessive noise."

The manager said, "My staff is very diligent. If anything unusual had happened, they would have reported the matter and it would have been recorded." He shrugged and smiled briefly. "Sometimes it happens. Couples argue. Throw things. You think something happened in this gentleman's room?"

"Perhaps. Perhaps not."

"I can check the daybook for complaints on that floor if you wish."

"I would appreciate it. Also, if this gentleman left anything behind in the room. Perhaps personal belongings. You can check?"

The manager nodded, then left them once more.

Sanchez rubbed his eyes and said to Volkmann and Erica, "The champagne and food ... I am puzzled. Why would Rudi want to order them?"

He picked up the ream of computer printout he had requested and unfolded the paper. The sequential list started with the first room number on Hernandez's floor. Slowly, carefully, he read through the printout, eyes scanning the information presented. Room number. Guest. Bill charges.

After a while, he blinked several times, rubbed his bloodshot eyes, then looked up.

"At last, a light shines in the darkness."

Volkmann and Erica Kranz stared at the detective.

"Someone booked a suite on the same floor as Rudi's room." Sanchez smiled broadly for the first time. "A Señor Nicolas Tsarkin."

The manager returned moments later carrying a thick ledger, open in his hands. He informed Sanchez that nothing had been recorded as left in the room and no complaints had been made concerning the first floor on November 25 or in the early hours of the following morning.

Sanchez asked if they could see the suite Tsarkin had hired.

"I'm sorry, it is occupied at present. But as soon as the guests check out this morning, I will arrange it." The manager shrugged. "I'm sorry I can be of no further help."

Sanchez nodded. "I am grateful for your assistance, Señor."

There was a knock on the door. Volkmann saw a man enter and speak quietly to Sanchez in Spanish. Sanchez asked to be excused, crossed to the man, and they both stepped outside the office.

Volkmann looked at Erica. He realized neither of them had slept for more than a couple of hours in the past twenty-four. Her exhaustion showed; she was restless, her eyes sleepy. A wisp of blond hair fell across her face; she brushed it away, smiled briefly at Volkmann.

Volkmann said, "If you want to go to your room and rest, I'll call you if anything comes up."

She shook her head. They both looked up as Sanchez came back into the room, talking to them directly, ignoring the manager's presence.

"That was Detective Cavales, the man I put onto Tsarkin's case. He managed to get a list of telephone calls made from Tsarkin's house in the last two weeks. There were two calls made to a radio-telephone link in the northeastern Chaco . . ."

Sanchez paused, let the information sink in. They were both exhausted, Volkmann and the girl, but now each looked intently at him.

"The radio-telephone link," Sanchez went on. "We've got a name, Karl Schmeltz. And an address. It's in an area up in the Indian country. Just north of the Salgado River near the border with Brazil. A desolate place, with not many people. Jungle and scrub land. The kind of place where a man shoots himself for something to do."

"How far?" Volkmann asked.

Sanchez shrugged. "Four hundred kilometers, maybe more. It takes perhaps ten hours to reach by car. The roads are bad, very bad. Jungle roads."

Volkmann checked his watch. Six-thirty. He needed sleep, to close his eyes, not to travel along rutted jungle roads. And by then, by then perhaps it would be too late.

"By helicopter," Sanchez said, "it takes two hours. Maybe a little less."

"You can arrange that?" Erica asked.

Sanchez nodded.

Asunción. 6:41 A.M.

Volkmann stared down through the helicopter's Plexiglas as the buildings of Asunción shrank below him.

It was cramped in the cockpit, the sun ahead of them, the military pilot wearing sunglasses to shield his eyes. The muted noise of the blades as they chopped the warm air filled the cabin.

There were five of them in the Dauphin helicopter apart from the pilot. Erica and Volkmann, Sanchez and Cavales, and another detective named Moringo.

Sanchez's two detectives were each armed with standard-issue thirty-eight pistols and pump-action shotguns. Two military M-16 rifles lay beside Sanchez, along with six spare clips of ammunition.

The second rifle was for Volkmann, Sanchez keeping the weapon by his side but Volkmann knowing it was for him, if needed.

The Dauphin bumped a little as they climbed higher, not too high, because in the heat, as Sanchez had explained, the blades couldn't grip the thin air. Volkmann saw the helicopter's altimeter rise to two thousand feet and settle.

They were over scrub forest and jungle already, adobes and huts of wood and straw and fields of sugar cane below, the landscape dotted with the ruins of old sugar mills. The Rio Paraguay flowed off to the right, a gray-green ribbon of water snaking through a patchwork of greens stretching as far as the distant horizon.

Volkmann could sense the tension and exhaustion in the cramped cabin.

Finally, the radio crackled and a metallic-sounding Spanish voice came over the speaker. The pilot switched to earphones, the noise in the cockpit too loud. He spoke for a few moments, then turned to talk to Sanchez in Spanish.

Sanchez nodded and said something briefly to Moringo, his
voice almost a shout to drown out the noise, then turned to
Volkmann and Erica.

"That was Asunción on the radio. I requested the local
policía to meet us near the house. Their orders are to direct
us to the property and assist us if we need them." He
glanced at his watch. "We will be in radio contact in just
under an hour. Moringo here knows the region, but not the
exact place. He thinks it is very remote."

Volkmann nodded. He sat back, his body aching now for
sleep as he stared down, mesmerized by the vast emerald
oasis of jungle below, the monotonous, rhythmic sound of
the chopping blades overhead almost sending him to sleep.

It was 7:00 A.M.

Northeastern Chaco. 8:25 A.M.

It was Volkmann who saw the vehicle first, rubbing his
eyes to make sure, the blue and white of the police car a
mere speck barely visible, waiting on the ribbon of desolate
road in the distance. The roads here were primitive, brown-
red strips of dirt cutting through the jungle, looking like
tape stuck onto the lush green earth.

Volkmann tapped Sanchez on the shoulder and pointed
downward. Sanchez nodded as his eyes picked out the blue
and white, pointed the direction for the pilot. The Dauphin
banked sharply, turned toward the place where the speck
of color waited.

They had been in contact with the local *policía* on a
special frequency for almost fifteen minutes. Sanchez was
translating the commentary for Volkmann. He looked very
tired but was coming awake now, staring out beyond the
Plexiglas, talking rapidly into the microphone to the sergeant in the car, almost directly below them now.

Sanchez turned to Volkmann. "The sergeant says the
property is straight ahead along the road another kilometer.
They will follow us there."

There was a cry from Cavales as he pointed beyond the
helicopter's Plexiglas. "There. To the left."

The pilot followed the line of his finger. The sky was

hazy with clouds, but even Volkmann could see the house now, less than a kilometer away. It stood alone in the midst of jungle, painted off-white, very large, one of the largest haciendas they had flown over in the last half-hour, a narrow, private road leading up to a clearing in front of the property.

As the tension rose in the small cabin, the helicopter began to bank sharply to the left. The pilot shouted something to Sanchez, who nodded, turned to Volkmann.

"The pilot says maybe he can land in front of the hacienda if there is a big enough clearing."

Volkmann glanced down, saw the blue-and-white car race below and behind them, moving fast along the narrow dirt road, plumes of russet dust in its wake. The helicopter suddenly slowed, hovered now, less than a quarter of a kilometer from the hacienda, the pilot shouting something to Sanchez.

"We go for the clearing, okay?" Sanchez said to Volkmann. "But two sweeps over the hacienda first, just in case there's trouble waiting."

Sanchez tapped the pilot on the shoulder and spoke rapidly. The helicopter began to move forward fast, dropping height, going in low. Volkmann tensed. Sanchez clenched his teeth and grabbed one of the automatic rifles and three clips of ammunition. He handed them over.

"For you, in case there's trouble. But make sure the girl stays in the chopper, *sí*?"

Volkmann glanced up briefly at the hazy sky, saw something glinting in the far distance, a flash of white light, and then it was gone. He tensed, checked the rifle, then looked down as the helicopter began its sweep.

Volkmann knew after the first sweep that the house was empty.

The pilot kept the helicopter in a steady angle of bank, circling the property in a perfect circuit, then sweeping out, coming in low again, barely clearing the surrounding jungle.

The place appeared to be deserted. There was a black stain on the landscape to the right side of the house, looking like an oil spill from the distance at first, but on the second sweep, Volkmann recognized the remains of a fire, the helicopter's blades causing the dark blot to lift and swirl as small black flakes rose and billowed into the air, eddying into a scattered mess.

The veranda was empty, the windows of the house bare of curtains, and a clutter of outbuildings stood at the rear, looking dilapidated and weathered, a small wooden outbuilding set off to the right of the house.

On the second pass, Volkmann glanced over at Sanchez, saw disappointment on his face but the eyes alert, awake, ready. But there was no need to be ready, Volkmann knew, seeing the blue-and-white police car coming up fast along the private gravel track that led up to the white hacienda.

As the car came to a sudden halt, four *policía* scrambled out, wrenching guns from holsters, crouching as the helicopter began to descend on a flat clearing to the right of the driveway.

As soon as they landed, Sanchez stepped out, followed by his men, pistols and shotguns at the ready, Volkmann close behind carrying the rifle, Erica remaining with the pilot, who was closing down the engines.

The heat and humidity of the jungle hit them as they crouched instinctively to keep their heads below the slowly dying blades. Then the swish of the rotors died, and it seemed to Volkmann that there was only utter silence and wilting heat, until seconds later, the clicking, shrieking sounds of the jungle erupted all around them.

Two uniformed *policía* from the car rushed forward, waving their guns, chattering loudly, pointing to the house.

Sanchez spoke to them briefly, then replaced his gun in his waist holster. He turned to Volkmann, the look of exhaustion on his face saying it all, knowing, as Volkmann knew, that they were too late.

He nodded toward the house. "Come, amigo. Let's take a look inside."

It became apparent to Volkmann that something was wrong. No one left a house this empty, this bare. No one picked a house this clean, leaving it like a corpse stripped of its flesh after the vultures had been at it.

Nicolas Tsarkin made his departure the same way, Volkmann reflected. *He cleared away everything with equal thoroughness.*

That is what the house, the property, suggested. A wooden skeleton. Echoing, hollow, the scrubbed floorboards inside creaking eerily underfoot, swept clean, swept of everything.

Erica joined them from the helicopter, only the pilot choosing to remain outside, indifferent, listening to a commercial radio station he had tuned into the receiver on board, oblivious to the heat as he stalked the area around the Dauphin, chewing gum.

The house was large inside, thirteen rooms, Volkmann counted, each sanitized, each bare, nothing covering the floorboards, not even a thread of carpet remaining. It seemed that even the dust had been swept away.

Sanchez ordered all the *policía* and his own men to go through the house room by room, checking for anything, for any clues. Then he went with Volkmann and Erica to look at the outbuildings.

There were three of them. Two had been garages, they guessed, big enough to accommodate a large car each, but nothing in either, nothing except faded, oil-stained patches on the ground.

The last was not much larger. It appeared to have been a storeroom, or a child's playhouse, built of wood. Again, nothing inside, only a number of very faint white paint marks on one of the walls. Volkmann and Sanchez moved closer, examined them. The marks had been painted a long time ago, and when they looked closely, they saw that they resembled faintly the pattern of a spider web, as if someone had started painting the interior and then changed his mind, or a child had been playing with a paintbrush.

None of them spoke as they examined the place, Sanchez smoking a cigarette, looking over the walls, the floors, until he seemed baffled and overcome by it all.

As they stepped out into the sunlight, Volkmann saw the remains of the fire. The ashes had been scattered in small, irregular clusters by the wake of the helicopter's blades. He knelt down and touched the center of the largest cluster. The ashes were soggy, as if water had been poured on them. He found a stick in a nearby thicket and poked at the remains until he had sifted through all the black clusters the helicopter's blades had scattered.

Nothing.

The sun was out now from behind the clouds, the heat becoming unbearable. Volkmann looked at Erica, then at Sanchez. There were small beads of sweat glistening on the detective's brow.

"Did the local sergeant tell you anything useful?" Volkmann asked.

"He's lived around here for most of his life," the detective answered. "The people here kept to themselves, he said. He scarcely knew of their existence."

"How far to the nearest town?"

"Twenty kilometers. The nearest house, ten."

Volkmann kicked a cluster of ashes, paused, then looked at Sanchez and said slowly, "What do you think, Vellares?" It was the first time he had addressed the man by his first name.

Sanchez wiped his brow with the back of his hand, looked at him, shrugged. "The Indians in my country, they have a word . . ." Sanchez said the word, a long, unfathomable word, a bewildered look on his sagging face as he said it. "It means . . . very strange. Very . . . *weird*." He stared at Volkmann. "You know what I'm saying?"

Volkmann nodded. In both the house and the small outbuilding, he had sensed something. He had shivered stepping into both of them. Something inside him felt touched by something, Sanchez sensing it too, and the girl, Volkmann could tell.

A feeling none of them could put into words.

He turned to Erica, who was looking at him.

There was a noise behind them. Volkmann turned, saw the helicopter pilot call Sanchez over, talking in Spanish.

Volkmann and Erica looked back at the white house, neither of them speaking. They heard Sanchez's footsteps moments later and turned. The detective held something in his hand.

"The pilot," Sanchez said to Volkmann, "found this lying in the bushes. The helicopter blades must have blown it from the fire."

Sanchez handed him a piece of glossy paper, the remains

of a very old black-and-white photograph. Half of it had been burned, the right side of the picture cracked and worn, but the image still discernible. The photograph was of a woman, a blond, young, pretty woman, smiling out at the camera, sky and snowcapped mountains behind her.

The young woman's right hand was linked through the arm of a companion, a man wearing some sort of uniform. Only the man's shoulder, his left arm and part of his torso were still visible. The rest of the photograph had been burned, its black edges ragged, flaking with cinder. But what caught Volkmann's eye was the conspicuous dark band around the man's arm: a black Nazi swastika set in a white circle.

Volkmann stared down at the photograph for a long time until Sanchez said, "Turn it over."

He did as the detective asked.

There was a date, in German, scrawled in the top right-hand corner in faded blue ink. *"Elfter Juli, 1931"*: 11th of July, 1931.

Volkmann looked up, shielded his eyes from the strong sun. He saw Erica and Sanchez stare over at the white house before both turned back to look at him.

"What does it mean?" Sanchez asked.

Volkmann flicked over the half-burned photograph, looked down again at the blond young woman in the picture, and wondered the same.

PART THREE

CHAPTER 16

Strasbourg. Thursday, December 8

The flight from Asunción to Madrid had been delayed and it was almost midday when Volkmann and Erica landed in Frankfurt.

When they arrived at Volkmann's apartment three hours later, he left her and drove to the office to type up a preliminary report. He put a copy in Ferguson's mailbox with a note saying he'd be in the next morning before noon.

At five, he had an early dinner with Erica in a small restaurant near the Quai Ernest, and they walked back to his apartment. After he had unpacked, he made up the spare bedroom and poured two brandies.

The afternoon before, Sanchez had driven them to a small cemetery on the outskirts of the city. The sky was cloudless, the heat unbearable, and Volkmann and the detective had waited under a jacaranda tree while the girl had said her prayer.

Later, Sanchez had taken them to the house in La Chacarita where the bodies had been discovered, and there had been brief interviews with Mendoza and Torres, but neither man had been able to add to their statements. They had visited Tsarkin's residence in the late afternoon, and Volkmann had seen the manicured lawns, the paintings on the walls, the open safe in the study. Sanchez's men had searched the rooms again, top to bottom, but found nothing of importance.

At the airport, Sanchez had promised to get the report on Tsarkin's background to Strasbourg as quickly as possible. His men were still digging through the files at the immigration office.

"I hope to have some information within the next twenty-four hours," Sanchez had said as he led them to Departures. Erica Kranz had thanked him, and the detective had smiled and said to Volkmann, "Look after her, amigo. Take care, and good luck."

Erica had been subdued and tired. On the flight back, Volkmann had explained that he wanted her in Strasbourg should Ferguson need to talk with her, and she had accepted his suggestion that she stay at his place rather than book into a hotel.

After she had gone to bed, Volkmann poured himself another brandy. Darkness had fallen beyond the window, the spire of the Gothic cathedral illuminated in the distance. No heat here, just a cold, chill wind rattling the windows.

As he sat there sipping the brandy, feeling the aching tiredness take hold, Joseph Volkmann heard the girl tossing restlessly in her sleep. He thought of the white house and the photograph of the woman taken a long time ago.

He wondered what Ferguson and Peters would make of it all.

Friday, December 9

The three men sat quietly in the warm office, Peters and Volkmann facing Ferguson's desk.

The tape machine beside Ferguson was on. When it finished playing through, Ferguson switched it off and shook his head.

There were three photographs lying faceup on the desk, copies made by the police in Asunción, and he stared down at them with interest. Faces to go with the story. One was a shot of Dieter Winter and Nicolas Tsarkin, taken with a telephoto lens. Another of Tsarkin himself, head and shoulders only, that looked like a copy from a passport. Hard eyes, a narrow mouth and a face that was thin and secretive. The third was a black-and-white photograph of the woman, her right hand linked through a man's arm. The Nazi armband was an interesting curiosity, Ferguson reflected.

He adjusted his glasses and picked up the photograph of the pretty blond woman and stared at it again. There was a note made by Volkmann, paper-clipped to the snapshot, mentioning the date on the back of the original photograph. Ferguson had written the date in pencil at the end of Volkmann's report: July 11, 1931.

He had also penciled in small asterisks and question marks in the margins of the report, points to be clarified by Volkmann when he arrived.

Now Ferguson scanned through the document once again. It had made interesting reading. Volkmann had spared no detail in describing the scene at the remote house in the Chaco. When Ferguson turned back moments later, he looked directly at Volkmann.

"The remains of the bonfire were analyzed?"

Volkmann appeared tired, but his eyes were alert. "Sanchez's people did a preliminary analysis of the remains. They were papers and photographs mostly. And wood and cardboard. But also some food traces, dried provisions. There was nothing in the house or outhouses. Every room had been stripped clean. For whatever reason, whoever these people were, they wanted every trace of their presence completely destroyed." Volkmann shook his head. "I've never seen anything like it before, sir. It looked like the whole property had been sanitized. As if whoever had lived in the Chaco house had gone through it with a fine-tooth comb and then scrubbed it clean."

Ferguson paused before speaking. He looked out toward the window, then back again.

"Leaving the question of the Chaco property aside for now, the question is, surely, where's the connection to Winter? What has all this got to do with Winter's death?"

Tom Peters leaned forward in his chair. "Might I make a suggestion, sir?"

Ferguson half smiled. "By all means."

"The report on the shooting in Berlin said the ammunition used was South American in origin. We know Winter was in South America. And not just once, but on at least eight occasions."

"Go on," Ferguson prompted.

"We know the ammunition used in both the Winter shooting and the killing of the businessmen in Hamburg a year ago was South American. We also know a lot of terrorist groups have been getting their supplies from there, since the Russians are no longer in the supply business." Peters hesitated, glanced at Volkmann. "And then there are the cargoes flown to Montevideo. There are countless possibilities, of course, sir. But it could have been weapons and munitions supplies. And it's a plausible reason why Winter would have been in South America."

Ferguson sighed, then stood up and crossed to the window. "Plausible, yes. But speculative. And I'm afraid it doesn't explain why Winter was killed in Berlin." Ferguson turned and raised an eyebrow, looked at Volkmann.

"What do you think the cargoes might have contained, Joseph?"

Volkmann hesitated. "It's difficult to say, sir. Weapons or narcotics seem likely. Or even precious metals. But if it was narcotics Rodriguez transported for these people, then the Chaco house wasn't used. The chemical agents used in the processing would have left behind trace elements." He shook his head. "But there were no chemical or narcotics traces on the property." He glanced at Peters. "What Tom says is still possible, sir. But there wasn't any hard evidence to support it."

"What about the land the property is on? Was it checked?"

"Sanchez had the local police check the land within a three-kilometer radius. There was a field that looked like it could have been used as a temporary airstrip about two kilometers from the house. There were deep tire marks on the surface and some faint oil stains in the soil. Nothing much else. But it could have been the place where Rodriguez landed."

"Was the aircraft this man Rodriguez used examined for narcotics traces?"

"The DC4 was impounded at Asunción. Sanchez had his lab people go over it."

"And?"

"There were minute cocaine traces in the aft cargo area." Volkmann shook his head as he looked at Ferguson. "But it proves nothing. According to Sanchez, Rodriguez could have made dozens of runs in between for other customers, ferrying narcotics."

Ferguson sighed and crossed back slowly to pick up a file from his desk. Inside were the original and two copies of the faxed report he had received an hour before from Asunción. He had delayed showing it to the men seated opposite, wanting to discuss Volkmann's report first. Now he opened the file, removed the contents.

"I received a report from Paraguay an hour ago. It's in

English. I think perhaps you had both better read it before we proceed further. There are copies for each of you. It rather deepens the mystery, I'm afraid."

Ferguson handed across the papers to Volkmann and Peters, the report Sanchez had promised. Volkmann took the three sheets and read slowly.

> To: Head, British DSE
> From: Captain Vellares Sanchez. Policía Civil, Paraguaya
> Subject: Visit of your officer, J. Volkmann, and his investigation
> Status: Highly Confidential
> After recent investigation the following can be reported:
>
> (1) The Chaco property your officer visited occupies a tract of land some 400 acres in size and was bought and registered in the name of Erhard Schmeltz in December 1931, one month after Señor Schmeltz, his wife, Inge, and their son Karl emigrated to Paraguay. Records reveal that Erhard Schmeltz was born in Hamburg in 1880, his wife one year later. According to his immigration records, Schmeltz served in the First World War in the German Army. His financial status upon arrival in Paraguay was five thousand U.S. dollars.
>
> The Chaco property was one of several that Señor Schmeltz purchased in Paraguay, beginning in December 1931, though the others were not in the same Chaco region. The Chaco property was used for the production of quebraco wood until 1949. Señor Erhard Schmeltz died in an automobile accident in Asunción in 1943.
>
> Police file sources disclose that from December 1931 to January 1933, he was in receipt of considerable sums of money sent from Germany. From February 1933 onward, money was sent to him in Asunción via the official German Reichsbank at exact six-month intervals, using bank drafts. Each draft was for the sum of five thousand U.S. dollars. After his

*death, Schmeltz's wife became the recipient. The drafts
finally ceased in February 1945.*

*Despite inquiries, which will continue, we have no
further information on the recent occupants of the
Chaco property. Señor Schmeltz's wife died in 1949.
The property register then recorded a change of own-
ership to the Schmeltz's son, Karl, born in Germany
in July 1931. No specific town or city of birth was
given in the immigration records, and there are no
photographs recorded in civil offices of Karl Schmeltz.
His present whereabouts are unknown.*

*(2) Regarding Señor Nicolas Tsarkin, the following
information has been confirmed:*

*Señor Nicolas Tsarkin arrived in Asunción from Rio
de Janeiro on November 8, 1946, and applied for Paraguayan citizenship two days later.*

*His immigration application stated his place of birth
as Riga, in Latvia, 1911. In his possession on arrival
in Paraguay he had the considerable sum of twenty
thousand U.S. dollars. Señor Tsarkin described himself on his application form as a war refugee and businessman. He was granted Paraguayan citizenship one
week after his application.*

*For your information, the application forms of the
time for citizenship were of two kinds: one for public
records and one that was held in the files of the seguridad—the security police—which contained information of a more confidential nature. Many refugees
came to South America from Europe after the war, and
the Paraguayán government of the time had pro-
German sympathies: thus ex-Nazis were admitted, particularly those with foreign currency or gold in their
possession. Depending on the subjects' influence and
financial status, some were helped to arrange a new
identity and residence within Paraguay.*

In Señor Nicolas Tsarkin's case, a seguridad *file
exists. I have seen the file but am not permitted to
transmit a copy. However, the following facts were
recorded:*

*(a) Nicolas Tsarkin was born in Berlin, not Riga,
in 1911.*

(b) Tsarkin's real name was Heinrich Reimer.

(c) He was a major in the Leibstandarte (SS) Division when the war ended in 1945.

(d) According to then-reliable sources named in the file, Tsarkin was responsible previously for a number of war crimes on the Russian and Allied fronts, and wanted by the Allied and the Russian authorities in this connection. It should be pointed out that at no time during his life in Paraguay was Tsarkin ever in trouble with the police. Nor were there any applications for his extradition, overt or otherwise. He apparently led an exemplary and successful business life and covered up his past successfully.

Tsarkin prospered in Paraguay, starting a number of businesses, importing farm machinery and mechanical parts. He also purchased a number of farms in the hinterland for cattle breeding and beef production. Tsarkin was unmarried. No business connection has been discovered between Tsarkin and the Schmeltz property. Tsarkin's holding company was sold six months ago to a native-born Paraguyan citizen.

(3) Immigration returns from border stations are still being thoroughly checked, but no additional immigration papers have so far been found or registered for Señor Dieter Winter other than those already discovered.

(4) One further interesting detail. A military radar installation at Bahia Negra northeast of the Chaco registered an unfiled flight thought to be a light aircraft or helicopter shortly after our arrival at the Chaco property. The unidentified aircraft was vectored proceeding northeast to the Brazilian border toward Corumba and was then lost from radar contact. This is being investigated further.

ENDS.

Sanchez.

Tom Peters had finished reading his copy and was shaking his head.

Ferguson looked perplexed. "As I say, it rather deepens the mystery, doesn't it?"

"You think there's a link to Winter's death in all this?" Peters asked, looking from Volkmann to Ferguson. "To the photograph of the woman? To what happened to the journalist and the young girl?"

"It's possible," Ferguson replied noncommittally.

Volkmann said nothing but looked out beyond the window. The sky was gray and it was cold outside, cold enough for snow. He looked back and saw Ferguson staring down at the photographs, at the one of the blond young woman.

"You say Tsarkin was responsible for booking the hotel suite?" Ferguson asked.

"That and every hotel suite used by Winter in the last two years during his visits to Paraguay." Volkmann shook his head. "But that tells us nothing, sir. Except that maybe Reimer was some sort of organizer for these people."

Ferguson made a steeple of his fingers. "I'll have a copy of the taped voices sent to the laboratory in Beaconsfield for analysis. Not that it can tell us much from the voice syntax and accents, apart from the approximate age of the speakers and their likely regional origin. But it may offer some clue. As of now, we're in the dark completely."

Ferguson paused, looked toward the window, then back again. "However, there is one curious but thin connecting strand, if either of you gentlemen have noticed?"

Ferguson saw both men stare at him. He held up the photograph of the young woman. "This man Erhard Schmeltz mentioned in the report. The money he received from Germany and the Nazi Reichsbank commenced the same year the photograph was taken, if the date on the reverse is to be believed." Ferguson paused, a perplexed look on his sallow face as he placed the photograph back on top of the file. "Erhard Schmeltz seems a rather curious proposition. He arrives in Paraguay in nineteen thirty-one from a depressed Germany with five thousand American dollars in his possession."

Volkmann looked across at Ferguson. He was troubled by a line in Sanchez's report, another connecting strand. Both Tsarkin and Erica Kranz's father had been officers in the Leibstandarte SS. Perhaps it was a coincidence, but still, it bothered him. He wondered if the others had noticed. For now, though, no one had commented.

"What did Hollrich say when you showed him the report?" Volkmann asked.

"I haven't," Ferguson replied. "With all the uncertainty about, just now I'm not sure the Germans would pursue it with much vigor. The file might be left gathering dust. Besides, for now, it's in our court."

"So what do you want me to do, sir?"

Ferguson thought for a moment. "The shipment talked about on the tape. It may connect to the Italian mentioned in the conversation. It may be worth asking the Italian desk to double-check their port entries for consignments from Montevideo after the twenty-fifth. But as we can't be very specific, I doubt if we'll have much success." Ferguson hesitated again. "Do either of you have any other suggestions?"

Volkmann hesitated, then said, "Maybe the girl knew students who were close to Winter at Heidelberg. People at the same university who might have known him."

"It's worth a try," Ferguson replied.

"You want me to go it alone?" Volkmann asked.

"For the moment, yes. Take the girl along, if she has no objections; she may be helpful, considering her contacts at the university. Bearing in mind her press connections, you had better explain that this is still a security operation. And if you need any help, let me know."

Volkmann stood up slowly. "The photographs, sir . . . I'd like copies."

"Of course. I'll have the lab get them."

"What about Erhard Schmeltz?"

Ferguson looked up. "What about him?"

"Could we have his background checked? It may turn up something. The fact that he was receiving drafts from the German Reichsbank may tell us something about the occupants of the house."

Ferguson nodded. "Very well, I'll have Tom send a request to the American Documentation Center in Berlin. Schmeltz would have left Germany before the Nazis came to power, of course. But who knows? Because of this Reichsbank business, he could have been a Nazi Party member, and the Document Center may have him on file. I'll also request information on Reimer, alias Tsarkin, to

confirm the information from Asunción. If what this fellow
Sanchez says is true, they ought to have his file. Leibstandarte SS. The same SS division as the girl's father, if I
remember from her file. Had you noticed?"

"Yes, sir."

"Another curiosity. Do you trust Erica Kranz?"

"In what way?"

"The fact that she knew this Winter at the university.
And that her father and Reimer were in the same SS division. One connection I could accept, but two I have questions about. And there's a third."

"What do you mean, sir?"

"She's been to South America and she knew the journalist. Do you think she's telling you everything she
knows?"

Volkmann shook his head. "I couldn't say, sir. She loved
the journalist, as far as I can tell. They were cousins," he
reminded Ferguson. "And they were very close. She knew
something about the story he was working on, and when
he was murdered . . ." He left the thought unfinished.

"So you believe her?" Ferguson asked quietly.

"Probably, but not certainly," Volkmann said. "Why
did she come to us in the first place?" he added. "She
came out of the blue. And if she had not chosen to come
to us, we'd have been the last to learn what we now know.
That leaves some possibility of deception, but . . ." He left
that thought unspoken.

Ferguson nodded to indicate the meeting was at an end.

"Very well, let's leave it at that for now. Good luck,
Joseph. And keep in touch so I can keep you informed if
anything comes in from Asunción."

After Volkmann had left the office, Ferguson turned to Peters. "You think he'll be able to handle it?"

"Sir?"

"You know how Volkmann dislikes the Germans."

Peters shrugged. "Would you prefer me to cover it?"

"No. Volkmann has the language and the experience. I
think for now, we'll leave it in his hands. By the way, Erica
Kranz is staying at his place."

Peters raised his eyebrows. "Who suggested that?"

"Volkmann took it upon himself." Ferguson smiled. "Either he's softened his attitude or he really doesn't trust the girl and wants to stick close to her."

"You mean if she's covering something up? Not telling us the full story?"

"I imagine so. But as Joseph pointed out, it begs the question as to why she came to us in the first place. And why she insisted on dealing only with the DSE and not the *Bundespolizei*." Ferguson hesitated. "Something's not quite right, Tom. And I don't like it." He looked at Peters. "By the way, what's she like?"

"Kranz? A bit of a stunner. A girl you'd crawl over broken glass to get a date with."

Ferguson smiled. "That'll be all for now, Tom."

"Right, sir."

The Oriental Restaurant in Petite France was empty except for the two of them.

Erica's blond hair fell loosely about her shoulders, and she had put on makeup. She wore a pale-blue sweater and a navy skirt, legs smooth in sheer stockings.

A waiter hovered, serving them attentively. Crisp beef and vegetables. A bottle of the driest white wine, ice-cold.

Volkmann had told her about the report from Sanchez, stipulating that it was confidential. He watched her face as he explained about Tsarkin's past and the owner of the Chaco property, and said that his people were checking on the backgrounds of Schmeltz and Reimer. He saw the look of puzzlement, and then Erica frowned.

"But the Reichsbank business with Erhard Schmeltz happened so long ago."

"We still need to check it out. The fact that the date on the back of the photograph and the first drafts being sent to Schmeltz happened in the same year may have some connection. Besides, it may tell us something about Schmeltz's son. Because apart from his name, we've very little to go on."

The girl looked at him and put down her glass. "I don't understand—you mean records are kept that far back?"

Volkmann explained that there were two ways that the post of someone like Reimer could be verified. There were two agencies in Germany that kept records of former Nazis and SS personnel. The first was in Zehlendorf in Berlin and called the Berlin Document Center. It was an American institution, funded by the German government, as a repository of Nazi Party organization documents. In 1945, American troops had captured almost the entire records of SS personnel and the Nazi Party and its organizations in various locations throughout Germany. These and other Party records were later stored in Berlin in special underground vaults, to aid in the prosecution of likely war criminals and to help determine which citizens of the Reich had been Nazi Party members during subsequent de-Nazification.

The second agency was run solely by the German government. Known as the Z-Commission, and located in the small town of Ludwigsburg in Württemberg, its staff consisted of a small number of dedicated operatives and attorneys whose function it was to investigate, and prosecute if necessary, known war criminals. Whereas the Berlin Document Center was a repository of Nazi organization and SS documents, the Z-Commission had actually hunted down Nazis and SS guilty of war crimes and mass murder, and most of the documented files it kept were copies of the ones in Berlin. But because many of those wanted for war crimes were either dead or had been prosecuted, or most likely had long ago managed to cover up their pasts successfully, the staff had found its funds from the federal government gradually diminished, and the Z-Commission was slowly being wound down.

Volkmann looked at the girl. "So the files and records of most former Nazis or SS will be in either Ludwigsburg or Berlin, but Berlin has all the original documents, so that's our best bet. They may have no record of Erhard Schmeltz, because he left Germany before the Nazis came to power in nineteen thirty-three, but it's worth a try."

He saw her hesitate and turn away, then look back again.

"Sanchez mentioned an aircraft in his report. Could he find out where it landed?"

Volkmann shrugged. "If it was anywhere other than a regular airport, I doubt it. It could have been another helicopter. In that case, it could have landed anyplace where there was a clearing big enough. And we're assuming it was the people from the Chaco house. It may not have been.''

Erica brushed her hair from her face. "So we still have nothing really to go on?''

"Maybe not. What about Winter's old friends from the university? People Winter associated with. Did you know any of them at Heidelberg?''

"I moved in a different circle. But there were a couple of girls I knew in Winter's circle. Why?''

"Did you know anyone who was close to him at Heidelberg?''

She hesitated for a moment. "Actually, there was Wolfgang Lubsch from Baden-Baden. You may have heard of him—the terrorist?''

"I know of him," Volkmann acknowledged. "Last I heard, he was leading an offshoot of the Red Army Faction, and he's on the *Bundespolizei* wanted list. But I can't say I know much about him or the organization he runs. I haven't had much to do with terrorists—especially German terrorists, thank God. They tend to be very nasty people.''

"Back when I used to run into him, Lubsch was terribly passionate and terribly intense. And nothing satisfied him. Nothing. Which is, I guess, the reason he's become so extreme." She caught Volkmann's eye. "Anyhow, I used to see Lubsch and Winter together now and again. It was actually kind of a funny relationship. Lubsch was very far to the left, and Winter was a right-winger. I guess they liked to spar together.''

"Jesus," Volkmann said, thinking out loud. "The one man who might give us a line on Winter turns out to be a terrorist, and probably unreachable.''

Erica raised a hand. "But not impossible," she said. "I knew his girlfriend, Karen Holfeld. We roomed together one year. I think she's living in Mainz somewhere.''

"You think you could find her?''

"I could telephone some old friends who might know. She may have lost contact with Lubsch. But if I do find her, what do I say?''

Volkmann thought for a moment. "How about telling her you want to write a story with a colleague from one of your magazines . . . a human-interest thing about people in-

volved in left-wing politics. Tell her you want to talk with
Lubsch in confidence. And that you won't use his name,
and won't identify the place where you interviewed him.
Maybe he will bite at the chance for some positive public-
ity. And maybe the old school ties will help. But keep it
low key. And if you can't find the girl through your own
friends, I'll put my people on it." He hesitated. "Was there
anyone else you remember who might have known Winter?"

"No. I'm sorry. But I really didn't know him well."

Volkmann hesitated, looked about the room. For a long
time he said nothing, then he turned to look back at Erica.
"I'd like to ask you a question. Did you sense anything
strange about the house in Chaco?"

"In what way strange?"

"Apart from the way the house had been left. A feeling.
Like an atmosphere."

She put down her fork and Volkmann saw the look on
her face. "I sensed something. But I'm not sure what. The
small house, the one next to the hacienda . . . I remember
that I shivered when I stepped inside, even though it was
a hot day." Erica Kranz shrugged, then hesitated. "It was
kind of like the feeling you get when you step into a house
in which someone has died." She looked directly at Volkmann. "Is that what you mean?"

"Maybe. I'm not sure."

"Is it important?"

He shrugged again and smiled. "No. It's not important.
Forget it."

When the waiter had taken away the dishes, Erica
reached across and touched Volkmann's hand.

"I would like to say thank you, Joe. Thank you for your
help."

Volkmann looked over at the blue eyes and the pretty
face and wondered if she meant it, or if she was just a good
actress.

He was awakened by the telephone ringing in the next
room. It was dark in the bedroom, the window open, curtains lifting and falling in a soft breeze. He switched on the

bedside lamp and looked at his watch. Midnight. He dressed and went into the living room.

Erica was sitting by the telephone, a notepad open beside her. She looked tired.

"I've made a lot of calls. And I think I've managed to trace Wolfgang Lubsch."

Volkmann looked at her questioningly.

"A girl I knew in Heidelburg . . . she gave me Karen's phone number." She caught Volkmann's eye. "When I called Karen, she seemed wary, afraid to talk to me."

"That shouldn't come as a surprise—especially if she and Lubsch are still lovers."

"I asked her if Lubsch was open to an interview. She told me he wasn't eager to talk to reporters these days. So I used the approach you suggested—with a few embellishments. I said I wouldn't use Lubsch's name but that the article was very important to me. And she seemed to think Lubsch might be interested in a story like that. She told me she'd phone and ask him. She rang back now and said it was okay."

Volkmann thought for a moment. "Fine work, Erica. Marvelous. So when do we get to meet him?"

"I've got the name of a bar. It's in an old wine town on the Rhine called Rüdesheim, about an hour's drive from Frankfurt. Tomorrow afternoon we're to be in a place called the Weisses Rossl at four o'clock. Karen asked me not to involve anyone else, apart from us. I assured her she could trust me."

Volkmann waited until Erica had gone, watching her retreat into the spare bedroom, before he telephoned the night-duty officer, Jan De Vries, and requested the files for Wolfgang Lubsch of Baden-Baden, a graduate of Heidelberg. De Vries promised to get back to him by eight that morning.

After Volkmann replaced the receiver, he crossed to the bookshelves. He found the *Times Atlas* and flicked the pages. He traced with a finger to the place on the border between Paraguay and Brazil named Bahia Negra, where Sanchez had said the radar had picked up the signal. From the map, it looked like a small, insignificant town straddling the border on the banks of the Rio Paraguay. He wondered if Sanchez had made any further progress, but knew the man would make contact if he did.

He replaced the atlas on the shelves, and a little later, he went into the bedroom and found the Beretta 9-mm service pistol, removed it from the holster and checked the action. There was a full clip of shells and a spare magazine in the plastic pocket. He left the weapon and the spare magazine on the bedside table and the holster on the dressing table. Then he went to sit by the window and read through the tape transcript again. When he finished, he looked up. It was cold outside and raining now, fine needles scratching at the glass. He lit a cigarette, inhaling slowly.

CHAPTER 17

The town faced onto the waterfront, a maze of cozy inns and narrow, cobbled streets.

In summer, the pretty wine town would have been flooded with visitors, the Rhine banks awash with the floating hotels and tourist barges that plied the river. But in winter, the visitors trickled to a few hardy weekenders who drove from nearby cities and towns.

Volkmann drove through the town to get his bearings, then made his way down toward the waterfront and parked the Ford near the railway station. He left the Beretta and his DSE identity card tucked under the driver's seat, and Facilities had provided him with a Press ID card.

A couple of squat tourist ferries were tied up for the winter season. It didn't feel like Christmas, but decorations hung in shop windows, and in the central Platz a giant pine had been erected, colored lights winking in the darkening afternoon light.

They walked back uphill through the narrow, cobbled alleyways toward the center of the old town. Most of the *weinstuben* were closed, but they found a café open and ordered coffee and pastries.

Although the girl had her blond hair tied back and wore hardly any makeup, her face was still strikingly pretty. As she sipped her coffee, Volkmann said, "You had better describe Lubsch to me."

Erica shrugged. "He wasn't the kind of guy most women would find attractive. Small. Thinly built. He wore glasses and had red hair. But he looked kind of vulnerable and at the same time, arrogant, if you know what I mean. A dreamer. But bright, very bright." She paused. "Does that help?"

Volkmann smiled. "It's enough. Does your friend Karen still have a relationship with him?"

Erica hesitated before she spoke. "I got the feeling she still sees him. She must, if she was able to contact him." She smiled. "And Karen always liked sleeping with intel-

ligent men. I think she thought at Heidelberg that by sleeping with enough bright undergraduates, she'd absorb
through osmosis what she needed to know. Maybe she did,
but she also got a reputation as a man-eater. Knowing
Karen, she probably still sleeps with Lubsch, even though
she's married now.''

"Tell me more.''

"She and her husband run a business together. It's in the
center of Mainz. And her name's no longer Holfeld, but
Gries.''

"What kind of business?''

"A sports boutique. You know, high-end athletic shoes,
designer active wear. Very fashionable. Very chic. Business
is booming, Karen claims.''

"Which faculty was she in?''

"Politics, the same as Lubsch.''

"So how did she get into sportswear?''

"Karen was always involved in politics, but she was into
her body more. She's very physical—running, swimming,
hiking, climbing, biking, sex—everything that makes you
sweat. At the university, she always had lots of guys.''

"What about you?''

"What do you mean?'' she answered, coloring a little.

"At the university. Did you have lots of male friends?''

"A few,'' she said carefully.

"You don't like to talk about that part of your life?''

She shrugged. "Not to someone I've just met.''

"Fair enough,'' he said with a slight smile. He changed
the subject then. "Tell me about the right-wing groups
Winter belonged to.''

She paused for a moment to collect her memories. "I
don't think they were particularly organized. Just guys who
got together to drink and tell each other how brilliant and
deep they were and—what's the expression in your language—to throw the bull?''

He laughed. "Close enough.''

"They'd throw the bull about the state of the country,''
she went on. "They liked to scapegoat immigrants. In their
view, Germany had become a half-breed state because of
its five million immigrants. When they were drunk, they
might shout insults at foreign-looking students—if those

students were stupid enough to drink in the places where Winter's friends drank. There were fights too, a few times, but nothing serious.''

She looked away, then back again. ''And when they were deeply drunk, they'd beat their steins against the tables and chant, 'Germany for the Germans.' I saw a Nazi salute or two now and again. But no one paid much attention. Most of us thought that what these guys were doing was stupid and silly.''

''And after they graduated, what became of them? Did they stay involved in extreme politics?''

Erica shook her head. ''I really can't say, Joe. I'm not a political animal. I didn't pay a lot of attention to them—except when I was in the same beer hall and couldn't avoid them. And none of my friends had anything to do with them, either.'' She smiled. ''My friends were more interested in drugs and rock music and sex.'' Her smile deepened, and she looked down at the cup held in both hands. When she looked up again, she said. ''You know, Joseph Volkmann, you're a very strange man.''

''Tell me why you think so,'' he said softly.

''You make me want to fill the silence by answering your questions. To even confide in you. I'm the journalist. And that's supposed to be my strategy. But with you, it doesn't work. Also, it's rather absurd.''

''What is?''

''I spend the night in a man's apartment about whom I know nothing. It's not the kind of thing that usually happens, Joe.''

''And what does usually happen?''

''Nothing to write home about, I assure you. I have my work. I listen to my music. I go out with friends. But mainly my work. I'm afraid I'm not *hausfrau* material.''

''You have a boyfriend, Erica?''

She shook her head. ''There's no one special right now.'' She looked across at him. ''Don't I get a chance to ask some personal questions?''

Volkmann smiled. ''What would you like to know?''

''Do you like your work, Joe?''

''It's what I'm trained to do.''

''You sound like a regular soldier answering a civilian

who's just asked him the same question.'' She smiled again. ''But do you really like your work?''

''Yes.''

He smiled back but looked away as if to avoid further questions. Dusk falling. Lights coming on in the cobbled street outside.

When he turned back, he said, ''I had Lubsch checked out. No surprises. His group operates from the Swiss border up to Frankfurt. He's been involved in at least two kidnappings and the murder of an industrialist in Freiburg. He also likes making withdrawals from German banks without having accounts in them. All, I'm sure, in the name of freeing the downtrodden and protecting the defenseless.''

He looked hard at her. ''But he is not an ivory-tower intellectual, Erica. He's a dangerous man. If you decide you'd rather not go with me . . .'' He left the rest of that thought unsaid.

''If it means finding the people who killed Rudi, I want to meet him.''

''Good,'' he said. ''I'm glad. But it also goes without saying that he musn't know I'm with DSE.'' Volkmann produced his Press ID. ''It's genuine. So what you told Karen ought to hold up. And no matter what, stick to our cover story.''

''What happens when we have to ask Lubsch about Winter?''

''Play it as it happens.''

He saw the girl hesitate, then nod her head. ''Okay.''

''You're sure you can go through with it?''

''Yes.''

Volkmann watched her for several moments, searching her face, but he couldn't detect any real fear. He glanced at his watch and when he looked back, he saw the girl's blue eyes looking at him intently before she turned away.

A few moments later, he paid the waitress and asked for directions to the Weisses Rossl.

They reached the tavern five minutes later, driving back down toward the waterfront to the ancient *bierkeller* of dark wooden beams that smelled of smoked sausage and candle wax.

They were the only customers, and Volkmann chose a table at the back next to a fire exit and ordered two glasses of schnapps.

The girl who served them had hardly left their drinks when a clean-shaven, stocky, dark-haired young man came in wearing a gray-plastic windbreaker. He ordered a beer and sat at the bar as he unfolded a newspaper.

Five minutes passed, and Volkmann became conscious of the young man observing them. He recalled Erica's description of Lubsch. The man seated at the bar in no way resembled the terrorist, and Volkmann guessed that if he was one of Lubsch's men, he was going to check them out and would make his move soon.

When the girl behind the bar went into a tiny kitchen, sure enough, the young man stood up slowly and crossed to their table. One hand remained inside his pocket.

He looked at Erica and said sharply, "Your name is Erica Kranz?"

"Yes."

Volkmann saw the man's brown eyes study him. "You're Volkmann?"

When Volkmann nodded, the young man hesitated, then said to Erica, "Wolfgang wants me to check you both out." He half smiled. "You understand, it's simply a precaution."

The man's eyes flicked momentarily toward the kitchen, where the girl had gone.

"There's an alleyway behind here, directly to the right. Finish your drinks and meet me there in two minutes. When you approach me, keep your hands out of your pockets and by your sides. All I want to see in your hands are identity papers. If you see anyone else approaching, pretend you know me and stop to talk. But don't attempt to put your hands in your pockets or do anything foolish. Do you understand?"

Erica began to speak, but the man barely perceptibly raised his hand. "Just do as I say. Otherwise, the meeting's off."

The man turned back toward the bar. He finished his drink and folded his newspaper, bade good-bye to the girl behind the counter as she came out of the kitchen. Volkmann saw him go out the front, veer to the right and disappear. He nodded to Erica.

"Okay, finish your drink and let's do like the man says. You've got ID?"

Erica nodded, searched in her coat pocket, removed her driving license.

"Keep it in your hand, like he says." They finished their drinks and Volkmann led the way.

The alleyway behind the *bierkeller* was long, narrow and poorly lit. They came out into a small cobbled yard, a light somewhere overhead flooding the area. Five meters away, Volkmann saw another narrow alleyway leading to a street. The young man was waiting at the mouth of the second alleyway, hands in the pockets of his windbreaker.

As they moved toward him, he said quietly, "To the right, please. Quickly. Hands up against the wall. And don't speak."

He said to Erica, "I'm going to have to search you, too."

The man's hands moved roughly but expertly over them, searching for concealed weapons. When he finished, he told them to turn around.

"Your identity papers."

They handed them over and he scrutinized them, turning the photographs toward the light, looking from photographs to faces. He handed them back and looked at Volkmann.

"You came by car?"

"Yes."

"Did you see anyone following you?"

"No."

"You're certain?"

"I guess so."

"I asked if you were certain, Volkmann."

"So far as we could tell, no one followed us."

The man hesitated, then said, "Okay. Follow me. And no questions." He turned abruptly and led the way down the alley behind him.

As they stepped through into a narrow, deserted street, the young man looked to the left and right. Then he raised his hand, and the dull growl of an engine filled the growing darkness.

A big gray Mercedes delivery van suddenly came out of

nowhere and pulled up sharply across their path. A man with pockmarked skin and wearing green overalls sat behind the wheel, gunning the motor.

The side doors of the van opened with a roll of metallic thunder and two young men jumped out. One of them held a Walther pistol in his hand and gestured with it for Volkmann and Erica to get inside.

The men pushed them forward into the Mercedes, and as they clambered in, they were forced down roughly onto the floor and then the door banged shut.

"Put these on."

One of the men thrust two black balaclavas at Volkmann and Erica. Each was eyeless, a small slit at the mouth to breathe through.

When Volkmann hesitated, the man seemed to lose his patience and kicked out at him viciously, his boot slamming painfully into Volkmann's thigh.

"Do it! *Now!*"

As Volkmann pulled on the balaclava, he saw Erica do the same, and then the blackness took over as the young man spoke again.

"Try to move or talk, either of you, and you're both dead."

The big diesel engine gave a deep, noisy roar and the van lurched and moved forward.

CHAPTER 18

The Mercedes van turned off the mountain road and drove down into the heavily wooded valley.

Darkness had fallen and the headlights were on. Five minutes later, the driver halted outside the mountain cabin. As he switched off the engine, the side door slid open and the two men in the back climbed out.

Volkmann felt a hand grip his arm and he was pulled out roughly. He could smell the woods, heavy and pine-scented, and hear the sounds of feet crunching on gravel. Seconds later he was being pushed through a doorway.

Now the smells were different: dry must, rotting wood, rancid food. Wooden floorboards shook under his feet. Almost a minute passed before a hand yanked the eyeless balaclava from his head, and in the sudden flood of light that followed, he was momentarily blinded.

He blinked. Erica stood beside him. She glanced at him briefly before she looked over at a young man wearing wire-rimmed glasses who stood by a shattered window.

The man wore a dark, padded windbreaker, blue jeans, and scuffed white sneakers. He was small and wiry, and his face had several days' growth of red stubble. His red hair was untidy, and he looked as if he hadn't slept for a week. His features didn't look German to Volkmann except for the eyes, which were very blue and sharp, like the small eyes of a nervous animal, but with a hint of arrogance. His jacket was unzipped and a Walther automatic was tucked into his trouser belt.

Volkmann guessed from the look on Erica's face that she recognized him and that the man was Wolfgang Lubsch. The young man stared over at them but said nothing.

A portable kerosene lamp hung from a meathook embedded in a ceiling beam. A second lamp stood on a wooden table in the center of the filthy room, throwing shadows about the bare timber walls.

Volkmann guessed that the room was part of a mountain cabin. A traditional *Berghütte*. One of the many thousands that dotted the German hills and valleys, used by hunters and woodsmen and holidaying families, but this one was old and it obviously had not been used for some time.

The two young men from the Mercedes stood nearby. One was tall and blond and carried an AK47 slung over his shoulder. The second was smaller and ruggedly built. His crooked nose looked as if it had been broken more than once, and a jagged scar ran across his forehead. He seemed like a man who relished physical contact, and he held a stubbed leather truncheon in his right hand as if to prove it.

Volkmann's wallet lay on the table, the contents scattered. The photograph from the Chaco of the blond young woman lay beside a clutter of paper money, his French driving license and Press ID, and the contents of Erica's handbag had been spilled out next to them.

The man with the truncheon pointed silently to the chairs.

When Joseph and Erica sat, the young man wearing glasses slowly stepped forward. He looked down at the items scattered on the table before his fingers probed among the pile. He finally picked up Volkmann's driving license and examined it for several moments, then threw it back down on the table.

He took a pack of cigarettes from the pocket of his jacket and lit one with a Zippo lighter. As he inhaled, his nervous blue eyes settled on Erica. She looked up at him but said nothing. The young man stared back at her.

"Erica. It's been a long time. You look as pretty as ever . . ."

"Wolfgang . . ."

"Forgive the dramatics in bringing you here like this, but I'm sure you realize that someone in my situation has to walk carefully." Lubsch paused to smile. "But then, I'm presuming you know why I've been cautious?"

Erica glanced over for a moment at the man brandishing the AK47, then back at Lubsch. "Because you're a terrorist."

"That's a question of perspective, surely? If the British had captured George Washington, he would have been hanged or shot, no? An eighteenth-century terrorist. And the terrorist founders of the State of Israel are now honored statesmen and Nobel Peace Prize winners." Lubsch smiled again. He removed his glasses and rubbed his eyes. "So, tell me. What do you want from me? I'm very interested in this article you want to write."

Erica slipped a quick glance at Volkmann, who nodded almost imperceptibly; then she looked back at Lubsch. "Joseph and I are working on a story," she said. "But it's not exactly the one I told Karen about."

"Oh?" Lubsch, said, his eyes intent and curious. "And what's the real story?"

"A man was murdered in Berlin ten days ago. Someone you knew at Heidelberg."

"Who?"

"Dieter Winter."

Lubsch paused, but his face showed no reaction. "I read about it in the papers. What's it got to do with me?"

"We're trying to find who killed Winter, and why."

"And why are you so interested in Winter's death?"

Erica Kranz hesitated. "Because we think his death is connected to other murders."

"Really. And what murders might these be?"

She told him about Rudi Hernandez and about what they had found in Paraguay.

Lubsch inhaled on his cigarette, then shrugged. "So what's this got to do with me?"

"The German connection," she answered. "The men in Paraguay are Germans. And Winter was killed in Germany. The police don't know who killed Winter, or why. They think there may be a drug connection, but they're really in the dark. I remembered that you knew Winter at Heidelberg. I thought you could help us. That maybe you knew people we could talk with who might know what Winter was involved in, or who his friends were. That's why we needed to meet with you."

Lubsch looked away for a moment, then back again. "Do you know what these cargoes from South America were?"

"No."

Lubsch stood there for several moments, not speaking, then stared at Volkmann.

"And what part do you play in all of this?"

"We're working on the story together."

Lubsch looked down at the table. "You carry a French

driving license, Volkmann. But you're not French, or German, are you? Your German is rather excellent, but your accent"—Lubsch shook his head as he looked back up—"a vowel here and there betrays you."

"I'm British."

The small blue eyes stared down suspiciously. "Is there any other reason you're both so interested in Winter, besides what you told me?"

"Should there be?"

"I asked the question, Volkmann. Answer it."

"There's no other reason."

For a second Lubsch hesitated, then suddenly he nodded his head, the merest of gestures.

The scar-faced man lifted a hand, and the stubbed leather truncheon swished through the air like a blade and struck the left side of Volkmann's face. The force sent him flying backward. The man with the truncheon caught the chair and pushed it back again. Erica screamed and a hand went over her mouth.

Volkmann felt the sharp, cutting sting the leather truncheon had left on his face, and when his hand went to touch his jaw, he felt the painful angry red welt where the weapon had struck flesh.

Lubsch suddenly gripped Volkmann's hair and yanked his head back. "Are you sure there's no other reason, Volkmann?"

"I told you . . ."

Lubsch stared into Volkmann's eyes. "Then listen to me, Volkmann. Listen to me, both of you. Number one, I don't help smart reporters who set me up for a meeting on the pretext of some stupid story. Number two, I take a very poor view of people wasting my time and putting me at risk meeting them. Do you understand?"

Lubsch waited for an answer. When Volkmann didn't reply, the terrorist yanked Volkmann's hair back savagely. "I asked you a question, Volkmann. Do you understand?"

"Yes."

"Good."

Lubsch released his grip and turned to Erica as the hand covering her mouth came away.

"And you. Don't try to contact Karen again. What Volk-

mann got was a friendly warning. Next time, there won't
be one. For either of you. And there's something else I want
you both to understand. You're on dangerous ground sniffing around Winter's friends. If you want to stay alive, forget about him and your story.''

Lubsch nodded to the man with the truncheon, who
turned and went outside. Moments later came the sound of
the Mercedes starting up.

The man with the AK47 removed the lamp hanging from
the meathook in the beam overhead and slipped outside.
Then came the rumble of the van door sliding open.

Lubsch picked up the second lamp and crossed to the
door. He looked back at Volkmann and Erica.

''Remember what I said. And be grateful you're both
still alive.''

Lubsch extinguished the lamp, and the small cabin
plunged into darkness. Footsteps crunched on the gravel
outside and a door slammed shut.

The van moved off down the track. Its engine noise faded
and there was only silence and darkness and the fetid smells
of the cabin.

They followed the track through the forest and it took them
half an hour to reach the village. The name on the sign as
they entered said ''Kiedrich.'' It was pitch dark and when
Volkmann and Erica stepped into the first inn they saw
open, the half-dozen customers inside looked at them warily.

The girl looked pale and her lips trembled. Their clothes
were covered in mud after the walk through the woods, and
they tried to ignore the stares. Volkmann went into the
men's room and threw cold water on his face. The welt had
swollen painfully and it hurt when the water touched his
skin, but the flesh hadn't been cut.

When he came out, Erica had ordered two brandies and
he asked the innkeeper for some ice. He put a couple of
ice cubes in a handkerchief and pressed it to his face.

According to the innkeeper, they were twenty kilometers
from Rüdesheim and there was a taxi service in the town,
but when Volkmann telephoned, he was told that the only
driver available had taken a local girl to the hospital in

Wiesbaden and it would be another half-hour before the taxi could pick them up.

The innkeeper asked Volkmann if he was all right or if he wanted to call a doctor, but Volkmann told him no and the man shrugged and inquired no further.

It was almost an hour before the taxi came and another half-hour by the time they arrived back in Rüdesheim. The Ford was still parked near the station and they drove back to Erica's apartment, arriving just after ten.

Erica looked at his swollen face and went into the kitchen. She came back with some ice cubes wrapped in a cloth and a bottle of schnapps. She poured two large measures and handed one to Volkmann after he had taken the cloth. She went to sit on the couch and looked over at him as he dabbed his face.

"Are you okay, Joe?"

Volkmann tried to smile and winced with pain. "Sure." He noticed that her hands were trembling as she sipped her drink. "What about you?"

She shivered. "I thought Lubsch was going to kill us. Do you think he meant what he said?"

"Yes, I do."

"You think he knows something about Winter?"

Volkmann put down the cool cloth. He picked up his glass and looked at her. "Lubsch is not telling us all he knows about Dieter Winter and his friends. Otherwise he wouldn't have warned us about them."

"Why do you think he wanted to warn us off?"

"I don't know, Erica. Only Lubsch can tell us that. I'd like to know why he wanted to know if we were interested in Winter for any other reason besides the one you gave him."

"You're not going to try to contact him again, are you, Joe?"

He looked at her and shook his head before he sipped the warm schnapps and put down his glass. His mouth hurt when he swallowed. "People like Lubsch don't give second warnings. If we try to contact him again, he'll do as he said."

"So what now?"

Volkmann hesitated and thought for a moment. "I want

you to drive down to my place in the morning and wait for me there. I'll give you a key. I think it's better after what's happened that you stay out of Frankfurt for now." He looked at her. "You've got a car?"

She nodded. "Yes, it's down in the parking lot. You're sure? About staying in your place?"

"It's for your own safety, Erica. I wouldn't rule out the possibility that Lubsch is in contact with Winter's friends. If so, they may come looking for both of us."

She was silent for several moments; then she stood up and asked, "Do you want me to get some more ice?"

Volkmann shook his head. "No, but another drink wouldn't go amiss."

She took the dripping cloth from him and poured him another full glass. He watched her as she went back into the kitchen. She seemed to have calmed down but still looked pale. The incident with Lubsch had had its effect and the girl hadn't turned down his offer to stay at his place. She seemed genuinely afraid.

He stood, crossed to the window and pulled back the curtain. The wind had died and it was a clear, calm night; the Rhine barges moved slowly back and forth on the water. Across the street by the river he saw a group of youths with shaven heads drinking from cans of beer as they strolled toward the Eisener Steg, their harsh, guttural voices carrying in the darkness.

She had made dinner for them and afterward turned on the radio, the Sibelius violin concerto playing softly in the background. They sat on the couch and after she poured them another drink, she looked over at him.

She hesitated before she spoke, brushed a strand of hair from her face. "You're such a strange man, Joseph."

"In what way strange?"

"I get the feeling that nothing frightens you. Me, I'm still trembling after meeting Lubsch. Doesn't anything frighten you?"

"The same things as most people."

"Tell me about yourself, Joe."

"What do you want to know?"

"Anything. Everything." Erica hesitated and smiled. "You're a stranger to me."

Volkmann picked up his glass. "There isn't much to tell."

"Are you married?"

"Divorced."

"You had children?"

"No, no children."

She looked at him. "Tell me about your family. In your apartment there was a photograph. Of you as a small boy, I think. The couple were your parents?"

When he hesitated, Erica lifted her glass, held it in both hands. She was ignoring his reticence, and Volkmann guessed that maybe she was talking out of nervousness.

"You've heard of Cornwall?"

"Yes. It's in the southwest of England."

"The photograph was taken there, by the sea. It's where my parents spent their summers when I was a child."

"What did your father do?"

"He was a lecturer at a university."

"Do you see him often?"

"He died six months ago."

"I'm sorry . . ." Erica paused, then looked back at him. "He looked very much like you. You never wished to follow in his footsteps?"

"For a time, yes. But after university I couldn't seem to fit into a teaching job, and office work bored me. So I took the king's shilling instead."

"The king's shilling?"

Volkmann smiled and his jaw hurt. "It's an expression. It means to enlist. I joined the army as an officer cadet."

"Was your father proud of you?"

"My father hated uniforms, Erica. He didn't particularly like the idea. But I had my mind made up."

"How come you ended up in DSE?"

Volkmann half smiled. "That's a long story. And probably covered by the Official Secrets Act. Let's just say I was seconded."

"Tell me more about your family, Joe. I'd like to hear."

Volkmann looked away a few moments, then back again.

"My mother used to be a concert pianist, but she doesn't play professionally anymore . . . arthritis."

"Of course, I know of her." She colored a little. "I don't know why I never made the connection. She was excellent."

He smiled. "Perhaps I don't look like a concert pianist's son."

"Oh, but you do," she smiled back. "You're deeply sensitive. It's just that you're not in a line of work where one expects to meet sensitive people." She paused.

"Were you like your father, Joe?"

"In some ways, yes."

"He didn't look like an Englishman."

"And how are Englishmen supposed to look?"

"I meant that he looked more middle-European. Tall and dark."

Volkmann was silent for a moment; then he said, "He was a refugee, Erica, he and my mother both. They went to England after the war. My mother was from Hungary, my father from the Sudetenland. My father's family lived there, in a town called Smolna."

"With a name like Volkmann, they must have been Germans."

"Yes, they were Sudeten Germans. Jews. Volkmann isn't exclusively a Jewish name but that's what they were." He saw a look of surprise on the girl's face and she blushed. "That's how I learned my German. For a long time it was the only language my father spoke. He always spoke English badly."

Erica said quietly, "And your mother's family? They were Jewish also?"

"Hungarian and Catholic. So I guess that makes me half Jewish."

"Do you go to the synagogue?"

"No. Because my mother is not Jewish, I'm not. And my father's family were Jews in name only. When I was a child, my father took me only once to the synagogue, just to show me what it looked like and satisfy my curiosity."

Erica put down her glass. For a long time she was silent; then she said, "The war must have been terrible for your father."

Volkmann hesitated. "He was in a camp, if that's what you mean. That's where he first met my mother. They were both sixteen. They used to meet at the wire separating the men's compound from the women's. When the camp was liberated, they lost each other. They met again in London after the war and married."

"I don't understand. Why was your mother there? She wasn't Jewish."

"Not only Jews were sent to the camps. Intellectuals, homosexuals, vagrants, Gypsies. Even respectable, middle-class ordinary people like my mother's family. Anyone whom the Nazis considered a threat to the Reich, however feeble the reasons. Surely you knew that?"

He saw the look on her face then and she turned away. When she looked back, she said, "It was a terrible time . . . for Jews, for Germany, for everyone. You must hate Germans."

Volkmann stared at her for a long time and then he said, "Not hate, but distrust. And not individuals. No people are more intellectual than the Germans; they're terribly rational and philosophical. And yet no people ever went as crazy as they did fifty years ago. I simply can't understand it. How your countrymen could let it all happen. I worked in Berlin for three years. I used to wake nights, thinking of what had happened here in this country of yours. To my parents and people like them."

She was silent for several moments; then she looked at him and asked, "Does that mean you don't trust me, Joe?"

There was a long pause before he answered. "To be honest," he said, "sometimes it's difficult."

She nodded. "I'll have to work on that problem then, won't I?"

He didn't answer her.

"There's something else I don't understand," she said after a time.

"What don't you understand?"

"You said your father hated uniforms. But you chose to wear one. Why?"

He shrugged. "Because maybe I always wanted to protect him."

"From what?"

Volkmann hesitated, turned his face away. He heard the Sibelius die in the background, the soft strains of the violin washing away.

"From anyone who might try to hurt him again."

When he turned back, he saw the girl looking at him. Was it compassion and understanding in her eyes, or something else?

Volkmann hesitated, then looked away again. "How in God's name did we get into that?"

"I'm sorry, forgive me, Joe. I shouldn't have been so inquisitive."

Volkmann stood up slowly. "I think I need some coffee."

He was standing over the sink rinsing a cup when she came in to him moments later.

"Joe?"

He turned, saw her standing there, looking up into his eyes. She spoke softly. "When you came to my apartment at first, I thought you were distant. Maybe even rude and arrogant. And that you didn't like me. Maybe that feeling was even mutual. But in Asunción when I cried, I felt that you cared. I felt that you knew what pain was." The blue eyes looked into his face. "Something terrible once happened to your father, didn't it, Joe?"

He did not reply but stood there, looking into her face.

She said, "Would it sound terrible if I asked to kiss you, Joe?"

She was standing close to him. Her fingers gently touched his lips before she moved her body against his, Volkmann feeling the softness of her figure, the warmth of her breasts comforting and full against his chest, her lips meeting his mouth softly at first, then more fiercely as they kissed and she pressed her body hard against his.

When they finally drew apart, she looked up at him and said, "I think I've wanted to do that since Asunción."

They could see the patina of sweat on Felder's fleshy face and almost smell the man's fear as they stood in the Grunewald. Spring was in the cold dawn air, and as the yellow sunlight filtered through the canopy of trees overhead,

*Volkmann remembered how absurd it was: the trees bud-
ding into life and Felder about to die.*

The big East German had his hands tied behind his back
and he was shaking as his eyes flicked nervously from Ivan
Molke to Volkmann. They both trained the silenced Berettas
on Felder, and he had started to tremble as soon as they
had emerged from the car.

As they stepped into the clearing, Molke said quietly,
"Turn around and look away, Felder. It'll be easier."

Suddenly Felder seemed to break, anger taking over.
"Anything I did was on orders, I swear it."

Ivan Molke shook his head. "You want to know something, Felder? Your people at Karlshorst will think we've
done them a favor."

There were beads of sweat on Felder's brow and he said,
"Yes, I killed two of your people. But I did it on orders. I
swear."

"That's not what your people are saying. They're saying
you went off on your own."

"It's a fucking lie."

There was a sudden noise from behind, and Molke and
Volkmann turned. A pigeon flew out of the low branches,
its wings beating furiously in the silence of the forest.

Volkmann heard the grunting noise from behind, and as
Volkmann turned back, he saw Felder make a run for the
trees.

Volkmann raised the Beretta and fired.

The first shot hit Felder in the back of the head, his body
punched forward; the second hit him in the shoulder as he
stumbled. The big man groaned, fell and rolled over on his
back, his eyes wide with pain. Molke ran forward and
pumped another shot into Felder's barrel chest. As he lay
on the ground, blood pumping from his wounds, a harsh
gurgling sound came from his open mouth.

Molke looked at Volkmann and said hoarsely, "Get the
shovels from the car."

When Volkmann hesitated, staring down at the body,
Molke said again, "Get the shovels from the car, Joe. We
haven't got all bloody day."

For a few moments more, Volkmann said nothing, just
stood there with the Beretta in his hand, staring down at

Felder in his last moments of life, the smell of cordite mingling with the fresh smell of the woods around him. He had killed and seen men killed before, but never so close that he could hear their dying breath. Then he looked up and was aware of the cold sweat on his forehead and the feeling of nausea in the pit of his stomach as he walked back toward the car.

As he removed the shovels from the trunk, he heard the faint crack of Molke's Beretta.

He came back and Molke said, "Are you okay?"

"Sure."

Volkmann looked down at the body. There was a trickle of blood at Felder's right temple where Molke had given him the coup de grâce.

After a moment, Molke spoke. "One of our contacts in Karlshorst said that even the Stasi and KGB guys were shocked by what he did to our two men."

Volkmann looked away and started to dig. The earth was soft and moist, the sweet humus of the forest rising up to their nostrils. A meter deep and then they would bury Felder.

"But the Stasi and KGB guys will know what happened to him when he doesn't turn up."

"Sure, and they'll put two and two together and be grateful. They'll know it was quid pro quo. We'd expect the same if any of our people acted like Felder did. There are unwritten rules, Joe, and Felder broke them."

There was a sharp crack as the shovel hit something hard, and Ivan Molke suddenly stopped digging and stared down at the soil, a look of horror on his face.

"Jesus!"

It was then Volkmann saw the top of the muddied skull in the fresh soil, and as Molke's shovel turned it over, there was another skull revealed beneath.

Molke had turned pale and as he knelt down, he took out his gloves and pulled one on, picked up the skull, placed it beside him, then the other, before he clawed at the earth with his gloved fingers. There was a tangle of bones, the remains of two bodies, and it looked to Volkmann as if they had been there for a long time. There were neat holes *drilled in the back of each skull. Molke turned away and vomited.*

"Cover it up again."

"But . . ."

Molke wiped his mouth with the back of his hand. "Just do it. Cover it up. We'll bury Felder some place else."

There was sweat now on Molke's face and brow, and Volkmann thought it absurd that Molke could be so calm at seeing Felder's bloodied corpse while the skeletal remains deeply affected him.

As they drove back toward the city an hour later, Molke was silent.

It had started to rain, and ten minutes from the Kurfurstendamm, Ivan Molke pulled up outside a café and filling station on the autobahn and switched off the engine.

"Let's have a drink."

His hands were shaking, and Volkmann followed him inside; they found a quiet table away from the groups of noisy truck drivers. Volkmann ordered a coffee; Molke asked for a double schnapps, then turned to look silently beyond the window at the early morning traffic. When the waiter had left, Volkmann looked at his colleague. The older man swallowed half his schnapps, then looked away again, his mind preoccupied as his hand gently massaged his neck.

"What do we do about the remains we found?"

Molke said quietly, "Nothing. Whoever they were, they've been dead a long time. I just didn't want a bastard like Felder buried beside them."

"I don't understand."

Molke looked at him. "The bodies have been there since the war."

"How can you be so sure?"

"Joe, I was born in Berlin. My father too. The Sicherheitsdienst and SS used to take people out to the Grunewald and put a bullet in the back of their skulls. Communists. Socialists. Jews. People they didn't want to bother sending to the camps or to prison. They simply took them out into the woods and shot them." He considered for a moment, the irony striking him. "Just like we did with Felder. Ex-

cept, these people were not like him. They were just ordinary people.''

''How can you know for sure?''

''About the bodies? My father was in Flossenberg.''

Volkmann looked at him. ''He was Jewish?''

''No, he was a socialist. He managed to hide out until 'forty-four. Then one night the Sicherheitsdienst raided the house where he was in hiding. They took him away, and the people who had hidden him. My uncle, his wife, their two young boys, they took to the Grunewald. They sent my father to the camps. Ravensbrück first, then Flossenberg.''

''Your father died there?''

Molke shook his head. ''He survived. He lived in Hamburg in an old folks' home until his death five years ago. I guess Berlin had too many memories for him.'' Molke looked away, toward the window and the cold spring morning and the passing traffic. ''When he came home after the war, he was in limbo. Nothing mattered. Flossenberg finished him. He was never the same. My mother and father split up. She said she couldn't live with a ghost. That's what he was, a ghost.''

There was a look of grief on Molke's face and then he said, ''You know what the strange thing was? The day he died, one of the old SS camp guards at Flossenberg was in a Munich courtroom. They'd been waiting fifteen years to bring the bastard to trial. But because he had such a good defense attorney, he'd managed to hold off the case with legal wrangling. The guy must have been nearly eighty. He'd killed men with his bare hands. But the jury took pity on him because he was an old man and near death and gave him a suspended sentence. One year.''

Molke grit his teeth. ''A week after I buried my father, there was a picture in the Münchner Post of the old SS guy coming out of court with a smile on his face and waving to his friends and family. He didn't look near death to me. I'd like to have put a bullet in the bastard's head. You know what his defense attorney said? 'Justice has been done.' '' Molke shook his head. ''The longer I live in this world, the more I realize there's no such thing as justice. Not real justice. There's an old saying: 'Every sin has its own Avenging Angel.' But it never works out that way. You* know what I mean?'' Molke hesitated, looked at Volkmann. *"What about your father? He's alive, Joe?"*

"Yes."

"You see him much?"

Volkmann looked away toward the window, wanting to tell Molke, but hesitating. Not then, not here. Another time.

"Sure."

"You're lucky, Joe. Sons need fathers as much as fathers need sons."

CHAPTER 19

Erica left at ten the following morning. Soon after that, he looked around her apartment, starting with the living room. He didn't know what he was looking for and he disliked having to search through her personal belongings, but he knew it had to be done.

Beside the computer terminal sat a neat stack of papers and a small wooden filing cabinet. He searched through the papers first. They were mostly rough drafts of magazine articles and correspondence related to her work: magazine and newspaper clippings highlighted in marker pen, and some copies of her own articles cut from popular German magazines. The filing cabinet was unlocked and he looked through it. There were more magazine articles under indexed headings and lots of filed correspondence from editors.

He was aware of the scent of Erica's perfume as he went through the closet and drawers in her bedroom. Her clothes and underwear were put away neatly, and under some panties and stockings he found a bundle of old letters addressed to her bearing Paraguayan stamps. They were all in Spanish, except for a couple of greetings in German, and they were all signed by Rudi Hernandez. He replaced them and looked through the other drawers.

He also found two old diaries, but many of the pages were illegible and most of the entries were simply shopping lists or reminders of meetings with girlfriends. He saw no references to Karen Holfeld or Gries, but the pages containing addresses at the back of both diaries had been torn out.

There were two slim photograph albums on the top shelf in the mirrored sliding wardrobe. One of them contained mostly photographs from Erica's childhood, and there were pictures of her and her mother and sister that appeared to have been taken in Argentina.

He flicked through the pages and at the end of the album he saw an old black-and-white photograph of a group of men and women standing around the pool sipping drinks with the blond woman, Erica's mother. The shot was slightly out of focus and the faces were blurred, but the men looked to be European rather than Latin. The second album contained mostly photographs of the girl in her teens and twenties, taken with friends at Heidelberg, and a couple of pictures with Rudi Hernandez, one of them a copy of the same photograph he had seen in Hernandez's apartment.

He put the albums back on the shelf. There were some boxes containing jewelry and trinkets and a stack of old records and tapes on the wardrobe floor. He looked through them all carefully. He checked through the rods of clothes, searching in pockets but finding nothing of interest. When he had made sure that everything was back in its place, he checked the bathroom. Perfumes and makeup and some pills and herbals in plastic bottles.

He crossed back into the kitchen, washed the coffee cup and replaced it on the hook, then went into the living room and sat on the couch. Joseph knew that he had to make contact with Lubsch again. He sat there for five minutes before he stood up, picked up the commercial directory by the telephone and found the name and address in Mainz.

He wrote down the address and then went to the bookshelves and took down the Rhine-Palatinate *Land* map. There was a street map of Mainz and he found the street near the cathedral where Karen Gries had her shop.

He spent the rest of the day trying to get some rest.

Mainz. Monday, December 12

Volkmann took the A66 autobahn to Wiesbaden and across the Rhine into Mainz, arriving just after ten.

He parked the Ford in a twenty-four-hour underground garage near the cathedral and walked to Karen Gries's address.

The MarktPlatz was busy with Christmas shoppers. A maze of alleyways and shopping malls branched off from the street proper, and Karen Gries's shop was on the first floor above a modern art gallery. Volkmann spent half an hour checking the street, referencing the layout of the minor roads and side streets with the tourist map he had studied in Erica's apartment.

It was cold and the sky overcast, and as he walked the street near the cathedral, he tried to figure out his plan.

There was a bar almost directly opposite, and the name overhead said "Zum Dortmunder." Maybe seventy meters away, there was a shopping mall. On the mall's first floor was a smart Konditorei whose panoramic window looked down onto the street, and Volkmann reckoned there was a clear view back to Karen Gries's premises.

He bought a copy of the *Frankfurter Zeitung* and went up to the café, sat by the window and ordered a coffee. He smoked a cigarette and watched the street below. The view on either side was unobstructed and he could see Karen Gries's place clearly, about fifty meters to the left, on the opposite side of the street.

When the waitress came with his coffee, he asked her what time the Konditorei stayed open to and the girl told him they stopped serving fifteen minutes before the mall closed at eight.

Volkmann sat there for another twenty minutes. When he had familiarized himself with the layout of the street, he folded his newspaper and tucked it in his pocket. He went downstairs to the mall and crossed the road.

There were two alleyways nearby within twenty meters of each other on the same side as Karen Gries's shop. One led to the back of a bakery shop and then onto a public parking lot. He knew that on the opposite side there were three alleyways before the street ended, because he had already checked them and two hadn't been noted on the map. For the plan to work, so much depended on luck and timing, even assuming that Karen Gries would take the bait.

A narrow flight of stairs led up to a landing and a glass-fronted door. There was red carpet on the stairs, and the sign on the frosted glass said, in English, "Sweatshop, Bruno & Karen Gries."

As Erica had said, it contained fashionable athletic wear, tastefully displayed. He saw a balding, middle-aged man fitting a woman with hiking boots.

Behind the man was a glass-fronted office, and beyond the glass, a woman with tight-cropped blond hair and wearing a leather jumpsuit sat talking with an Oriental woman. Volkmann guessed that the young woman with the cropped blond hair was Karen Gries and the middle-aged man was probably her husband.

He went to look around, and a few moments later, he heard voices behind him and saw the two women walk to the door. The blonde kissed the other on the cheek and handed her a plastic shopping bag, and when the woman had gone, she came over to Volkmann.

"Can I help you?"

She was smiling at him. She could have been pretty, Volkmann thought, but she wore too much makeup. It made her look a bit trashy—not the kind who might be attracted to someone like Lubsch, unless the danger of the affair gave her a kick, but from the way her eyes wandered quickly over him, Volkmann could tell she liked men.

"Karen Gries?"

"Yes."

"My name is Volkmann, Frau Gries. I'm a colleague of Erica Kranz's."

Her smile faded instantly, and at that moment the door opened and a couple entered the shop. As they began to browse, Karen Gries looked over at them and forced a smile as they waved to her, then she turned back to Volkmann. The smile vanished again as she looked at him.

"What the hell do you want?"

"I'd like to talk with you about Wolfgang Lubsch. Is there somewhere quiet where we can talk, Frau Gries?"

"What did you say your name was?"

"Volkmann. Joseph Volkmann." He flashed the Press ID.

"Why did you come here?"

"Your friend Lubsch had a talk with Erica and me yesterday. Only it wasn't very helpful. I need to talk with Lubsch again."

Karen Gries's face flushed with anger. "You're wasting your time coming here, Herr Volkmann. And Lubsch is not a friend, he's someone I knew a long time ago. Erica asked if I could help her find him because she wanted to talk with him. But that's as far as I was prepared to go. So if you don't mind, Herr Volkmann . . ."

The young woman turned away impatiently and looked toward the balding man, who was finishing a sale. He no-

ticed her look at him and he half smiled and stared at Volkmann warily before turning back to his customer.

Volkmann said, "We can do this one of two ways, Frau
Gries."

She hesitated. "What do you mean?"

"Either you listen to me and do as I ask, or I call the
police and tell them what a bad girl you've been. I'm sure
they'd be interested to know that you're associating with a
wanted terrorist. Before you know it, the antiterrorist squad
will be crawling all over this place and questioning you and
your husband. And I'm quite sure your customers will read
about it in the papers. Do you understand me, Frau Gries?"

The woman's eyes blazed at him. "Are you threatening
me, Volkmann?"

"I'm asking for your help. I could also tell your husband
you're still screwing Wolfgang Lubsch."

Karen Gries stared at Volkmann. Her mouth tightened
and her neck flushed red with rage. "Who the hell do you
think you are, making an accusation like that?"

"You do still see him, don't you?"

The balding man went to open the door for his customer.
Volkmann saw him stare across before he came to join
them, as if he sensed something was wrong, ignoring the
other two customers in the shop.

"Is everything all right, Karen? Can I be of any assistance?"

Karen Gries turned to him quickly and said, "Bruno, this
is Herr Volkmann. He's a colleague of a friend of mine.
I'd like to talk in private. Can you be a sweet and look
after things here?"

The man shook Volkmann's hand. "Glad to meet you,
Herr Volkmann." He looked at his wife and his hand
touched her waist. "You're sure everything's okay?"

"Of course, Bruno." Karen Gries smiled. "You better
look after the customers." She turned back to Volkmann
and said in a businesslike manner, "We'll use the office,
Herr Volkmann."

Volkmann followed her. The office was small and cluttered. The desk that dominated the room was covered with
fashion magazines and paperwork.

When she had closed the door, Karen Gries sat stiffly

behind the desk and glared at Volkmann. Beyond the glass, he saw her husband talking to the two other customers.

"What the hell do you mean by coming here?"

"Lubsch wasn't very helpful when we met." Karen Gries looked back at him impatiently, as if she knew already. "Do you know where he is, Frau Gries?"

"No, I don't."

"But you can get in touch with him?"

Frau Gries leaned forward, placed her manicured hands on the desk. "Listen to me. Lubsch isn't the kind you play around with. Do you realize the trouble you could find yourself in by coming here and threatening me? You could get hurt, Herr Volkmann. Badly hurt." She looked at his face. "And I'm not just talking about a bruised jaw. That goes for Erica as well as you. You call the police and Lubsch won't take it lightly. Do you understand me?"

"I want you to contact Lubsch. Tell him to meet me again."

"Are you crazy? Go to hell, Volkmann, get out of here."

As Karen Gries stood up, Volkmann looked at his watch. "It's eleven-fifteen, Frau Gries. I want Lubsch to meet me at seven this evening. That ought to give you enough time to get in touch with him. Otherwise, I make my call."

"Volkmann, you're crazy. I want you to leave. Now, this minute."

"You want to know how crazy I am?" Volkmann picked up the phone on the desk and punched in a number as the girl stared at him.

They both heard the line click, and Volkmann said, "*Polizei*?"

He looked at the girl's face and saw her eyes open wide; then her hand reached across and slammed down hard on the cradle.

Karen Gries said, "I never should have listened to Erica."

Volkmann put down the receiver. "Seven o'clock. If Lubsch is a minute late, I make my call."

Her face flushed red. "Where?"

"Across the street in the bar called Zum Dortmunder. Tell him to meet me inside at seven exactly. Tell him I want to talk with him alone. Just talk. There's no need for any rough stuff, do you understand? And don't try to contact Erica, she's no longer in the country.''

"I hope you realize what kind of fire you're playing with.''

"Let me worry about that.''

Joseph turned and went out the door.

He walked back to the underground garage and drove over the Rhine bridge to Wiesbaden.

He still had almost eight hours to kill and he took the roundabout road north, up into the hills behind the Rhine. When he reached the picturesque spa town of Bad Schwalbach, he forked east and drove into the Rhine-Taunus Nature Park. The journey took him under forty minutes.

In summer the big park would have been busy with tourists and campers but in winter it was a vast, desolate place, wind whipping through the banks of pine and fir trees that rose and fell in undulating waves. It was bitter cold, and fifteen minutes beyond Bad Schwalbach, he saw a sign that pointed toward the lake.

He drove off the track and was fifty meters into the forest before he saw the sign for the lake. He climbed out of the car, locked the door and walked along the path through the trees. Five minutes later, he reached the small lake.

The area was deserted and the water was choppy. Nearby stood a narrow wooden pier jutting ten meters out into the cold gray lake, and at two-meter intervals there were wooden tie beams for the small boats in season.

The water was deep at the end of the walkway, and Volkmann stood there looking at the scene, smoking a cigarette, as he went over the possible scenarios in his mind. If his plan worked out, the lake was remote enough and quiet enough for him not to be disturbed.

If the plan worked.

He drove back into Wiesbaden and found a hardware store on the outskirts. He purchased a twenty-meter length of orange-colored nylon rope, a rubber-wrapped flashlight and four spare batteries. Volkmann put his purchases in the glove compartment, then drove back to the apartment in Frankfurt.

When he went up, the windows in the front room were

closed, but the air smelled of fresh lavender and he poured himself a scotch from the bottle in the kitchen, then went to lie on the couch.

He checked his watch. Two-fifteen. He would try to sleep for a couple of hours.

He awoke at four and drove back into Mainz, arriving a little after five.

He didn't know whether he would need the Ford or not, and it depended on how many men Lubsch would have with him and what kind of transportation they had. There was no doubt that Lubsch would make an appearance, but he guessed that the terrorist wouldn't come alone and would certainly be armed.

He had dealt with people like Lubsch before; they wouldn't think twice of shooting in a crowded street, and Volkmann knew that for his plan to work, he'd have to act quickly.

He decided to use the same twenty-four-hour underground garage again. It was a block from Karen Gries's place and not as close as he would have liked if the car was needed, but the street where Gries had her shop had metered parking and he didn't want to risk being towed away. He checked the Beretta before he got out of the car, made sure the safety was on, cocked the weapon and slipped it into his right-hand pocket. He placed the flashlight and spare batteries in his other pocket, and put the nylon rope in the pouch inside his overcoat.

It was just after five and darkness had fallen, but there were Christmas lights strung across the streets and above the buildings. He walked along the illuminated one-way street, mingling with the shoppers. If he guessed right, Lubsch and his people would arrive early. He thought maybe in an hour, but just to be certain, ninety minutes. He guessed Lubsch would send a runner to the bar first rather than appear himself, and he'd have someone watch it long before Volkmann was due. Lubsch or his people wouldn't expect him to be armed, and they wouldn't expect him to go on the offensive.

He bought a newspaper and walked back to the Konditorei where he had sat that morning; he had to wait for ten minutes at the door before a seat by the window came free. He ordered coffee and unfolded his newspaper, but he kept his eyes on the road outside, looking up only to check his watch.

It was five-thirty-one.

It wasn't the Mercedes van this time, but a dark-blue Opel sedan.

The car came down the one-way street half an hour later, then disappeared around the corner. It did the same thing three times before it pulled up fifty meters away on the same side of the street as Karen Gries's premises. There were three men: two in front and one in the back.

Volkmann recognized Lubsch sitting in the driver's seat, his face illuminated by a string of colored Christmas lights above the street. The little red-haired man wore the same padded dark windbreaker and his face was clearly visible, but Volkmann couldn't see the faces of the other two men from where he sat.

Five minutes later, the man in the rear of the Opel stepped out and closed his door, then walked toward Gries's shop. There was a pharmacy beside the art gallery, its neon sign on overhead, and the man went to stand in the alcove. He pulled out a newspaper and began to browse through it. Volkmann recognized him as one of the men from the Mercedes. He was going to watch the bar from across the street, and Volkmann guessed he had a walkie-talkie.

Joseph knew he had to move quickly, and he was aware of his heart pounding in his chest and the sweat on the palms of his hands. The street below was still crowded with shoppers, which would give him cover, but it was also open, vulnerable and dangerous. If Lubsch or his men started firing, there was a real danger that someone in the crowded street could get shot.

Volkmann rechecked his watch. There were still forty minutes to go before the meeting, and he knew he had to make his move before Lubsch left the car or drove around the block again.

The man in the passenger seat beside Lubsch would be a problem, and so much depended on timing and on whether the terrorist who was watching the Zum Dortmunder had left the rear door of the car unlocked. Volkmann wasn't worried about the people in the street seeing anything, because their eyes would be on the shop windows.

He saw Lubsch's face peer out through the glass and then look away impatiently. The third terrorist, standing in the alcove, looked over at the bar from behind his newspaper every few moments. There was a Christmas tree in the pharmacy window, its lights winking on and off; the lurid colors illuminated the man's face and fogging breath as he stared across at the Zum Dortmunder.

Volkmann felt the stress tensing the muscles of his neck.

He folded his newspaper and paid for his coffee.

It was time to go.

He stepped out onto the street and crossed over. He was ten meters behind the Opel and as he walked toward it, he strained his eyes to see if the door lock in the rear was up. Five meters from the car, he saw that it was.

The man sitting in the passenger seat was wiping the side window with the sleeve of his coat, and Volkmann got a glimpse of his profile. It was the same man who had wielded the truncheon, and he was grinning as he spoke with Lubsch.

Volkmann turned and went back down the street. The alleyway behind the bakery was empty and as he entered it, he unfolded his newspaper, slipped the Beretta under the fold in the pages and flicked off the safety.

As he went back out onto the crowded street, he looked toward the blue Opel. The man in the passenger seat was still wiping the side window, and Volkmann saw the man standing in the alcove glance toward the Opel, then step back out of view.

Volkmann came up alongside the car from behind, wrenched open the door and clambered into the back seat, the Beretta already out and the safety off. The two men in the front turned and Volkmann saw the surprise on their faces as Lubsch said, "What the fuck . . . ?"

And then Lubsch was reaching frantically in his jacket and the passenger was doing the same.

Volkmann's fist smacked twice into the passenger's face

hard and the man's head cracked against the window.

As Lubsch struggled to remove his gun, Volkmann pressed the Beretta firmly into the terrorist's neck.

"Don't."

Lubsch's face had turned chalk-white. "Slip the gun out of your pocket. Hand it to me, very slowly, grip-first. You try anything and I take your head off."

Lubsch said palely, "Volkmann, you're dead . . ."

"Do it."

Lubsch slowly removed a Beretta from his jacket and handed it over, his fingers around the barrel.

Volkmann said, "Turn around. Face front. Keep your mouth shut and start the car. Drive straight to the end of the street and turn right. Keep going until I tell you. And don't try anything as we go past your friend."

"Volkmann, when this is over . . ."

Volkmann reached over, yanked Lubsch's collar tight and pulled him back, pressing the Beretta harder into the terrorist's neck.

"Behave yourself and you and your friend here walk away from this alive. You don't and I drop you. Understand? Now start the car. Drive."

He let go of Lubsch, and the young man leaned forward and started the Opel. As he did so, Volkmann's free hand was already moving over the passenger. The man was out cold, and he found a Walther PPK in his right pocket and a CEL walkie-talkie in the other. Volkmann put them on the floor beside Lubsch's weapon.

As the Opel pulled out from the curb and picked up speed, Volkmann kept the Beretta steady.

He saw Lubsch's man in the alcove stare at the Opel in disbelief as it went past the pharmacy, and then suddenly the man dropped his newspaper and was running after them.

Volkmann said to Lubsch, "Keep driving. Move it."

As the car picked up more speed, the third man caught up beside them, running fast. Volkmann put down the locks just as he reached and began wrenching at the door handle. The man's face was up against the window, and when he couldn't open the door, his fists hammered madly on the glass, his face convulsed in confusion and anger.

Volkmann pressed the Beretta into Lubsch's neck and said, "What's your friend's name?"

Lubsch answered through clenched teeth. "Hartig."

Volkmann smiled out at the running man. "Happy Christmas, Hartig."

And then the car picked up even more speed and rounded the corner, and the face was gone from the window.

CHAPTER 20

Thirty minutes later, they turned into the town of Bad Schwalbach and Volkmann told Lubsch to take the turnoff for the Taunus Nature Park.

As the headlights of an oncoming car swished by in the darkness, the passenger beside Lubsch started to come around. Volkmann slid his thumb into the concavity behind the man's left ear where jaw met skull, his other four fingers sliding around the man's neck and locking in a vise. He applied the pressure quickly and heard a small cry.

Lubsch's eyes flicked angrily at Volkmann, who kept the Beretta aimed at the terrorist and said, "Keep your eyes on the road."

He knew exactly how much pressure to apply to the point behind the ear, and seconds later, he felt the man's body sag. Hard pressure would have killed within a couple of minutes, but the amount Volkmann had used would keep him out for no more than a couple of hours.

As the body slumped back in the seat, he heard the man's breathing, heavy at first, then slow and regular. Volkmann slipped his thumb and forefinger around the limp wrist and felt the pulse. Though it was a little slow, he reckoned there wasn't a problem. There was a stream of blood on the man's mouth and chin, but the flow had stopped. From the crack of bone when he had hit the man, Volkmann guessed he had broken the man's nose or fractured his jaw.

Lubsch asked, "Who the fuck are you?"

"Keep driving and shut up."

When they reached the forest road ten minutes later, Volkmann told him to turn off onto the narrow track that led down to the lake. There was a half-moon, but the night sky was patchy with black clouds. Twenty meters from the lakeshore, Volkmann ordered Lubsch to stop and get out of the car.

The trees at the edge of the forest tossed furiously in the wind, and as Volkmann stepped out, he flicked on the flashlight and told Lubsch to move down to the jetty. The moon illuminated the choppy lake with faint silver streaks, and

Volkmann shone the light ahead of the terrorist as he followed him down to the water.

They were a couple of meters from the boardwalk when Lubsch suddenly made a run for it. He veered sharply to the right and started to run frantically toward a bank of trees. Volkmann sprinted after him and when he caught up, he dropped the flashlight and gripped the terrorist's shoulder. As Lubsch spun around, his small, wiry frame crashed into Volkmann in the darkness and then his fists were pounding into Joseph's body.

The terrorist grappled for the weapon in Volkmann's hand and tried to wrench it free. Lubsch was strong but Joseph was stronger; his free arm came around and locked the little man's neck in a vise. Volkmann heard his gurgle as he fought for breath, but he kept up the pressure on the man's throat. Moments later, Lubsch's body sagged and slid to the ground.

Volkmann went back to retrieve the flashlight and shone it in Lubsch's face. The man wasn't unconscious but his eyes were dilated from lack of oxygen, and as his hands massaged his neck, he started to cough up his lungs on the grass.

As he gasped for breath, he looked up at Volkmann. "When this is through, you're dead, Volkmann. Dead."

His voice was hoarse with pain, and as he lay there, Volkmann pointed the Beretta.

"Get up, Lubsch. Walk down to the pier."

Lubsch struggled to stand, and when they came down to the water, Volkmann said, "Now tie your shoelaces together."

"What?"

"You heard me. Do it."

Volkmann pointed the gun and watched as Lubsch did as he was ordered. When he finished, Volkmann flashed the light and checked them. He told Lubsch to take off his belt and then lie down on his stomach. When Lubsch hesitated, Volkmann forced him down. Once the terrorist had removed his belt, Volkmann used it to tie the man's hands behind his back, then he pulled Lubsch up into a sitting position. It was bitter cold, and the wind coming in off the black water clawed at their faces.

Volkmann said, "We can do this the easy way or the hard way. The easy way is for you tell me what I need to know. The hard way is for me to deliver you and your friend to the nearest police station."

There was anger in Lubsch's face as he looked up at the harsh light. "You think you'll get away with it, Volkmann? My men would hunt you down and find you. Who the fuck are you? *Polizei?*"

Volkmann ignored the question and said, "Think about it. A high-security prison for maybe twenty years. And that's if the judge is in a good mood. Guards watching your every movement. No visits except from your lawyer, if you were lucky enough to find one who'd take your case." Volkmann slipped the Beretta into his pocket, removed the nylon rope and held it in front of Lubsch's face. "So what's it to be? I wrap you and your friend up like a Christmas present and drop you outside the nearest police station, or you talk?"

Volkmann shone the beams in Lubsch's face; the terrorist blinked and looked away. The wind blowing across the black waters in the darkness was icy-cold and the only sounds were those of the lapping water and the wind sweeping through the trees in ragged, harsh gusts.

Lubsch sat there on the freezing pier, not moving, as if considering his predicament. When he looked back, he shivered and his face was red from the cold.

"And if I talk, what's in it for me?"

"I let you and your friend go."

"What the fuck do you want to know, Volkmann?"

"What I wanted to know the last time we met. About Dieter Winter and his friends."

"How do I know you'll keep your word?"

"You'll have to trust me, Lubsch. But if you don't tell me the truth, or if I find out you lied to me or didn't tell me everything, your friend Karen gets a visit from the police."

Lubsch's voice sounded thick with anger, and his small blue eyes squinted as he looked up at the white beam and grimaced. "You really are fucking crazy, aren't you? Just like Karen said you were . . ."

Before the terrorist could finish his sentence, Volkmann

reached over and gripped the collar of Lubsch's jacket and dragged him over to the edge of the jetty. He gripped a handful of Lubsch's red hair and pushed the terrorist's face down into the freezing-cold water. Lubsch fought to get free; his body bucked and squirmed, his legs kicking wildly in the air.

Volkmann saw the air bubbles rise as he counted to ten. Then he pulled Lubsch's head back up. The terrorist gulped in deep breaths as his lungs fought for air.

". . . Okay, okay. I'll tell you."

Volkmann dragged him back into the middle of the pier and waited until Lubsch had caught his breath. His hair was plastered over his forehead, water dripped from his face, and he shivered violently.

Volkmann said, "I want to hear it from the beginning, Lubsch. From how you first met Winter. Leave nothing out. Do you understand?"

Lubsch coughed again and spat. For several moments he sat there, his chest heaving as he took deep breaths. When his breathing had returned to normal, he looked up at Volkmann for a moment, then turned his face away before he spoke.

"I first met Winter at Heidelberg. He was a member of the history faculty."

"You were friends?"

"No, just acquaintances. We used to meet sometimes to drink and talk."

"Tell me about Winter."

Lubsch sniffed, then spat out into the water. "What do you want to know?"

"I told you. Everything."

"Winter and I, we were on different sides of the fence politically. He was a right-wing fanatic. And me, I went the other way. But Winter was always a convincing speaker. For a time, he even managed to convince me that we had something in common."

"Tell me."

Lubsch looked up at Volkmann, then turned his head away again. "The future of Germany."

"What do you mean?"

"It was a pet topic with Winter. He and his friends had

this idea that they could change the country.''

"And who were his friends?''

"Fellow students. Others who shared his views.''

"Tell me about his friends, Lubsch.''

Lubsch hesitated, then said, "What's this got to do with me, Volkmann? The murders you spoke about, or something else?''

"Just carry on talking until I tell you to stop. What about his friends?''

Lubsch hesitated, looked away again toward the cold lake. "Six months into our second year at the university, I'd gotten to know Winter pretty well. Whenever we'd drink beer together, we'd argue about politics. Winter was a drinker and a talker, but our talk was never violent, just heated discussion because we had opposing views. Then one day he asked me to join him and a group of his friends for a weekend on Lüneburg Heath. There were to be seven of us. Some were students, but only Winter and I were from the Heidelberg campus. The others came from different parts of Germany and from different backgrounds, most of them working-class. Toughs, a couple of them, and out of their depth intellectually, but Winter had asked them along. We stayed in a rented house in the forest and drank in the local inns. We walked and talked day and night. About politics. Philosophy. History.''

"And the others, they all knew Winter?''

Lubsch looked up for a moment. "Sure. It was like a fraternity. Like they all knew each other pretty well.''

When Lubsch paused, Volkmann asked, "Who were these friends of Winter's?''

"Winter had asked them along. I'd never met them before.''

"I want names, Lubsch.''

Lubsch hesitated. "I remember only one. A science student. His name was Kesser. Lothar Kesser. He was about my age and he came from Bavaria.''

"Where in Bavaria?''

Lubsch shook his head. "Some small town, I don't remember where.''

"You said the group was like a fraternity. What did you mean?''

Lubsch shrugged. "It was like they had some bond between them. It was kind of weird. Like a secret society. Don't ask me to explain it, Volkmann, because I can't. But it was like I was outside the circle, not one of them. I was there only because Winter had asked me. I guess they liked me because I was an intellectual who wasn't afraid of action. And because I liked to spend time talking with Winter, maybe they thought they could convert me."

"Go on."

"One night after everyone's gone to bed, this guy Kesser suggests we go for a walk in the forest. Just him and me. It's dark and gloomy outside, and we've had a few drinks. But I agreed because I got the feeling Kesser wanted to talk with me in private.

"So we walked together for maybe an hour. Kesser kept talking about Germany's past. Not the bad things. The good things. How Germany had always come through in times of great suffering and upheaval. Overcome all obstacles. Created order out of chaos. That sort of shit. Like Kesser was giving me some sort of political speech. He said that Germany would go through a phase of disorder again. There were definitely going to be problems in the future. Not only in Germany, but in all of Europe. Politically. Economically. Socially. But there were also going to be opportunities. And that we were all Germans together and that when that time came, we should strive together to seize the opportunity to create a better Fatherland. I was pretty drunk, but I thought Kesser was talking foolishly. I told him it all sounded like undergraduate, idealist shit to me."

"How did Kesser respond?"

"He got annoyed and said that when the right time came, he and the others who supported his beliefs would have financial support for their cause. When I asked him to explain, he wouldn't elaborate. But he said he knew I was involved with the Red Army Faction. Kesser said he and Winter didn't see me and my friends as terrorists, merely as disenchanted Germans who sought a different Germany. He said we could join him if we wished."

"And what did you say?"

"I said it was kind of him, but he was wrong. I wasn't involved with any group. I was drunk, Volkmann, but I

was careful. Besides, I thought Kesser was playing some
kind of trick. Maybe Winter and Kesser were *Bundespolizei*
plants. They do that, you know. Send their brightest cadets
into German universities to spy on extremist undergraduates. Lead them along and then trap them.''

''What was Kesser's reaction when you refused?''

Lubsch shrugged. ''He said I was making a grave mistake. He didn't say any more, and that was the end of our
conversation. But after that, Winter kept away from me on
campus. He rarely talked to me, and whenever we met, he'd
keep his distance.''

The wind gusted across the lake and Lubsch shivered.

Volkmann asked, ''Did you see Kesser again?''

Lubsch said nothing for several moments. ''A friend of
mine gets a call one night. The guy wouldn't say who he
was. But he wanted to pass on a message to me. He said
Lothar Kesser wanted to meet me. That he had an important
proposition that would interest me. He gave a number and
a time to call back and asked my friend to pass on the
message. So I called. Winter answered. He sounded pretty
friendly and when I asked him what it was about, he said
he and Kesser wanted to meet me again and that what they
wanted to talk about couldn't be discussed over the phone.
But he said it was very important.

''I was curious, so I agreed to meet outside a small town
in the Black Forest. I took along a couple of men to check
out the location first. But Winter and Kesser were there
alone. We drove up into the mountains and the three of us
went for a walk. When I asked them what it was about,
Kesser did all the talking. He said he had a proposition for
me. For me and my group.''

''What sort of proposition?''

''He said he could offer us everything the Russians had
supplied us with in the past.''

''What do you mean?''

''Weapons. Explosives. Whatever we needed.''

Volkmann paused. ''Did Kesser say where he got the
supplies?''

''No, he simply said it was none of my business. That
the offer was genuine and I could take it or leave it. It was
up to me and my people.''

"And what did you think about this proposition?"

Lubsch smiled grimly. "I thought it was crazy, Volkmann. A right-wing radical supplying a left-wing terror group with weapons. There was no sense to it."

"You didn't accept?"

Lubsch half-smiled. "Of course I did, eventually. I might have thought Kesser was crazy, but I wasn't. Our weapons dumps were pretty depleted. There wasn't much coming from the Soviets. And after the Wall came down, they did an about-face."

"What kind of weapons did Kesser's people deliver?"

When Lubsch hesitated, Volkmann said, "What kind, Lubsch?"

"Small arms and explosives mostly. Machine pistols, assault rifles, handguns. Grenades and Semtex. And once a rocket launcher we needed to take out a politician's car."

Volkmann looked down at the terrorist and hesitated for a moment. "What conditions did Kesser make?"

"My people had to pay for the weapons. But it was a token payment. To cover costs."

"Didn't your people question Winter's motives?"

Lubsch shook his head and laughed quietly. "Volkmann, we would have taken weapons from the devil himself, as long as they were reliable and shot straight. We were just grateful for the supplies."

"How long did Winter and his people supply you?"

"About eighteen months."

"Why? What happened?"

Lubsch turned to look at him, and Volkmann played the flashlight beam away from his face. "There was one other condition Kesser made."

"Tell me."

"Every time we'd get a supply, we'd get a request. A favor to do in return. They'd suggest we hit certain targets."

"What sort of targets?"

"Banks. Financial institutions. State property. Those Allied bases that still remained on German soil. Some of the hits suited us. They fit in with our scheme of things, and we were happy to oblige. But some didn't. When they didn't, we still did it because we needed the supplies."

"So why did Winter and Kesser stop supplying you?"

Lubsch paused. "About six months ago, Kesser's demands started to become more outrageous. He wanted us to start bombing immigrant hostels. That wasn't our style. And he wanted us to hit some people. He gave me three names he said he wanted dead."

"Did Kesser say why he wanted these people killed?"

"No. Just that they were part of the deal."

"So who were the people?"

"Two of them I'd never heard of before. But one of the names on the list I knew, and I wouldn't go along with it."

"Go on."

"He was a liberal politician in Berlin. I told Kesser it wasn't our style. We'd hit politicians or businessmen who suited us. But we wouldn't do the names on the list."

"What did Kesser say?"

"He just smiled and said he'd handle it himself. But after that, things were strained between us. We were due one more delivery a month later, but it never came. And Kesser or Winter didn't contact me again."

"Who did Kesser want dead?"

Lubsch paused. "A guy in East Berlin. His name was Rauscher, Herbert Rauscher. Another was a woman in Friedrichshafen, near the Swiss border."

"Her name?"

"I can't remember."

"Think, Lubsch."

"Hedda something. Pohl or Puhl. I'm not sure."

"Who was she?"

"A nobody. The widow of a businessman."

"And the man in East Berlin, Rauscher?"

"A small-time businessman. Another nobody."

"Your people checked their backgrounds?"

"Of course. We weren't going to kill just for the sake of it, Volkmann. That's not our style. We only hit selected targets we think deserve to be hit. Big businessmen who corrupt this country. Politicians who support them. The police and the armed forces."

"Who was the politician in Berlin?"

"His name's Walter Massow." Lubsch looked out at the cold lake and shivered violently, his lips trembling with cold. "He's not a political animal, just a good and honest man trying to do his best for the downtrodden in this country. That's why I told Kesser, "No way." We weren't racists and we wouldn't go along with his fascist ideals. I also told him that if Massow was hit, I'd take it personally." The terrorist looked back. "And after that, I told you, the supplies halted."

Volkmann thought for a moment, then said, "Did you ask Winter or Kesser why they wanted you to carry out the attacks on the immigrant hostels?"

"Sure. Kesser said some of the immigrant groups in Germany had set up their own terror groups and were hitting right-wing supporters. Kesser said he was going to hit back. But Kesser was a right-wing fanatic. It was the sort of thing you'd expect someone of his background to use as an excuse for his action."

"What do you mean?"

"That time on Lüneburg Heath, I overheard him talk about his father. He was some bigshot SS man during the war. I heard him say the old man had helped draft the Brandenburg Testament for Adolf Hitler, whatever that was. But Kesser said it like a boast, as if it were proof enough of his pedigree."

"What's that?" Volkmann asked quickly, remembering the words on the tape. And there was that other word as well, "pedigree." *What do they mean? Kesser was proving his pedigree with reference to the Brandenburg Testament?*

"What?" Lubsch was saying.

"The Brandenburg Testament."

"I just told you. I have no idea."

Volkmann looked away, then back again. "The politician, Massow, what happened to him?"

Lubsch shook his head. "Nothing. He was left alone."

"And the others?"

"I don't know. Dead, I guess." Lubsch shivered violently as a gust of icy wind blew in off the lake.

Volkmann said, "Why do you think Massow wasn't killed?"

Lubsch shrugged. "Maybe Winter thought it more tactful to let Massow live after he understood my views. I don't know, Volkmann. Either way, Kesser or Winter didn't contact us again. Besides, they had others to do their dirty work for them."

"What do you mean? What others?"

"We learned that Kesser and Winter were supplying other groups, not just ours."

"You mean terrorist groups?"

Lubsch half-smiled and his lips trembled with cold. "It's a question of perspective, isn't it, Volkmann? But yes, let us say terrorist groups in your idiom."

"Which ones?"

"Pretty nearly all you could mention. Those of significance anyhow. He did the same deal for them. Weapons in return for hitting the kinds of targets I told you about."

Volkmann hesitated. He stepped down to the edge of the jetty, felt the icy wind slash at his face.

He looked back at Lubsch and said, "What you've told me, none of it makes any sense, Lubsch. What was Winter's angle? What was in it for him and his friends? Why did Winter want you to kill these people? Why didn't his group do it themselves? They had the weapons."

Lubsch smiled bitterly. "I don't know, Volkmann. None of our people understood it. I had a theory. Some of it made sense, some of it didn't."

"Tell me."

"Maybe the plan was to spread anarchy. Winter and his people supplied weapons. Had those weapons used on certain targets they wanted eliminated. Businessmen. State and private institutions. Soft-line military personnel. But people blame the Red terrorists for hits like that, and the right-wing groups gain more support."

"You said that some of your theory didn't make sense. What part?"

Lubsch shrugged. "The people Kesser wanted killed, besides Massow. And something else. Whoever was behind Winter, they must have had money and good organization to buy and ship arms and supplies in such quantities. Maybe a right-wing group within the police or the army. Or a cabal of wealthy business people could do it. People with something at stake."

"Where did the weapons Winter and Kesser supplied come from?"

Lubsch shrugged. "I don't know."

"Winter's death. Was that your people?"

"No."

"So who killed him?"

"I don't know. Winter lived on a knife-edge. He dealt with groups like mine. He also had a big mouth. And when he was drunk, he liked to talk." Lubsch shrugged. "You play with fire, you get burned. So maybe one of them burned him."

"When was the last time you saw him?"

"Six months ago, when I met Kesser."

"How do I find Kesser?"

The terrorist looked up; his face was blue from the freezing cold. "I don't know, Volkmann. But I'll give you some advice. The advice I gave you before. If you're wise, you'll keep away from him and his friends. Unless you and the girl want to end up dead."

"The names Karl Schmeltz or Nicolas Tsarkin. Did either Winter or Kesser ever mention those names?"

"No."

"You're sure?"

"Kesser or Winter never mentioned names. Never. Apart from the names on the list I told you about." Lubsch's teeth chattered. "Are you going to untie me now, Volkmann? Or am I going to sit here all the fucking night and freeze to death? I've told you everything I know."

Volkmann shone the flashlight slightly to the right so it didn't shine in the terrorist's eyes, but so that he could still see the man's reaction clearly.

"One more question. Erica Kranz."

"What about her?"

"How well did she know Winter at Heidelberg?"

"What are you asking me for, Volkmann? Ask her yourself."

"Just answer the question, Lubsch."

Lubsch shrugged. "A couple of times I saw them talking together at parties." The terrorist's face looked frozen as he stared up at Volkmann. "I thought she was a friend of yours."

Volkmann ignored the question and stood up. "I enjoyed our talk."

"Fuck you."

He saw the look of rage in Lubsch's eyes. As he moved away, he hesitated and turned back, shone the light in Lubsch's face.

"I did you a favor tonight, Lubsch. By rights, you ought to be behind bars for the rest of your life. Only I'm keeping my word. But if I learn you've been lying to me, or if you try to come after me, the police will pay your friend Karen a visit. And one more thing. Keep away from Erica Kranz."

Volkmann flicked off the flashlight and the wooden walkway plunged into darkness.

"You'll find the car somewhere near Karen's place. I'll leave your friend behind to keep you company."

As he walked back toward the Opel, he heard the wind raging across the lake in the freezing darkness, and Lubsch grunting as he struggled with the belt on the pier.

CHAPTER 21

When he let himself into the apartment, it was almost midnight and Erica was asleep in the spare bedroom.

He telephoned Peters's home number. When Peters had activated the scrambler, Volkmann told him what had happened with Lubsch.

"Christ, Joe, you took a risk. You want me to pass on the girl's name to the BfV?"

"No. Let's see what happens. If Lubsch tries to come back at me, we'll do it then."

"You think Lubsch told you the truth?"

"Your guess is as good as mine, Tom. I'd say yes, but I'll have to check it out."

"What do you want to do? Ferguson's going to be away for a couple of days."

"I'll carry on."

"Okay. But if you need help, let me know. About Erhard Schmeltz, we got some information from the Documentation Center in Berlin."

"What did they say?"

"They've got records of the Nazi Party going back to nineteen twenty-five, when the party really started to officially document its membership. There's an Erhard Johann Schmeltz, born in Hamburg and listed as party number six-eight-nine-six. His party application was made in Munich in late November of nineteen twenty-seven, and his year of birth is the same as in Sanchez's report. Considering the date he applied and the fact that the party had over ten million members in Germany at its peak, Schmeltz would have joined pretty much at the start."

"What else did they say?"

"They have his original application and his file and photograph from the master files of the Nazi Party headquarters in Munich. He was also a registered member of the Brownshirt SA, the *Sturmabteilung*. And Schmeltz didn't quit the Nazi Party when he went to South America. His party dues were paid until his death in nineteen forty-four. He arranged payment in absentia."

"How can they know that for certain?"

"The Nazis had something called the *Gau Ausland*. The best way to describe it is as a department that dealt with party members in foreign regions, people who had left Germany but still kept up their party membership. Committed Nazis. Schmeltz was registered with the *Gau Ausland* from November of nineteen thirty-one." There was a pause before Peters spoke again. "There's something else, Joe. The Documentation Center said Erhard Schmeltz's party application had a recommendation attached to it."

"What do you mean?"

"Apparently every application for party membership had to be recommended and endorsed, usually by the local party group leader for the region in which the person applied. But in Schmeltz's case, there was a letter sent from Prinz-Albrecht Strasse in Berlin, the SS headquarters, at the time Schmeltz applied, which was pretty unusual, apparently. The letter was signed by Heinrich Himmler, and it recommended Schmeltz's immediate acceptance. It suggests that maybe Schmeltz was a close or trusted acquaintance of Himmler's, or had contacts pretty high up in the party."

Volkmann paused, let the information sink in. "Anything else?"

"The information on Reimer. The Document Center had him on its list of personnel files on SS officers. Apparently they've got pretty good records of SS officers that the Americans captured at the end of the war. But there's really nothing much in there that could help us. I'll have the copies of the information on Schmeltz and Reimer on your desk tomorrow, the stuff Berlin sent from their files. What about you, you need anything else?"

"Lothar Kesser, scientist from Bavaria. I want him checked out. It's not much to go on, but you may get lucky. And I'll need a return ticket to Zurich, first available flight tomorrow morning."

"Why Zurich?"

"Remember Ted Birken?"

Peters laughed. "I thought they put the old fox out to grass years ago."

"They did. But he still has contacts and he may be able to help."

"Okay. I'll organize the ticket with Facilities right away. Keep in touch. Goodnight, Joe."

" 'Night."

When he put down the telephone, Volkmann heard a sound and looked around. Erica Kranz stood in the doorway. She wore a dressing gown and the blue eyes looked over at him, a hint of anger there.

"I heard you talking on the phone. You said you wouldn't contact Lubsch or Karen. Is that where you went today?"

Volkmann said nothing, and the blue eyes continued to look at him accusingly. "You know what kind of man Lubsch is. You know what he's capable of. Why did you do it, Joe? Why have you put us both in danger?"

"He won't bother you, Erica. I've made sure of that. If he does, I tell the police about Karen. You've nothing to worry about, believe me."

She hesitated. "I think there's something that worries me more, Joe."

"What?"

"That you didn't trust me enough to tell me what you were going to do."

When Volkmann didn't reply, she sat down. "Tell me what Lubsch said."

He told her and she watched his face. "Do you trust him?"

"Trust him, no. Believe him, yes."

Erica Kranz shook her head. "Don't you think he could have been trying to mislead you? Why would Winter's people want to kill those others? Why would they want Lubsch to carry out racist attacks on immigrants? To attack state institutions? The targets seem so diverse. There isn't any sense to it."

"Maybe. But I don't think Wolfgang Lubsch lied, Erica. I think he told me the truth."

"And what if he and Winter's people are still doing business together, despite what Lubsch said? If that's the case, then Lubsch will tell them about you and me."

"It's a risk we'll have to take." He looked at her. "You want to find the people who killed Rudi, Erica. Getting Lubsch to talk was the only way."

The girl said nothing and looked away. The anger had subsided, but she didn't speak. Volkmann crossed to the window. When he looked back at her, he said, "Do you have access to any newspaper libraries?"

Erica hesitated. "The one at the *Frankfurter Zeitung.*"

"How about checking through the files there? The people Lubsch talked about that Kesser and Winter wanted killed. Rauscher, and the woman Hedda Pohl or Puhl. See what you come up with."

"Your people can't check on that?"

"It would mean going through the German desk at DSE. And I'd rather we kept it to ourselves for now." Volkmann paused. "And the politician in Berlin—Massow—that Lubsch spoke about. See if you can contact his office and arrange a meeting. I can fly up there and talk with him if he agrees."

"What do you want to talk with him about?"

"If what Lubsch said is true, there must have been a reason Winter's people wanted Massow dead. Maybe Massow knows why. I'll give you a number where you can reach me if anything turns up. If I'm not there, you can contact Peters or leave a message."

"You won't be in Strasbourg?"

Volkmann shook his head. "The information Sanchez sent—about the money transferred from the Reichsbank to Schmeltz in Paraguay before and during the last war—there's someone I'd like to talk to about it in Zurich. Someone who may be able to help."

He told her the news Peters had given him about Erhard Schmeltz. There was a puzzled look on the girl's face.

"You think Schmeltz's past has something to do with what's going on now?"

"I don't know, Erica. We know almost nothing about Erhard Schmeltz, or his son, apart from the fact they were the registered owners of the Chaco property and the information the Berlin Document Center had on him. Let's wait and see what I can turn up in Zurich tomorrow."

"This man Lothar Kesser. Can your people find him?"

"If there's a file on him, yes."

As she stood up, she said, "What time are you leaving for Zurich, Joe?"

"Before nine, I guess. Why?"

She said, "Then I better let you get some sleep." She looked at him for a long time, hesitated as if about to speak, then changed her mind. She turned, and Volkmann watched her go into the bedroom.

CHAPTER 22

Zurich, Switzerland. Tuesday, December 13

He had made the telephone call to Ted Birken early that morning, and Peters had arranged a ticket for the first flight out of Strasbourg to Zurich.

The plane was full and when it landed, Volkmann took a taxi out to the house overlooking the Zürichsee. It was bitter cold but the sky was clear, and in the distance he could see the snowcapped mountains beyond the lake.

The house was small compared to some of the lakeside villas nearby, but it was pretty and neat, and set in its own tidy gardens twenty meters back off the shore road. Volkmann saw Ted Birken come out to the front door and wave a greeting.

The man's shoulders were hunched beneath a loose-fitting cardigan, and he looked older than his seventy-odd years. Volkmann realized it had been almost ten years since they had last met, when Birken had lectured at the house in Devon.

The blue eyes twinkled as he shook Volkmann's hand. "Good to see you again, Joe. Come inside."

Volkmann paid the driver and followed the tall, gray-haired man. The house was warm, and in the study Birken had set out a small wooden tray with glasses and a bottle of cherry kirsch. A fire blazed in the hearth and the wide study window looked out onto the lake.

Ted Birken had been an intelligence officer for most of his adult life. A Jewish refugee from Germany, he and his family had escaped to Switzerland in 1940, when Birken was eighteen. The son of a once-prominent and wealthy banker, he soon grew tired of sitting on the sidelines and within a year had left his family and the safe comfort of a neutral country behind him and made his way to Nice with forged papers. From there he began a hazardous journey to Lisbon and then England, where he attempted to join the British Army. Interned ignominiously on the Isle of Man for the rest of the war because of his doubtful and uncorroborated background, he had to wait until the summer of

1945 to offer his services. By then the war was over, but the officer who interviewed him realized that Birken's unique talents—he spoke German fluently and had connections through his father with many major Swiss banks—could be put to better use, and passed him onto the intelligence service.

Thus began a career that for four years saw Birken track down and interrogate senior Nazis and SS who had secretly helped to dispose of many millions in gold and currency from the Nazi Reichsbank and death camps in the last months of the war. When his work came to an end, Birken had become a British citizen and joined SIS, in later years becoming a senior intelligence figure before retiring to Switzerland.

Volkmann saw the elderly man puff on his meerschaum and fill the two glasses with kirsch before the sparkling blue eyes swiveled to look at him. Volkmann had explained on the telephone his reasons for wanting to see him, and Birken was a businesslike man; he got straight down to business.

"You had three questions, one about the money that was sent to South America by the Nazi Reichsbank. The other concerning these men, Schmeltz and Reimer, and the Leibstandarte SS. Let's start with the first, shall we?" He took a sip of his drink, then sat back, puffed on his pipe before speaking.

"First, perhaps I had better explain the background behind Nazi funds, so you get a fix on things. At the end of the war in May of nineteen forty-five, the equivalent of almost two billion in today's terms had gone missing. That included lots of valuable art objects too, but mainly gold and silver bullion, the so-called property of the Reichsbank. Some of it—quite a lot, actually—had been plundered from invaded countries." Birken paused to smile. "There was enough to equip another German Army, and I think that was the vague intention of the Nazis, especially Himmler, when the plans to hide the caches were first discussed. But of course as the war situation became more hopeless, that idea was quickly forgotten, and many of the people whose job it was to hide the caches actually started working for themselves."

Volkmann sipped his drink, then asked, "So what happened to the bullion and money, Ted?"

"Some of it we located. But a lot of it vanished. It ended up in Switzerland or South America, and some in the Arab countries that had been favorably disposed toward Hitler. A few unscrupulous Americans helped themselves to some of the gold or did deals with the Nazis they apprehended, but it was small scale and to be expected. Quite a number of Nazis escaped to South America, as I'm sure you know. And quite a lot of the bullion and currency went with them. The people involved ranged from lowly privates up to high-ranking SS and Gestapo. They slipped out of ports all over Europe, but mainly from Italy. We tried tracking both them and the caches down in South America, but it proved a rather hopeless exercise. Most of the South American countries still had pro-Nazi sympathies at the time and did nothing to help us."

"What were the reasons behind taking the gold and currency to South America?"

Birken smiled indulgently. "It was considered a relatively safe and distant place. Some countries there had been openly supportive of the Nazis, and those with large German colonies especially so. Paraguay is a good example. General Stroessner was the military dictator there for quite some time. He was part German himself, and pro-Nazi. And there were many other countries in the region with the same sympathies. Most of the loot that ended up in South America lined private pockets, though a considerable portion of it was controlled by *Die Spinne*—the Spider—the secret organization of former SS who set up down there. Otherwise known as the *Kameradenwerk*, and before that, as Odessa. There was a rather loose plan to regroup and eventually finance another Nazi Party in Germany when the time was ripe once again, but of course it came to naught."

Birken paused, and the watery blue eyes looked at Volkmann. "*Die Spinne,* you're familiar with its original function?"

"No."

"Well, it had quite a few, actually. But the primary ones were to protect former SS men from prosecution and to help establish those same former Nazis and their families in commerce and industry. And, of course, to continue to propagandize the ideals of the Third Reich.''

Volkmann looked out toward the gray, choppy lake for several moments. When he looked back at Ted Birken, he asked, "Did you ever hear of funds being sent back to Germany with that purpose in mind, Ted?"

"In what respect?"

"To finance extremists. Neo-Nazis."

Birken relit his pipe and said, "Mossad had a theory that some of the neo-Nazi resurgences in Germany over the last thirty years were financed in part from *Die Spinne* funds, but there was never any evidence of that. Of course, *Die Spinne* was notoriously secretive, and defied any attempts to infiltrate it. The Israelis tried to on a number of occasions, but their people involved in such missions usually disappeared, never to be heard of again."

The blue eyes regarded Volkmann keenly. "I presume this has something to do with these men, Schmeltz and Reimer, you asked me to check on?"

When Volkmann nodded, Birken said, "Do you mind me asking why? Of course, if you'd rather not talk, I quite understand."

Volkmann told him the story. It took him almost ten minutes to outline what had happened, and Birken sat there quietly smoking his pipe, pausing only to refill the meerschaum. When Volkmann had finished, Birken leaned forward.

"Do you have the photograph of the young woman with you?"

Volkmann removed the snapshot from his wallet and handed it across. Birken looked at it for a long time, then handed it back as he shook his head.

"I'm afraid I don't recognize her. Of course, that date would have been before my time. And of course the young woman could have been anyone. A public figure or simply an anonymous girlfriend of some Nazi officer."

"What about Schmeltz and Reimer?"

Birken nodded. "After you telephoned this morning, I had a look back through my notes and diaries. I kept copious notes when I was tracking down the missing Reichsbank funds. As I told you once many years ago, the team I was involved with at the end of the war had to go right back through the books, back to nineteen thirty-three, to try and figure out where most of the money and bullion had come from. What part was party funds, what part belonged to the German people, what part had been spoils of war, and so on." Birken smiled. "I had hoped to write a book one day, but somehow I never seemed to get around to it. That's the reason I kept copies of almost all the major accounts serviced over the twelve years of the Nazi regime."

Volkmann nodded. "That's why I contacted you, Ted."

"Well, I'm afraid I found nothing on this man Reimer, alias Tsarkin. He wasn't one of the people we were chasing. The ten thousand American dollars you say he had in his possession when he arrived in Paraguay could have been a little nest egg he had stashed away during the years of the war, or it quite possibly could have been paid to him from *Die Spinne* funds."

When Birken hesitated, Volkmann asked, "What about Erhard Schmeltz?"

Birken again shook his head. "I found no record of money being sent to any Schmeltz in Paraguay. Not that I expected to. That's not to say, of course, that the Reichsbank didn't send him the funds you spoke of. Such an account could have been serviced secretly, and most likely was. But the amounts sent to Schmeltz's account would have been small beer by comparison to some of the others the Reichsbank serviced abroad, both before and during the war. Those were mainly for espionage work, for propaganda purposes, and for secret accounts that high-ranking Nazis could rely on if things went wrong. The amounts to Schmeltz were considerable, but still relatively small. The real question is, why was Schmeltz sent money before the war? And why did the money continue to be sent to his wife after his death?"

"Do you have any ideas, Ted?"

Birken smiled at Volkmann. "God only knows. It could have been for anything. Some Nazis set up slush funds through German immigrants in South America in the belief, I suppose, that one day they'd need them. As I recall, there were always quite a number of German colonies in Paraguay, and most of them were fervently pro-Nazi.'' Birken shrugged. "Maybe the Schmeltz couple was simply playing bank manager for someone.''

"What about the fact that Schmeltz's Nazi membership was endorsed by Himmler himself?''

Birken smiled again. "Now that *is* interesting. But I'm afraid I still can't give you an answer. It suggests that Schmeltz was a close personal friend or acquaintance of Himmler's or some high-ranking Nazi, obviously.'' Birken shrugged. "But if Himmler or someone at the top of the Nazi Party was using this man Schmeltz as a channel for siphoning away a secret money hoard for the future, I'm sure the amounts would have been much, much larger.'' Birken paused. "Perhaps Schmeltz did someone a favor or kindness. Perhaps he was being repaid a stipend for it. It's the only explanation I can think of when one considers that Schmeltz retained his party membership despite being thousands of miles away. Either that or Schmeltz was being used to set up a slush fund for someone in the party. Blackmail is another possible reason for the drafts, of course. But it's unlikely that Schmeltz would have remained in the party if that were the case, although you never know. And I can only assume that the reason the monies ceased in February of nineteen forty-five was because by then, the Reichsbank was finding it increasingly difficult to transfer funds out of Germany, even through its Swiss accounts.''

"What was the bullion that made its way to *Die Spinne* actually used for?''

Birken looked out toward the view beyond the window for a few moments, then turned back to face Volkmann.

"I think I'd have to agree with the Mossad's theory, at least in part. I'm sure some of it was used to finance neo-Nazi and right-wing movements over the years. And not only in Germany, but all over Europe, and in America and South Africa in particular. But until now, Germany's been too prosperous a country to have its keel unsettled by that kind of thing.'' Birken shrugged. "I imagine a lot of the money's still in South America, keeping a certain number of very elderly Nazis and their sibling families in considerable comfort.''

"Are we talking millions here, Ted, or what?''

"Oh, much more than that, my boy. Probably as much as a quarter of the original amount that disappeared. Especially when you consider that the original capital would have been put to work."

"How?"

"In business ventures mainly, and land purchase. Much of it in South America." Birken paused. "That's where your last question comes in. What do you know about the Leibstandarte SS Division?"

Volkmann shook his head. "Very little. Just that they were an elite within the SS. And that Hitler's personal bodyguard was drawn from its ranks."

Birken nodded. "They were the elite of the *Waffen*, or armed SS, all right. And principally Hitler's bodyguard. First formed after the Night of the Long Knives, when the SA leadership was destroyed by Hitler because he saw them as a threat to his own future and survival. Sepp Dietrich, a fanatical and dedicated Nazi officer and a close friend of Hitler's, decided to set up a special SS unit to act as Hitler's bodyguard in any future crisis. The men were all hand-picked, hardened Nazis, and fanatically loyal supporters of Hitler. The unit later grew to become a division. They were also instrumental in setting up *Die Spinne* and helping to get much of the Nazi gold to South America." Birken paused and smiled. "It's interesting, but there is a slim connection between this fellow Erhard Schmeltz and Reimer."

"What kind of connection?"

"Reimer was Leibstandarte SS. Erhard Schmeltz was SA. A Brownshirt."

When Volkmann nodded, Birken went on. "Well, the Brownshirt SA was initially set up as Hitler's bodyguard. But after the Night of the Long Knives in nineteen thirty-four, when they were purged, some of their members, the ones ardently loyal to Hitler, were inducted into the ranks of the Leibstandarte SS." Birken shrugged. "It's a small connection, but a connection nonetheless."

"What happened to Sepp Dietrich?"

"He survived the war and was sent to trial, but served only about ten years for war crimes. He died in Germany during the seventies."

Volkmann glanced at his watch, then at the telephone on the study desk. "I'm booked on the twelve-thirty flight back, Ted. Do you mind if I use your phone to call a taxi?"

"Not at all. Let me do it for you."

It was ten minutes later when they saw the cab pull up on the gravel path outside. Volkmann finished his drink and Birken stood up shakily.

"One last question, Ted. Did you ever hear of the Brandenburg Testament?"

The old man thought for a moment, scratched his chin. Finally he said, "No, I'm afraid not. What is it?"

Volkmann shook his head, smiled. "I'm afraid I've no idea. Thanks for your help, Ted."

"Sorry I couldn't be more useful." Birken paused, then said, "About Schmeltz, there *is* something I could do that may be worth a try if you're looking to get a fix on him."

"What?"

"So many of the old Nazis are dead, of course. But there are still a few of them alive. I have a contact in the German Federal Archives Office in Koblenz. I could ask him to check and see if he can come up with some numbers close to Schmeltz's party membership number and check them with the WASt."

"What's that?"

"It's an acronym for the *Wehrmacht Auskunftstelle*. That's the German Army Information Agency. It's in Reinickendorf in north Berlin, and it's one of the main German military-personnel records offices. The WASt keeps information on all former German Army personnel, going back to before the last war. That includes the SS, which was actually part of the army. Whenever former German military personnel wanted to claim state or federal pensions, either because they were war invalids or they had reached retirement age, they had to apply through the WASt. Only when the WASt had confirmed their military service records could the pensions be paid."

"You mean former members of the SS are paid pensions?"

"Dreadful as that seems, yes."

"How can the WASt help?"

"Well, if we can get a list of Nazi Party membership

numbers and names that were close to Schmeltz's, and those people served in the German military or the SS during the war and are still alive, they ought to be receiving pensions. The WASt will have a record of their addresses when they applied. There can't be too many of the old boys still around, especially those whose party numbers were close to Schmeltz's number. And even if they knew of Schmeltz, they may have long forgotten him, or not even want to talk. But it's the only hope you've got.''

''What if these people have changed their addresses in the meantime?''

Birken smiled. ''That's where German thoroughness comes in. Until a couple of years ago, it used to be the law that whenever any German citizen changed his address, he had to inform an office called the *Einwohnermeldamt*. It was a special registration office, run by the police. So finding addresses for these people isn't really a problem. Your real problem is the fact that so many of them will probably be dead by now. But leave it with me for now, and I'll see what I can come up with.''

''Thanks, Ted. I appreciate your help.''

''Not at all, my boy.''

Birken led him to the front door, and the blue eyes sparkled as he gripped Volkmann's hand. ''I'll be in touch if anything turns up.'' He smiled. ''Do call again sometime. It's so seldom one gets visitors these days.''

It was almost noon when the taxi pulled up outside the Departures terminal, and as Volkmann paid the driver, he noticed the dark green Citroën pull up across from the terminal. He had spotted the car in the rearview mirror on the way in from the lake road.

It was too far away for him to get a good look at the two passengers inside without making it obvious, but when he went to check in, he noticed the blond young man with the newspaper standing by the Hertz desk. He wore a long, dark winter overcoat and his hair was cropped close to his skull. Volkmann thought there was something familiar about him until he felt certain he remembered that he had seen him that morning at the airport, standing by the information desk as he came out of Arrivals.

When he was handed back his boarding pass, Volkmann looked around. There was no sign of the young man with the newspaper.

He walked back out to the Departures entrance and stepped outside. The green Citroën had disappeared, and the blond man wasn't among the crowd on the concourse.

Volkmann waited another ten minutes, going through the old routines, but he noticed no one watching him and he was certain he wasn't followed as he walked back toward the boarding gate.

CHAPTER 23

Strasbourg. December 13

He arrived back at DSE headquarters at three. He telephoned Peters's office and was told by the secretary that Peters had left early. There was a message for Volkmann from the duty officer, and when he was put through, Jan De Vries came on the line.

"An unclassified signal came through the Italian desk," the Dutchman said. "They say they're rechecking all sea-port cargo manifests that arrived from South America within the last month. If they come across anything, they'll get back to you." De Vries paused. "Also, a voice-analysis report just came in from your place in Beaconsfield. You want me to pass it on to Peters, Joe?"

"I'll pick it up myself, Jan. Thanks."

There was some correspondence on his desk but he ignored it for now. He felt certain that the blond young man at the airport in Zurich had been watching him, and that the two men in the green Citroën had followed him out from the Zürichsee. But why? And who were the men? Had he seen the blond man outside the departures terminal, he would have turned the tail around, only that hadn't happened. The business at the airport made him feel uneasy. Apart from Facilities and Peters, only Erica had known he was traveling to Zurich. He remembered that she had asked him what time his flight left. Or had she asked him simply when he was leaving? He couldn't remember the words exactly, but the thought bothered him.

He signed for the Beaconsfield report, then went back up to his office and read the two-page document.

The report had determined that there were three voices on the tape, each male.

The first was approximately in his late forties, and the diphthong and syntax analyses had regionalized the accent to within the Munich area, most likely the western region. The man was a nonsmoker, his build suggested as medium to heavy, the social class determined as middle.

The two other voices, the report stated, had proven more

difficult. In both cases, the German they spoke was a softer version of *plattdeutsch*. But it was not a native-spoken dialect and the analysis suggested that both men were bilingual, their voices softened by a Latinate tongue, most likely Spanish. Class in both cases impossible to determine exactly, but possibly middle.

Of those two voices, one was of a speaker roughly in his middle thirties, a smoker, likely of stocky build. And the other was of a man in his early to middle sixties. Possibly thin to medium build, and a nonsmoker.

The German they spoke was regionalized to non-ethnic German colonies within either Paraguay or Argentina, but again difficult to determine which exactly, and the report suggested it could be a border region straddling both territories.

Volkmann read through the report several times, then made two copies and left one each marked for the attention of Ferguson and Peters.

When he went through the correspondence on his desk, he found a large envelope from Peters, containing photocopied material from the American Document Center in Berlin.

There were two manila folders inside, each containing a sheaf of pages. There was a note paper-clipped to the front of one of the folders. It explained that one set of copies was from Heinrich Reimer's file and the second from Erhard Schmeltz's, and that they were copies of the original documents held at the Berlin Document Center.

Volkmann picked Reimer's first.

All the relevant information was in the file. SS number, Nazi Party number, and application forms for each, filled out and signed by Reimer himself. There were notes concerning his education, medical history, his officer-training courses, his transfers and promotions, up to October 1944. The space for his marital status said he was single; the spaces to record the names or births of any children Reimer had fathered were blank. There was also a four-page copy of Reimer's family tree, dating back to 1800, to show the Aryan purity of his background.

Three of the pages were copies of a typed questionnaire, called a *Fragebogen*. According to the notes from the Document Center, this was standard practice for SS officers. The replies were neatly written in Reimer's own hand. His age at the time was given as twenty-five and his place of birth as Lübars in Berlin.

There was a handwritten, one-page personal biography. Reimer started with his date and place of birth and went on to describe his education and family background; the son of a bakery worker, his involvement on the fringes of the Nazi Party in his late teens in 1929, his joining the party in 1930, his entrance into the Leibstandarte SS in July 1934. Most of the information was unremarkable and described his involvement in helping at party rallies and his attendance at party education seminars, and it was all written in a stilted fashion, the last paragraph a gushing statement of Reimer's dedication to Adolf Hitler and the Nazi Party. It was signed and his rank given as *SS Untersturmführer*, lieutenant.

The third page contained three black-and-white photographs of Reimer. Two were head-and-shoulders shots, one front and one side profile. The third was a full-length photograph in the black uniform of *Untersturmführer* SS, taken against a white background. His hands were clasped in front of him and he wore polished, high black boots and wing trousers. His SS rune flashes were visible on his collar. On the left sleeve of his officer's uniform was a swastika armband, and above the sleeve cuff another armband that said, "Adolf Hitler."

All three photographs were of a solemn-looking young man with cropped blond hair and a sharp face; they bore little resemblance to the photograph Sanchez had shown him. There were the same thin lips and high forehead, but that was where the similarity ended.

Reimer's promotions from his entry into the ranks of the SS officers' corps in 1934 to 1945, when he had attained the rank of *Sturmbannführer*, major, were all recorded. He had seen service in Austria, Poland, Russia, France and the Balkans. His last posting was recorded in October 1944, when he was transferred to a Leibstandarte SS training school in Berlin's Lichterfelde district.

Volkmann put Reimer's file aside and opened the folder on Erhard Schmeltz.

There were four pages inside; one was a copy of Schmeltz's original Nazi Party application form. At the top of the application it read: *Nationalsozialistische Deutsche Arbeiterpartei*, and underneath: *München Braunes Haus*, the address of the Nazi Party headquarters in Munich. Below the head was the application proper.

There was a line for the applicant's signature and it contained Erhard Schmeltz's, the letters firm and bold. For "Profession" or "Occupation," the words *Fabrik Werkmeister*, Factory Foreman, were written in Schmeltz's handwriting. The place and date of birth were given as Hamburg, March 6, 1880. In a box in the top right-hand corner was stamped the number 6896.

Schmeltz's address was given as 23 Brennerallee in Schwabbing, and the date of application was November 6, 1927. Underneath the official's scrawl were the words *Verweisung: Hauptquartier.* Refer to headquarters.

Volkmann guessed it referred to the endorsement of Schmeltz's application that Peters had told him about, and when he looked at the next page, he saw a copy of a letter headed Prinz-Albrecht Strasse, Berlin, the headquarters of the *Reichsführer* SS.

The letter was dated three days before Schmeltz had applied for party membership and addressed to Gau: Munchen. There was a terse message that simply said, *"I recommend immediate acceptance of party applicant Erhard Johann Schmeltz into Gau Munich. Any queries, contact me personally."* The letter was signed *H. Himmler, Der Reichsführer SS*, and the signature bore an official stamp.

The other two photocopies were front and back shots of Schmeltz's original master file card from Nazi Party records.

Schmeltz's card contained very little information: name and address, party membership number, date of entry into the party, and the Nazi Gau and Ortsgruppe to which he belonged. There was a head-and-shoulders photograph of Schmeltz on the reverse side, in a black-bordered frame.

The face in the photograph showed a plain, middle-aged man with a broad, rural face and a thick, bullish neck. His dark hair had partly receded, and what remained was oiled and combed over his scalp. He wore a dark, ill-fitting suit that looked tight over a stocky, muscular body, and an old-style wing collar and tie. The eyes were narrow slits, and his dark bushy eyebrows were knit together as if he were trying to concentrate as he stared at the camera.

Volkmann stared down at the photograph for a long time, wondering again what had made Schmeltz leave Germany and travel to South America with his wife and child. And why he had received such large sums of money. There was nothing in his file to suggest why, and the only thing unusual was Himmler's letter, but Volkmann guessed that many party applicants had asked senior-ranking Nazis to look favorably on their application.

It was almost half an hour later before he finally put the folders back in the envelope. After that, he tidied up his desk, left the office, and drove to his apartment.

It was after five and dark when he let himself in, and he saw that Erica had set the table for dinner. She told him she had gone shopping in Petite France, bought fresh fish and vegetables and two bottles of Sauterne and intended cooking dinner for both of them.

She looked good in jeans and a tight sweater, and her hair was down and fell about her shoulders. Over the meal he told her about the voice-analysis reports and his visit to Zurich, but he made no mention of the man at the airport who had followed him.

"Did your friend in Zurich have any idea of why Erhard Schmeltz received the money from the Reichsbank?"

Joseph told her what Ted Birken had said, then shook his head. "But he was just speculating, Erica. So anything is possible. Even blackmail could have been the reason Schmeltz received the money. What about you, did you turn up anything?"

"I spent the day at the *Frankfurter Zeitung* office, going through the library clips."

"And?"

She hesitated. "Lubsch must have told you the truth. At least about the two people Kesser wanted him to kill."

"Why?"

"A man named Herbert Rauscher was murdered in East Berlin five months ago. It's got to be the same man. The

Berlin papers ran stories and they were picked up by the major dailies.''

"Tell me."

"The reports said Rauscher was shot at his apartment near the Pergamon Museum. Two bullet wounds in the head. He died immediately. According to the newspapers, there were no witnesses and the Berlin police had no leads. I telephoned the Berlin homicide office, but they wouldn't give me any information other than that the case is still under investigation and no one has been arrested."

Volkmann looked across at her. "What about the woman?"

"Her name was Hedda Pohl, and she was murdered too."

"Where?"

"Not far from Friedrichshafen in southern Germany, where she came from. It's near the Swiss border, beside Lake Konstanz. The murder happened a week before Rauscher was killed. All the Munich papers ran stories, but I rang the local paper in Friedrichshafen and I spoke to one of the reporters. She said the woman was murdered between midnight and two o'clock in a woods outside the town. She was shot three times in the head and back. The reporter knew very little except that the case was still open. She just gave me what details she could. Hedda Pohl was in her early sixties, the widow of a businessman, and had two grown children. She seemed pretty highly regarded in the town. There was no motive for the murder, and the police didn't seem to be making much progress."

"Did you contact the local police in Friedrichshafen?"

Erica shook her head. "No, I thought you'd want to do that. But I've put a file together with all the newspaper clips I could get on the murders."

"What about Rauscher's background? Did the newspaper reports say?"

"Just that he was a businessman, that's all."

Volkmann sighed and thought for a moment. "What about the politician, Massow?"

Erica brushed a strand of blond hair from her face. "Still very much alive. He's got an office in the Kreutzberg district in Berlin. It's a place where mostly poor immigrants live. I telephoned and his secretary said Massow was away for several days at a convention in Paris, but she penciled you in for an appointment in two days' time. Ten o'clock in Massow's Kreutzberg office.''

He wondered whether to mention the man at the Zurich airport, but decided not to. He told her he would be gone the next morning for a day or two at most, but he did not tell her where and she didn't ask him. The blue eyes were looking back at him and he smiled across at her as he cleared away the dinner table. ''Now, how about some coffee?''

She had opened another bottle of wine, and he spent a half-hour reading through the file she had made from the newspaper stories on the murders. There was very little detailed information in the articles apart from what Erica had told him, but when he finished reading, he decided he needed to talk with Jakob Fischer in Berlin. Fischer was a detective in the Berlin Kriminalamt whom he knew well and the only contact he could think of who might help him keep his inquiry into Rauscher's murder unofficial. He knew no one in Friedrichshafen, and there it would be a matter of figuring out how to get the information on Hedda Pohl's death from the local police.

Several times he had gone to the window when Erica wasn't in the room and looked down at the parking lot and the street opposite, but he saw nothing suspicious and if he was being watched, then whoever was doing the watching was good. He had left the Beretta in his overcoat pocket.

As Erica came to sit beside him on the couch, Volkmann saw the soft nape of her neck as she leaned forward to refill their glasses. He thought she looked very beautiful. When she sat back, she noticed him staring at her.

''What are you looking at, Joe?''

''You.''

She didn't blush, but turned away. When she looked back, Volkmann said, ''Did you love Rudi?''

There was a look like pain on her face and she closed her eyes, then opened them again before she answered the question.

''Yes, I loved him. But not in the way you might mean.

He was good to me. He always made me laugh. And there were times in my life when Rudi was the only person I could turn to. There were certain things I had to face up to, unpleasant things, and he was there when I needed to talk. Even if only on the telephone.''

"You think he loved you too?''

She hesitated, then said, "Yes. I think he did.''

"What were the times you say he was the only one you could turn to?"

She hesitated again. "Why do you want to know?''

"For the same reason you wanted to know about me.''

She looked over at him and then turned away. When she finally spoke, her voice was almost a whisper.

"There was a time when I felt ashamed. Ashamed of certain things in my family's past.''

She hesitated, bit her lip, and Volkmann knew she wouldn't go on. He said quietly, "You mean about your father?''

The blue eyes turned to him again, but this time he saw the startled look on her face.

"How did you know?''

"Erica, the German police keep files on most of your country's citizens, you must know that.''

"You mean especially on the children of war criminals?''

Volkmann nodded. "It's your government, Erica. And it's been so for almost fifty years.''

She said nothing for a long time. Then she said quietly, "Tell me what you know.''

He didn't repeat all the details in the file, but there was no need to. "Your father served in the Leibstandarte SS Division. The same division as Heinrich Reimer.''

"What else do you know?''

"At the end of the war, he escaped to South America. The war-crimes people tracked him down to Buenos Aires, but he died before he could be extradited.''

Erica said nothing for several moments. Then finally she said, "The first day I met you, did you know about my father?''

"Yes.'' He looked at her as she spoke.

"That first time we met, I sensed that you found it dif-

ficult being near me. It was in your manner, in the way you
looked at me. That maybe you hated me a little. Did you
hate me a little, Joe?''

He shook his head. ''No, I didn't hate you, Erica. Hate's
too strong a word. Distrust maybe.''

''Because I was the daughter of an SS officer? Because
of what happened to your parents? And now you must distrust me even more because my father was in the same SS
Division as this man Reimer.''

He did not speak and she looked at his face. ''Was that
the reason you didn't want to sleep with me, Joe? Because
of who my father was?''

''Yes.''

She shook her head. ''You know, it is a terrible thing
that hate or distrust can be carried from one generation to
another. That it can be passed from father to son. Because
if that is so, then there is no hope for any of us, not ever.
Don't you see? You are blaming me also for my father's
sins.''

Volkmann hesitated, then shook his head. ''I'm not
blaming you for anything, Erica.''

''Oh, but you are, Joe, you are. Even though maybe you
don't want to. I want to tell you something. When I was a
little girl, my father was everything to me. But I didn't
know what he had done. Killed people in cold blood. Men,
women, children. I didn't know that the hands I had held
had inflicted so much suffering and death. I trusted him.
And when he died, I felt I had lost someone that I had
looked up to. I was sixteen when I first heard the rumors.
And it was a year later before my mother finally told me
the truth. From that moment on, he was no longer the papa
I had loved, but a beast. He had let me love him and trust
him when he didn't deserve my trust or love. But no, your
files will never tell you that. They will never tell you of
the pain and suffering and the humiliation of the families
and children of these people who shamed Germany so. Do
you think every child of every Nazi is proud of his parents'
past? Do you, Joe? Some, maybe, but they are sick people.
Decent people, ordinary people, they suffered because of
what their parents did. I carry a scar around as much as
you.''

"Tell me."

The blue eyes looked at him intently. "We are both victims. You a victim of your father's past, I of mine. But you cannot see that, Joe. You think all Germans are untrustworthy and barbarians."

"I never said that."

"You don't have to. It's in your eyes. In the way you distance yourself. Just like now. You still don't trust me, do you, Joe?"

Volkmann said nothing. Finally he looked at her. "I was followed in Zurich today."

"What do you mean?"

"The man I went to meet in Zurich. Two men in a green Citroën followed me from his home to the airport."

"What are you saying?"

"Apart from my office, you were the only one who knew I'd be in Zurich."

Volkmann saw the girl's face turn red, and her eyes blazed back at him. "What are you saying? You think I told someone?" When Volkmann didn't reply, she said, "Who could I have told, Joe?"

"I don't know, Erica."

She looked at him for a long time before she shook her head. "You can't trust anyone. I won't even dignify your question by telling you what I think of it."

He saw the wet eyes and the struggle to keep back tears and he wondered if she was genuine. She didn't cry but simply looked at him, her lips quivering.

As she stood up slowly, she said, "And now I am tired. I will say good-night, Joe."

He watched her leave the room and he sat there, not knowing what to say or whether to believe her.

Before he went to bed, he remembered that he would have to speak with Jakob Fischer in Berlin about Rauscher's case, and he made a note in his diary to call the detective at the Berlin Kriminalamt the next day.

He went to bed just after eleven, slept fitfully and awakened at two. He crossed to the hallway and opened the door to the girl's room. The bedside lamp was still on but Erica was asleep. He could see her bare tanned shoulders, and her blond hair lay strewn about the pillow. For a long time he stood there looking down at her, and he thought how beautiful she looked.

Erica was right: he didn't trust anyone. He wondered if he had been too harsh with her, and too distrustful. And what she had said about him not sleeping with her had been true. He felt attracted to her, though his distrust had held him back. And he knew it was really the thought of what men like her father had once done to his father. But how could it not be so? He had loved the man, and had there been any way to cancel out his father's pain or to repay the people who had caused him so much suffering, he would have done it a long time ago.

A car hooted in the distance and distracted him. He looked at the girl's sleeping face one last time before he flicked off the lamp and crossed over to the window and pulled back the curtain. The window looked out toward Strasbourg, and the lights of the city peppered the darkness. He thought briefly of the report from Beaconsfield. Three voices. Three men. A little more substance to go with the shadow, but still things were moving too slowly.

Sie werden alle umgebracht. They will all be killed.

He went through the taped conversation again in his mind, trying to unravel what he had learned in the last few days, trying to find threads that connected. There were two separate but perhaps parallel lines: what was happening now and what had happened in the past. The people from the Chaco house and what they were doing now. And Tsarkin, and Schmeltz and his past, and the photograph of the young girl, and how they related to the present.

How and why did they connect?

He wondered if Sanchez had made any progress. There was a link between Paraguay and Europe. But what was it? And what Lubsch said had disturbed him more than he let Erica know. Yet still he was floundering.

He heard the soft rustle of sheets and turned around, saw her sit up and look at him sleepily in the light washing through the window.

"Joe?"

"It's me. Go back to sleep."

And as she sat there looking at him, he realized how much he wanted her.

"Some of the things I said . . . I'm sorry, Joe. Can you forgive me?"

Her voice was husky with tiredness, and he could smell the scent of her body as he went to sit on the edge of the bed.

"Maybe it was my fault. Maybe you were right."

"Then will you do something for me?"

"What?"

"Try to trust me, Joe."

He placed a hand on her face. She pushed her cheek into his open palm and then kissed his fingers. It seemed to happen so naturally, and as she pulled him toward her, he found her mouth and kissed her. His hand cupped one of her breasts and as he moved onto the bed beside her, she was already pulling him on top of her urgently, kissing his neck and face and lips, her nails raking the sensitive flesh of his back and tearing at his clothes.

There was a savagery to their lovemaking that surprised Volkmann. It was as if both of them were in the grip of some uncontrollable frenzy, and when they finally spent themselves, their bodies were drenched in sweat.

For a long time afterward they lay there, the girl's head on Volkmann's chest.

Her voice came to him out of the darkness. "Tell me about your father, Joe. Tell me what happened to him."

"Why do you want to know?"

"Because I want to know everything about you."

He looked away then, toward darkness, toward nothingness, and when he spoke, his voice was soft.

"When the Germans came to the Sudetenland, my father's family moved to Poland, to a village near Cracow. My father and his parents and his two young sisters. Then the war came and it wasn't safe anymore. The *Einsatzgrüppen* were moving through the villages, rounding up and killing Jews. They were the special groups of mobile killing squads the Nazis used before they organized the extermination camps. One day my father's parents went out to get some food. They never came back and my father never saw them again.

"My father was fourteen. The two little girls were eight and ten. On the fifth day when his parents didn't come back, he knew something had happened. He learned in the village that one of the *Einsatzgrüppen* had come and taken them away. He decided to try to make it over the Tatra Mountains to reach Budapest, where his mother had relatives. He got some food and wrapped up the little girls in warm clothes and they set off.

"On the third day, they reached the border. One of the killing squads caught up with them. They took them into a forest clearing with a group of other Jews and made them stand in front of a shallow pit. My father knew what was going to happen. Everybody did. His sisters were trembling and crying, and so was he. My father begged one of the guards to spare the little girls.

"The guards pulled my father aside and called him a filthy Jew and made him watch while they stripped the small girls. They raped them in front of his eyes. Then they threw the girls into the pit and shot them.

"After that, they made my father kneel down in front of the pit. The guards were drunk. The one who shot my father in the face wounded him but didn't kill him. My father lay in the pit with the bodies of his sisters, pretending to be dead. When the Germans had finished their work, they just covered all the bodies with clay and left.

"My father lay there, bleeding, too shocked to move, barely able to breathe. When it was dark, he managed to free himself from the pit and the tangle of corpses. He buried his sisters in a shallow grave and wandered the mountains for days with a bullet in his face. This time he made it to Budapest and his relatives.

"Then the Germans came again. His relatives were taken away. My father was caught in a roundup and they sent him to Dachau, then to Belsen. The others were sent to the ovens. My father survived, but he could never forget what had happened to his two young sisters."

He lay there silent in the darkness and he could hear the girl breathing. He couldn't tell if she was crying, and he didn't speak or make a sound. It was such a long-ago pain that he couldn't cry, and all he could do was think of his father.

It seemed the silence went on forever in the darkness, and it was a long time before her hand came to touch his face. But Erica said nothing. There was nothing to say.

PART FOUR

CHAPTER 24

Berlin. Wednesday, December 14

On the morning of the fourteenth, Volkmann telephoned Jakob Fischer at the Berlin Kriminalamt, but the policeman who answered said that Fischer was out of the office and wouldn't return until late that afternoon. Volkmann left a message saying that that he had called and would ring back later.

That afternoon he got a seat on the Lufthansa flight to Berlin. It was after four and growing dark when he landed at Tegel. It was half an hour later before he made the call to Jakob Fischer. He had to wait five minutes before Fischer came on the line.

"It's been a long time, Joe. How are you, my friend?"

"Good. And you?"

"Six months from retirement and I can't wait to throw off the harness. What can I do for you, Joe?"

"You got my message?"

"This morning."

"I need to ask you a favor, Jakob."

Volkmann explained about Herbert Rauscher, and when he had finished, Jakob Fischer said, "Is this official, Joe?"

Volkmann told him he wanted to keep it unofficial and low-key for now, and Fischer said, "You better tell me what you want."

"I'd like to know what your people have on Rauscher's death. And whatever background information you've got on him."

"You say this Rauscher lived over on the East side. It's off my patch, Joe. Our people handle the eastern side of the city now, of course, and I'm Kriminalamt. But the homicide boys may get suspicious if I ask them to look at the file. You think this Rauscher was involved in any criminal activity?"

"I don't know, Jakob."

"Okay. I'll try to get a look at the file anyway and see what happens. We keep most stuff on computer and I may be able to get access."

"I'd appreciate it, Jakob."

It was almost two hours later when Fischer rang back.

"I'm afraid I only got limited access to the file on the computer, Joe, and there wasn't much there. So I decided to call the guy who handled the case, but it turns out he's on leave. I spoke to one of the other detectives at the same station and he told me what he could. It wasn't much but it may help you."

"You want to tell me over the line?"

"I think it's best we meet, Joe."

The main bar in the Schweizerhof was empty except for a couple of men in business suits talking at the bar. Volkmann was near the door an hour later when he saw Jakob Fischer appear. The detective was in his sixties but his walk was still brisk, his blue eyes bright, and his full, dark head of hair only slightly flecked with gray. He shook hands with Volkmann and slumped into one of the big armchairs opposite.

Joseph asked him if he'd eaten but Fischer settled for a club sandwich and a glass of Weizenbier. They spent five minutes talking about old times and when Fischer finished his sandwich, he wiped his mouth and said, "What's this case about, Joe?"

Volkmann told him the bare facts and Fischer said, "Sounds like a lot of trouble. So why are your people handling it and not ours?"

When Volkmann told him, Fischer nodded and said, "Okay, you want to hear what I've got?"

"Tell me."

"Background first, just to fill you in. Herbert Rauscher was born in Leipzig. Forty-nine years old at his last birthday. Moved to Berlin twenty-eight years ago. Single, never married. Worked in a small publishing firm as a manager until the Wall came down. They published tourist guides, a bird-watcher manual, and assorted books like that. He was a model citizen, from all reports. The Stasi Kriminalamt people had a file on him. What was in it, I don't know for sure because a lot of the files disappeared or were destroyed after the Wall came down. Rauscher's file vanished too. Our people managed to get a few details from former Stasi personnel after Rauscher was murdered, though not much.

"He had bought himself a secondhand Merc and moved to a better apartment, but still on the East side. Then six months ago, someone hit him. It happened late at night, about eleven. Two shots to the head. According to the detective I spoke to, there were powder burns on the skull, so it was a close hit."

"What did forensics say about the ammo or the weapon?"

"They think a Beretta was used, with a silencer. But I've no info on the ammo, except that it was nine-millimeter."

"Where was he killed?"

"At his apartment. It's near the Pergamon Museum. His girlfriend came home and found him. According to the file, she was checked out but came up clean."

"Where's the girl now, any idea?"

"I'm trying to find out, because I reckoned maybe you'd want to talk with her, but no luck so far. Her name's Monika Worch. That's all I know."

"What about Rauscher's death, did your people turn up anything?"

The detective shook his head. "Nothing, Joe. They tried the usual angles. People in the same business, but they didn't turn up anything, according to the investigator I spoke to. But Rauscher must have known who his killer was because there was no sign of anyone breaking into his apartment and it happened in the front room. One of the janitors who was on duty in the building said he heard nothing and saw nothing. Same with the neighbors."

"Was Rauscher political?"

Fischer frowned and shook his head. "Not that our people know of. And from the type of guy he was, I'd say probably no. He seemed more interested in making money than in politics. Why, do you think Rauscher's death was political?"

Volkmann hesitated. "I don't know, Jakob. What about Rauscher's girl?"

"What about her?"

"You think you could find her for me?"

Jakob Fischer shrugged. "Sure, if she's still in Berlin.

But it may take time. My guess is she's still in the business. I'll ask around.''

Volkmann said, ''Is Rauscher's apartment still unoccupied?''

''I believe so.''

''Can I take a look?''

Fischer smiled. ''I guessed you'd want to. My car's outside. Finish your beer and then I'll drive you over. We'll see if my ID can get us in.''

It was after nine when they pulled up to the apartment block near the Pergamon Museum.

It was one of the luxury modern apartment blocks the Soviets had built for their liaison personnel in East Berlin over thirty years before. It was still well kept, and there were neat gardens at either side of the entrance. There were eight stories and according to Jakob Fischer, the apartment was on the top floor.

Fischer ignored the intercom system and banged authoritatively on the glass doors like a true policeman. A couple of minutes later, the night porter appeared. Fischer flashed his ID and told the man he wanted to see Herbert Rauscher's apartment. The man seemed intimidated by the authority of Fischer's voice and badge and once he'd led them inside, he scurried off to find the keys.

When he came back five minutes later, Fischer told him they'd go up in the elevator by themselves. The porter handed over the keys, and Volkmann and Fischer took the creaking elevator to the penthouse apartment on the top floor.

There was a sign pasted on the door by the Berlin homicide police forbidding anyone to enter the apartment, and they had put a third lock on the door. Fischer had to go back down to his car and it took him almost half an hour to open the third lock with a filed key from the big set he had on a metal ring.

When they stepped inside, Volkmann was surprised by the lavishness of the apartment. There was a panoramic view of the granite facade of the Pergamon, and in the distance they could see the illuminated top of the Brandenburg Gate and the narrow, cobbled streets of the old eastern quarter, softly lit by yellow streetlights.

The apartment smelled of dry air and must, and it was expensively furnished with black hide furniture. There was a Sony TV and video in a corner and an expensive Bang and Olufsen hi-fi by the window.

When Volkmann stepped toward the window, he saw the dark-red bloodstain near the coffee table. It was a big, dark patch and it looked like someone had once spilled red wine there. The police hadn't left the rooms in disarray, and Volkmann had a good look around the two bedrooms and the rest of the apartment.

The closets were full of expensive suits, but there were no women's clothes; Volkmann guessed Rauscher's girlfriend had cleared out all her belongings. The drawers in the bedrooms were empty of any personal belongings except for some underwear and monogrammed silk shirts. There was nothing to hint that Rauscher had had any involvement in politics, and the only books were glossy coffee-table types.

It was eleven when Jakob Fischer drove him back to the Schweizerhof, and the detective told him he'd get back to him as soon as he had any news on Rauscher's girlfriend. Volkmann told him to leave a message saying where he could be contacted in case Volkmann wasn't there and Fischer said he'd do that.

CHAPTER 25

He took a taxi to Walter Massow's office in Kreutzberg the next morning.

It was in a drab, prewar building just off the Blücher-strasse, right in the middle of a block of neglected tenements that teemed with Turkish and Asian immigrants, in the old, still war-scarred suburb in the southeast of the city. The front of the building had been daubed with painted slogans that someone had painted over again, and the windows on the first two floors were boarded up.

It was ten when Volkmann arrived; a young man was seated behind a desk on the ground floor. He looked up cautiously as Volkmann entered. When he had checked Volkmann's identity card, he pressed a button under his desk and a door sprang open that led upstairs.

Four flights up, a young secretary sat typing in an outer office and she asked Volkmann to wait while she went to fetch Massow. She returned moments later followed by a man of about fifty. Big, powerfully built, wearing glasses, and whose gentle manner and soft voice belied his physique.

"Herr Volkmann, I'm Walter Massow."

He shook Volkmann's hand firmly and led the way down a corridor into a spacious but cluttered office.

Bright winter sunlight filtered through a large window, and there were metal filing cabinets against the peeling walls. The office overlooked a small park below, and there was a clear view to several blocks of dilapidated flats opposite.

The secretary brought them coffee and when she had left them, Massow sat back in his chair. He selected a toothpick from a small cup on the desk and played it around in his mouth as he looked across.

"May I ask what this is about, Herr Volkmann?"

It took Joseph several minutes to explain the reason for his visit. He kept his information to a minimum and told Massow that he was investigating the murder of a man

named Dieter Winter and that the investigation had revealed
a connection with a threat to Massow's life. Volkmann
spoke briefly about Winter's background and the circumstances of his death.

Massow didn't seem unduly surprised or perturbed, but
simply listened calmly. When Volkmann finished, the politician sipped his coffee and sat back farther in his chair
and it creaked under his weight.

"May I ask why a British DSE officer is investigating
this case? Surely it would be an internal matter for our
police. . . ."

Volkmann explained that the weapon used to kill Winter
had been used before in the shooting of a British-born businessman in Hamburg, and when Massow nodded his understanding, Volkmann said, "Have you ever heard of
Dieter Winter before, Herr Massow?"

The big man shook his head firmly. "No, I haven't."

Volkmann looked across at the politician and said, "Do
you have any idea, Herr Massow, why this man Winter
might have wanted you killed?"

Massow smiled as he chewed on the toothpick. "You
say this Winter was a right-wing extremist?"

"It would seem so."

Massow shook his head and smiled ruefully. "Herr
Volkmann, if I had a deutschmark for every death threat or
hate letter I received from people like that, I would be a
wealthy man by now." He suddenly stood up. "Let me
show you something."

The politician crossed to a filing cabinet and removed a
file. He flicked through a thick sheaf of papers and crossed
back to his desk, where he spread the papers out.

"Letters," explained Massow. "Rather unpleasant letters. These are copies, the police have the originals, not that
it means much. They never find these people."

Massow selected one and handed it across. The single-
sheet copy page had been constructed from cutout
newspaper-headline type.

Across the top of the page a single line said: *JEW
LOVER. WE'RE WATCHING YOU.*

When Volkmann had looked at it, Massow handed across

another. This time it was another single page but in writing, the letters big and bold and threatening.

IMMIGRANTS OUT! MASSOW, YOU ARE DEAD!

Massow said, ''Those are some of the milder threats. There are others much worse.'' He smiled. ''It comes with the territory, as they say.''

The politician sat back again and gestured to the window.

''This area I represent, Herr Volkmann, the people here are mainly of immigrant stock, as you are probably aware. Turks. Poles. Slavs. Asians. Greeks. People from the African countries. I do my best for them. But there are those, as there are in every country, who think people like my constituents should be sent back to wherever they or their parents came from. No matter that they have perhaps been born here and are as good citizens as the next.'' Massow shook his head. ''It happens in every country you care to mention, Herr Volkmann. France. Germany. England. Italy. And no doubt, if the extremists and racists had the chance, they would send people like me back with them.'' He shrugged his big shoulders. ''Now and then the thugs who call themselves Germans throw a pipe bomb or deface our building. But we've become used to it. And my staff are dedicated, diligent people. I'm not saying such things don't worry us, but we go about our work nonetheless.''

Volkmann gestured to the letters and asked, ''Who are the people who send you these?''

''People like your friend Winter, I should imagine. Extremists. Neo-Nazis. Immigrant haters. People haters. Lunatics.'' Massow shrugged, smiled. ''I think I've covered all the possibilities.''

Volkmann said, ''Have you ever heard of a man called Wolfgang Lubsch?''

Massow frowned. ''The terrorist?''

''Yes.''

''Yes, I've heard of him.''

''How well do you know him?''

Massow raised his eyebrows, then smiled and said guardedly, ''Herr Volkmann, the man is a wanted terrorist. Many years ago when he was a student, I met him briefly at a political rally in Hamburg. He is not a friend, if that's what you are implying. And on that subject, I say no more.''

"And the death threat I spoke about?"

"What about it?"

"Do you have any idea who might have been behind it?"

"No, Herr Volkmann, I don't. Except the kind of lunatic fringe I just talked about. Like I said, I receive so many threats." Massow smiled. "In fact, if they stopped, I might get worried that the racists and bigots have come to like me. And that would *really* frighten me."

"Why would such people want you dead?"

"Because to the extremists and the racists, people like me are a thorn in their side."

Massow stood up, took a step closer to the window. The bright winter sunshine pouring through washed the big man's face, made him squint. He looked down at Volkmann. In the harsh light, Massow's clothes appeared shabby, his big, kindly face was creased with worry lines, and he looked serious.

"Do you have any idea of how immigrants are treated in this country, Herr Volkmann? There are five million people of immigrant stock in Germany. In France, in Italy, there is a similar problem, but my real concern is Germany. Many of them came here in the years after the war, when there was a labor shortage and ordinary Germans had become too affluent and proud to do menial work. They came as laborers and did the dirty work most Germans refused. They settled and had families and made a life for themselves in this country. Now they are almost seven percent of the population, a figure greater than the Jews before the last war. But unlike the majority of Jews of that time, many are caught in a poverty trap. There was a time when these people were needed. Now we have Germans from the former East bloc, along with immigrant ethnic Germans, who are quite willing to take their jobs.

"The German employment laws demand that every worker be treated equally, but the reality is somewhat different. Wages among immigrants are lower than average and unemployment runs at twenty-five percent. So they live in ghettos and immigrant hostels. The problem, then, is real and troubling. But even more troubling is Germany's response. When the racists and neo-Nazis provoked violence, it caused not only indignation, but demands for a limit to the number of foreigners entering this country. As if the victims were at fault and not those people persecuting them.''

Massow frowned. ''Now, when there is terror, the politicians say they don't have enough police. Yet when the terrorists rack this country, the police manage to guard almost every important businessman and executive in the land.''

Massow looked out at the bright sunlight, then back at Volkmann. ''When you leave this office, Herr Volkmann, take a walk through the streets. Look at the living conditions. Look at the faces of the people living in this neighborhood. *Really look.* They are frightened people. Frightened of the shaven-headed toughs who attack their homes. Frightened of the future. What you see outside, Herr Volkmann, is a tinderbox waiting to be ignited. Because someday these people are going to raise their voices and organize themselves and fight back. And then you will have big trouble. The whole damned country will be set ablaze.''

Massow shook his head ruefully. ''Sometimes I wonder if things have really changed in over fifty years.''

''What do you mean, Herr Massow?''

''Before the last war, the rally call of the Nazis was *Judenfrei.* Free of Jews. These days, it's *Ausländerfrei:* Free of foreigners. Today there are hardly any Jews left in Germany. But there are immigrants who might become the nation's next scapegoats. And the same feelings are there. The same undercurrents. Because these people are not Aryans with blond hair and blue eyes, they are not considered Germans.'' Massow sat forward. ''Let me give you an example. The ultra-right Deutsche Volksunion Party alone once used a simple anti-immigrant slogan in the state of Bremen during the elections there. ''The Boat is Full,'' they said. And for that, they gained six more seats in Parliament.''

Massow sat down again slowly and said, ''Forgive me, Herr Volkmann. This is not what you came here to talk about. You asked about this man Winter and I end up giving you a lecture on what's wrong with Germany.''

Volkmann said, "Herr Massow, you're certain you never heard of Dieter Winter?"

Massow shook his head. "Never."

As Volkmann stood, Massow offered his hand and said, "I wish you luck with your investigation. Good day, Herr Volkmann."

He walked back through the streets to the U-Bahn Station.

The winter sun was still shining and the air clear and cold. The suburb was a busy maze of thoroughfares and as he walked, he did what Massow had suggested. Massow's claims seemed slightly histrionic as befitted a politician, but Kreutzberg had been a working-class area since before the last war, and the immigrant tenements he passed were derelict and shabby.

Near the station he bought a bratwürst from a Turkish vendor and as he stood eating and waiting for the train, he noticed the station walls daubed with racist slogans, and here and there, the hastily painted swastikas.

The people on the platform had the same dark, haunted brown eyes of his father, and for a moment Volkmann thought of the faces in the old black-and-white photographs of the ghettos at Warsaw and Cracow.

He pushed the thought from his mind as the train pulled into the station, the doors opened and he stepped on board.

When he got back to the hotel at noon, there was a message for him saying that Jakob Fischer had rung ten minutes before and given a number to reach him. When he called, he heard Fischer's voice.

"I found the girl, Joe."

"Where is she?"

"Still in Berlin, but she's a Westie now."

"You've got a telephone number, Jakob?"

"Sure. I rang her a little while ago. She said she didn't want to talk about Rauscher's murder. I told her I didn't want to have her brought to the station and go through all that routine and that I wouldn't take up much of her time. Just a quick, friendly chat."

"What did she say?"

"She'll talk to us. She'll be at home about eight. Can I pick you up about eight-thirty?"

"Sure. I'll be in the foyer."

The apartment was south of the city in Friedenau, and when they came out of the elevator on the third floor, Fischer rang the buzzer.

She was about thirty, with long blond hair and very good-looking. She wore tight black ski pants and flat shoes, and her white T-shirt was tucked tightly into her pants. She was a big girl, and Volkmann watched her as she closed the door and led them into the living room.

The apartment was done in a modern style and the lighting was soft. There were framed modern paintings on the walls and a couple of charcoal nude drawings in expensive metal frames.

Jakob Fischer showed the girl his ID, but she didn't pay much attention to it and she hardly looked at Volkmann.

"I told you on the telephone: I told your people everything I know."

"I understand that, Frau Worch, but my colleague would like to ask you a few questions. We won't take up much of your time."

Volkmann looked at the girl and she looked back at him indifferently.

"How long did you know Herbert Rauscher, Frau Worch?"

"Two years."

Volkmann looked at the girl's eyes. "Did you ever hear of a man named Dieter Winter?"

"No."

"Are you sure Herbert Rauscher didn't know of anyone with that name?"

The girl shrugged. "I don't know."

Volkmann went through the other names, but the girl just shook her head indifferently. "I didn't know any of his business acquaintances or friends. The only people I knew that he was friendly with were a couple of the photographers he used."

"And you never heard him mention those names?"

"No."

The girl looked back at him steadily and he guessed she was telling the truth.

"Was Rauscher involved with any political group?"

The girl looked at him. "What do you mean?"

"Did he ever express any political opinions to you?"

The girl frowned, then shrugged. "He sometimes said how shitty it used to be living under the Soviets. Is that what you mean?"

"Anything else?"

The girl half smiled, then the smile left her face. "Mostly he talked about himself—his business, office gossip, projects he was working on. He was an easygoing man. Likable. He didn't put pressure on you. Some people may have found him boring, but I liked him."

"Was he ever racist in his remarks?"

"I don't understand."

"Did he ever say how he felt about the immigrants in this country?"

The girl looked at Fischer. "What is this?"

"Please just answer the questions, Frau Worch."

The girl looked back at Volkmann. "No."

"Did he have any right- or left-wing acquaintances, or friends or enemies?"

"What do you mean?"

"Extremists. Neo-Nazis. Terrorists."

The girl laughed and her breasts heaved under the flimsy cotton. "Is this some kind of joke?"

Jakob Fischer said, "Please just answer the question."

"Herbert didn't mix with anyone like that."

"What about his background?"

"What about it?"

"Did he ever talk about his past? His parents? His family?"

The girl shrugged. "Once or twice, sure. But he didn't say much."

"Tell me what he did say."

"His mother died when he was twenty. His father he never knew."

"Why?"

The girl shrugged again. "He died in some camp."

"A concentration camp?"

The girl grinned. "No. One of those places in Siberia the Russians sent our soldiers to after the war."

"Why was Rauscher's father sent there?"

"He was a Nazi. Some kind of officer. I don't know what. Herbert only mentioned it once. When he was drunk."

"What did he say?"

"That his father had been wounded in Berlin at the end of the war and had been captured by the Russians and sent to one of their camps in Siberia. That he was a Nazi officer."

"Do you remember anything else he said about his father?"

"No. Just what I told you. He didn't really talk about his past."

"But you're sure his father was a Nazi officer?"

"That's what Herbert said." The girl sighed impatiently and looked at Volkmann. "Look, is this going to take much longer?"

"One more question. Do you have any idea why your boyfriend was murdered?"

The girl shook her head and said impatiently, "No, I don't. And I told your people that a hundred times already."

Volkmann looked at Jakob Fischer and nodded. Fischer stood up and said, "Thanks for your time, Frau Worch."

He had one drink in the Schweizerhof bar with Jakob Fischer. He thanked the detective for his time and help, and when they had finished their drinks, he walked with Fischer to the foyer.

"What about Rauscher's father, Joe? You going to check up on his background?"

"There's not much point, Jakob. I could try the Russians, but I doubt they'll be much help. And I don't have a rank or any background information for the Documentation Center to be of much use. They'd need a date of birth and a Christian name at least. There could have been hundreds of officers named Rauscher."

"Anyhow, let me know how it works out."

"Sure. I'll call you. And thanks again for all your help, Jakob."

"It's been good seeing you again, Joe. Take care."

He watched Fischer go and then he went up to his room and poured himself a scotch. He opened the window and stood at the cold balcony.

None of it made any sense to him. If what Monika Worch had said was true about Rauscher's father being a Nazi officer, then Rauscher would have been the least likely target for Winter's people. But there was nothing in the man's background to suggest that he was involved with either right- or left-wing groups. And besides, Herbert Rauscher would have been a small child when his father had been captured by the Russians and probably never knew the man, as the Worch girl had said.

He wondered if the fact that Rauscher's father had been a Nazi was a mere coincidence. So many people of Rauscher's age had had parents in the German Army; he guessed that maybe it was irrelevant and there was another angle to it.

He phoned Erica at the apartment before he undressed for bed. He told her about his meeting with Walter Massow and what he had learned about Rauscher.

He heard the frustrated sigh and then Erica said, "What about the woman, Hedda Pohl?"

"We can drive down to Lake Konstanz tomorrow, see if we can turn up anything."

"When will you be back, Joe?"

"I'm taking the first flight back tomorrow."

There was a pause, then Erica said, "Joe . . . ?"

"Yes?"

"I miss you."

"I miss you too."

CHAPTER 26

Volkmann could see the snowcapped mountains of Switzerland across Lake Konstanz as they drove into the pretty lakeside town of Friedrichshafen. There was a light fall of snow as they pulled up on the lake promenade in the late afternoon. Volkmann parked the Ford and they walked back along the lake. Christmas trees twinkled in the windows of the old Bavarian-style houses and the whole town was lit up with colored lights.

He and Erica had lunch in one of the attractive restaurants that overlooked the lake, and Volkmann decided that the best approach was to visit the police station in the town. He couldn't use his DSE identity card without arousing the suspicion of the local police, but he still had the Press ID that Facilities had issued him and he decided to use that. He left Erica in the car and walked back to the station, near the lake front.

There were two officers on duty at the desk. Volkmann showed his ID and asked to speak with one of the senior detectives on duty. He had to wait for ten minutes before a middle-aged man appeared from one of the offices. He was big, ruddy-faced and heavily built, his beer belly protruding over his belted trousers. He introduced himself as Detective Heinz Steiner. When Volkmann showed him the Press ID and asked to speak in private, Steiner shrugged and led him back to a small office down the hall. When they were seated, the detective looked at Volkmann.

"What can I do for you, Herr Volkmann?"

Volkmann told the detective that he was a journalist writing a series of articles on unsolved homicides for a popular German magazine and that he wanted to talk with him about the murder of a local woman named Hedda Pohl five months before. When the detective raised his eyebrows and queried Volkmann's interest further, Volkmann told him he had picked up Hedda Pohl's case from the Munich dailies and thought it would interest his readers. Steiner's eyes flickered with curiosity but he didn't move in his chair.

"What do you want to know exactly, Herr Volkmann?"

Volkmann smiled. "About the woman's background, Herr Steiner. The newspapers didn't go into much detail at the time. And if you have any idea of why she was killed or by whom, I'd be grateful for your help."

Steiner shook his head and his tone became less formal. "We have no idea of why she was killed or by whom, Volkmann. But the case is still open, I assure you."

Volkmann took his notebook and pen from his pocket. "Can you tell me how the woman was murdered?"

Steiner lit a slim cigar and blew smoke up to the ceiling. "Three shots, one in the chest, two to the back of the head at close range. Thirty-eight-caliber slugs. She went out one night in her car, told her son she was going for a walk on the promenade. But she didn't go to the promenade so far as we know. And she didn't come back. Her body was found by a hiker two days later in a forest about two kilometers inland. Her handbag had been rifled through and her purse had been stolen." Steiner frowned and his ruddy face creased with lines. "But the murder was very strange."

"In what way strange, Herr Steiner?"

"You're a journalist, Volkmann. You ought to know that that kind of crime isn't prevalent in this area."

"Of course, but I thought you meant something about the case."

"That too. Hedda Pohl was not your typical victim for that kind of death."

"Tell me."

"Lots of reasons why. The style of murder was more like a gangland killing. Hedda Pohl was sixty-two. A widow. Well-off, but not rich. No vices. Absolutely no criminal past or convictions. The woman hadn't ever been given a parking ticket, in fact. A very upstanding lady who was involved in her community and church." Steiner hesitated and drew on his slim cigar. "And there was something else. We found her car nearby in the woods. It was like she went to meet someone she knew. But her family knew of no prearranged meeting."

Volkmann scribbled a few notes in his pad and asked, "Was she active politically?"

Steiner's eyebrows rose. "No, definitely not. Why do you ask that?"

"No reason, just trying to get a fix on the lady. How well did you know her, Herr Steiner?"

Volkmann thought for a moment that the detective was going to say something, but instead, Steiner leaned back in his chair.

"Quite well."

"Is there anything else about her background you think might help me?"

Steiner shrugged. "Her husband used to be a respected businessman. He's dead maybe ten years."

"What about him, did he have any criminal background?"

Steiner laughed and shook his head. "He was as clean-living as a Lutheran minister. A good man. Very upstanding."

"How did he die?"

"Heart attack, so far as I recall."

"What about her family?"

"All upstanding. And as I said, she was a good woman and well-liked locally." Steiner shrugged. "As to the murder, the only scenario we can think of that makes sense is that she picked up a hitchhiker. Some crazy who decided to rob her and kill her."

"What about clues?"

Steiner puffed on his cigar and shook his head. "Nothing. No fingerprints. No clues. Whoever did it must have been very careful. A professional criminal perhaps. Or someone who had killed before. And we checked every usual angle. Family, friends, acquaintances. But nothing that gave off a whiff of suspicion."

Volkmann looked at his watch, then said, "Thanks for your help, Herr Steiner. I'm sure you're a very busy man, so I won't take up any more of your valuable time."

"You're welcome, Volkmann. You'll send me a copy of your article?"

"I'll do that, certainly."

The snow had stopped and a cold, fresh breeze blew in off the lake as they walked along the promenade.

Erica slipped her arm through his, and when they sat on one of the benches that faced out toward the water, she said, "There's no obvious reason why Winter's people would want to kill her. She had no terrorist connections. No criminal past."

"There has to be a connection somewhere between Rauscher, Hedda Pohl, and Massow, Erica. We just can't see it."

"So what happens now?"

Volkmann shook his head. "I wish I knew."

She pursed her lips, as if she were about to say something; then she seemed to change her mind. She shivered, and Joseph looked at her.

"What's the matter?"

The blue eyes smiled up at him. "I'm just cold. Take me back to the car, Joe."

As Volkmann stood, he looked out at the gray choppy waters of Lake Konstanz. There was a small boat with a blue sail tossing in the swell, and as it tried to hug the shore farther along the lake, the image seemed oddly fitting. He felt hopelessly lost, and there and then he made up his mind to leave aside his reluctance to deal with the Germans and to talk with Werner Bargel of the Landesamt in Berlin.

The Landesamt was the German equivalent of MI5 or CIA and the section responsible for keeping track of terrorist and extremist organizations in all categories. Volkmann knew it was the only hope he had of turning up more information on Kesser and Winter. If there was anything of significance in either man's past, then the Landesamt would have it in their files.

As he looked out at the choppy waters, he wondered what Sanchez was doing. If he had made any headway, the man would have called him, he was certain of that. He turned back and joined Erica and she leaned in close as they walked back to the car.

CHAPTER 27

Berlin. Saturday, December 17

Werner Bargel sat in his office in the building on the corner of Auf dem Grat and Clay Allee in Berlin's Dahlem district and waved to the chair opposite for Joseph Volkmann to join him.

At forty-two, Bargel was one of the youngest men ever to hold the position of assistant director of the *Landesamt für Verfassungsschutz* in Berlin, the state office for the Protection of the Constitution, otherwise known as LfV.

The function of the LfV is similar to British MI5, in that its purpose is to gather intelligence on terrorists, extremist organizations and espionage networks that are a threat to security, except that in the case of the Landesamt, its responsibilities usually concern only the city and state of which it is a part, and generally not the country as a whole. For unlike MI5, the German intelligence service is regionalized.

Its offices are divided up into nineteen departments, each called a Landesamt, or State Department, with each Landesamt responsible for intelligence-gathering within the state to which it belongs. However, all Landesamt offices come under the umbrella of the central federal office in Cologne, called the *Bundesamt für Verfassungsschutz*, or the federal office for the Protection of the Constitution, and while each Landesamt is autonomous, it is ultimately responsible to the Cologne main office.

The beige-painted, two-story Landesamt building in the leafy Berlin suburb of Dahlem looks unremarkable to the passerby, but its offices house almost a hundred staff members who are daily engaged in gathering vital intelligence information—on terrorism, extremist organizations, and those engaged in espionage against the state of Berlin—and it keeps comprehensive files on anyone who is or was engaged in such activities in the past. The building overlooks a neat park, and most Berliners are unaware of it. And just two doors away is the home of the CIA head of station in Berlin.

Like all Landesamt in Germany, the director, or head, is a political appointment, and can change with each election. But the assistant director and next in line is always a senior, professional intelligence officer, and it is he who bears responsibility for the day-to-day running of the department.

Tall, thin, and boyishly fresh-faced, Werner Bargel looked more like a young, bespectacled accountant than a senior intelligence officer.

"Well, Joe, what brings you to Berlin?" He looked across at Volkmann and smiled. "It must be at least a couple of years since we last met?"

"I'd like to pick your brains, Werner. And ask you a favor."

Bargel raised his eyebrows. "Is this something you're working on that directly concerns my people?"

"It's too early to say."

"What kind of information are you looking for?"

"Have you been getting much trouble from the extremist groups recently?"

Werner Bargel sat back in his seat, placed his hands behind his neck. "Whenever you get a recession, you always get an upsurge in left- and right-wing activity, you know that, Joe. You get our monthly and annual reports from Cologne?"

"Sure."

"As I recall, there's a piece in this month's report about a percentage rise."

"What about the right wing, any new groups?"

"A couple, none that have caused us much grief. But the old ones have been pretty active of late. The usual stuff. Last month in Hoyerswerda another refugee center was evacuated after a three-day siege by right-wing gangs. Two black street vendors were stabbed in Leipzig a week later. A Turkish boy was tossed from a second-floor window in Essen and died from his injuries the same day. I could go on. But it's all in the report I told you about."

"Are your people worried?"

Bargel smiled thinly. "That kind of thing always worries us, Joe. We try to keep it under control. But there's always going to be that fringe element in every country, isn't there?"

"What about the immigrant extremist groups? Are they hitting back?"

"At who?"

"The right wing, the neo-Nazis."

Bargel shrugged. "There are a few organized gangs that hit back after right-wing attacks. But it's small-scale, Joe. They're mainly defensive groups, not offensive." Bargel stared at him. "Is that the real reason for your visit? All that stuff you can get in our reports you receive."

"A few weeks ago, a young man named Dieter Winter was shot to death in Berlin. You recall the case?"

Bargel frowned, thought for a moment. "The incident at the Zoo Station?"

"That's the one."

"What about it?"

"I'd like to know if you kept a file on Winter. I saw a BP report on him, but there was very little in it."

Bargel smiled. "They don't plumb to the same depths as we do, naturally. I can have it checked. Anything else?"

"I'm flying to Munich tomorrow. Winter had an address there, but the BP had no record of it. I'd like you to contact the Landesamt people in Munich. I need to take a look at Winter's place if they know where it is. Also, a guy named Lothar Kesser. Comes from somewhere in Bavaria. Graduated from Munich University about four years ago in computer science. If you've got a file on him and a photograph, I'd like to see them too."

"That'll probably be Munich, but it shouldn't be a problem. If they or any of the Landesamt offices have a file on him, they can send us a copy within minutes. Was Winter involved with a right-wing group?"

"That's what I'm trying to find out. The weapon used in the Zoo Station shooting was used on a British industrialist in Hamburg a year ago. That's why Ferguson is interested."

"What about this guy Kesser?"

Volkmann hesitated. "I'm only fishing at this stage, Werner. There may be no connection."

"You think some immigrant extremist group could have hit Winter?"

Volkmann shook his head and smiled. "You're way ahead of me, Werner. I really don't know."

"But you'll keep me informed if anything comes up that we ought to look into?"

"Sure."

"I'll get you a copy of last month's report as well. And a preview of the month's to come." Bargel stood up.

"I'd appreciate that, Werner."

"You're staying in Berlin tonight?"

"At the Schweizerhof."

"I can have my secretary book a table for us at Le Bou Bou, if that's okay with you."

"Why not? We can have a chat about old times."

The restaurant on the Kurfurstendamm was almost empty but the service superb, as always.

Bargel had brought along the reports and the files that Volkmann had requested but he did not discuss them, except to say that he had arranged for Volkmann to be met in Munich by a Landesamt man and taken to Winter's last known address, an apartment in Haidhausen, and that the Munich contact would fill him in when he arrived. They spent almost two hours talking about the old days in Berlin and when they had finished their meal, Bargel walked with Volkmann back to the hotel.

As they strolled along the Kurfurstendamm toward the Budapester Strasse, Bargel said, "Do you ever see Ivan Molke now, Joe?"

Volkmann shook his head and said, "You know he took early retirement. Before he did, we used to talk now and again, but we've been out of touch for the last couple of years. I hear he's in Munich."

Bargel nodded. "Right." He caught Volkmann's eye. "Maybe you should call him up when you go south. I suspect he could be useful to you. I can give you his number before you go."

Volkmann brightened, liking the idea. "A good thought. I think you're right."

"You and he were pretty close."

"Sure, you could say that. I feel bad that we've gotten out of touch. But you know how it is."

Bargel shrugged. He did know how it is. Then he asked, "Can I ask you a personal question, Joe?"

"Sure."

"What did you and Ivan do with Felder?"

"I thought you knew." When he saw Bargel shake his head, Volkmann said, "We took him out to the Grune-wald."

"I always wondered. The bastard deserved what he got." He looked at Volkmann and said, "It was a lousy business in those days."

"Your people have still got the boys who do the dirty work?"

"You mean the killing?"

"Yes."

"No way, Joe. In those days, it was the Stasi and the KGB we were up against. Our group who looked after that kind of thing was disbanded after the Wall came down."

"For sure?"

"For sure. Molke will tell you so himself." Bargel smiled. "Nowadays we're clean as green."

Volkmann hesitated, then asked, "Where do your police and armed forces stand politically? How do they feel about right-wing activity?"

Bargel shrugged. "They're apolitical, or supposed to be. What they think personally, of course, is quite another matter. But sure, I guess some might sympathize with fascist groups. But there's nothing we can do about that, so long as it doesn't interfere with their work." The intelligent eyes regarded Volkmann carefully. "Why do you ask, Joe?"

"The number of right-wing attacks is increasing. But your people don't seem to be having much success stopping them."

Bargel said, "It's a difficult area, you must know that. You've got the usual calls to put all these extremists away. But if you started doing that, you'd get the bleeding-heart liberals who oppose them saying we're becoming a police state again, putting people in concentration camps. And for us Germans, that's a touchy subject." Bargel shook his head. "There's no easy solution. Some of the right-wing groups have been proscribed. That's dampened the activity a bit, but not entirely. But then, you only have to read the papers to know that."

"Do these people have much support?"

"You mean the right-wing groups, the neo-Nazis?"

"Yes."

"Some, but their extreme policies wouldn't appeal to the majority of Germans, that goes without saying."

"What kind of numbers are we taking about?"

"In Germany? A conservative figure would be sixty thousand."

"Hard-line?"

"Pretty much hard-line. You could probably triple that figure with softer supporters."

"That's a lot of support, Werner."

The intelligent eyes looked at Volkmann. "What you're really wondering is, could it happen again? Could a political party like the Nazi Party ever come to power again in Germany? Are you asking me that, Joe?"

"If I remember my history, the Nazis had fewer than five thousand supporters when Hitler led the beer-hall *putsch* in nineteen twenty-three. When he started his campaign to become chancellor of Germany, the Nazi Party had fewer than a quarter of a million members."

Bargel shook his head fiercely. "It couldn't happen again, Joe. Politically and legally, it's enshrined in our Constitution, surely you know that? Only those parties that conform to the Constitution are admitted to the political system. Which is why the communists and neo-Nazis were banned from political office in the past. And then there is the five-percent barrier. In simple terms, that means that any party polling less than five percent of the vote in an election cannot enter the Bundestag, which effectively excludes extremists and independents from entering our Parliament. But besides all that, people are wiser, Germany would never tolerate another Nazi Party or anything like it.

"Sure, we have a problem with extremists. There's a neo-Nazi riot in the streets of a German city and the world's press prints banner headlines that suggest the Fourth Reich is imminent. But in Germany, these groups have never had great support. And the people who do support them are cranks and misfits. Not responsible Germans. The shaven-headed thugs who beat up immigrants and desecrate Jewish graves are not organized. It's a fringe element. And the ones who are organized are small-scale and we keep them under control as best we can.''

Volkmann looked across at Bargel. "But there are similarities, Werner. The street riots. Immigrants being attacked instead of Jews. The call to have foreigners expelled. All the social and economic problems you had in the past when the Nazis came to power.''

Bargel nodded. "Of course, you can draw parallels in any situation. But another Nazi Party in power? Joe, it's not possible. Germans would not allow it. You may say they allowed it in nineteen thirty-three. But that was different then. Germany was different. The circumstances may appear the same, and in some ways, they are, but they are intrinsically different. And besides, every day we Germans see reminders, on television, in the press, of the sins committed in our name, and the vast majority of us have no wish to repeat those sins." Bargel shook his head vigorously. "That another Nazi Party would ever come to power in Germany? Joe, for that to happen, it would have to be presented to the German people as a fait accompli. And that, I could never envisage happening. I admit there are problems and that some of them appear to be getting worse. But the problems will be resolved, believe me.''

"How?''

"You know of Konrad Weber?''

"The vice-chancellor? Sure.''

"He's also the interior minister, responsible for federal security. He's a good man, Joe. Tough, conservative, but responsible. Weber's already banned some of the more extreme groups. And he's been making more noises lately about the level of extremist activity. Says it's still unacceptable. Between you and me, I hear that he wants to bring in some tough changes in the law to put a brake on these people for good.''

"What's he going to do?''

Bargel smiled. "Even if I knew, I couldn't tell you that, Joe. But my ears in the Interior Ministry tell me Weber's going to crack the whip pretty hard and put a stop to it once and for all.''

They had reached the hotel, and Bargel handed across the large envelope containing the files and reports. "You'll destroy the file copies when you're through with them?"

"Of course."

He shook Volkmann's hand. "If there's anything else you need, give me a call."

"Thanks, Werner."

As Bargel turned to go, he touched Joe's arm and the sharp eyes looked at him. "And don't forget, Joe, if anything comes up that concerns me, let me know."

He read the reports in the hotel room of the Schweizerhof.

There was very little new in Winter's file except that he had been brought up in a Catholic orphanage near Baden-Baden, and there was no mention of his parents' past. Judging from his institutional background, Winter was a classic joiner: a loner who needed to identify with a cause. There was also a report going back three years, stating that Winter had taken part in a right-wing march in Leipzig in which two policemen had been seriously injured. But there was no further evidence of his involvement with such groups.

Kesser's file was a précis that contained very little: a head-and-shoulders photograph of a handsome young man with thinning fair hair and high cheekbones. Graduating from Munich University the same year as Winter, he had worked as a programmer for an unnamed government research establishment on a year's contract before moving to a commercial bank in Nuremberg. Volkmann guessed that the unnamed research organization was military.

There was no mention of Kesser ever having been a member of any right-wing party, and his address was given as the Leopoldstrasse in Munich's Swabbing district. There was no indication given of his present employment. Volkmann guessed the file had been deliberately kept brief because of Kesser's involvement in military research and that the file was probably classified, hence the précis.

The monthly reports Werner Bargel had included mentioned an eighteen-percent rise in the rate of right-wing incidents and attacks, and the preliminary report for the present month estimated a further three-percent rise, but observed that with seasonal unemployment taken into account, such rises should be expected. There were several more incidents noted, including an attack by right-wing extremists on an apartment building in Hamburg four days previously, in which two Turks had been badly wounded.

The report concluded that further incidents were expected over the coming months and that two new neo-Nazi cells had sprung up, one in Regensburg, the second in Cottbus, near the Polish border.

When Volkmann had finished reading the files and reports, he replaced them in the envelope and poured himself a scotch from the mini bar. He stood by the cold balcony, wondering what Erica was doing at that moment.

As darkness fell across the bare winter landscape of the Tiergarten, he could see the Brandenburg Gate, illuminated by sulfur-yellow light, and the winged statue on the gilded Victory Column was lit up so clearly it could be seen for miles.

He remembered the news pictures that had flashed across the world the night the Wall came down, and the happy crowds waving the colors of the Bundesrepublic; the young men climbing on top of the Brandenburg Gate in a rush of fervent nationalism, the looks of joy and energy on their faces that night as he watched in his apartment in Charlottenburg, hearing the passionate voices singing *Deutschland über Alles*, and himself wondering if the character of a nation had really changed that much in fifty years.

The distant roar of a lion in the Zoo distracted him and as he closed the window, he took one last look at the Brandenburg Gate and the Reichstag building, standing close together in the distance, their colonnaded pillars and granite facades illuminated by yellow arc lamps; then he locked the window and went to bed.

CHAPTER 28

Munich was bitterly cold, and it was almost ten when the Landesamt delegated to meet him at the airport pulled up outside Winter's address in Haidhausen.

It was a modest apartment building, and Winter's rooms were on the second floor.

When the man unlocked the door and stepped inside, he handed Volkmann the key and told him he'd wait outside in the car until he had finished.

The studio apartment smelled musty and unused, and a colony of spiders dangled on silken threads from webs in the ceiling fixture. The tiny kitchen was filthy, and in the cupboard under the sink were three empty Bushmills whiskey bottles and a couple of unopened cans of Dutch beer.

Two bookshelves ran along the far wall above the bed. The mattress had been tossed askew, and Volkmann guessed the police had searched the place thoroughly. Among the books were several copies of Spengler's works, and Volkmann noticed a tattered copy of *Mein Kampf*, the Zentner edition, which was standard reading for German history students like Winter, but apart from those, the rest were paperback thrillers. There were no photographs on the shelves and no inscriptions in any of the books.

The driver had told him on the journey in from the airport that after Winter's death, they had received a request to go over the apartment but it had looked as though someone had beaten them to it. Most of Winter's belongings appeared to have been taken, and several of the desk drawers had been emptied. It had been a professional job, and the police hadn't found anything of interest and hadn't wasted their time in taking prints.

Volkmann spent half an hour looking through the apartment before closing the door and stepping down into the cold street to join the driver.

He had booked a room at the Penta on the Hochstrasse, and after he was dropped off, he checked into his room and telephoned the number Bargel had given him for Ivan Molke.

The woman who answered was Molke's sister, and she told Volkmann that her brother was in Vienna on business and wouldn't be back until late that afternoon. He thanked her and said he would phone again in the evening.

Fifteen minutes later, he had showered and unpacked his overnight case and telephoned the Hertz office on the Hochstrasse to hire a car.

The address off the Leopoldstrasse in Swabbing turned out to be a fairly prosperous-looking block and Volkmann found Kesser's name on the intercom outside.

It had started to rain as he walked back down the street. He found an office-supplies shop in a mall around the corner and bought a plastic clipboard and large notepad. When he walked back to the apartment block, he wrote down the names of all the residents on the intercom on his pad and then pressed all the intercom buttons except Kesser's. During the barrage of questions that followed, the door lock buzzed and sprang open. Someone expecting someone.

As he stepped inside, an elderly woman appeared and looked at him quizzically, her eyes going to the clipboard.

Volkmann smiled and said, "Block management. A problem with the plumbing."

The woman nodded and went back into her apartment.

He climbed the stairs to the second floor, knocked on Kesser's door, and when there was no reply the second time, he removed the filed penknife from his pocket and probed the lock. It took him less time than he had thought; he stepped into Kesser's apartment and closed the door after him.

Volkmann checked the bedroom first and looked through the mirrored clothes closets. There was a suitcase containing old clothes and a pair of worn-looking climbing boots. In one of the drawers he found several parcels of new baby clothes still in their cellophane wrappers. He checked under the bed and mattress and then looked in the kitchen and bathroom.

He left the living room until last. There was a photograph of Kesser and a pretty young blond girl on the windowsill.

There were a couple of dozen books on the shelves, computer-programming titles mostly, and Volkmann came across a recent Bundeswehr signal-operations codebook marked *"Geheim"*—"Secret"—and some books on Ada, the military programming language. An album on one of the shelves contained photographs from Kesser's youth and university days, and in one of them Volkmann saw a picture of Kesser and Winter together, taken in a beerhall, the two young men smiling out at the camera.

When Volkmann leafed back toward the front of the album, he saw a photograph of an older man who slightly resembled Kesser. But it was a snapshot taken long ago in black-and-white and the man was in the uniform of a Leibstandarte SS general, posed beside a burned-out Russian tank. He looked young for a general, and there was a written inscription at the bottom of the photograph: *"To Hildegard with love. Manfred. October 1943."*

On one of the pages there was another picture of the same man, but this time in color, and the man much older, sitting outside a house somewhere in the mountains, a young boy on his knee, and Volkmann guessed from the resemblance that the boy was Lothar Kesser as a child, the features unmistakably similar. There was a date written in the bottom right-hand corner: April 4, 1977.

He heard the faint sound of a car pulling up in the parking lot below. Volkmann closed the album and replaced it on the shelf. He crossed to the window. A young man had stepped out of a gray Volkswagen and as he locked the door, a blond, attractive girl in her early twenties, and looking obviously pregnant, stepped out of the passenger side, her stomach bulging under a floral maternity smock.

Volkmann recognized Kesser and the girl from the album photographs.

He took a note of the telephone number and then stepped out into the hallway and closed the door. He passed Kesser and the girl on the first-floor landing, the couple ignoring him as they juggled flimsy plastic bags of groceries. The girl looked much prettier close up, and Volkmann noticed that neither Kesser nor the girl wore a wedding ring.

In the parking lot, he took the registration number of Kesser's Volkswagen, and five minutes later he drove back to the Penta. He poured himself a scotch from the mini bar and thought about the photograph in Kesser's apartment of the man in uniform. The Leibstandarte SS general could have been Kesser's father, for the family resemblance was unmistakable.

It took him an hour to walk to the Victualan Markt and another ten minutes to find the *Bierkeller*.

The tables and chairs at the front were full, and when he stepped down into the warm bar, he heard a group of young people singing in the corner. He had almost forgotten it was less than a week from Christmas, and then he saw Ivan Molke sitting alone at the end of the bar, hunched over a beer.

He looked older, his hair graying at the temples, and he wore a gray business suit instead of the casual clothes he always used to favor. He recognized Volkmann at once and beckoned to him.

"It's good to see you, Joe," Molke said as he shook his hand firmly.

He looked younger when he smiled, and then he said, "There's a room in the back where we can talk."

He ordered a beer for Volkmann and when it came, he led the way into the small room. There were two trestle tables laid out end to end, thick pine benches at both sides, and the dark, oak-beamed ceiling gave the room a traditional look. Molke explained that the owner was a friend and he thought the room would be more private.

They sat facing each other, and Molke said, "I heard about your father, Joe. I was sorry to learn of his death." There was a pause. "I presumed when you rang me that this wasn't going to be a social call. So maybe you better tell me what it's about."

"I need your help, Ivan."

"What's it got to do with? DSE?"

Volkmann nodded and said, "You're still in the business?"

Molke half smiled. "You know what they say: once in, never out. I quit officially two years ago and came south. But then, you would have heard." He paused to sip his drink. "I'm in partnership in an agency in the city. Countering industrial espionage." He smiled. "Not as exciting as the old days in Berlin, but it pays the bills."

"But you're still in?"

"The State Interior Ministry here calls me in on a consultancy basis maybe once or twice a year." Molke paused. "So what is this about, Joe?"

It took Volkmann almost fifteen minutes to fill Molke in, and when he had finished and shown him the copy of the black-and-white photograph taken of the woman in the Chaco, Molke stared at it a while before frowning.

"Interesting. But what's the connection between the past and the present? Between South America and Germany?"

"That's what I need to find out, Ivan."

"Can you discover who the young woman in the photograph might be?"

Volkmann shook his head. "I haven't had any luck. Besides, it was such a long time ago. And the girl may have been no one important, not even related to Schmeltz. But the man in the photograph may be a clue."

Molke thought for a moment. "Back over twenty years ago, when Willy Brandt got tough on our institutions in Germany responsible for hunting down wanted Nazis, they used several experts to verify identities from photographs. The people they used were mostly academics who specialized in the Nazi period, and some ex-Nazis themselves. I can ask around if you like. If the girl in the photograph was somebody important, they may be able to help identify her."

"Thanks, Ivan."

Molke smiled. "I'm not saying you'll get lucky, but no harm in trying. This guy Kesser whose apartment you checked. What do you intend doing?"

"I'd like to tag him for a few days. Maybe it'll turn up something. If you agree to come in on it, I'll see you get paid consultancy rates."

Molke smiled and waved dismissively. "When do you want to start?"

"Tonight, if that suits you?"

Molke checked his watch. "Okay. I'd better make a call first, to cancel an appointment that's not important. Where are you staying?"

"I'm at the Penta. Room One-two-eight."

"I can meet you there in an hour."

"I appreciate it, Ivan."

"No sweat, Joe. You want to use two cars or one?"

"Two."

"I'll bring along a couple of talkies in case we need them. That way we can keep in touch. They're long-range. The latest stuff."

It was eight-thirty when they pulled up in their cars around the corner from Kesser's apartment. It had stopped raining and the light was on in Kesser's living room, the Volkswagen parked in the lot out front.

They walked back and drove Molke's green BMW back around and parked across the street by the park, from where they could see Kesser's apartment block. Molke gave Volkmann one of the two-way radios, and Volkmann showed him the head-and-shoulders photograph of Kesser.

They sat in the BMW until well after midnight, when the lights in Kesser's apartment went out. A little after one, they decided to call it a night and arranged to meet back at the park at five-thirty.

CHAPTER 29

Thick, juicy steaks and fat sausages sizzled on the charcoal barbeque, and sunlight washed the garden.

Vellares Sanchez gazed down at one of the slabs of meat with no appetite as he speared it with a fork, turned it over to reveal the pink and bloodied rare underneath. Many things were bothering him. Many things, but all connected to one thing.

The face of Rudi Hernandez flashed before his eyes. Lying on the morgue slab, white sheet pulled back, wounds uncovered.

Sanchez grimaced and looked away from the unappetizing meat toward the sunlit garden. Clusters of neighbors, friends, and relatives stood chatting, drinks in hand. A special day. Maria, his youngest daughter, had made her Communion.

Innocent girls in white Communion frocks and boys in ill-fitting suits sipped lemonade and ate chocolate cake and traipsed about the lawn, bored now the ceremony was over. Not that Sanchez necessarily wanted to be here this day himself. But family duty was family duty. He saw Maria catch his eye and wave at him and smiled. He waved and smiled back.

The girl was very pretty, a tribute to her mother's good looks. One day the boys would be falling over themselves to catch her eye. But not yet. Innocence was to be savored.

The girl came up to him, flouncing her white frock.

"Is the food ready yet, Papa? I'm hungry."

Sanchez patted her head of dark, curly hair. "Not yet, my sweet." He saw his wife, Rosario, coming toward him from the patio. She had gone inside the house earlier, to freshen up, Sanchez had thought, but now she had a frown on her face.

He tapped his daughter's shoulder. "Do Papa a favor, precious. Go see if everyone is okay for drinks."

The girl nodded and skipped away.

Rosario came up beside him, still frowning.

"I thought this was your day off?"

"It is."

"Is everything okay?"

He nodded. "The food's almost ready."

"I didn't mean the food." She saw him look at her with sleepy, curious eyes and she said, "Detective Cavales is inside. I asked him to join us, but he said no. He'd rather speak to you in private."

"Then I had better see him. Do me a favor. Take care of the steaks."

As he turned to go, his wife said, "And I thought you were going to be free today."

He shrugged. "So did I." He kissed her cheek as she frowned again. "A policeman's lot is not a happy one."

"Nor his wife's. But you should have told me that before you asked me to marry you."

Sanchez smiled. "And risk losing such a beautiful woman?"

She frowned in mockery, then smiled back at him, picked up two cans of beer from the buffet table and handed them to her husband.

"Take one in to Cavales. He looks as though he could do with a drink."

He took the beers, crossed to the patio and stepped inside. The house was cool after the heat of the garden. Plants and flowers everywhere. Why had women such an obsession with flora, he wondered. It was a mystery he had never been able to solve. He closed the door and crossed to where the detective stood and handed him the beer.

"Compliments of Rosario. She said you looked like you needed one."

Cavales nodded. "It's hot." He looked toward the scene on the lawn outside. "Nice day for a barbeque."

"Maria's Communion," Sanchez explained. Cavales was single. No ties. No responsibilities. But a good cop. Ambitious, in a quiet way. And thorough.

"So," Sanchez said finally. "What brings you to this neck of the woods on my one day off? It's not a social call."

Cavales shook his head. He appeared tired. Like Sanchez, he had been working hard. Days and late evenings working on the case. Manpower was limited right now, with people on summer leave. Sanchez gazed out the window and sipped the cold beer.

"Tell me."

"I've been over at Tsarkin's house again."

Sanchez turned to look at his colleague. "Go on."

"I know we searched it three, maybe four times and found nothing."

Sanchez smiled. "But you wanted to pick over the bones?"

Cavales nodded. "Something like that."

"So what did you find that the rest of us couldn't?"

"What makes you think I found something?"

"You see enough of my face at the office. And I'm not such an attractive man."

Cavales smiled. "You're right."

"That I'm not such an attractive man or that I was right?"

"The second."

"Good. For a moment I thought you were going to hurt my feelings." Sanchez half smiled, sipped his beer, blinked. "So, tell me."

"I went through all the rooms again. Top to bottom. Just in case we missed something." Cavales paused. "We did."

Sanchez raised his eyes. "And what did we miss?"

"Photographs."

Sanchez blinked. "Explain."

"Photographs. Everybody keeps them. Albums. Of friends. Acquaintances. Relatives."

Sanchez shook his head. "There were none. I remember. Except one. A photograph of Tsarkin himself. On a dressing table in his bedroom."

"That's what I mean. There were no other photographs besides the one in the bedroom," Cavales said quietly. "Old people. They always got photographs."

Sanchez smiled. The man had a perceptive mind. "Go on."

"I spoke to Tsarkin's butler about it. He was very uncomfortable when I mentioned the photographs. Even more than when we spoke to him before. Like he had something to hide."

"And did he?"

Cavales nodded. He put down his beer and lit a cigarette, offered one to Sanchez, who accepted. .

"You bet." Cavales glanced toward the scene beyond the window, then back at Sanchez again. "I told him if there was anything he knew and hadn't told us, he could be in big trouble. I told him I wanted him to come down to the station. The old guy got upset. Said he hadn't done anything wrong."

"But what *had* he done?"

"He said the day after Tsarkin committed suicide, and before we thoroughly searched the property, a man came to the house. An acquaintance of Tsarkin's who occasionally visited, a businessman, the butler thought. He asked what the police had done and wanted to know if there were any papers left behind by Tsarkin. When the butler said no, he said he wanted to look just in case. The butler protested, but the man persuaded him it might be better if he cooperated."

"This man threatened him?"

Cavales shrugged. "Implied, rather than outright."

"Continue."

"He searched the house thoroughly, then took away some photograph albums Tsarkin kept."

"And?"

"That's it. He also ordered the butler to tell no one he had been there, or that anything was missing."

Sanchez sighed, blew out smoke. He sat on the edge of the chair by the window. "Did you get a name?"

Cavales smiled and nodded. "After a little friendly persuasion."

"The name?"

"Franz Lieber."

"Who is he?"

"All I know right now is that he was an acquaintance of Tsarkin's. But the name is obviously German."

Sanchez glanced out the window toward the sunlit gardens and the cheerful knots of visitors. Maria was comparing dresses with another little girl. His wife stood among a circle of female friends, laughing. He loved that woman, loved her to distraction. Many times he wished he wasn't a cop, had chosen a different vocation so that he could spend more time with her and Maria.

He turned to Cavales. "Give me an hour. I'll meet you at the office. I want Lieber's address and information on his background."

"I'm checking already. Two of the day shift are working on it."

Sanchez nodded. "An hour then."

When Cavales had left quietly without finishing his beer, Sanchez moved closer to the window.

Sunshine swamped the lawn. The sound of laughter reached him. A day to enjoy. Rosario wouldn't like it if he left, but he had work to do. He checked his watch; half an hour, then he'd drive to the office.

He stubbed out his cigarette and went to rejoin his guests.

4:35 P.M.

The brothel was near the railway station and the Plaza Uruguaya.

Despite its shabby exterior, inside, the decor was sumptuous. Coral-blue stucco walls, expensive cotton-print drapes. Silk-sheeted beds. Saunas and steaming showers for clients. Private rooms were decorated with panache and with an eye for the discerning patron.

The girls were equally attractive, reputedly the prettiest in Asunción. And the most expensive.

Lieber had picked a girl no more than seventeen. His companion had preferred a more mature woman. Large-busted, thirty, voluptuous hips. Two bottles of champagne had been brought.

When they had been drunk and the sex was over, Lieber found his wallet and peeled off some notes and handed them to the girls as they threw on flimsy gowns. The second man still lay on the bed, a glass of champagne in his hand, a grin on his weasel face.

"Take it," Lieber said to the girls. "A bonus."

As the girls went to leave, Lieber said to the older of the two, "My friend and I have some business to discuss. Tell Rosa to make sure we're not disturbed."

She nodded and left with her friend, Lieber watching the
pair of pale, retreating buttocks through her flimsy gown
with diminishing pleasure.

He took two fresh glasses and a half-finished bottle from
a nearby table and turned to the still-naked man sitting on
the bed.

"Well, Pablo . . . you're satisfied?"

The man opposite Lieber was small and wiry. His name
was Pablo Arcades. For ten of his thirty-five years he had
been a *seguridad* officer, an invaluable acquaintance of Lieber's. Especially since the man had two universal vices:
money and women. As vices, they were weaknesses to be
exploited.

The man grinned as he pulled on his trousers. "You
know me. I could fuck all day." He zipped his pants and
slipped on his shirt. "You brought the money?"

"Afterwards. First, let's talk."

6:02 P.M.

Lieber drove back through the darkening Asunción streets.

He had made the call on the mobile phone ten minutes
before. He'd remembered her name from the list. He verified that. Yes. Her name was one of those in the web. She
would have to be contacted as a matter of urgency, of that
much Lieber was certain, to confirm what had happened,
the ramifications of any further progress made clear to her.

The rest of Arcades' information he would pass on. It
would have to be acted on quickly. The men would have
to be dealt with. Volkmann. Sanchez. But Volkmann's part
he couldn't understand; a *British* DSE officer, and not
German. If anything, it should have been German. Lieber
shook his head in confusion; the girl would be able to explain. He didn't understand why she hadn't been contacted
before now. What was the bitch up to?

His mind was preoccupied as he went through a list of
what had to be done. First contact security, then Kruger in
Mexico City. They were there for another forty-eight hours.
There was business to be discussed with old Halder and the
Brazilian, Ernesto. And there would be visitors, old faces

calling to pay their respects, and offering their advice for the days ahead.

Arcades' information would have to be discussed, decisions made; the girl's position clarified, take her out of the web or keep her in.

Lieber turned the Mercedes into the driveway of his house, going fast, tires burning on gravel.

Out of the corner of his eye he caught sight of two men standing behind the open gates. Lieber, startled by their presence, was already fifteen meters beyond them, about to slam on the brakes and look back, when his eyes caught sight of a second irregularity.

The lights were on in the porch, and another two men stood there, an unfamiliar white car parked directly outside the front door.

Panic gripped him but there was no time. Already he had reached the top of the gravel path and come to a sharp halt in front of the car.

Lieber climbed out warily as the two came quickly forward.

"What's going on? Who are you?" Lieber demanded.

One of the two men spoke. He was a large, hulking man, his grubby suit loose on his oversized body.

"Señor Lieber, I presume?"

Lieber said nothing.

The big man smiled thinly as he looked up. "My name is Sanchez. Captain Vellares Sanchez."

CHAPTER 30

Asunción. 6:32 P.M.

Every light inside the house appeared to be on, the *mestizo* butler nowhere to be seen.

They were in the study. The two detectives and Lieber. The big detective smoked a cigarette as his companion sifted through the contents of Lieber's polished walnut desk. The locks had been forced; papers and documents lay scattered on the floor and on top of the polished wood.

Lieber looked at the big detective palely.

"You have no right . . ."

"Señor, I have every right."

"May I remind you that I am a personal friend of the police commissioner's . . . ?"

"And might I remind you that my search warrant is in order?"

Lieber had seen the warrant, signed by a magistrate.

"There is no need to subject me to such treatment. If you would only tell me what it is you are looking for . . . ?"

"I told you already."

"I don't know what photographs you're talking about. All I know is that my property has been damaged. And that this is a flagrant abuse of—"

"Please, Señor. Spare me." The hooded, sleepy eyes regarded Lieber carefully. "If you simply tell us where the photograph albums, are, it would help matters."

"I really don't know what you are talking about."

Sanchez ignored the gaping look of acted innocence on Lieber's face. "As I explained already, they were taken from the house of a friend of yours the day after he killed himself. Tsarkin's butler already told us. Really, Señor, you are wasting my time."

Lieber swallowed. "I refuse to speak until I have contacted my lawyer."

"As you wish. You have a safe in the house?"

"A safe?"

"A safe for personal belongings. Businessmen usually

have one, and you own several businesses in Asunción, Señor. An import-export agency. A property-development company. A plush office on the Calle Palma.'' Sanchez paused, letting Lieber know he'd done his homework, saw the man's eyebrows rise. ''So, do you have a safe here in the house?''

''That is none of your business.''

''Señor, you can be agreeable and cooperate. To do otherwise will certainly not help your situation.''

''And what *is* my situation?''

The big man scratched his ear. ''If I am unsatisfied with your replies, you may find yourself under suspicion of being an accessory to the murder of one Rudi Hernandez, journalist. And two other murders, also.''

''That is quite ridiculous,'' Lieber said hoarsely. ''I don't know what you are talking about.''

The detective ignored Lieber's words. ''You haven't answered my question. You have a safe?''

Lieber thought for a moment, then slowly took a set of keys from his pocket, handed them to the big detective. ''In the bedroom upstairs facing onto the driveway, you will find a painting. A Vermeer copy. Behind it you will—''

Sanchez took the keys. ''I know.''

He spoke quietly to the two detectives for several moments before handing one of them the keys. The men left. Lieber heard their footsteps quickly climb the stairs.

Left alone with the big man, Lieber glanced around, then said amicably, ''Amigo, there must be some mistake. You know, I have friends in high places, people who could—''

The detective raised his hand to silence Lieber's words. ''Please. Spare me.'' He sat down and produced a cigarette, lit it. ''My men will search the rest of the house again. To be certain. This may take a little time.''

''My lawyer . . .''

Sanchez waved his hand dismissively once again and drew on his cigarette, blew smoke out into the warm air. ''I suggest you remain silent.'' He smiled thinly. ''I'm sure you are quite happy to do that.''

Lieber pursed his lips and said nothing.

* * *

It took almost an hour of waiting yet he felt strangely confident. There was nothing in the house to incriminate him. Nothing to connect him to what had happened to the journalist and the girl. Not a shred.

He saw the two detectives come into the room as he sipped a scotch. One of them carried an album of photographs. Lieber frowned. It was an old album he kept in his bedroom. It hadn't been added to in years.

He saw Sanchez take it in both hands and examine it, begin to flick through the cellophaned leaves. After a time he pursed his lips and looked up, walked over to where Lieber stood.

Sanchez held up the album. "This is yours?"

Lieber hesitated, then said, "Yes, it belongs to me."

Sanchez leaned forward and pointed to a photograph in the album. Lieber swallowed.

"This snapshot," Sanchez asked. "Where was it taken?"

The picture was of a white house. Three men together, Lieber one of them. Jungle flora cutting in on the right of the frame.

"I can't remember," he said hoarsely.

"*Think*. In the Chaco perhaps?"

"I told you. I can't remember. It's an old photograph."

The detective saw the look on Lieber's fleshy face and pointed again to the photograph. "The man on the left is you. The other two . . . who are they?"

Lieber shook his head as he saw the detective's finger point out the men in the photograph, taken many years before, one stocky, dark-haired and young, the other older, tall, silver-haired, handsome.

"I told you. It was taken a long time ago. I don't recall."

Lieber saw the detective stare at him, frustration on his face. The man was unsure of himself, Lieber could tell. Searching. But lost.

"Señor, on the evening of November twenty-fifth and the early morning of November twenty-sixth where were you?"

Lieber frowned. "I was at home."

"Alone?"

"Apart from one of my staff, yes."

"How can you be so certain?"

"I had important paperwork to attend to."

"No doubt your member of staff will attest to this if necessary?"

"No doubt, yes."

Sanchez glared at the man.

The detective to whom Sanchez had given the keys to the safe returned, shook his head as he handed them back. Sanchez grimaced, placed the keys on the coffee table in front of Lieber.

Lieber said, "Have your men finished?"

The detective hesitated, then said, "For now. *Sí.*" He turned to the other man and gestured for him to leave them.

"You intend arresting me?"

"No."

Lieber suppressed a sigh. "Then I want you and your people off my property." He stood to his full height, towering over the other man. "Your commissioner will hear about this intrusion of my privacy. Now leave. At once."

Sanchez put down the album on the study desk. For a long time he said nothing, simply stood there, staring at Lieber. When he spoke, his voice was low, but threatening.

"Señor, I will be back. Again and again, if necessary. I wish to assure you of that."

"That's harassment."

"No, Señor." Sanchez smiled grimly. "I prefer to call it thoroughness. It is a terrible trait of mine. You must have patience with me."

Lieber felt the anger rise in him. "Be assured, your commissioner will hear from me."

Sanchez's smile broadened. "Yes, I'm certain he will." The detective hesitated, then said, "But you see, Señor, there is a certain matter of a tape. A tape recording of a conversation in a certain hotel. I'm sure you know what I'm talking about. So be assured, you will see me again."

The smugness vanished. Perplexed, Lieber felt the blood rise uncontrollably to his cheeks, saw the detective's hooded eyes stare at him, search for a reaction.

He checked himself, then said hoarsely, "Go."

He watched as the big detective turned and left.

*   *   *

Forty minutes later, Lieber was on the Plaza del Heros. He parked the Mercedes outside and checked the street. He had checked the rearview mirror on the way and so far as he could tell, he had not been followed, deciding to use a public phone in case the scrambler wasn't safe, or the telephones in his house were bugged.

In a hotel near the Plaza he got change in the bar and crossed to the telephone kiosks near the restrooms. He made the two calls he needed to make, listened to the incredulous voices as he sweated in the tiny, hot enclosure. He kept the conversations as short as possible, all the time his eyes searching the hotel lobby to make sure he wasn't being watched. He told them his plans and received their immediate approval.

The third call he made to an unlisted number on the outskirts of the city. Lieber told the man what he wanted done, then put down the telephone and waited for the reply call.

It came less than five minutes later. He listened to the voice and noted the instructions. Less than a minute later, he stepped from the hotel and walked back toward his car. His eyes scanned the busy streets for anyone following him.

No one did.

Sanchez stood at the office window looking down at the fronds of the palm trees along the Calle, a mug of steaming coffee in one hand, a cigarette in the other.

Almost nine o'clock. Traffic streaked below, the blue-and-whites pulling up outside every now and then, disgorging their nightly cargo. Hookers. Pimps. Thieves.

He heard the door open loudly and turned. Cavales came in, closed the door.

Sanchez said, "Well?"

"It was just like you said, he went to make a call. I had four teams following him. Twenty minutes after we left, he drove to the Plaza del Heros and went into a small hotel, the Riva. We think he made just a couple of telephone calls, but we can't be sure. The girl watching him said he was pretty uncomfortable so she didn't push it."

"Go on."

"He drove back home, stayed half an hour. Then he left

and had the manservant drive him to the outskirts. He walked for five minutes, then hailed a taxi. He changed taxis twice. The second took him to the airport, where he picked up a suitcase at the baggage carousel. We tailed the servant too. He drove to the airport after he dropped Lieber off and stashed the suitcase in the carousel, where Lieber picked it up.''

''You managed to check the suitcase?''

Cavales nodded. ''It contained a couple of shirts and a suit. Underwear and toiletries. The usual stuff. Nothing interesting.'' Cavales paused. ''There's something else.''

Sanchez raised his eyebrows but said nothing, waited for Cavales to continue.

''He picked up a package at the information desk, along with the ticket for his luggage. Two of our people followed him to the departure area.''

''They didn't stop him?''

''There was something much more interesting to consider.''

''Tell me.''

''He had a passport in a different name and checked onto a flight for São Paulo, with the first connection to Mexico City tomorrow night. I guess the passport was in the package he picked up. He must be running scared.''

''The name he used?''

''Monck. Julius Monck.''

Sanchez sighed.

Cavales said, ''You want me to get immigration in São Paulo to pick him up?'' He checked his watch. ''The flight doesn't land for over another hour. Possession of an illegal passport is one thing. Using it is another. On that alone, he's got some questions to answer.''

Sanchez said nothing, his eyebrows knit closely together, as if the act of thinking was painful.

After a long time, he looked up.

''Bring me the map from the wall.''

Cavales crossed to the facing wall and unhooked the large hanging map of South America, placed it on Sanchez's desk.

The big detective stared down at the multicolored patterns on the laminated, nicotine-stained cardboard, then be-

gan to trace a finger from the northeast, Chaco, to the
Brazilian border.

After a few minutes' silence, he looked up again.

"The report from the radar people at Bahia Negra. They
said the flight they vectored disappeared toward Corumba,
over the Brazilian border."

"*Sí.*"

Sanchez's finger traced a line on the map. "It's only a
short distance from there to Campo Grande."

Cavales scratched his chin. "I guess so."

"There's an airport at Campo Grande. With a shuttle
service to São Paulo, I believe."

Cavales frowned. "I don't see the point."

"*Think* about it. From Paulo there's a connecting flight
to Mexico City. Lieber's destination. Maybe the people
from the Chaco house took that route. Maybe they went to
Mexico City also. Now Lieber's worried. He needs to talk
to them. In person."

Cavales smiled. Sanchez said, "It's possible, no?"

"*Sí.* Either that or Lieber's running for good."

Sanchez shook his head. "I doubt it. He's scared about
something. We frightened him tonight. You saw the look
on his face when I mentioned the taped conversation? It
really worried him." Sanchez thought for a moment, then
said, "Get onto Chief Inspector Eduardo Gonzales in Mexico City. Inform him of Lieber's likely arrival there in the
name of Monck. And have our people check the passenger
lists on flights from São Paulo to Mexico City in the last
ten days. If the name Karl Schmeltz turns up, let me know.
I doubt that it will; considering that our friend Lieber used
a false passport, Schmeltz could have done the same. But
no harm in checking."

"Is Gonzales a friend of yours?"

Sanchez nodded. "We met at a police conference in Caracas. Have a photograph of Lieber wired to him. Lieber's
connecting tickets are in the name of Monck, so just in case
he has another passport, they should be able to identify him
from the photo. And get onto São Paulo too. Ask them to
watch Lieber when he arrives, make sure he makes the
connecting flight he has booked. If he uses a hotel, ask them
to observe his movements. I want to know of anyone he

meets. But also ask them to be very discreet, to use their best undercover people. It's top priority. I don't want it blown.''

"You want this Gonzales to pick up Lieber?"

"No. Simply followed. I want to know where he goes. Who he meets."

Cavales nodded, went to leave.

"And Cavales . . ."

"Sí?"

"The first available connecting flight to Mexico City. Book two seats." Sanchez smiled thinly. "But not the same route as Lieber, obviously."

Cavales smiled back, nodded and left.

Sanchez opened his wallet and stared down at the photograph. It was the one he had removed from the album in Lieber's house. He had pocketed it deftly. Theft, but justifiable. He doubted that Lieber had noticed, the man had been too distracted.

Now he placed it on his desk and blinked. He stared at the two men flanking Lieber in the picture. From the cut of the clothes, he guessed Lieber hadn't lied when he said the photograph was taken a long time ago. Ten years, maybe, but difficult to say. There was a veranda behind the three men, painted white like the house in the Chaco jungle. And every sense told him it *was* the house in the Chaco.

He scanned the photograph again. He would have the faces of the two men flanking Lieber checked out. Perhaps the files would turn up something.

He sighed now as he thought of the work ahead, ran a hand through his thinning hair. He would telephone his wife and tell her of his plans. No more than a day or two in Mexico City, if he was lucky. He stared down at the photograph of the three men once more as he picked up the receiver and went to dial his home number.

Rosario would understand.

This one was for Rudi Hernandez.

This one was personal.

CHAPTER 31

Munich, Monday, December 19

Volkmann slept until five, then showered and shaved.

As he pulled up outside the park half an hour later, it was still pitch dark but Molke's BMW was already there. The light was on in Kesser's living room and Volkmann could see a shadow move back and forth behind the drawn shades.

As he climbed in beside Molke, the older man said, "The light went on ten minutes ago, just after I got here. Looks like he's getting ready to move. You want to do first tag?"

"Sure."

"Don't forget to keep the radio on. We can change tag every ten minutes. The traffic's going to be pretty thin while he's driving."

"Okay, Ivan."

As Volkmann climbed out of the BMW, Molke grinned and said, "Let's hope Kesser's not just taking an early morning jog in the park, my friend. I'd hate to have got up this early for nothing."

Kesser came out of the apartment half an hour later wearing a blue rainproof anorak and carrying a briefcase.

It had started to rain heavily and when Kesser's Volkswagen pulled out of the parking lot, Volkmann gave him a fifty-meter start before following, seeing Molke's lights behind him.

Fifteen minutes later, the Volkswagen pulled up at a filling-station restaurant on the Munich ring road and Kesser took half an hour over breakfast and read a newspaper before filling his car and taking the road south to Bad Tolz.

The traffic was already busy by seven-thirty, and it was over an hour later when Kesser turned off from the Tergen See road and the Volkswagen began to climb into the mountains. The traffic was light, and several times both Molke and Volkmann had to drop back until they saw the gray Volkswagen turn off to the right and climb up a steep, narrow mountain track.

Volkmann halted the Opel a hundred meters beyond the track. The narrow mountain road Kesser had taken wasn't signposted, but a sign said that the property beyond that point was private and trespassers would be prosecuted. When Volkmann looked up, he saw a steep, rocky outcrop patchy with snow rise above a thick forest of pines, the top of the mountain smothered in a halo of low rain cloud.

Molke pulled up, climbed out of the BMW and moments later slid in beside Volkmann. He rubbed the fogged window and stared up at the pine slopes.

"What do you think, Joe? You want to risk going up after him?"

Volkmann hesitated. "You know what that mountain is called?"

"I saw a sign a kilometer back that said the Kaalberg was this way." Molke smiled. "There's got to be something up that mountain for Kesser to drive all this way. You want to risk playing lost tourist? The last town we passed through had a hunting shop. I could go and get us a couple of walking canes and waterproofs. A little exercise might do us both good."

"Sure, why not?"

Molke smiled and as he climbed out of the Opel into the drizzle, he said, "If Kesser appears again, give me a buzz on the radio. I'll be as quick as I can."

Volkmann moved the Opel just off the shoulder of the road about fifty meters beyond. There was a steep tier of pines leading up to the mountain, and below and to his left lay a deep, wooded valley. The quaint wooden houses of a Tyrolean village were barely visible in the distance through the thin membrane of rain.

As he sat there smoking a cigarette and listening to the radio, he saw the green BMW return almost an hour later. Ivan Molke climbed out carrying two sturdy mountain walking sticks and olive-green waterproof capes. He removed a pair of powerful Zeiss binoculars from the trunk before joining Volkmann.

They decided to keep off the dirt track Kesser had taken and instead climbed up through the thick pines. There were patches of snow in the clearings and the rain had softened to a light drizzle. On the two occasions they crossed the dirt track, they saw that it had been covered with a surface of cracked pebbles and when they had gone a hundred meters into the forest on the far side, Ivan Molke tapped Volkmann's arm and pointed through the trees.

With the powerful Zeiss, Volkmann could make out a narrow wooden sentry hut and two men standing outside. To the right of the hut a gray-painted metal barrier gate was lowered in place. Both men wore civilian clothes and had Heckler and Kochs draped across their chests, and one of the men was smoking a cigarette. Past the gate, Volkmann could make out a narrow road leading up.

Beyond the cover of the trees they could see the sloped, gray-slated high roof of a large traditional berghaus, but the view was too obscured for them to see the place clearly, and the top of the mountain that rose above and behind it was still covered in low cloud. Volkmann thought he saw what looked like a low-walled balcony jutting out from the back of the berghaus, but he couldn't be certain. Beyond the house stood what appeared to be the top of a big, square drab-looking concrete or metal building, maybe twenty meters square, but it was difficult to judge from the distance. To the right of it were what looked like two old, traditional wooden barns with sloped roofs.

Fifteen minutes later, they had moved back down through the forest and were sitting in Ivan Molke's BMW.

"What do you make of it, Joe?"

Volkmann shook his head. "Has the government got any covert research establishments in this part of Germany?"

"Why do you ask?"

"Kesser worked for a government research unit a couple of years back. And those guys at the sentry box wore no uniforms, but they carried Heckler and Kochs."

"There're a couple of hush-hush places in Bavaria, sure. But where, I couldn't say. You want me to try and check it out for you?"

Volkmann thought for a moment before replying. "It'll have to be done discreetly, Ivan. I don't want Berlin or London coming down on Ferguson for playing off-pitch."

"Okay, I'll check it out. But if it gets too hairy, I'll back off quietly. You want to call it a day?"

Volkmann nodded. "But I'd like to have Kesser watched
for the next couple of days. A record of his movements
kept. Who he talks to, who he visits."

"You want me to do it?"

"I'd appreciate it, Ivan. I want to keep it low-key. Otherwise I'll have to call in my own people and that may
cause problems with the German desk. By the time they're
briefed, we'd have lost a few days."

Molke nodded. "I'll get a couple of the men from my
agency, it shouldn't be a problem." He paused. "What
about a bug on Kesser's phone?"

"You think you could do that?"

Molke shrugged. "If his girl stays out of the way long
enough, it might be possible."

"You better warn your people to be careful, in case Kesser is armed. Can I contact you at home?"

"Sure. And if I'm not there, leave a message. I'll start
the watch tonight."

Volkmann checked out of the hotel and returned the rental
car. It was two hours later when they came off the Brienner
Strasse and turned right for the airport.

As they passed the signpost for Dachauer Strasse, a
white-and-green tour bus was turning off toward the
concentration-camp road.

The old camp at Dachau had been preserved after the
war and lay a couple of kilometers to the north, a place the
tourists and the curious came to see and one of the few
remaining legacies of the Third Reich preserved for pos-
terity. He had visited it once before, after his last term at
Cambridge; stood on the infamous Appellplatz where his
father would have stood on cold winter mornings, waiting
for the five-o'clock roll call, the barbed-wire perimeter and
the watchtowers and the gas chamber and the ovens all grim
and tangible reminders of his father's nightmare.

Beyond the rain-streaked glass of the tour bus he could
see the faces of the passengers. Young faces pressing som-
berly against the damp glass. Volkmann saw that several
of them wore skull caps, and a sign against the glass pro-
claimed that they were a student tour group from Tel Aviv
University.

As they overtook the bus, Volkmann noted the grim look on Ivan Molke's face, but neither man spoke.

It was almost seven when he arrived back in Strasbourg, but he drove to the office and checked his desk. There were no messages, and neither Peters nor Ferguson was in his office. There were two Italian officers still on duty, and they stood by the coffeemaker talking with Jan De Vries. Volkmann lingered with them for ten minutes before he telephoned Erica and drove over to the apartment.

She seemed glad to see him and he realized he had missed her in the past forty-eight hours. He booked a restaurant in Petite France, and over dinner she asked him what he had been doing in the last two days. He didn't go into detail and he didn't tell her what had happened with Kesser, just that he had got more information on him and Winter but that for now, it was classified. She didn't question him, and she didn't ask him what the information was, although he could see the curiosity in her eyes.

After dinner, they walked back through Petite France. The old town with its pretty period houses and its narrow, cobbled streets and babbling river was deserted, and at one of the weirs Volkmann stopped to look down at the water. He was aware of her looking at him, and when he turned to look back, he saw the blue eyes linger on his face.

Before he could speak, she had stepped closer and as her lips brushed his cheek, he could smell her perfume.

She slid her arm through his and they turned and walked back through the empty cobbled streets.

He looked back twice, but could see nobody following them.

CHAPTER 32

Strasbourg. Tuesday, December 20

On Tuesday morning, Volkmann had gone into the office at ten to find two telephone messages on his desk. One was from Ted Birken in Zurich, asking to be rung back, and the second was a call from Ivan Molke, urging him to contact his Munich office.

He tried Molke's number first, but the secretary who answered said he was at a meeting and she would have him return Volkmann's call.

When he telephoned Ted Birken's number in Zurich, the line was answered promptly and he heard the polite, cheerful voice of Birken reply.

"I've made a little headway, Joe. Have you got a pen and paper ready?"

"Is it good news?"

"Difficult to say, but it's better than I expected. My contact at the Federal Archives office in Koblenz was transferred, but he passed the request onto a friend, the director of the Berlin Document Center, a chap named Maxwell. He asked him to check back through the early Nazi Party numbers and try to come up with a list of those whose membership was close to Erhard Schmeltz's.

"Maxwell knew about the request from your people for information on Schmeltz and he rang me, wanted to know what it was about. I told him the story, that you had asked me to help, and that we needed to find anyone still living who had had a number close to Schmeltz's. After he had me checked, he got back to me and agreed to have his people go through the files of fifty numbers, twenty-five numbers above Schmeltz's party number and twenty-five below.

"Then I checked with the WASt and the relevant authorities. Out of the fifty names, only four were still alive, and two of those are living in South America. Both of the other two are registered as living in Germany. The first is a man named Otto Klagen, born in Berlin nineteen-ten. He was a fairly young man when he joined the party. His membership application was dated November one, nineteen twenty-seven.''

''Where's Klagen now?''

Volkmann heard Ted Birken sigh at the other end. ''That's the problem. His last address was in an old folks' home in Düsseldorf. I telephoned the home and they said Klagen had a stroke about two months ago and was still in pretty bad shape, hardly able to talk. He's now in the city hospital on Gräulingerstrasse. His mind's not the best apparently, and he's not very coherent, so I doubt if Klagen's going to be of much use to you, even if he had heard of this fellow Erhard Schmeltz. You can try him if you wish, but I wouldn't bet on getting anywhere. Besides, Maxwell said the German authorities investigated Klagen twenty years ago. He was a diehard SS man. The war-crimes people wanted to nail him on atrocities they said he committed in Poland during the war, but the prosecution didn't have enough evidence and had to let the case drop. All a long time ago, of course, but a leopard doesn't change its spots.''

Volkmann took a note of the hospital and said, ''What about the second man?''

''Wilhelm Busch. Like Schmeltz, the place of application was given as Munich.''

''Have you got an address?''

Ted Birken gave Volkmann an address in Munich's northern suburb of Dachau.

''The man will be in his early eighties now. I hope he's in better shape than Klagen. Otherwise you'll be completely wasting your time.''

''Have you got a telephone number for Busch?''

''I'm afraid not. I checked with the operator for the number, but it's unlisted. You'd probably be best just calling cold and catching him unawares; otherwise he might not even consider talking to you.''

''What was his war record like, Ted, any idea?''

''According to Maxwell, Busch ended up in military intelligence—the *Abwehr*. One of Admiral Canaris's people. He wasn't wanted for any war crimes, and his last rank in nineteen forty-five was *Hauptmann*—captain. Surprising, really. Usually those who joined the Nazis before nineteen-thirty were considered the party aristocrats. Busch really ought to have risen higher in rank considering his *Abwehr* background, unless maybe he dirtied his bib along the way."

"What's his background after nineteen forty-five?"

"Maxwell had a quiet word off the record with the Berlin CIA station, who had Busch's background checked. Busch spent ten years in the Gehlen organization, the forerunner of the German security services. It was riddled with ex-Nazis, as you probably know, so his credentials would have served him well. He retired from that outfit over thirty years ago and went into private security. But he's a very old man now, long retired and living on his pension."

"Thanks, Ted, I appreciate your help."

"Not at all, my boy. And if you need any more help from the Document Center in Berlin, you can contact this chap direct. Just ask for Ed Maxwell and mention my name. It's been good talking with you."

It was noon when the telephone buzzed on Volkmann's desk. It was Ivan Molke returning his call.

"We need to meet and talk, Joe."

There was an urgency in Molke's voice, and Volkmann said, "Is there a problem, Ivan?"

"I think you could say that. I've pulled off my men watching Kesser."

"What's wrong?"

"I'd rather not talk about this over the line, Joe. Can we meet? There's something I think you ought to see."

"I could drive down to Munich, be there about three."

"Let's meet in Augsburg. It'll shorten your journey, and besides, I need to get out of the office. You know where the Hauptbahnhof is in Augsburg?"

"No, but I'll find it."

"I'll be there by two-thirty, in the main bar. One last thing. Do me a favor."

"What?"

"When you drive down, check your tail."

Volkmann frowned. "What's up, Ivan?"

"I'll tell you when I see you, but just do as I ask," answered Molke, and then the line clicked dead.

* * *

It was almost two-thirty when Volkmann stepped into the Hauptbahnhof. He had parked in an underground garage near the railway station and walked back.

On the drive down to Augsburg, he had watched in the rearview mirror and taken note of the cars behind, but none were tailing him, and he had stopped at half a dozen filling stations en route to be certain.

He saw Ivan Molke sitting over a cup of coffee and smoking a cigarette in a corner of the bar. He appeared tired and his face looked tense. He nodded for Volkmann to join him and when he had ordered a beer and sat down, Volkmann saw the dark rings under Ivan Molke's eyes.

"No tails on the way down?"

"Clear all the way. What's the problem, Ivan?"

Molke stubbed out his cigarette. "You came clean to me on Lothar Kesser, Joe? You told me everything I needed to know?"

"Of course, why?"

Molke looked across at Volkmann. "I put two of my men on Kesser the day before yesterday. One of them managed to get into Kesser's apartment yesterday evening. His girl's been there most of the time, she left only once with Kesser to visit a local doctor. Her name is Ingrid and she's Kesser's live-in girlfriend. By the look of her, she's about six months pregnant."

"Go on."

"My man had maybe ten minutes in the place before Kesser drives back alone. The second man tagged Kesser back from the doctor's office. The guy at the apartment hadn't much time, but he managed to find a notebook belonging to Kesser and a spare set of keys to the apartment. He didn't have time to plant a bug on Kesser's phone, but he photographed a couple of pages from the notebook and got out just before Kesser came up the stairs. My men made their report to me last night about nine and gave me a mold of the keys and the photo prints they took of the pages in Kesser's notebook."

Molke sighed, quickly lit another cigarette and inhaled. "In the middle of the night, I get two calls within the space of ten minutes. It's the two guys I put on Kesser. One of them says his wife wakes up about three o'clock and goes downstairs for a glass of water. She sees the door to the study is open. She flicks on the light and there's this guy searching through her husband's briefcase. She screams. The guy pulls a gun and points it at her like he's going to blow her head off. By the time her husband gets down the stairs, the intruder's gone and his wife's fainted on the floor.''

Molke saw the look on Volkmann's face. He paused before he went on. ''The next time the phone rings, it's Pieber, the second man. He's at his girlfriend's place and he leaves late. He notices he's being followed home. Two guys in a dark-colored Volkswagen, but he didn't get the number because the license plate was muddied. When he gets to his apartment, he goes to his bedroom and checks the window but sees no one below. But half an hour later, he hears whispered voices outside the apartment door. He puts on the hi-fi, walks around the apartment, making noise like he's very much awake, then he telephones me. I get there ten minutes later, but there's no one outside the apartment. But someone's been at the door lock, no question.''

For a long time Volkmann was silent, then he looked over at Molke.

''You're certain this has something to do with watching Kesser?''

Molke said, ''Joe, there's nothing my men are working on at present that would bring that kind of flak. And certainly nothing that would involve guns.''

''What do you propose to do?''

''My men are off Kesser since last night. Your people have official authority and they carry weapons. My boys can't and it's getting too dangerous.'' Molke shook his head vigorously and crushed his cigarette in the ashtray. ''I just won't risk them getting hurt, Joe. You understand?''

Volkmann nodded. ''You think Kesser knew your men had been in his apartment?''

''That's the funny thing. I asked them the very same question. They said they were sure Kesser suspected nothing, didn't know he was being watched.''

''And they didn't see anyone else watching Kesser's place?''

''Not that they were aware of, but I guess they were too

busy watching Kesser to take much notice.''

"What about Kesser's movements since Sunday evening?''

Ivan Molke removed a notebook from his pocket, flicked
it open. "Twice he's driven up to the mountain. It's called
the Kaalberg all right. Yesterday and the day before, he
drove up there early, about seven in the morning, and left
about noon.''

"Did your men see any other movement up there?''

"No one came or left apart from Kesser, and the armed
guards are still there.''

"What about checking out the place like I asked?''

"You mean to see if it's a government research place?''

"Yes.''

"I talked with a few people I know at the ministry. They
confirmed that there's maybe a dozen places in Bavaria
used for hush-hush lab work. Military communications
mainly, and a couple of government-funded weapons and
missile research labs. But I got the feeling they didn't want
to talk, so I backed off, tried another tack. I went back to
the village where I bought the mountain gear and asked
around.''

"And?''

"Nobody I spoke with seemed to know anything except
that there's a lot of private land up there. Maybe a couple
of square kilometers. Pretty rocky, forested ground. The
solid rock outcrop that tops it off—that's the Kaalberg. Un-
suitable for skiing or pretty much anything else. There's a
big mountain house up there, the one we saw. A couple of
wooden barns, and a flat, concrete building directly behind
the house that could be a laboratory, but there're no other
buildings apart from the sentry hut on the road leading up.
The mountain and all the land around used to belong to a
private sanatorium, but it closed down maybe ten years ago.
Someone bought the site a couple of years back, but none
of the locals seem to know who it belongs to now or what
goes on up there. They think the government owns the
place, they're not sure. They say the site's been marked off
with 'Entrance Forbidden' and 'Private' signs all over the
place.''

Volkmann sighed and looked away toward the crowds

on the concourse outside, then back again. "What do you think, Ivan?"

Molke shrugged. "It could be a government research place. You said there were some books in Kesser's place, military communications stuff, so it's possible Kesser might be involved on some hush-hush project up there when you consider his background. And after what happened to my two men, I'd say it's likely. It sounds like a Landesamt job. They keep watch on their people and if they're being followed or something suspicious happens to them, they investigate. Only in my business, Joe, I don't need that kind of heat. I could have my license pulled and I'd be out of a job. That's why I think it's best to back off and let your people handle it."

Volkmann thought for a moment, then said, "If Kesser was working for the government and I asked the Landesamt to see his file, I doubt if they'd let me."

There was a puzzled frown on Ivan Molke's face. "What do you mean?"

"Werner Bargel let me see a précis of Kesser's file. Government research personnel files usually have restricted access. So it doesn't make sense that Bargel would let me see Kesser's."

Molke shrugged. "Not unless Bargel suspected that your people were on to something that might involve Kesser. And if Kesser is still involved in government research work, that way it might make sense. Did Bargel ask you to get back to him if you came up with anything?"

"Yes."

"Then maybe that's it."

"Maybe. What about you, you have any doubts?"

Molke hesitated. "Something doesn't make sense. The pages in the notebook my men found in Kesser's apartment. According to Pieber, there were maybe a couple of dozen pages of lists of names and what looked like some pages of diagrams of some sort. But Pieber only had time to photograph a couple."

The girl serving behind the bar came to replace the ashtray with a fresh one and wipe the table, and when she had gone, Ivan Molke reached into his pocket and took out an envelope. He slid it across to Volkmann.

"Maybe you ought to take a look at the photographs."

Volkmann opened the envelope and slid out the contents. Inside were two enlargements of narrow, faint-ruled pages. One of the pages had a list of three names with an X marked beside each. The second contained what appeared to be a roughly drawn map of some sort of building. Beside it was another map, this one giving directions, and underlined were the names of several towns. On closer examination, Volkmann saw what looked like the word "Kloster" circled in ink above the drawing. The German word for "monastery." Volkmann looked at the names again.

Horst Klee.

Jürgen Trautman.

Frederick Henkle.

He looked up at Molke. "Any idea who they are?"

"None. And like I said, there were lots more names. Dozens. My man only had time to shoot one of the pages with names on it."

"What about the map?"

"I checked it out this morning."

"And?"

"The directions were clear enough. It's an old deserted monastery off the main autobahn to Saltzburg, an hour's drive from Munich. It hasn't been used in years. Looks in pretty good shape, but there's no one there, you can check it yourself. I've drawn a proper map for you with directions on how to get there." Molke took an envelope from his inside pocket.

As Volkmann took the envelope, he said, "Who owns the monastery, do you know?"

"After the religious order moved out over twenty years ago, the German government bought it, but it hasn't been put to any use since." Molke shrugged. "If Kesser's still working for the government, it could be someplace they're planning to set up and use. So I'd tread carefully if I were you, Joe. The ministry people responsible for special projects are pretty sensitive about security."

Volkmann hesitated, then tapped the photographs of the two pages from Kesser's notebook. "You mind if I keep these, Ivan?"

"On one condition."

"What's that?"

"If the Landesamt come knocking on my door, I want your word you'll explain that what my men did was sanctioned officially, that I was working for you."

"You have it, Ivan."

Molke reached into his pocket, slid across a set of keys. "They're for Kesser's apartment. I had them made from the molds, in case you still wanted to take it further. But I'm out, Joe. From now on, your people will have to handle it. And you didn't get these from me."

Volkmann nodded and slipped the keys into his pocket.

"I also think it would be best if I had something on paper, Joe. Just in case."

"I understand. I'll have Ferguson sort out your expenses and I'll write up a letter personally. Thanks for your help, Ivan."

"One more thing. The photograph of the girl. The one you found in the Chaco."

"What about it?"

"I checked up on the specialist people our government used during the Nazi trials." Molke paused. "There was a woman, a historian. She specialized in the Nazi period and pretty much knew all the players. She just may be able to help with the photograph, or maybe know someone who can." Molke shrugged. "It's all I can come up with, Joe."

"What's her name?"

"Hanah Richter. She was on the history faculty of Stuttgart University. But that was over twenty years ago and she wasn't young even then, so I'd say she's well retired by now. And I'm assuming she's still alive."

"Okay, I'll have my people check on her."

Volkmann walked back to the underground garage and went through the routines to make sure he wasn't being followed.

The streets were crowded with Christmas shoppers but no one was tailing him, and when he reached the car, he climbed in, lit a cigarette and sat there for ten minutes, thinking over what Ivan Molke had told him about Kesser. None of it made any sense, none at all.

Apart from Wolfgang Lubsch's word and the two photographs in the apartment—one of the men in uniform he assumed was Kesser's father, and the photograph of Kesser and Winter together—there was little to implicate the man. And all the clues seemed to suggest that Kesser was still involved in government research work.

He decided the best thing to do was to concentrate on the information he had: the two names Ted Birken had come up with whose Nazi Party numbers had been close to Schmeltz's—Otto Klagen and Wilhelm Busch—and the sketch Ivan Molke had given him from Kesser's notebook. He could phone the duty officer later and have him check the three names on the list in Kesser's place. It occurred to him they could be research people Kesser worked with, and if that was the case, he would have to back off. He shook his head in confusion and frustration and started the Ford.

At the first hotel he saw, he used one of the phone booths in the lobby. He got the number for the hospital in Düsseldorf where Klagen was a patient, called and told the girl who answered that he was a relative of Otto Klagen's and asked if the old man was still a patient. She checked the patient register while he held on, and when she told him Otto Klagen was still in the hospital, he asked to speak to a doctor on duty who was familiar with Klagen's case.

He had to hold on for another ten minutes before a female doctor came on the line. He told her he was Otto Klagen's nephew and that he was phoning from Bavaria to inquire about his uncle's health. He wondered if it was possible to visit and speak with him.

"You weren't told about his condition?"

"I'm afraid I've been abroad and just heard the news. Is my uncle that bad, Doctor?"

"I'm sorry to say he's had a cerebral stroke, Herr Klagen. He's paralysed down his right side and his speech is still virtually incoherent. He couldn't really communicate if you visited, but of course you're welcome to see him."

"When do you think he'll be able to talk again?"

"That depends on his progress and therapy, Herr Klagen, but at this stage, the prognosis isn't good and he isn't making much progress. And at his age, I'm afraid . . . you understand?"

Volkmann said he did and that he'd call again to check on his uncle's condition. He thanked the woman and hung up.

The next call he made was to his apartment. When Erica answered, he told her where he was and explained about Ted Birken's information and what had happened with Klagen, but he made no mention of what Ivan Molke had told him. When she heard him sigh, she said, "What about the second man, Busch?"

"It's an hour from here to Dachau, so I'll carry on. I just hope I have better luck than I did with Klagen."

"When will you be back?"

"That depends on whether I can locate Busch or not. And even if I do, he may not even want to talk. You're sure you'll be okay on your own?"

"I'm going to take a long walk in the Orangerie and then come back and drink your wine and watch television. Isn't there anything I can do?"

Volkmann smiled. "Keep the bed warm. And keep your fingers crossed that Busch is in better health than Otto Klagen. Talk to you soon."

It was almost four when he reached the old town of Dachau. Dominated by an ancient castle, the pretty Bavarian town looked a picture of rural charm. But it seemed somehow absurd to Volkmann that the place that had once lent its name to the infamous concentration camp should be lit up with glittering seasonal lights.

He found the address Ted Birken had given him in a street of drab prewar detached houses, a ten-minute walk from the road that led down to the old concentration camp. There was a Christmas tree in the window of the house, but when Volkmann walked up the concrete walk and rang the doorbell several times, no one answered.

As he stood there wondering what to do next, a young woman pulled up in a white Volkswagen and stepped out. She looked to be in her late twenties and as she carried several bags of shopping up to the front door, Volkmann went to help her.

"Danke schön."

The young woman smiled as she reached in her purse for her key.

Then she looked at Volkmann rather warily and said, "I'm sorry, I don't think we've met before."

Volkmann saw that she wore no wedding ring. "I'm looking for Wilhelm Busch. I believe he lives here."

"Are you a friend of my grandfather's?"

"No, we've never met." Volkmann produced his ID, and the girl stared at it for a moment.

She turned suddenly pale. "Are you with the police? My grandfather isn't in any sort of trouble, is he?"

Volkmann smiled. "No trouble at all, I assure you. May I speak with him?"

"I'm afraid he's not here."

"Can you tell me where I can find him?"

"My boyfriend's driven him to Salzburg to visit a relative. My grandfather's sister hasn't been well."

"When will he be back?"

"Sometime tomorrow. Perhaps you can call back. Can I tell him what this is about?"

"It's a private matter, Frau Busch. I'd really rather discuss it with him."

The woman shrugged. "Very well, I'll tell him you called."

And with that, she turned the key in the door and stepped inside.

He found a small hotel opposite the park near the S-Bahn Station and checked in for one night.

His room overlooked the small park facing the station, and when he had shaved and showered, he decided to drive back up to Busch's house just to check to see if the old man had come back early, but there was still only the white Volkswagen in the driveway. The light was on downstairs, the Christmas tree winking in the window.

At the end of the street, he turned left to come back into the town and saw the road that led up to the camp. He skirted back to the town, and when he had parked the car in the hotel's back lot, he went up to his room and phoned the duty officer in Strasbourg.

It was a young French officer named Delon who came

on the line, and Volkmann explained that he wanted three names checked. He read out the list from Kesser's notebook and spelled them phonetically.

"You've got addresses or descriptions?"

"I'm afraid not, André."

"That's going to make it difficult. What are you looking for, Joseph? Anything in particular?"

"Just to see if those names come up on our files and if there's any connection among the three men."

"Which area—criminal?"

"I don't know, André, so you better leave it open. But the main thing is to try and link them."

The young Frenchman sighed. "If you're trying to link them, that means we will have to do a random check on the names first. It may take some time."

"I'm aware of that, but it's priority. If you have no luck with our computer, ask the German desk to help. It's more than likely their territory, anyway, judging by the names. But there's a chance the three are government research employees, so if the German desk tells you their files are restricted, just back off and don't explain. So see what we can come up with first."

He gave the Frenchman the details on Hanah Richter that Ivan Molke had provided Delon to do what he could to locate her.

"Okay. This ought to keep me busy for the shift. Where can I contact you?"

"If I'm not in the office, leave a message at my apartment. If a woman answers, just say you called."

"A woman? You want to tell me what she looks like?"

"Pretty, very pretty. Be good, André."

He took a walk through the town to get some air, aware of his restlessness.

The old castle on the hill was lit up with yellow lights, and Volkmann realized that there was nothing to suggest to the casual visitor, unaware of the town's past and the nearby camp, the brutality and murder that had taken place here.

A small town in Germany like so many others, with young people in good spirits filling the streets and inns in

the days before Christmas. He looked at them as he passed
the crowded bars, their glasses raised, their voices loud and
harsh and full of confidence.

It was almost midnight when he got back to the hotel.
As he lay in bed in the darkness, he could hear the voices
in the street below as the bars emptied. They carried up to
his window, some of them shouting drunkenly. Then they
faded, and a little after midnight a train rumbled past in the
station across the street.

CHAPTER 33

Chief Inspector Eduardo Gonzales was a thin, energetic man of fifty. He had the gnarled face of a tough street-fighter, an appearance that belied his sharp intelligence.

And despite his pugilistic appearance, he was unhealthy: he had managed to smoke his way through three packs of cigarettes a day for the past thirty years. As a result, his voice was hoarse, he coughed constantly and his fingers were stained brown with nicotine. Yet his pale-gray uniform with red epaulettes was crisply ironed, the creases sharp as blades.

His office overlooked the Plaza de San Fernando and had an excellent view of Mexico City; the sprawling, ragged metropolis, part of which was his dominion. The office itself was functional and tidy, the only suggestion of untidiness being overflowing ashtrays, strategically placed about the room to accommodate his habit: one by the panoramic window, another on top of a metal filing cabinet near the door. Two on the desk, one of them of functional glass, the other a beautiful, ornate affair of quebraco wood in the shape of a half-cut coconut shell, carved by the Indians in Paraguay's Chaco, resting on a base that was a sparkling slice of jagged quartz. A present from his friend, Captain Vellares Sanchez.

The dark wood had a pungent aroma that could still be smelled faintly despite the years of stale cigarette ash. Despite its appearance, it was a work of art. Ugly, brooding mulatto faces with closed eyelids were cut into the dark, granite-hard wood; the receptacle was clasped and cupped by a perfectly carved wooden hand, the firm hand so in contrast to the ugly carved faces that it resembled on first sight some hedonistic chalice; the wooden faces looking like the shrunken heads of Amazonians one saw in the museums. But not frightening. Rather, they served to remind that evil had to be controlled by good; a strong hand holding evil in check. Beauty and order controlling evil and ugliness.

According to the Indians.

So Sanchez had told him when he presented the gift in Caracas years before, but with a smile on his face that suggested the story might be apocryphal.

Now strong December sunlight poured into the office. Hot, despite the season. A freakish warm front in from the Gulf of Mexico. An air-conditioning vent in a wall below the ceiling blew out a faint, ineffective stream of chilled air.

A metal tray cluttered with bottles of sparkling water and a jug of fresh, iced lime juice and four glasses lay on Gonzales's desk. Despite the heat, they had remained untouched since a young *policía* had brought them in fifteen minutes before.

The four men sat around the desk. Gonzales and his senior detective, named Juales, a rugged, short-necked man with a squat body and bushy eyebrows, sat on one side; Sanchez and Cavales on the other.

Eduardo Gonzales inhaled on a cigarette, coughed throatily, blew thick smoke out into the warm air. He tapped ash into the dark-wood ashtray and then looked across at his two visitors. Both men were tired, their eyes red-raw after their long journey. And the high altitude of the city must be making them dizzy, Gonzales thought.

It took tourists and visitors at least forty-eight hours to accustom their lungs to the rarefied oxygen, and the two men seated before him had been in Mexico City less than an hour. A police car had taken them directly from the airport, siren blaring, lights flashing. Their lungs must be on fire, Gonzales thought, their minds fogged and hurting from altitude sickness. But neither visitor complained.

The formalities had been dispensed with, the greetings and well-wishings over. Sanchez had briefly explained his reasons for wanting Franz Lieber, alias Julius Monck, followed.

Gonzales had listened attentively, his brow furrowed in concentration while Sanchez had spoken. Now it was Gonzales's turn. He coughed. "Okay. Let's take it from the beginning. Okay with you?"

Sanchez and Cavales nodded. Gonzales nodded in turn to Juales. The man leaned forward. His voice was thin, but his Spanish had an educated timbre. He wore a shirt and tie, and a portable phone was clipped to his belt, on the opposite side to his holstered, blunt-nosed Smith & Wesson thirty-eight. He spoke slowly, glancing up at Sanchez and Cavales every few moments as he read from written notes.

"The subject, Julius Monck, alias Franz Lieber, arrived in Mexico City two hours ago. One-sixteen local. I had six men watching him in the arrivals terminal, another two on the airport ramp, dressed as airport staff so as to identify him as soon as he stepped off the plane. We got an ID, no problem, from the photograph you sent." Juales glanced at Sanchez, then back at his notes.

"As soon as he collected his luggage, he went straight through customs. I had briefed one of the customs men to stop him, and he checked the luggage thoroughly. Nothing of interest. There's a list of the contents of the single suitcase, if you want it."

Sanchez waved his hand in reply. "Later, please go on."

Juales looked down at his notes again.

"The subject went to the exchange counter, changed U.S. bills into pesos, and got some change. Then he made one telephone call at one-forty-seven. The officers watching him couldn't get close enough to see the numbers dialed, because the subject was blocking their view. The call lasted just under one minute. Lieber seemed anxious. Soon as he finished the call, he went to a taco stand outside the terminal and bought a glass of fresh fruit juice, drank it, then went to the taxi stand at one-fifty-six. One-fifty-seven, he took a taxi to the City Sheraton, arrived there at two-thirty-nine and booked in straightaway under the name of Julius Monck." Juales looked up from his notes. "He was still there as of fifteen minutes ago. Room Two-one-five."

"And now?" Sanchez asked.

Juales tapped the portable phone clipped to his belt. "I've got six undercover men at the Sheraton. If Lieber goes in or out or anybody visits him or he makes a call, my men will let me know."

Gonzales interrupted. "The call Lieber made, you've got something on that yet?"

Juales shook his head. "Not yet. I've assigned one of my men to check it with our technical people." He turned to Sanchez and Cavales. "I ought to explain. After Lieber made the call at the airport, I had one of my men wait by the telephone until a colleague from the technical division came with a tape recorder. They hit the re-dial button and recorded the digital dialing pips. They can play it back and decode it in the tech lab and find the number. Then we can trace to wherever it was called." Juales glanced at his wristwatch. "We ought to have that soon."

Sanchez nodded, saw Gonzales smile through stained-yellow teeth.

"Technology," said Gonzales, waving his cigarette. "It's beyond an old policeman like me. These young boys in the basement lab are like Einsteins. They play with computers all day. Me, I'd go crazy down there." He smiled.

Sanchez nodded his head and smiled faintly. His bones ached to the marrow, his chest hurt when he breathed, and his brain was fogging with a deep, throbbing pain. He glanced at Cavales. The detective stared ahead blankly, then rubbed his raw eyes. He must be feeling the same, Sanchez thought. A bed would be welcome; a cold shower first, then sleep. But there was no time for that. Not yet. His mouth felt dry and the iced fruit juice looked tempting, but he ignored it.

He turned to look at Juales and Gonzales. "The passport Lieber used. Did he ever use it to visit Mexico before?"

Gonzales went into a fit of coughing, pounded his chest with his fist before he replied. "I had that checked too, Vellares. The answer's no. Never. No Julius Monck with that number on the passport."

Sanchez looked at Juales. "How many nights did Lieber book at the Sheraton?"

"He told the desk clerk one, possibly two. He couldn't be certain."

"And the hotel people are being cooperative?"

"We spoke with the manager," Juales replied. "No problem. He's been very discreet. Even gave us a room two doors away. We've got two men there. If Lieber comes out, we've got a copy key card. We can plant a bug in his room, no problem, just in case he entertains visitors."

"What about his telephone?"

Juales said, "We've got that covered already. We're going to wire into the hotel telephone system. The manager wanted to see our permission first. Chief Inspector Gonzales has organized it.'' Juales glanced at his watch. ''Our people are on their way and should be patched into Lieber's telephone within the next half-hour.''

Sanchez looked at Gonzales, inclined his head gratefully. ''You're being more than helpful, Eduardo. My thanks.''

Gonzales shrugged, coughed again, waved his hands dismissively and looked at the carved ashtray as he ground out his cigarette, the dark, ghoulish, blank-eyed faces staring up at him. He smiled across at Sanchez. ''It's the only way we beat the devils of this world. No?''

Sanchez smiled back, faintly.

Gonzales stood up, hitched his gray-cotton trousers farther up his thin waist, glanced at the liquid refreshments still untouched on his desk. The atmosphere in the office felt charged. Expectant. Like worried fathers outside a maternity ward. Not a place to relax.

Gonzales said, ''There's nothing more we can do until Lieber makes a move. We've got a hospitality room for visitors down the hall. Why don't we all go down there? I'll have some tacos and fresh drinks sent up and you can rest yourselves. Juales here will come with us. If a call comes through from any of his men, we'll get it there.'' He looked down at Sanchez and smiled. ''Besides, it will give us a chance to catch up on gossip since Caracas. Okay?''

4:40 P.M.

Franz Lieber stood at the window on the fifth floor of the Sheraton. He swallowed his second scotch-and-soda, gripped the empty glass tightly in his big hand as he stared down at the city below. The air-conditioning was on, the hum distracting.

Tiredness racked his body, pains arcing intermittently across his broad chest in spasms, like tiny jolts of electricity. Rivulets of sweat ran down his back and temples despite the coolness of the room.

Stress.

Lieber ran the back of his hand across his forehead.

The flights had been bad enough. Asunción to São Paulo. An overnight in Paulo, then the long haul to Mexico City. Throughout his long journey, anxiety gnawed like a rodent inside his skull, eating away brain tissue, making his head ache. Even now. Not just the altitude.

He took a deep breath, let it out slowly. Did the same again three times, trying to relax, but knew it was useless.

Mexico City out there and beyond—a ragged, noisy, dirty sprawl of human ants on a high-altitude dungpile. Cities like this drained him. Claustrophobic, chaotic, orderless. They made his headache worse.

A woman would help relieve the tension. But Kruger had expressly forbidden visitors or phone calls.

Just wait. For the return call.

The hotel would be checked first. To make sure he had no tails, no one watching him. Lieber had tried to tell Kruger it was okay when he had phoned him from the airport, that he had been careful, but Kruger had refused to accept his assurance.

"Just stay in your room. I'll get back to you."

"How long?"

"As long as it takes; just wait for my call," came the curt reply before Kruger hung up.

Lieber shook his head and swore to himself, felt the trickles of sweat tickling his spine. The waiting wasn't helping his stress.

How long before they checked him out? He'd been in the room almost two hours now. As he went toward the mini bar to pour himself another scotch, the telephone rang. Startled, he felt as if a shock of electricity had jolted his body.

He hesitated, but only for a moment, put down the glass and wiped his brow again, then went to pick up the receiver.

Sanchez sat quietly in the small hospitality room. White walls. Thick, deep-pile carpet the same gray-blue color as Gonzales' uniform.

For ten minutes he and Gonzales had spoken, until the tiredness had overcome Sanchez. Now he sat sipping freshly squeezed orange juice from a paper cup. A half-eaten taco and a hot chili sauce dip lay in front of him on a paper plate, beside it a dish full of grilled *charals*. Hunger was in his stomach, but not on his mind. He had eaten some of the taco out of courtesy, the hot chili sauce burning his tongue, until he had washed the fire away with two glasses of iced orange juice.

The others sat and talked. Mainly, Gonzales. Cavales listened out of courtesy to the older man's rank. Stories about the old days in Mexico City, the problems, the interesting cases.

Juales sat there nodding occasionally at his boss, his neck lost in his shirt so that it looked like he had no neck at all. Sanchez guessed he was very capable. A thorough man. His boss had chosen well. The narrow, careful eyes flicked to Sanchez as Juales smiled briefly and turned away.

"You think Asunción's bad," Gonzales was saying to Cavales, each man puffing on a cigarette, "you ought to try a month here. Twenty-three million people, amigo. Like a cross between a zoo and a lunatic asylum. But without walls."

Sanchez closed his eyes tightly, eyelids aching, opened them again. The view beyond the panoramic window was stupendous, as far as the high Sierras surrounding the city. He wondered how Gonzales and his people managed to cope. Lots of crime, lots of crooks. The organization itself must be a headache like no other.

His own head throbbed. The high altitude had a dizzying effect, tightening his chest, dulling his mind, making the effort of thinking and talking a slow process. As if the thin oxygen slowed your body clock, made you wind down.

But something was happening.

He could sense it.

The next move was Lieber's.

He wondered what it would be.

He looked up absentmindedly as a lull in the men's conversation distracted him, heard a soft click as the door behind opened. Sanchez turned, saw a good-looking young man in a cream-colored linen suit standing in the open doorway. He clutched a sheaf of papers in one hand, smiled

warily at the two visitors and Gonzales before his eyes
shifted to Juales.

"Captain . . . may I speak with you?"

Juales stood up, crossed to the man and they stepped out
into the hallway together. Gonzales stood and hitched his
trousers, puffed on a cigarette as he frowned and looked at
the two men in the hallway huddled in conversation. Juales
returned after a brief interlude holding a single sheet of
paper.

"We traced the call made at the airport."

"And?" Gonzales prompted.

"It was to an address in Lomas de Chapultepec."

"An expensive area," commented Gonzales. "Did you
get the name of the occupant?"

Juales shook his head. "No, not yet. But my man did a
little quick checking. The property is owned by a company
called Cancún Enterprises. It's run by a man named Josef
Halder. He's a businessman. Old guy. Very wealthy."

"I know who he is," Gonzales said quickly. He looked
at Sanchez and Cavales. Both men had stood up.

Gonzales drew on his cigarette, blew out thick smoke.
"Halder is German-born. Rich. A retired businessman.
Owns a lot of property in the city." He coughed and
smiled. "Maybe this fits in with what you told me about
this other old guy . . ."

"Tsarkin?"

"Sí."

"Tell me."

Gonzales sighed. "Halder came here from Brazil maybe
forty years ago. Started in business in the city. He must be
in his eighties now. But well-known, lots of powerful
friends. I remember him because there was a problem with
an extradition warrant from France when I worked in headquarters. The French said Halder was wanted for war
crimes he had committed there. Claimed Halder was in the
Gestapo. Long time ago, I know, but Halder must have
greased a lot of palms, because the charges were refuted
by our people. At that stage, Halder was tied into the business life in the city. Lots of businesses, lots of employees.
And more important, lots of powerful political friends. The
French persisted for a while, but eventually Halder swore

an affidavit of innocence and that was the end of it." Gonzales smiled. "Simple when you have money, *sí*?"

Sanchez nodded. "And this is one of his properties?"

"It would appear so," said Gonzales. "It's in a pretty wealthy area up in the Chapultepec Hills. A long way from the working-class *colonias*. It's a very beautiful place. Hilly, forested ground. Huge mansions and villas in the middle of landscaped parks and rocky ravines. Very chic. Where only the very rich live." He smiled. "And maybe a few corrupt police chiefs and judges as well."

"Can you make a check on the occupants?"

"I could, but that would mean going through Halder's company people. Like waving a red flag." Gonzales shook his head. "Better that I get some people over there straightaway. Undercover. Have them watch the place, see how the land lies, who comes and who goes. How does that sound?"

Sanchez nodded. "I would appreciate that, Eduardo."

"No problem, amigo. Juales will organize it straightaway."

A shrill sound startled them as Juales's portable buzzed. The man unclipped it, flicked it on and listened.

Sanchez heard nothing, only Juales's sharp replies as he frowned.

"When? You got the number? Put out an all-cars alert. But tell them don't approach. Just observe and report their position. Understood?"

Juales let his hand fall, looked at Gonzales. "Lieber got a call in his room three minutes ago."

Gonzales smiled. "Our men were tapped into his phone?"

Juales shook his head. "No. The technicians were still working on it. They missed the call. By the time they got to the operator, Lieber had put down the phone."

"Shit!"

"That's not all. Lieber left the Sheraton two minutes ago. Went down to the lobby and crossed the street and bought a newspaper. A car came by and Lieber climbed in and the car moved off like a bat out of hell."

"The car was a taxi?"

"Not a taxi. A civvy. Volkswagen Beetle."

"Our men followed?"

"*Sí.*"

"And?"

Juales swallowed. "As of just twenty seconds ago, we lost him."

CHAPTER 34

Lieber sat in the front seat of the white Volkswagen as it wove through the chaos of traffic.

Lunatic Mexican drivers, chili and pepper smells, and all the time the pressing, claustrophobic sensation of sweaty bodies. Everywhere. Millions of the dago bastards.

His head ached. Sweat still poured through his shirt, a fresh one he had hastily dragged on before he left the hotel after the call. He was clear, according to Kruger. Two of Halder's men had checked out the hotel and lobby for almost two hours. Waited and watched. No *policía* or plainclothes so far as they could tell.

If he had been watched, the watchers were very good. But Lieber doubted that. He had moved too quickly, too carefully. Besides, dagos were notoriously inefficient. Except for the women. Hourglass bodies of curvaceous flesh made for pleasure. And the cop, Sanchez, was not one to underestimate. But still a cretin. All dagos were when it really came down to it.

The cramped, whining Volkswagen felt claustrophobic, despite the open windows. The man in the driver's seat was one of Halder's people. He wore a sweatshirt and tennis shorts, and his forehead was creased as he concentrated on the traffic.

Outside the windows of the tiny Volkswagen, darkness fell, lights coming on, the traffic thickening—if it could get any thicker—a scene of utter chaos. But the driver knew the city, wove down side streets and alleyways, ignoring the irate screams and cries of street vendors whose barrows got in the way, until now the small white Volkswagen was climbing up into the hills, the streets becoming cleaner, less cluttered, the air fresher, cooler. But still skull-crushing pressure as the whiny-engined Volkswagen strained ever upward. The car had been well chosen. Mexico City thronged with Volkswagens.

Now whitewashed adobes and filthy *colonias* were replaced by middle-class homes, were replaced by splendid villas with walled gardens. Armed, uniformed guards, some with leashed guard dogs, stood behind gates, carefully watching the roads.

Lieber had been in the city many years before: the lava ravines and soaring rocky outcrops of the Chapultepec landscape familiar to him; flowered walks and tiny lakes dotted with clumps of *camelotes*. Narrow, winding streets with unobtrusive but guarded entrances that often belied the sumptuous properties beyond. A place for the very rich and elite.

Suddenly the Volkswagen turned into a quiet avenue and halted outside a double wrought-iron gate. In the semi-darkness a man appeared beyond the gate and peered into the car. Moments later, he opened the gates manually and let them through.

The Volkswagen strained up a winding gravel road, a white villa waiting in the distance, set amidst lush gardens. Jacaranda trees and thick-clumped flower beds of poinsettias and *zempoazuchitl*. The flower of death, old Halder had once told him it was called.

Sulfur-yellow light washed over the vast lawns dotted with palm trees, and lights blazed in windows. The villa was sumptuous. Lights on everywhere outside. A big place. Impressive. Private. Secure.

Now the road swung around so that Lieber could see the swimming pool, a kidney-shaped shimmering of turquoise light. He saw the patio and the French windows at the side of the house. And then he saw the guards, Werner and Rotman. They wore shorts and sneakers and light rainproof jogger jackets as they patrolled the gardens, carrying Heckler and Koch MP 5K machine pistols.

He glimpsed big Schmidt, standing away from the other two men, a pistol in a shoulder harness across his chest, no sign of the big sheathed bowie knife, but Lieber knew the man went nowhere without it.

Inside the windows, the lights were on and he could see the figures waiting for him. There were four men present. The tall, silver-haired man and Kruger standing; old Halder seated in a comfortable armchair, lost in the leather, an inhaler clutched in one of his hands. Wrinkled, wheezy old Halder, face like a dried prune; thin lips, emaciated fea-

tures, looking like an old buzzard. They said he had killed
men with his bare hands in the old days; strangled them,
gouged out eyes, raped. But to look at him now, he could
have been a grumpy, harmless old grandfather near the end
of his days. But still important. Still part of the web.

The fourth man, Lieber knew, was Ernesto Brandt. A
mischling. German father, Brazilian mother. Brown, thinning hair, brown eyes, tanned skin, metal-framed glasses
with thick lenses, and a high forehead that made him look
like some science-fiction humanoid or an eccentric professor. Maybe fifty, but youthful-looking. An unusual physical
combination. But the man was important, had been one of
the vital keys to the plan.

Lieber looked around as the Volkswagen came to a sudden halt in front of the porch.

5:20 *P.M.*

In the growing darkness, the traffic was bumper to bumper.

As the unmarked police car inched forward in the heavy
traffic, Gonzales, sitting in the front passenger seat, said,
"To hell with this, amigos," as he grabbed the blue light,
reached out and up through the rolled-down window,
clamped it on top, flicked a switch on the dashboard.

The piercing scream of the flashing siren tore into the
growing darkness like a banshee. Traffic separated, horns
honked, and then they were through.

"Take the next left," Gonzales commanded.

Juales swung the car down a one-way street of two-lane
traffic. He let out an uncharacteristic whoop as he nudged
onto the pavement, the car tilting, driving for thirty meters
like this, children and passersby staring.

"The only way to travel," Gonzales remarked with a
smile.

The news had come over the mobile radio five minutes
before, and Juales had repeated it aloud, a look of triumph
on his face: *"They caught sight of the Volkswagen, heading
up to the Chapultepec Hills. We're in luck."*

Now Sanchez said, "What happens when we get there?"

Gonzales swiveled around to face him and Cavales. "We

look and watch." He paused. "There's a couple of Browning pump-actions in the back in case we need them. You both know how to shoot those damned things? I don't want my ass ending up like a colander."

Sanchez and Cavales smiled, said yes, they knew how to use the Brownings. The traffic suddenly thinned and the car began to climb, the streets becoming less crowded, the houses less shabby, the air slightly cooler. Gonzales switched-off and removed the siren.

Juales' phone buzzed on his lap and he picked it up. He listened for several moments and then said, "Good. Wait there. We'll be with you in ten minutes."

Then he turned to the others and said, "The Volkswagen just turned in through the front gates of the address in Chapultepec. There's a guard at the gate. No way of getting past him. My men are parked and waiting with the others a hundred meters down the street."

Gonzales smiled. He turned to Sanchez and said, "You think the people you want will be at this place waiting for Lieber?"

"I hope so."

"You understand, Vellares, I can't go in without a warrant. And this place is full of rich people. The rich protect themselves. And someone like Halder's got lots of friends in high places, you can count on it. So we better do it strictly by the book."

"What do you suggest?"

"Well, we need a search warrant, to protect my ass." Gonzales hesitated. "There's a judge named Manza. He often helps me. Law-and-order type, straight down the line. I think he's my best bet."

"What about the periphery of the property?"

"The area is all hills and narrow, winding streets. Difficult sometimes to know where one property begins and another ends. But I'll have one of the other cars take a quick run around. Have a look for rear exits and try to find a good vantage point where we can observe the place. But let's talk to the judge first."

Gonzales picked up the mobile. "Control. This is Chief Inspector Gonzales here. I want you to patch me through to Judge Ricardo Manza . . ."

* * *

The avenue was well lit and Juales had moved the car in the shadows between two street lights on a hill overlooking the villa, under a copse of sweet-smelling eucalyptus. The place was a perfect vantage point in the bright moonlight: the property lay almost two hundred meters below, and beyond them, the walled perimeter, the gates, the path leading up to the villa itself clearly visible, obscured only in places by occasional clumps of trees.

The windows of the car were rolled down, the air cool. The smell of eucalyptus and poinsettias. Big houses all around.

Sanchez had listened while Gonzales had spoken with the judge for at least five minutes, arguing his case. The conversation had been heated, but the judge finally gave in. He would agree to sign the search warrant.

"Don't compromise me, Gonzi. Don't fuck me up," Sanchez heard the judge say over the mobile.

"You have my word on it," Gonzales had replied, then said his polite good-bye, turned to the others after he had put through a second call.

"One of my men is picking up the warrant. He should be here in ten minutes."

"What happens then, Eduardo?"

Gonzales looked back at Sanchez. "If we go up to the gate with the warrant and demand entry, whoever's at the gate can stall us and let whoever's up at the villa know we're coming. So it's best if one of my men goes over the wall just before Juales hits the guy on the gate with the warrant. With one of our men inside, he'll make sure the guard doesn't have time to alert the villa. It's risky, I know. They could have armed guards patrolling the grounds, and they might start shooting in any confusion. But it's the only way we're going to surprise them. Let's just pray they don't have guard dogs loose on the lawns, or an electrified perimeter. Whoever goes over the wall could get chewed or crisped."

"What then?"

"Our man lets us through the gate and we drive up to the house, quick as we can. One of the other men can take over from Juales and we move in with another car behind us, go up the driveway fast as hell. We put the sirens and lights on at the last moment. That way, there can be no mistake. They'll know it's police, but they won't have time to think. And if they run, they run like scared rabbits." Gonzales paused. "But leave any talking to me once we're inside, okay? After I've done the preliminaries, you can have Lieber and whoever else you want for questioning."

Cavales said, "The people inside, they may be heavily armed."

Gonzales shrugged. "Up here in Chapultepec, everyone's heavily armed, amigo. They're probably legally held weapons. But once they know we're police, they'd be crazy to open fire. Unless they want to get out of that place pretty bad."

There was a tap on the roof on Juales' side and everyone started. A man stood outside and Sanchez realized it was one of the plainclothes policemen.

"What's the problem?" Juales said.

"There's some movement around by the side of the villa. A group of men just came out onto the patio. They're sitting at a table by the pool. Looks like they're having a meeting." The man paused and held up a nightscope. "You want to take a look, sir? You can see them pretty well if you move up the rise."

Juales took the scope and handed it across to Gonzales, who said to the man, "You've found the rear entrance?"

"I believe so, sir. I've got a car there, with three men."

"Good. You've got another scope?"

"Yes, sir, Barca has one."

"Then we'll hold onto this one. Thanks, Madera."

The man turned and walked away into the shadows.

Juales looked across at Gonzales. "You want to try and see the men by the pool?"

When Gonzales nodded, Juales drove up the rise for twenty meters and halted. They could see the side of the villa now, the faint turquoise shape in the distance that was the swimming pool. Gonzales stepped out of the car and looked through the scope across the narrow valley, then handed it to Sanchez.

"You can't see too good, Vellares. Just a bunch of people. No faces, just blurry green blobs."

Sanchez got out and peered through the scope. The swimming pool looked bright green, and when he swung the finder a little to the left, he saw a group of static figures seated at a white table beside the pool. But too far away to get a clear view, the images hazy.

There was a sound behind him moments later and the same detective who had given them the scope handed Gonzales a folded sheet of paper, explaining it was the authorized warrant. Gonzales took it, flicked on the interior light, scrutinized the sheet.

When he looked back up, Gonzales considered for a moment, then said to the detective, "Can the pool at the side be reached directly from the driveway?"

The man shook his head. "The driveway cuts only to the left, past the pool. But you could maybe make it across the lawn. There're some trees in the way, but you could cut around them, drive straight over toward the pool area."

"Thanks, Madera."

Gonzales went to dismiss the man, but before he did, he explained that he wanted him to go over the wall just before Juales served the warrant. The man looked unhappy about the arrangement, but didn't argue.

"You got a pair of thick gloves in the car?"

"No, sir."

"Well, get a pair from one of the others. And quick. Someone's got to have a pair. Try one of the uniforms. Put them on before you go over the wall, because if you don't and that wall's electrified, you end up with stumps. And tell the others to prepare to move, but wait for my call."

Madera moved off at a jogging pace.

As they sat there in the darkness, Gonzales said, "Okay, we've got five cars. Three men to each car, except this one. Sixteen men in total. Six uniformed." Gonzales paused, lit a cigarette, blew out smoke. "The three other cars stay outside, two covering the front and one the rear. So that leaves us and one more car to go through the gates. Any questions before we go?"

Nobody spoke.

Gonzales turned and peered through the nightscope quickly, then handed it to Sanchez. The images through the lens were grainy, eye-straining green, but Sanchez could still see the figures by the pool. Very little movement: a figure shaking its head, another leaning forward.

Sanchez put down the scope.

Gonzales said to Juales, "You want to hand out the pump-actions?"

Juales went to the back and unlocked the trunk, came back with two pump-action Browning shotguns and two boxes of cartridges. He handed a weapon each to Sanchez and Cavales, and a box each of cartridges.

They stepped out and loaded the weapons, then climbed into the back seat again. Gonzales took the scope once more, made one last check on the figures by the pool, then turned around in his seat.

He looked at Sanchez. "There are a couple of guys wandering around the lawns. But it's difficult to see them clearly."

"They look like they're armed?"

Gonzales shrugged. "I can't tell, Vellares. But we'll have to risk it. Everyone ready?"

They nodded.

Gonzales slid his own Smith & Wesson from its holster and placed it on his lap, then picked up the mobile and pressed the transmit button.

"One to Nightwatch units . . ."

6:02 P.M.

On Gonzales's command, Juales stepped quickly from the car, unholstered his gun and began to move down the hill at a jogging pace. Sanchez saw him raise his Smith & Wesson to chest height as he moved.

They saw the detective, Madera, come out of the shadows where the other police car was parked twenty meters away.

The man wore a pair of white gloves, and when Gonzales saw him, he smiled and said, "Jesus . . ."

As Gonzales slipped across into the driver's seat, Sanchez watched Juales, outside on the street, ten meters from the gates, slowing now, the gun held down by his side, the white warrant visible in his hand. A couple of meters from the gates, Juales halted, pushed himself back against the wall and waited.

Madera joined him moments later. Juales laid down the gun and warrant, cupped his hands, and Madera slid in his foot. Juales lifted him up. It took three attempts before Madera gripped the top of the wall. He pulled himself up warily, and seconds later they saw him hesitate, then disappear as he dropped over.

Juales retrieved his gun and warrant and began to move toward the gate. Sanchez noticed a police car a hundred meters down the street begin to move slowly out of shadows, ready to follow Gonzales's car through the gates.

He looked back to Juales where he waited next to the wall.

There was a sudden loud explosion, a gun discharging, followed by another shot, and Gonzales said, "*Fuck . . .*"

Everyone in the car tensed and they saw Juales race to the gate, his weapon raised and clutched in both hands. Then the gate swung open and Madera appeared.

Gonzales let out a deep sigh as they saw Juales slip inside, his gun raised in his right hand with the warrant waving at them frantically, but not looking at them as he moved in.

At that moment, Gonzales said, "Okay, amigos. Let's go."

He hit the accelerator, and the unmarked police car scudded quickly down the hill and raced toward the entrance gates.

The five men sat around the poolside table.

Turquoise water shimmered under lights. Two butlers had served them drinks, then left them alone. They had moved out to the pool at Halder's request, the villa humid, his wheezy old chest unable to stand the cloying air.

Lieber had told his story while the others remained silent. Told his story and waited for the reaction.

Old Halder coughed and sucked on his inhaler, took a deep breath. Everyone around the table looked at him. Very slowly he rose from his sunken position in the chair. He was a small man, smaller still with the weight of years on his buckled old shoulders.

There was spittle on his lips as he spoke to Lieber. "How, Franz? How could there have been another tape?" Halder's voice sounded like a whispered, throaty death rattle.

Lieber sighed deeply. "Either we destroyed the wrong tape or there were two tapes. There's no other explanation."

There was a long silence at the table. Halder's wrinkled claw of a hand went to his brow, massaged the flesh there. Thinking. Thinking hard.

"Is your *seguridad* source absolutely certain about the information?"

"Certain."

The old man hesitated. He looked across at Ernesto Brandt, then at the silver-haired man. He was about to speak further when they all heard the crack of a gunshot somewhere in the distance, then another.

Kruger sat bolt upright, then jumped to his feet, his eyes fixed on something over Halder's shoulder. Halder turned, saw one of the guards come running across the lawns, machine pistol in hand, the big man's body pounding hard across the grass.

Kruger was already moving toward the man, meeting him on the lawn ten meters away. The man spoke rapidly and Kruger turned and raced back just as everyone around the table heard the whine of car motors straining in the distance.

Kruger reached them, his face deathly pale, urgency in his voice. "We've got company. Two cars just came in through the gates." He turned back smartly, called out to the guards. *"Rotman . . . Werner . . . cover us!"*

Just as Kruger wrenched the Walther from its shoulder holster, there was a sudden shriek of sirens, a ghostly flashing of blue light visible through the shrubbery and trees, and then the growling nose of a car screamed around the gravel driveway and bumped onto the lawn. Sixty meters away, heading straight toward the poolside, lights blazing.

"Everyone! . . . Inside!" Kruger screamed at the top of his voice, and as they moved toward the patio, he turned, saw the first car, then the second, racing toward them out of the darkness, sirens wailing.

The guards were already reacting. Werner raised his machine pistol and the weapon chattered in his hands, flame leaping from the barrel.

Kruger saw the windshield of the first car shatter, heard the thumping report of lead ripping through metal. The car careened across the lawn and scudded into a tree, its blue light suddenly dying, its siren fading like a dying wheeze.

The second car, thirty meters away now, weapons prickling from its windows. A blaze of fire erupted from the vehicle, guns exploding in the darkness. Werner was blasted in the chest, his big body flung backward.

Kruger swore, reached the patio doors just as a blast of lead pellets peppered the wall to his right. He saw the look of alarm on the faces of the others as they moved into the villa through the French windows, saw the sudden paleness on the face of the silver-haired man as he called out to Kruger, "The back way, Hans. Quickly now!"

Schmidt had already torn the Magnum from its holster, and now he aimed at the oncoming car, squeezed the trigger twice.

The explosions rang around the lawns, echoed about the patio.

Kruger roared, *"Inside!"*

He pushed them in through the patio doors, hesitated long enough to see Rotman fire a long burst at the second car, the chattering weapon puncturing the vehicle, screams erupting into the night, windshield shattering, figures inside trying to shield their faces as the driver was hit in the chest and the car wove aimlessly across the lawn, shot halfway across the turquoise pool and nosed into the water.

As the guard fumbled for a fresh magazine, Kruger roared: "Keep us covered, Rotman!"

The guard didn't even look behind, simply raised his hand as he went to slam another magazine into the Heckler and Koch and moved for cover.

Suddenly, Kruger glimpsed a movement to the left of the first car, saw a figure crawl out of the wreckage where it had hit the tree.

Kruger raised the Walther, aimed, fired three quick shots, then turned and disappeared into the villa.

CHAPTER 35

Sanchez lay on the grass and watched the man disappear into the house.

The car had come to a halt in a thicket of shrubbery, the left side of the vehicle embedded in the trunk of a eucalyptus tree. When Sanchez tried to move, he felt a jolt of pain shoot down his right leg.

He had flung himself from the car at the last moment, landed hard on the grass. Now his right hip was on fire, excruciating when he moved. The car was five meters away. He couldn't see inside, the windshield shattered and frosted, riddled with bullet holes.

Sanchez still had the shotgun, gripped in both hands, and he ignored the pain in his hip, grimaced as he called out, "Gonzales! Cavales!"

There were a few seconds of silence and then he heard a groan before an answer came back—Gonzales's voice—pain in the reply.

"Over here . . . !"

Before Sanchez could reply, he heard a movement off to the right and turned. A man crouched near the pool, a machine pistol in his hands. At that moment a blaze of light erupted from his weapon and a rake of fire razed the grass beside the big detective.

Sanchez rolled to the right, into shrubbery, then aimed at the moving figure. The pump-action exploded in his hands and the recoil shook his body, but the man by the pool had moved out of sight and into the shadows of a clump of palm trees.

Rear guard. To slow them, Sanchez guessed.

The shrubbery Sanchez found himself in was poor cover, but better than nothing. Twenty meters away, the second car sank in the turquoise pool, its blue light still flashing but no sound from the siren, bubbles rising like froth, crimson patches here and there in the pale water. The left rear-passenger door was open and riddled with holes, one of the bodies of the men hanging half in, half out. Sanchez could make out a head thrown back in the driver's seat, mouth open in death.

He suddenly thought of Cavales and Juales. Dead or still alive?

He heard Gonzales swear from behind the wreckage of the car by the tree. Sanchez called out, "Stay where you are."

Suddenly another burst erupted from near the pool, fire raging across the grass, raking the car. Then the firing stopped. Gonzales swore again.

Sanchez whispered, "Are you okay?"

"I'm alive," came the reply. "Can you see the bastard with the machine gun?"

"Thirty meters away, by the pool. Can you cover me?"

"I'll try. But take it easy, amigo."

Sanchez turned, rolled deeper into the shrubbery, ignoring the pains that shot through his hip, conscious of the passing seconds, of the urgency to move into the villa after the men. He crawled quickly on his belly through the thorny undergrowth, the pain making him wince. He came out ten meters away, at the base of another eucalyptus tree, eyes trying to pick out any movement in the darkness where the figure had darted.

Nothing.

If he was going to pursue Lieber and his people, he would have to move quickly.

Suddenly a movement off to the left caught his eye and he heard a faint rustling of bushes. He strained his eyes, then saw the man crouched low among the shrubbery, caught in a shaft of moonlight. The man was waiting, hesitating, as though he was trying to decide whether to take the risk and move across the lawn. Sanchez inched forward slowly, came to within a dozen meters of the man before he saw him turn, a startled look on his face as he saw Sanchez.

The pump-action in Sanchez's hands rose and exploded. The blast hit the man in the chest, a muted cry as the man's body was hurled back into the shrubbery.

At that moment Sanchez heard sirens wailing in the distance. He turned, moved quickly back to Gonzales, ignoring the terrible pain in his hip as he knelt down beside him. In

the wash of light from the side of the house he could see
the sweat glistening on Gonzales's brow, the man's face
contorted in pain. A patch of dark below the right elbow
where a bullet had penetrated flesh.

"Your arm . . ."

"It's nothing. Just a flesh wound. We're getting too old
for this, amigo. Let's stick to conferences. You got the bastard?"

Sanchez nodded as he quickly examined Gonzales's forearm. A bullet had rutted the flesh, chipped bone. Nothing
serious, but painful.

As Gonzales tried to push himself up, he said, "The
others . . . ?"

Sanchez looked back into the silent, bullet-riddled car,
saw the frosted glass and ruptured metal where lead had
punctured neat holes, aware of his heart beating wildly as
he moved forward to look. Bile in his stomach, anger in
his head like a wild thing, knowing what to expect.

Even in the poor light he could see the bodies clearly.
Juales in the front passenger seat, his head to one side,
mouth open, a slash of red across his chest, blood everywhere below the torso and waist. Sanchez put a hand to the
man's mouth. A faint breath. He moved as quickly as he
could to the rear, unable to ignore the excruciating pain in
his hip.

In Cavales's case, there was no doubt: the top of the
man's skull had been torn apart, a gaping hole in the lower
cheek where the handsome face had once been, dark treacle
spilling out, running down his jacket. A sickening mess.
Sanchez took a deep, angry breath, wanted to vomit, held
it, fury welling up inside him, almost taking over, wanting
to rush into the villa after Lieber's people, blow them away.

He heard a sound behind him, looked around. Gonzales
had stood up, a hand on the hood of the car as he stared at
the scene inside.

Sanchez said, "Juales is barely alive, see if you can help
him."

"Where are you going, Vellares?"

But Sanchez wasn't listening. As he moved away toward
the villa, the shotgun gripped in both hands, he was aware
faintly of the police cars roaring up the driveway, the wail

of sirens coming closer. He looked back at Gonzales.

"I'm going in after them, Eduardo. Tell your men."

He heard Gonzales's voice call out after him, "Are you crazy? Wait . . . Vellares . . . my men are coming."

Sanchez didn't reply. His eyes were fixed on the patio door and the darkened room beyond, and he cocked the pump-action as he moved toward the villa.

6:08 P.M.

As they moved through the rooms, Kruger was in control, covering the rear, the emergency plan clear in his mind: move to the garage as quickly as possible, across the open space of the lawn first—a problem, of course, too vulnerable—then drive down the narrow private road through the warren-like park to the safe house. Speed vital.

Keep moving.

Five rooms to the exit that led to the lawn and the escape route. They were in the third room. No more than two minutes to the garage. But already things were not going according to plan. Kruger swore. Halder was the problem. The old man moving slowly, joints buckled and gnarled.

He ordered Lieber and Brandt to carry Halder between them, and now the six men moved through the house more quickly, old Halder, feet dangling in midair between Lieber and Brandt.

Schmidt held the Magnum .357 in his right hand, eyes watchful. The house was lit up like a Christmas tree. *Too much light.* Kruger extinguished each light as they left each room. It would slow anyone who followed.

Suddenly up ahead, a butler appeared, stepping out of a room to the right, face pale, eyes wide. Everyone startled.

Before the man had a chance to move, Schmidt raised his Magnum and fired. The explosion reverberated throughout the house, the force of the bullet sending the man sprawling backward against a wall, blood erupting on his white jacket.

Kruger swore. The noise of the big Magnum would alert anyone coming after them.

They stepped aside, passed the crumpled body.

Up ahead now, Schmidt opened another door, moved quickly inside, weapon at the ready. Another door. Then they were through and into the deserted kitchen. Stainless steel, copper, dark wood. The door at the end led outside, to the garden, darkness beyond, and Kruger saw through the windows the vast stretch of silvered lawn.

Vulnerable. Too open. Sixty seconds to cross it at a trot. More because of the others. Maybe ninety. He heard old Halder moan and ignored it. Almost there. They could make it.

Keep moving.

Schmidt moved to the kitchen backdoor, opened it slowly, peered left, right, ahead, toward the vast silvered lawn, then turned back and nodded the all-clear.

Schmidt stepped out, the others following, old Halder wheezing and groaning now. Kruger swore again. He ought to put a bullet in the old bastard, he was slowing them up as they moved across the lawn.

Kruger was the last to step out, and as he did so, he saw the light switch by the door and hesitated.

He heard a noise behind him, faint but distinguishable, coming from somewhere back in the house. A door opening?

This time he left the light on, then followed after the others.

He was moving backward across the lawn ten seconds later, still covering the rear, the Walther ready in his hand, when he saw the kitchen door move. Barely discernible.

They were perhaps twenty meters across the grass, moving fast—as fast as old Halder would allow—Lieber and Brandt grunting under the weight of the old bastard as they carried him between them, another forty meters to go, breaths gasping, hearts pounding.

Kruger had left the kitchen light on deliberately, knowing that if anyone came through, they would be at an immediate disadvantage: light looking into dark.

But Kruger would be able to see. Able to see and respond.

And Kruger *definitely* saw the movement. Seconds later, the door burst open, a figure appearing, but only for a glimpse and then the figure disappeared from view.

Kruger swore, went to fire, but knew the shot would be wasted. He swore again . . . heard the panting and groaning of the others behind him.

"Keep moving!"

He hesitated, knelt, raised the Walther, aimed toward the lighted kitchen, waiting to see the figure move again, judging the distance—a difficult shot . . . eyes scanning the room for movement, counting the seconds . . . two, three, four, five, six, seven . . . and then a shotgun blast erupted and the kitchen light went out.

Fuck!

The bastard was clever, knocking out the light, guessing his strategy. Dark looking into light so easy, dark into dark difficult, leveling the odds.

Kruger waited . . . eyes narrowing, straining desperately to see into the silvery darkness, counting . . . eight . . . nine . . . ten . . . eleven . . .

A faint movement, to the left?

Kruger fired off three rapid shots . . . heard the crack of lead smack into glass, plaster, heard the kitchen window to the left shatter.

Then nothing.

A shout from behind him. "Kruger!" Leiber's voice. "It's Halder! Something's wrong!"

"Keep moving!" Kruger shouted back, not turning. *Fuck Halder.*

But he heard Halder's wheezing gasps, and his eyes darted back; the others still moving, almost at the garage, but Lieber and Brandt slowing, holding the sagging, ancient body of Halder between them, something up with the old man, his heart probably, not able to take the strain. Kruger wiped sweat from his brow, tried to control his breathing as his eyes went back to the kitchen.

A movement. To the right.

Kruger fired three more quick shots in a short arc, heard the smacks as the lead hit glass, then concrete, wood, concrete.

And then suddenly he saw the figure.

Moving toward them out of shadow: a large man in a light suit moving quickly out onto the silvered lawn like a specter, long barrel of a weapon at waist height visible as he advanced steadily toward them.

Kruger aimed and fired three quick shots at the ghostly figure, saw the man buck and then spin.

Kruger went to fire again, but the hammer clicked. Empty. He tore out the spent magazine, slammed home a fresh one from his pocket.

He focused on the man again. The bastard was still coming, his body listing to one side.

Kruger brought up the Walther, aimed at the center of the target, squeezed off one round, was about to squeeze the trigger again when at almost the same moment, he saw the man's hands swing up the shotgun, the weapon exploding and a blast of air whistling past Kruger's left like a hurricane, then another, and another . . .

Jesus!

Screams erupted in the night. Something stung Kruger's left shoulder and he was spun around, the Walther wrenched from his hand, and as he spun, Brandt and Lieber were flung back onto the grass, hands flailing, old Halder collapsed between them.

Kruger searched frantically on the grass for the pistol, but couldn't find it . . . a numbing, prickling pain in his left forearm and hand . . . heard a groan from the tangle of bodies on the grass, then silence.

Forget the weapon . . . the man fifteen meters away . . . halting, loading again in the darkness, calmly . . . like it was no big fucking deal.

Kruger saw the moment and seized it.

He scrambled backward on his hands, past the pile of bodies—Lieber, Brandt, old Halder—oblivious to his pain, not caring whether the three men on the grass were dead or alive, as he ran toward the garage where the others had entered.

As he ran, gulping deep mouthfuls of air, he waited for the shotgun blast to hit him in the back.

It never came.

Panting, he reached the garage door and stepped into darkness.

*   *   *

Sanchez stood in the middle of the lawn reloading the shotgun.

He saw the man run toward the building at the end of the lawn, half hidden behind a clump of trees. Too far away now to get a good shot.

There was a numbing, prickling sensation in his right shoulder where two bullets had hit him with the force of sledgehammers, sending him reeling. No pain there, not yet, but it would come.

He loaded five shells and cocked the pump, stepped forward, pain shooting through his thigh and hip like fire.

The man on the lawn had given him no choice but to fire. Not to have done so would have meant death. He had fired but missed, the shotgun exploding in his hands, firing to the right, hitting the group of men instead as they moved with their backs to him across the lawn.

Shit.

These were the men; these were the people. No doubt in his mind.

And he had wanted them alive, hoped they still were.

As he approached the bodies on the grass, he held the shotgun at the ready. He saw Franz Lieber's face clearly in the moonlight, contorted, twisted. The blast from the pump-action had hit him in the back. Lieber wasn't moving. Sanchez grimaced; he had especially wanted Lieber alive.

He heard a groan, halted, looked down. Another body, arms twisted to either side. A man with glasses, big forehead. This one was still alive. A gurgling sound came now from the man's throat, his eyes closed, face screwed up with pain. There was a dark patch of blood on his left arm and shoulder.

Sanchez saw a third figure between the two men, lying facedown. There were bloodstains on the back of the pale suit where the shot had blasted the man's body. Sanchez bent, turned him over. A small, wizened old man. It was the pale suit he had seen on the dark lawn and aimed toward. One of the old man's clawlike hands was raised as if in supplication. Sanchez stared at the face. Not one of the faces in Lieber's photograph. Nor the man lying on the grass near him, the one still alive. The man groaned again.

Sanchez ignored him. Gonzales's men would deal with him.

From behind him there suddenly came muted, distant noises. He turned sharply, saw no one. Gonzales's men, probably somewhere in the house. Sanchez ignored the noises and turned back, toward the building. The man who had escaped had gone inside after the others, and he knew the only real hope lay in finding them.

He began to step toward the building behind the clump of trees.

Sweat drenched the back of his neck, images burning in his skull. Rudi Hernandez and the young girl, the savage wounds inflicted on their bodies. The body of Cavales, face blown away. Gonzales's men: Juales and the men whose car had been raked with fire and plunged into the pool.

The images drove him on, made him oblivious to his own safety, desperate to find the men who had escaped.

The bodies on the grass behind him: he had seen how the man had ignored them, unconcerned about his comrades, caring only for his own safety. A coward. Ruthless.

He stepped closer to the building, no longer aware of the ache in his hip and leg, the pump-action held firmly in both hands.

Ten meters from the building, he saw the door, silver light washing on wood. He approached cautiously and raised the shotgun. He squeezed the trigger twice: the blasts shattering silence, fragmenting wood, sending what remained of the door smacking back against the inside wall, where it bounced and shuddered off concrete, then settled on creaking hinges as the peppering lead rattled against metal somewhere inside the building.

Then the noise died.

Darkness inside, beckoning. Sanchez pressed himself against the outside wall. There was a crack where the door had abutted the frame. He peered in, listened. No sound. But if the men were inside, they could be waiting. He stepped around warily, the pump-action at the ready, eyes narrowing, concentrating on the darkness facing him, trying to discern shape, form.

The smell of oil. And gasoline. A garage? He peered again, could make out the faint shape of a big car parked in the center of the building, a dull glint of polished metal, a sheen of glass reflected. Now that he looked closely, he saw another door, ajar, at the end of the building, a thin crack of silver moonlight shining through. Had the men escaped there? Or were they waiting for him? If they were waiting, this time he would have to wound, not kill. Difficult with the pump-action. He would have to be careful.

He listened.

Still nothing.

He couldn't wait forever.

He took a deep breath, felt the sweat coursing down his face as he leveled the shotgun, swung around from the wall, moved inside.

And then . . .

A light suddenly went on overhead and blinded him.

Sanchez barely heard the barked command: *"Schmidt!"*

In the sudden, blinding light, he saw the form of a huge man lunge at him from behind the car—big, blond, a crazy look on his face like a wild animal, the glint of jagged metal in his hand.

Sanchez swung the pump-action up and around and squeezed the trigger. The deafening roar that followed raged through the garage like a sonic boom.

Sanchez saw the look on the man's face: ugly, snarling, his body like some boulder of granite bearing down on him as the shotgun exploded half a meter from the man's chest.

The force of the blast halted his body in midair—his chest and belly exploding, a cavernous hole appearing in the center of his huge torso, gut spilling out and a wave of gushing blood, the animal look on the man's face becoming a look of horror.

The man collapsed on top of Sanchez, pinned him against the wooden wall, the crushing weight knocking his breath out, the face up against Sanchez's own, eyes open wide.

Sanchez smelled the wheezing, foul breath.

The man was still alive.

Sanchez's fingers tried frantically to unpin the shotgun, struggled to push the man off, but the weapon was wedged between them. The terrible weight pressing down on him, making him helpless.

Two other men were visible now in the corner of his eye: a young, dark-haired man carrying a big Magnum pistol, and another man, older, tall, silver-haired, coming toward him out of nowhere, Sanchez recognizing the faces from the photograph in Lieber's house.

Sanchez made a supreme effort, pushed with all his strength. The huge blond man moved and his huge hand swung up. Sanchez saw the blade of the bowie knife arc. Sanchez found the pump-grip, reloaded, pulled the trigger just as the jagged knife thrust into his shoulder, cut through bone and flesh, pinned him to the wall.

Sanchez screamed in pain and the shotgun exploded again. This time the man's face and head disintegrated, flesh peeling from bone, his body flung backward, another wave of blood drenching Sanchez as shotgun pellets deflected back, prickled his body.

And then everything seemed to happen at once.

The two men came forward.

The younger man held the big Magnum in his hand, rage on his face, Sanchez realizing that the dead man had been expendable, a diversion. The man pointed the gun at Sanchez's temple, his other hand reaching to grasp the pump-action, wrench it away.

The silver-haired man stepped quickly forward. His tall frame towered over Sanchez. Kind, soft blue eyes, but something in them Sanchez couldn't fathom.

Did it matter now?

The man's voice whispered something to his companion, but Sanchez didn't hear. Voices—Gonzales's men—coming from outside now, distant, too distant to save him, muted, carrying across the lawn.

The distant voices had decided his fate.

The man holding the Magnum pressed the big pistol hard against Sanchez's head.

It exploded.

6:20 P.M.

The silvered lawns seemed awash with uniforms in the moonlight. Gray uniforms and flashing blue lights.

Ambulances came and went. A little later, a detective took a dazed Gonzales to the old garage, past the bodies on the grass.

When they showed him the body of Sanchez, he wanted to weep but didn't.

He looked at the corpse for a long time; the pitiful, life-less corpse pinned against the wall, the jagged blade driven through his shoulder into the wooden wall, the powder-burned hole drilled through his forehead, the floor awash with blood.

Then he looked at the body of the big blond man. What was left of it. There was a pervading smell of human ex-crement. Both bodies had defecated after death. Normal.

Sanchez had taken four of the bastards. It was little con-solation. None really. Besides, there was no pistol near the body of the blond man; someone else had done this. A detective had already told him that roadblocks were being set up around the perimeter of Chapultepec. But it was a big area. Some hope.

When he finally stepped outside, he threw up on the lawn. In the silver light, someone lit him a cigarette and he took it, wiped his mouth, inhaled deeply.

Another detective stood beside him now. After several moments of silence, Gonzales gripped the man's arm.

"Did Juales make it?"

The detective shook his head. "Dead before they got him to the ambulance."

Gonzales closed his eyes in grief, opened them slowly again, said in a dazed voice, "How many others dead?"

The detective's eyes were glazed over with incompre-hension, not that Gonzales noticed; he himself stared into nothingness.

"Four of our own men. The two friends of yours from Asunción. Six from the villa. That includes Halder and their man on the gate who got it from Madera when he tried to pull a gun." The detective paused. "I'm having roadblocks set up all the way to the city. Every possible route. A rookie says he thought he heard a car move off just after he heard the last gunshot. But in the confusion and noise, he's not exactly sure. Difficult to smell exhaust fumes with the smell of cordite and shit in there." He swallowed. "But the garage doors were open. Some traces of dark paint on the garage doors but we'll have to wait for forensics.'' He nodded back toward Halder's villa. "It's possible some of them got away."

"I want the roadblocks, tight. You understand?" Gonzales sighed, said impatiently, "Only trouble is, we don't know who or what we're looking for. What about the man you found alive on the lawn?"

"He's wounded, not badly, but he's lost a lot of blood. Two of our men went with him in the ambulance. We'll make him talk just as soon as he's patched up."

"What about staff from the villa? Anyone alive?"

"A butler. One of two. We found him hiding in the basement. The other's dead. I forgot about him; we found him in the house. Shot in the chest. He must have got in the way of their escape. That makes thirteen dead in all. But the butler who's alive is too shocked to make sense. He took some pills to calm down."

Gonzales jabbed a finger at the detective. "*Make* him make sense. Have him and the one from the back lawn brought to the Central. Find out how many people were here. Get descriptions, names." He shook his head. "Thirteen men dead . . . I don't believe it." He drew on his cigarette; his hands trembled.

He spat out bile on the lawn and said hoarsely, "And they're allowed no calls, understand? To hell with procedures, I want answers first."

The man nodded and walked away.

Gonzales looked back toward the scene of the carnage—all for what? Who *were* these people? What the fuck was going on?

The sound of an ambulance wailing up the driveway distracted him. Too late now. Far too late. Sanchez never had a chance. To do what he did was *loco*. Stupid. He must have wanted these people from the villa badly.

Another sound distracted him; this time footsteps, a soft voice saying, "Sir?"

He turned, in a daze.

A young *policía* stood there awkwardly. "Sir, there's a man out front who says his name's Cortes. Judge Felipe

Cortes." The young man put the emphasis on "Judge," hesitated, looked pleadingly at Gonzales.

"What does he want?"

"He says he wants to talk to the officer in charge. He seems pretty angry. Wants an explanation for all the noise and shooting. He asked if we knew where we were." The *policía* swallowed nervously. "He said this was Lomas de Chapultepec, a respectable area, not some tin-and-cardboard *barrio*."

Gonzales grimaced. He knew the judge: a fat and pompous bastard. He lived not far from here. Big Chapultepec house with servants and a fat wife. As corrupt as many of his neighborhood friends.

"Did he?" Gonzales was barely able to contain his rising anger. "Tell him I'm busy."

"Sir, I told him. He refuses to listen."

"Then"—Gonzales said it slowly, but frustration edged his voice—"tell him to go fuck himself. And if he's not careful, I'll have him arrested for hampering the police in the course of their duty."

He saw the young *policía's* eyes open wide at the disrespect, the anger.

Gonzales stubbed out his cigarette on the lawn. "Don't worry, I'll tell him myself."

He turned and left the young man standing there, walked slowly back up toward the villa, each step an agony.

CHAPTER 36

Dachau. Wednesday, December 21

He awoke at eight in the morning and after breakfast checked out of the hotel and drove by Wilhelm Busch's house again.

It was unlikely that the old man would be back that early, but he had wanted to try just to be certain. The white Volkswagen wasn't there, and when he rang the doorbell, there was no reply.

He drove back into town and walked through the streets for almost an hour, still with the feeling of restlessness.

He spent a frustrating hour in the park outside the S-Bahn Station, reading the *Frankfurter Zeitung*. There was snow forecast in the next twenty-four hours, and he decided that if Busch hadn't appeared by the middle of the afternoon, he would drive down to the old monastery off the Salzburg road before the weather turned bad and return to Dachau later.

There was nothing to do but wait, but his mind was seeking action. He walked back to the Ford and drove up the hill at the end of the town, and when he had descended the far side and crossed the Amper River, he saw the sign that said "Niebelungenstrasse."

When he reached the old camp five minutes later, the parking lot reserved for the tourist buses was empty. He parked the Ford near the new entrance and walked up to the gate. The railway tracks were no longer there, but the old moat was, its trough overgrown in places with dockweed and bramble, and he could see the guard towers that still stood along the perimeter.

The gate was open, but a sign on the wire fence said the camp was closed to visitors. He saw a truck with building materials parked inside, but when he couldn't see anyone around, he decided to step through.

The camp remained much as it had looked during the war, but cleaned up and prettied. The *Blockhaus*, the U-shaped barrack house that had once served as the stores and administration building, was now a museum and cinema.

To the right were the cells that had housed the maximum-security prisoners, kept in isolation by the SS.

The camp was still ringed by the original slatted concrete walls and barbed-wire, but the only testament to the rows of prison huts that had once stood there were two solitary wooden replicas, constructed to show visitors how the prisoners had existed in the squalidness of the camp. Facing the *Blockhaus* building was the Appellplatz, where the prisoners had assembled each morning. At right angles ran the Lagerstrasse, the long street down the center of the camp, once flanked on either side by the crowded prison huts.

The original gates to the camp, still bearing the words *"Arbeit Macht Frei,"* were off to the left, set in the center of the concrete guardhouse that had controlled the entrance into Dachau. Volkmann could see a red-bricked chimney through a clump of fir trees in the distance, where the old crematorium still stood.

There was a sign on the wall outside the modernized annex to the left of the *Blockhaus* that said: *"Verwaltungsgebäude."* Administration building.

Volkmann opened the door and found himself in a large, empty office. There were rows of metal shelves stacked with books, and a sign on the wall said in German "Reference Library." Another door led off to the right, and another sign said "Museum."

He opened the door. The *Blockhaus* museum was long and wide. Someone had left the lights on overhead, and there were windows in the thick walls at two-meter intervals, pale, watery winter sunlight pouring in, dust motes rising in the air.

Blown-up photographs were hung from the walls, and there were several exhibits in glass cases. A tangled mound of eyeglasses in one, looking like some grotesque work of art; a tattered, striped prison uniform in another, a ragged yellow Star of David sewn on its sleeve. In the middle of the long room stood a grim reminder of the brutality inflicted in the camp: a wooden whipping block, used by the SS guards.

On the wall to the left was a series of photographs: victims of the camp experiments, a cattle train loaded with corpses, lines of emaciated flesh that had once been men, women, children, laid out in the sun. In one, a frail young woman, wide-eyed in death and clutching a dead little girl with matchstick legs, was propped up against the wall of a barrack building as a grinning SS officer stood looking down at their bodies, his hands on his hips.

He did not know why he had come here, but for a long time he stared at the pictures, until he was overcome by the images of brutality and torture.

There was a noise behind him and Volkmann looked around. A woman stood in the doorway, carrying a sheaf of papers.

Volkmann guessed that she was one of the administration staff, and she seemed startled by his presence.

"Are you with the building-repair people?"

When Volkmann shook his head, the woman said, "The camp is closed to visitors right now. Didn't you see the sign outside on the gate?"

He walked past her but said nothing and went outside.

As he drove out of the parking lot minutes later, he was thinking of his father and he never noticed the dark green Volkswagen pull out a hundred meters behind him.

When he drove by Busch's house again, there was still no car in the driveway, but he decided to stop and try the bell just the same.

When he rang for the second time, he saw the shadow behind the frosted glass and then the door was opened by a man. Despite his obvious age, he was big and burly and he looked fit and tanned. He wore tinted, thick-lensed glasses and a heavy gray-woolen cardigan, and his head of snow-white hair was swept back off his deeply wrinkled face.

He peered at Volkmann sternly.

"Yes?"

The voice was sharp and aggressive, and when Volkmann looked closely, he saw that the man's skin was a pale yellow, and the color wasn't from sun, but from ill-health.

"Herr Busch, I wonder if I might speak with you."

"About what? Who are you?"

Volkmann produced his identity card. The old man held out a wrinkled yellow hand and took it, stared at the ID for several moments before looking back at Volkmann.

"You're the fellow who called yesterday. My grand-daughter told me. What do you want?"

There was an impatient tone in the old man's voice as he handed back the ID card.

"I was hoping you might be able to help me, Herr Busch. I'd like to ask you a few questions."

"Questions about what?" the old man demanded.

"Could we talk inside?"

Busch started to reply but broke into a sudden fit of coughing. He removed a handkerchief from his pocket and covered his mouth. Volkmann heard the wheezing breath. When he had recovered from the fit of coughing, Busch wiped his mouth with the handkerchief and said brusquely, "You better come in."

The old man led him into the hallway. As soon as they stepped through, Busch broke into another fit of coughing. He took out the handkerchief again and coughed into it, then pointed to a door on the right. "Wait in there, in the conservatory," he said gruffly.

The old man left him, opened a door into another room, and Volkmann did as Busch said.

The living room he stepped into was long and wide, and at the end of it, steps led down to a sunken floor that formed part of a conservatory. Strong winter sunlight poured in through the glass and the room was very warm. The framed photographs hanging on the living room walls were of Busch's extended family, he guessed, and Volkmann saw an old one in black-and-white of Busch in officer's uniform.

Volkmann went to sit in a cane chair while he waited. Busch came into the room moments later. He was still good on his feet considering his age, but when he sat opposite, he placed a hand on his chest as he looked at Volkmann.

"The consequences of old age and too many cigarettes, Herr Volkmann. The medicine helps for a while. Now, what is this about?"

There was still a gruffness in the man's voice that irritated Volkmann; it suggested he was used to giving orders. The images on the walls of the camp museum were still fresh in Volkmann's mind, and when he glanced at the

photograph of Busch in uniform, he felt a flush of anger.
He looked at the man and his tone was businesslike.

"You're familiar with DSE, Herr Busch?"

"I've heard about it, yes."

"You were with the Gehlen organization after the war.
You were an intelligence officer."

"That is correct, yes. But what's this got to do with—"

"During the war, you were also an officer in the *Abwehr*."

Busch's watery blue eyes became suddenly wary. "That
was a long time ago. Perhaps if you tell me what this is
about?"

"A case I'm working on. I hoped you might be able to
help me."

Busch hesitated, and his tone seemed to mellow slightly.
He half smiled. "Herr Volkmann, I retired from intelligence work many years ago. I am no longer involved, even
indirectly. So I don't understand why you would want my
help."

Volkmann explained about Hernandez's murder and the
story the journalist had been working on. When he told
Busch about the house in the Chaco and the man who
owned it, he saw the confused frown still on Busch's face
and said, "Herr Busch, the man who owned the house
joined the Nazi Party in Munich in nineteen twenty-seven.
His party number was six-eight-nine-six. Twelve numbers
away from yours."

The look on Busch's face went from puzzlement to understanding; then the old man said, "I see." He looked
away for several moments, then back at Volkmann. "And
how did you find me, Herr Volkmann?"

"I had the Nazi Party membership files checked for a
recent address and cross-referenced with the WASt, where
your military records were confirmed before you received
your state pension. There are only two men still alive in
Germany who had party numbers relatively close to the
number of the man I spoke of. You are one of them."

Volkmann explained about Otto Klagen, and Busch simply nodded. The old man looked away toward the garden
for a few moments. The heat that lingered in the conser-

vatory had become stifling and Busch shifted uncomfortably in his chair.

"You said this man in Paraguay was dead. I don't understand. What relevance has he to the murder of the journalist you spoke of?"

"None, obviously, Herr Busch, but he originally owned the house and property where we found the photograph, and his past is very unclear. Someone was living in the house who was related to him and who may be implicated in the murder. It might help if I knew more about this man whose number was close to yours. It may help fill in some gaps in the investigation." Volkmann paused. "I also learned that while living in Paraguay, the man who had owned the property had received large sums of money from Germany, both before and during the war. I don't know why. Your party number was close to his. I was hoping you might remember him and shed some light on the matter." Volkmann paused again and looked at Busch. "I realize it's unlikely, Herr Busch, but you are the only connection I have."

Busch half smiled and shook his head. "Herr Volkmann, we're talking about a long, long time ago."

"I realize that. All I ask is that you just look at the photograph and tell me if you recognize the man."

Before Busch could reply, Volkmann removed the photograph of Erhard Schmeltz from his wallet and handed it across.

The old man sighed, then slowly took the photograph. He looked down at it, then back up at Volkmann and shook his head.

"The face . . . I'm sorry, I can't remember. Besides, my eyes are not what they used to be. I'm sorry you've wasted your time." He looked at Volkmann as he went to hand back the photograph. "The man, what was his name?"

"Erhard Schmeltz. He came from Hamburg. But like I said, he joined the party in Munich."

Something flickered in the old man's watery eyes and he stared down at the photograph again. When he finally looked up, Volkmann saw the look of disbelief on the wrinkled face.

Volkmann said, "You remember him?"

Busch said slowly, "Yes, I remember him."

"You're certain?"

Busch's yellow skin had turned pale. "I met him many times." He paused for a moment. "And the name, yes . . . I remember. Erhard Schmeltz. From Hamburg."

Volkmann said, "Can you tell me anything about him?"

Busch hesitated, then looked out at the garden; he suddenly looked very uncomfortable. He turned back to Volkmann and his tone softened.

"Would you mind if we stepped out into the garden, Herr Volkmann? The heat . . . I need some air."

When Volkmann nodded, the old man stood up shakily. After they put on winter coats, he led the way to the door.

They sat facing each other on the wooden chairs at the picnic table. Busch still held the photograph of Erhard Schmeltz in his hand and he looked down at it. His voice sounded shaky, and when he looked back up again, he didn't look at Volkmann but toward the bare fruit trees at the end of the lawn.

"Erhard Schmeltz, from Hamburg. Yes, Herr Volkmann, I knew him."

"What sort of man was he, how did you meet him? Anything at all may help."

Busch looked back as if he were still lost in reverie.

"He knew my father. That was how I first met Erhard Schmeltz. He had served in the First War, so he was much older than I. He and my father worked together for a time. The kind of man Schmeltz was? Physically, he was a big man. Tough and dependable. But a peasant, not an intellectual. The type who takes orders, not gives them."

"How did you meet him?"

Busch hesitated. "It was the winter of nineteen twenty-seven, just before I joined the party. In those days, the Nazi movement was gaining ground. Germany had come out of a war with nothing." Busch stared at Volkmann. "People say things are bad now, but in the old days it was worse, believe me. Do you know what it's like to see a man wheeling a barrow full of banknotes to the bakery shop to buy a loaf of bread, Herr Volkmann? Crazy. But that's how it was in the nineteen-twenties.

"Every day there were riots and protest marches and armed anarchists roaming the streets. No one could find decent work. And when people saw university professors reduced to selling trinkets and matches on street corners, they knew they were lost." Busch removed his glasses, rubbed his eyes. "My father had been a soldier in the First War, like Schmeltz. And when he returned after the armistice, there was nothing for him but a long list of menial, badly paid jobs. We went from lodging house to lodging house, barely eking out an existence, never enough bread in the house to feed a hungry family.

"And then came the Nazis. They promised prosperity. They promised work. They promised hope. They promised to make Germany great again. Drowning men will grasp at straws, and we Germans then were drowning, believe me. There was a price to be paid of course, but that came much later."

Busch stopped rubbing his eyes and stared at Volkmann.

"You might ask what has all this got to do with Erhard Schmeltz? Nothing, except that I want you to understand the background and how we came to meet."

Volkmann said quietly, "Tell me about him."

"Schmeltz worked in the same factory as my father in Munich. One day in the early winter of nineteen twenty-seven, the factory closed down. That evening my father and his colleagues went out to get drunk to forget their sorrows, and later my father brought some of the men home to meet my family."

Busch paused. "My father and his friends were very drunk and very despondent. One of the men present was Erhard Schmeltz. They all sat around the table in our kitchen having soup and bread. They talked of Germany's hopelessness. I sat with them. Schmeltz, I remember, was a quiet man. He had been a factory foreman. Diligent and trustworthy. The loss of his position had upset him completely. At the table, he brought up the subject of the Nazis. Most of the other men present were communist or socialist party supporters. My father was apolitical. But Schmeltz declared that he was going to support the Nazis and become a party member. He said they were the only hope for Germany and suggested that my father and the others do likewise. When they declined, Schmeltz tried to interest me. I was a youth and easily impressed by Schmeltz's enthusiasm, plus the fact that Schmeltz said he knew Hitler and had served in the First War with him and some of the other top Nazis. A week later, I applied for membership and was accepted.''

"How often did you meet Schmeltz?"

Busch shook his head. "After that night, I didn't see Erhard Schmeltz again for at least another year. I joined the party without Schmeltz's help or recommendation. He and I were not close friends—he was much older than I, but I got to know him."

"You say he knew some of the top Nazis personally. Who did he know?"

Busch paused for a moment, looked out at the bare winter trees. "Himmler, Goering, Bormann. And he and Hitler were old comrades. They had served in the same regiment. I later heard that Heinrich Himmler himself had proposed his Nazi Party application. But that's all I know. I didn't hear Schmeltz mention his connections again after that night. He was really a very private man. But it gave him a certain amount of status in the party."

"What was Schmeltz's function in the party?"

Busch shrugged. "Nothing important. He was just a functionary. He helped at elections and played bodyguard. Many times I saw him at party rallies, or in the Munich beerhalls with some of the bigwigs. Especially Bormann and Himmler. But he wasn't the type who would have made it to the top himself. He was more brawn than brain, but a loyal and trusted party man."

"Did Schmeltz wear a uniform?"

Busch nodded. "Yes, black jackboots and kepi and brownshirt. Standard SA uniform."

"Did you know that Schmeltz emigrated to South America, Herr Busch?"

"No, I didn't. And by telling me, you solved an old mystery."

"How?"

"Sometime in nineteen thirty-one, Erhard Schmeltz disappeared. No one knew where he had gone. But if what you say is true, now I know."

Volkmann paused, looked at the garden, then back again. "Do you know of any reason why Schmeltz might have gone to Paraguay? If he was the loyal Nazi Party member you say he was, why did he leave Germany?"

Busch turned back. The old man regarded Volkmann solemnly.

"Why is this so important, Herr Volkmann? All this happened over sixty years ago. What relevance has it to now, to the present?"

"I don't know how exactly, but I believe it has. Do you know why Schmeltz ended up in Paraguay, Herr Busch?"

Busch paused, then slowly shook his head. "No, I don't. But I do remember there were rumors after he disappeared."

"What rumors?"

"That he was in trouble with someone high up in the party and had been killed." Busch shrugged. "But there were so many rumors. That he had been sent away on a mission. That he had got into someone's bad books and been forced to leave the country. But which story is true, I cannot say." Busch hesitated. "You said there was a photograph . . . of a woman? May I see it?"

Volkmann removed the photograph from his pocket and handed it across. Busch squinted down at the image.

Volkmann said, "Do you recall ever having seen that woman before, Herr Busch?"

The old man looked up. "Herr Volkmann, at my age, faces are difficult to remember. The girl could be anyone. And my eyes . . . they're not the best, I'm afraid. You know the young woman's name?"

Volkmann shook his head. "No. There was just a date on the back of the original photograph. July eleventh, nineteen thirty-one."

Busch peered intently at the image once again, then shook his head. "I'm afraid she is not familiar to me."

"Could she have been a relative of Erhard Schmeltz's?"

Busch thought for a moment, looked again at the photograph more closely, then shrugged, handed it back.

"Perhaps. It's possible. I thought perhaps his sister. I met her many times, but it's not her."

"What about his wife, or a girlfriend?"

Busch shook his head firmly and smiled. "No, definitely not. Most definitely not. Schmeltz wasn't a womanizer. He was a big, awkward countryman who always appeared ill at ease around women." He paused. He began to say something, then appeared to change his mind.

Then, as Volkmann replaced the photograph in his pocket, Busch said, "You're not telling me everything, are you, Herr Volkmann?"

The light was fading to gray now, the sun gone behind clouds.

Volkmann said, "Erhard Schmeltz emigrated to Paraguay in November of nineteen thirty-one. According to records in Asunción, he had with him his wife, Inge, and their child, a boy named Karl. Schmeltz also had five thousand American dollars in his possession. Two months later, he received a bank draft from Germany for another five thousand American dollars. At exactly six-month intervals afterwards, he received further drafts of five thousand American dollars each. At first the drafts were sent privately. But after the Nazis came to power, they were sanctioned and sent secretly by the Reichsbank, right up until Schmeltz died in Asunción in nineteen forty-three. After that, his wife received the money, until February of nineteen forty-five, when the drafts ceased." Volkmann paused. "I'd like to know why Schmeltz received that money, Herr Busch. It may or may not have relevance to the case I'm working on, but I'd like to know. It's part of the puzzle."

Even in the fading light, he saw that the old man had turned pale again, and he stared into Volkmann's face. He opened his mouth to speak, then closed it.

Volkmann said, "Is something the matter?"

Busch hesitated, shook his head slowly. "No."

"Something I said, did it surprise you?"

Busch was silent, then he said, "Everything you have said so far about Erhard Schmeltz has surprised me." He looked away, stared out into the fading light. His face was as white as chalk. "Do you know who sent the money that Schmeltz received from Germany?" he asked.

"I've no idea. But someone with authority. It had to be, once the Reichsbank was involved."

"Why do *you* think the money was sent?"

Volkmann shook his head. "I've no idea." He looked at Busch. "But it surprises you that Erhard Schmeltz was sent such large sums?"

"Of course. He wasn't a wealthy man. At least not while I knew him. And I can't think of a reason why he would have received such amounts."

"You think it's possible Schmeltz was playing banker for someone, helping someone to put away money secretly? Someone high up in the party?"

Busch thought for a moment, then shrugged. "It's possible. When I worked in the Gehlen organization after the war, certainly information like that came to light. Germans abroad helped Nazis set up secret bank accounts. But that happened mostly toward the end of the war, when everyone knew defeat was inevitable. Not before. And most of those accounts were kept in Switzerland."

"Did you ever hear of Erhard Schmeltz being mentioned in that regard?"

"No, Herr Volkmann, I didn't."

Volkmann looked at the old man. Something seemed to be troubling him, but he remained silent, his brow furrowed.

Finally, Volkmann said, "One last question, Herr Busch."

Busch looked around absentmindedly and Volkmann said, "When you were an intelligence officer in the *Abwehr*, were you familiar with any of the officers in the Leibstandarte SS division?"

"Some, yes."

"The names Heinrich Reimer or Manfred Kesser, do they mean anything to you?"

"They were Leibstandarte officers?"

"Both of them. The first held the rank of major in nineteen forty-four. The second was a general."

"The name Heinrich Reimer is not familiar to me. I don't recall any Leibstandarte officer of that name. But Manfred Kesser, I believe I may have heard of. But only in passing. I don't believe I ever met the man."

"Did you ever hear of something called the Brandenburg Testament?"

Busch's wrinkled face came up sharply to stare at Volkmann.

"Has this got something to do with what we're discussing?"

"Let's just say it came up in conversation. Why, you've heard of it?"

"Yes, I've heard of it."

"Tell me what it was."

"Just old Nazi propaganda, Herr Volkmann."

"What do you mean?"

"In late February of nineteen forty-five, two months before the war ended, a meeting was said to have been held in Berlin in Hitler's bunker, in the Reich chancellery grounds near the Brandenburg Gate. It was supposed to be top secret, but we heard rumors about it afterward in the *Abwehr*. Hitler's most loyal SS were said to have been present at the meeting. Mostly Leibstandarte SS, his bodyguard. The people he thought he could most trust. Even they knew defeat was imminent by then, but none would dare admit it publicly. Instead, they talked about regrouping to carry on the war. The Testament was said to have been a legacy proposed by Heinrich Himmler, and sanctioned by Hitler."

"What kind of legacy?"

"Herr Volkmann, it was really only propaganda nonsense, I assure you."

"Tell me anyhow."

"In the event of the Reich being defeated, gold and bullion held by the Reichsbank and SS were to be secretly shipped to South America, and also hidden in parts of Germany. The belief was that when the time was right again, the party would be resurrected. You could say it was a blueprint to secretly reestablish the Nazi Party." Busch paused. "When we heard about the plan in the *Abwehr*, we laughed. As with so much that was promised at the end of the war, we knew it was an empty promise. The foolish hope of desperate men, Herr Volkmann. Like Goebbels's Werewolves, the underground army that was supposed to destabilize Germany after the Allies had occupied the country." Busch looked at Volkmann. "Besides, the Testament came to nothing. Certainly gold and other bullion made its way to South America after the war. But most of it was used for no other purpose than to keep a chosen few in comfort and security for the rest of their lives. But the amounts of money Schmeltz received and when he received it, that would eliminate him from any connection, surely?''

Volkmann nodded.

For a long time, Busch was silent. It was growing cold in the garden; he finally looked at his watch and stood up slowly. ''I'm afraid I must take my leave of you. I have things to attend to.''

Volkmann stood up also and said, ''Thank you for your help.''

Busch led him inside, and when they reached the front door, he said, ''The smuggling operation you spoke of, Herr Volkmann, you think it's gold?''

''I really don't know, Herr Busch.''

Busch half smiled, and the blue eyes looked at Volkmann keenly. ''I really wouldn't place any credence in the Testament you asked about, Herr Volkmann, believe me.''

Volkmann nodded. Busch seemed about to say something more, but hesitated. Then: ''There is one more thing. Something perhaps you should know. I don't know if it's relevant, and I meant to say it earlier, but our discussion was somehow deflected.'' The old man paused as Volkmann looked at him. ''According to your information, Erhard Schmeltz went to South America with his wife and child.''

''That's what the records in Asunción say.''

''The boy's name again?''

''Karl.''

''And when was the boy born?''

''The records say four months before Schmeltz arrived in Paraguay.''

Busch shook his head vigorously. ''Herr Volkmann, it couldn't have been Erhard Schmeltz's wife, and it couldn't have been his son.''

Volkmann stared back at the old man in confusion.

''Why?''

''Because Erhard Schmeltz never married, Herr Volkmann. At least not in Germany. Nor did he have any children that I knew of. And the woman who emigrated to South America with him would have been his sister. I thought perhaps it was she in the photograph you showed me, but it wasn't. Her name was Inge, I remember. She was a rather unattractive, awkward countrywoman who had never married or had children. She lived with her brother as his housekeeper, and she disappeared at the same time as Erhard Schmeltz." Busch paused and shook his gray head. "So whoever the boy was that you say they took with them to Paraguay, he wasn't their child."

CHAPTER 37

Mexico City. December 21, 12:00 A.M.

It was warm in the basement interview room, the atmosphere charged with tension.

Tension and frustration.

The gray walls were awash with bright light, and Gonzales grit his teeth as he stared down at the Brazilian, Ernesto Brandt, seated behind the table. The man's left shoulder and arm were bandaged, his arm in a sling, and he looked to be in pain.

Gonzales himself had been attended to by a paramedic at the villa; the man had given him a couple of yellow pills and told him to see a doctor immediately. The throbbing in Gonzales's arm wouldn't go away, but the doctor would have to wait; there was too much to do, too little time.

He stared down at the Brazilian.

The man had thinning brown hair and wore metal-framed glasses with thick lenses. His high forehead made him look like a professor or some sort of academic. He sat there impassively, except when his face showed his pain, but silent throughout the one-sided conversation that had gone on for almost three hours.

Gonzales had put his two best interrogators on the job, and they had questioned Brandt for an hour before Gonzales himself arrived. Now he glanced at his watch. After midnight.

The interpreter, a shy, young bespectacled man, sat opposite, his presence a waste of time because Brandt was saying nothing.

He had been read his rights, in Portuguese, by the translator. Gonzales spoke a little Portuguese himself; not much, but enough to get by. There would be no lawyer until Brandt spoke. No food, no water, no painkillers. Nothing. Extreme, for this was an extreme situation. But hours had gone by now, and Gonzales might as well have been talking to a mute.

When he had first come into the room, after speaking to the Mexico City commissioner of police—a heated discussion that had left Gonzales angry and drained—Brandt had already been interviewed by the two senior detectives, using the translator.

Gonzales had spoken briefly to one of the detectives outside in the hallway before entering the interview room and had seen the look of frustration on his face.

"I'm talking to myself," the detective had said.

"Tell me," Gonzales almost spat.

"His name's Ernesto Brandt."

"He told you?"

The detective shook his head. "He told us nothing. He hasn't spoken a single word. Just sits there. When we searched him, we found a key card for the Conrad Hotel. I had a man go over and check out the room."

"And?"

"Our dumb friend checked in two days ago off a flight from Rio. Our man went through his luggage. The usual garbage. But also a Brazilian passport in the name of Ernesto Brandt with our friend's photograph. Age fifty, born in Rio. The passport looks good."

Gonzales had raised his eyebrows. "You checked it out with the Brazilian Embassy?"

The detective nodded. "They're checking with Brasilia. They'll get back to us as soon as they have anything."

Gonzales had sighed. The detective had said, "Any luck with the roadblocks?"

Gonzales had shaken his head. No luck. But then, they didn't know what they were looking for. An immediate disadvantage in a city of over twenty million. Brandt would know how many people had been in the villa and who they were. Or what type of car the person or persons who had murdered Sanchez had escaped in.

The only people at the villa that had any sort of identification were Lieber—the false passport in the name of Monck—and the two butlers.

The second butler, who had survived, had been able to tell them nothing. They had learned from the contents of his wallet that he worked for a catering company often used by Halder. But the butler had been in a state of shock. Immediately after the shooting at the villa, he had swallowed a hundred and fifty milligrams of Largactil and twenty milligrams of Serenace. A strong cocktail of calmers. Now he was muttering dazedly, tranquilized to the eyeballs in the psychiatric unit of the Valparaiso Hospital on Calle Ciudad. A zombie.

The psychiatrist attending him said that maybe in twenty-four hours the police could talk with him, but right now, the drugs were in control. "You might as well talk to the wall," the doctor had said. A detective was beside the man's bed in case he became coherent. But it was unlikely for many hours.

And time was one thing Gonzales did not have.

He had learned that the old man named Halder wasn't quite dead when the shooting stopped. He'd suffered a heart attack. The old bastard had died as they stretchered him to the ambulance, just like Juales had. He could have been useful.

The detective had nodded back toward the interview room and said, "You want to try with Brandt? Personally, I think you'd get more response from a chimp at the city zoo. The guy has got glue on his lips."

Gonzales scowled and nodded toward the room. "Okay, let me talk to him."

The man had watched him enter the room. Watched and said nothing. Gonzales felt the vexation rise within him, wanted to lash out, beat the silence out of Brandt, pummel him with angry fists. Juales dead. Cavales dead. Sanchez dead. And ten other s.

Thirteen bodies. A bloodbath.

And yet this man said nothing. No sign of fear on his face. Calm. Controlled, despite his pain. Hours of frustrated questioning, threats, pounding the table in front of him, had produced nothing.

Gonzales tried again. "Your name?"

Silence.

"Why were you at the villa?"

Brandt continued to look straight ahead at the far wall. Gonzales grit his teeth. "Tell me the names of the men who were with you at the villa."

Brandt licked his upper lip, but his eyes didn't move or flicker.

Gonzales said, "One last time I'll tell you. The charges against you are serious. Complicity in the murder of six police officers. Resisting arrest. Attempting to flee the scene of a crime. I could go on but I'm losing my patience. You realize that?" Gonzales's fist pounded the table. "So talk! Why were you at the villa? Who were the men meeting Lieber?"

Gonzales reached over, wrenched Brandt from his seat by the lapel nearest his wounded arm. Then he made a fist, clenched into a tight, angry ball.

For once, Brandt reacted. He screamed in agony.

Gonzales let fly.

The fist halted a hairsbreadth from the man's face. Gonzales let out a deep sigh of frustration. Out of character, this behavior, but born of frustration. From the corner of his eye, he saw the detectives and the interpreter stare at him. Grudgingly, he let go of the Brazilian's lapel.

Brandt's face was contorted in pain. Slowly he sat down. He stared up at Gonzales for a moment, but remained silent. No sign of fear, but a little anxious now.

Controlled again, Gonzales said quietly, "I want you to listen to me, Brandt, or whoever the hell you are. Listen well. Thirteen men are dead. Some of them were policemen, close personal friends of mine. Good friends. Good men."

Gonzales hesitated, took a deep breath, let it out, then went on: "The charges you face are serious. But if you can help me with names, descriptions, the number of people in the house, anything, no matter how small, I will make certain that your help is considered by the court, you understand?"

Gonzales left the words hanging, waited for a response. In the silence that followed, he could hear his own breathing, the breathing of the others in the room. The bright lights blazing on gray walls were giving him a headache.

Finally, after what seemed like an age, there was a brief flicker in Brandt's eyes. He looked up at Gonzales, stared at him.

He's going to talk, thought Gonzales.

Then Brandt opened his mouth and the words came out in Spanish, contempt in every syllable.

"I have nothing to say. Except that I want to speak with a lawyer."

Gonzales exhaled with a terrible frustration.

The man was tall and gray-haired, and wore an expensive, well-tailored suit. His face was tanned and handsome.

They sat in Gonzales's office, the two of them alone. The lights of the city sprawled and winked beyond the window.

In his left hand Gonzales held the embossed personal card the man had handed him in the basement hallway minutes before. Serif type in raised-gold lettering. Gonzales ran a finger across its shiny rough-smoothness.

First Secretary to His Excellency, the Ambassador of Brazil. The man's name below his title.

The man said in perfect, cultured Spanish as Gonzales looked up, "Perhaps you had better explain the situation to me."

Gonzales ignored the niceties and told it straight. What had happened at the villa. Thirteen people dead.

The diplomat had showed no reaction until Gonzales mentioned the body count. At that, he raised an eyebrow faintly and sighed.

When Gonzales had finished, there was a long pause; then the diplomat said, "After your detective phoned the embassy, we contacted police headquarters in Brasilia. The passport this man Brandt carried is legitimate. And concerning Brandt, I believe our chief of police in Brasilia will be contacting his opposite number here in Mexico City to discuss the matter."

The man hesitated, and Gonzales saw the perspiration on his upper lip. He was worried. When Gonzales had met him in the hallway, he had asked to see Brandt, to see him but not to talk with him. The diplomat had looked at Brandt silently for a long time. His face had turned pale; then he had nodded to Gonzales before being led upstairs to the office.

"Go on," prompted Gonzales.

The diplomat paused again as if uncertain, then said,

"This is a rather . . . sensitive matter. I believe I ought to speak with your commissioner first."

Gonzales frowned, took a deep, angry breath, then let it out and looked the man in the eye.

"I am in charge of this case. You talk only to me. Thirteen people are dead and your countryman downstairs is implicated in some way. I want answers, and fucking fast. Who's Brandt? Why are you people so interested that the first secretary himself comes here? Tell me, and tell me quickly."

The diplomat's face flashed red with anger. He was not used to being talked to in this way. *Fuck you*, thought Gonzales.

The man looked across at him. He removed a silver cigarette case from his pocket, selected one and lit it. For a long time the man said nothing, the tanned face looking sullen, as if Gonzales' lack of respect had offended him deeply. A picture of upper-class privilege, but still looking worried. Perspiration still glistening on his upper lip and brow.

Gonzales said impatiently, "I haven't got all day, Señor."

For a second or two, the diplomat glared at him, the curtness of Gonzales's tone and manner an affront. He inhaled deeply on his cigarette, then his tone changed, became almost familiar.

"Very well, Chief Inspector. Your superior will no doubt confirm this once our chief of police has spoken with him. However, I will tell you myself. What you are about to hear is highly classified and sensitive information." He paused, inhaled again, then said, "You may be aware that during the time the military was in power, Brazil developed a program for the production of nuclear weapons. After the return of democracy, the program was canceled, but not before several kilos of weapons-grade plutonium were produced. This material was not disposed of."

Gonzales watched the man without replying.

"Señor Brandt was involved in that program," the diplomat continued. "And it has come to light that he has managed to steal some of that material . . . in small quantities. But over time, the small quantities add up."

"So you're saying that some people out there have enough Brazilian plutonium to build a bomb?"

"In short, yes."

"Shit."

The story continued for five minutes, but its essence was contained in the diplomat's first words, the enormity of what he was saying making Gonzales understand Brandt's reluctance to talk.

When the diplomat had finished, Gonzales was silent for a long time, and when he was satisfied that the man had told him everything, Gonzales thanked him and led him to the door, then crossed quickly back to his desk.

The call from the commissioner came immediately.

The conversation lasted for almost two minutes; then Gonzales tapped the receiver and made the necessary phone calls immediately. All border posts, all air and sea ports—on alert.

As for the plutonium, the diplomat had no idea of where it had been taken. Perhaps it was still in South America. Perhaps radical Muslims had it. Perhaps it was in Europe or North America. The proper, international authorities would have to be notified about it. And then God only knew what they could do about it. Meanwhile, the *policía* in Asunción—Sanchez's people—might have more immediate leads.

Shit.

In a moment he tried the number of the Central Police Office in Asunción himself, but the lines were busy. He called the operator on the ground floor, gave him the number and told him to keep trying until he got through. He checked his watch. In a little while he would have to drive out to Tacubaya and tell Juales' widow of her husband's death. An unpleasant thought and deed. The man had been a good and competent policeman, and a close friend.

His head ached. He stood, lit a cigarette, and inhaled deeply as he crossed to the window. His arm still throbbed painfully, but he tried to ignore the discomfort of the tight dressing the paramedic had applied around the wound.

Beyond the glass, stardust lights stretched to the Chapultepec Hills and the Sierra de las Cruces. A big city. So many places to hide in a city of over twenty million souls, so many routes of escape. He didn't hold out much hope. People like Halder had connections, and there were other Halders. What did they call it in the old days? *Die Spinne.* The Spider. He remembered hearing the stories told to him by the old detectives when he was a rookie. The Germans who had come to Mexico with gold and money after the war and bought the big villas in the Chapultepec Hills and down along the coast. And their organization—the Spider— that was secretive and efficient in the extreme.

The chances of catching the men were slim. Without question, he would try—dig out the old dusty files, make telephone calls to the retired men who had worked on the old cases—but something was telling him that the men from the villa were already gone. It was going to be a difficult, tiring, frustrating day. Still, he had to make the effort. For Juales and his men, for a dead Sanchez and his dead compatriot, lying now in the police morgue.

The telephone buzzed. He turned, startled.

Asunción, he hoped. His call to Paraguay.

They would need to know about Sanchez and Cavales, how they had died. And just as importantly, why.

And now that he himself knew, he shook his head in disbelief. No wonder the men had been so desperate to escape the villa. He crossed back to his desk, stubbed out his cigarette and picked up the phone.

CHAPTER 38

Wednesday, December 21

It was almost five-thirty when Volkmann reached Schliersee. Twenty minutes later, he had already left Hundham behind and the Ford was climbing easily up the gentle slopes where the Wendelstein begins.

He consulted Ivan Molke's drawing. There was a minor road that led to Hundham, and Molke's map had placed the monastery eight kilometers from the town going southeast toward the Wendelstein, on the road for Waldweg. For another ten minutes there was traffic behind him, until he turned off the narrow road and found the sign that said "Waldweg."

It led down an unlit, desolate winding road and Volkmann followed it until he came to the end. The road appeared unused and was lined on either side by tall fir trees. As the headlights of the Ford swept around a corner, the roadway came to an end and he saw a narrow granite bridge, and beyond it, the two massive wooden doors of the monastery entrance, set in high sandstone walls.

He left the headlights on and as he climbed out of the car, some instinct told him to take the Beretta. He flicked open the glove compartment, slipped the pistol in his pocket, and took the flashlight and the spare batteries.

The sandstone was cracked in places and the pointwork crumbling, but the solid walls that appeared to ring the old monastery were still standing and unbreached. There was a metal crucifix high over the ancient wooden gates, its iron rusted and flaking, a brown rust stain running down the pale sandstone. A judas gate was set in the middle of the gates, and Volkmann turned on the flashlight before he doused the headlights.

As he stood there in the silence that followed, he shone the light toward the judas gate. When he pushed it, the gate swung open on creaking hinges and he stepped inside.

He found himself in a broad, cobbled courtyard. As he played the flashlight about the shadows, he saw the arched cloisters that ran along the sides. With the beam, he picked

out an ancient rusted handcart and mounds of debris that
were littered about the cobble. His footsteps echoed in the
darkness as he walked toward the center of the cobbled
square.

Beyond the courtyard, he saw what appeared to be a
building of some sort, its roof pitched higher than the cloister, and beside it stood what looked like a belfry tower.

He stepped into the arched cloister to his left.

The plaster had crumbled in places, and here and there
were several doors leading off. One of them hung on broken hinges, and Volkmann walked past it. He was in what
appeared to have been an office. There were the remnants
of old furniture, an ancient broken chair and a heavy
wooden desk. The wood smelled of decomposition. For a
few moments he stood there, the rotting stench filling his
nostrils until he found it overwhelming and stepped outside
into the cloister again.

A sandbrick archway led into another open space. Here
and there was a scattering of withered fruit trees, and
cracked paving ran around what had once been a tiny garden. An old fountain stood in the center, its stone bowl
filled with rainwater. As Volkmann stood there in the
moonlight, he shone the flashlight about until the shaft of
light caught the building and the tower again at the end of
the garden.

It was a small church, consisting of belfry and nave and
tiny chancel. A vestry door stood half open, the arched
doorway covered with bare, overgrown withered ivy. When
he pushed open the nave door, the sound cracked inside
like a roll of thunder. There were broken stained-glass windows set high in the walls, and here and there an ancient
pew rested on its side.

The place smelled of must and decay, and as Volkmann
went to step outside again, he hesitated. The wash from the
flashlight caught a shadow on the wall to his left, the entrance to a stairway. Stone steps led down into darkness.
Volkmann played the light over the walls and stairwell but
could see nothing beyond.

He followed the steps down warily, until he found himself in the cellars beneath the church. At the end of the
stairs was an ancient, solid wooden door. Volkmann

gripped the rusted ball knob and twisted. The door gave in easily, but its unused hinges yawned with a jarring screech.

He found himself in a large storeroom.

Bags of plaster and cement were stacked against the walls and cans of paint piled neatly. There were other building materials. The storeroom was filled with them. Volkmann examined these briefly. They appeared fresh and unused, and there was a considerable supply. As he stood up again, he heard a noise.

He froze.

Footsteps echoed from somewhere above.

He slid the Beretta from his pocket and flicked off the safety. The noise sounded as if it came from the church.

He moved back toward the door and crossed to the end of the stairwell. When he arrived at the top, he peered out into the shadowy moonlight of the church, but saw and heard nothing.

Moments later, he heard a noise again, off to the right where he had entered the vestry, and it sounded like the click of a shoe.

He raised the Beretta and moved out into the darkness. When he reached the entrance to the vestry, he halted and listened. The doorway was open a crack and there was a faint scraping noise coming from somewhere inside.

He felt the sweat rise on his brow as he crossed silently to the door. He heard another scraping sound, and then more footsteps.

Volkmann leveled the Beretta and moved quickly into the room, playing the light on the walls as he tried to find a target.

The room was silent and empty.

Another door led out. As he stepped through, he found himself in another garden, much larger this time. There were three arched cloisters, the fourth leading out to open space and darkness beyond, and he could make out the dark, tilted forms of ancient headstones in the watery moonlight.

He heard the footsteps again, but this time they were slow and echoing. He saw a shadowy figure dart back toward the garden behind him. As it vanished into the shadows, he heard the footsteps echoing hard on the cobblestones.

Volkmann raced back toward the first garden that led to the main gates, the Beretta at the ready, and as he came around into the courtyard, he saw the figure move between the cloisters.

At that precise moment, the figure halted, turned, fired twice, all in one fluid movement. The bullets cracked into the wall several meters away. Volkmann pulled back into the shadows for cover.

The Beretta came up fast and he fired off three quick shots into the dark cloister, the bullets smacking into sandstone and ringing about the courtyard. But the figure had vanished.

Volkmann was already moving toward the monastery gates, and as he stepped through the judas gate, he saw the taillights of a car disappearing down the roadway. Some instinct told him to check the Ford and when he raced toward it, he saw that the two front tires had been shot through.

He swore out loud and when he looked up again, he could just make out the red of the taillights fading through the trees before they disappeared into the darkness.

It took him almost an hour to reach the service station on the autobahn, driving on one flat tire after fitting the spare. It took another half-hour to have two new tires fitted and give a tip to the station mechanic. By then, it was almost nine, and he drove back to the monastery to take another look around, this time leaving the car half a kilometer from the Waldweg road and walking back, taking the flashlight and spare batteries with him.

There were marks on the gravel where the fleeing car had burned rubber, but apart from that, he found nothing unusual as he walked the perimeter before venturing inside again. At the stone bridge he stopped, shone the light and noticed a stream that ran in a moat around the perimeter.

He estimated that the property stood on several acres walled with sandstone, and that despite its years, it was still in solid condition, but there was nothing in the monastery or the outhouses or the gardens that suggested anything unusual, and he wondered again what significance it must have to be drawn in Kesser's notebook.

He shone the flashlight under the cloisters where the fleeing figure had fired, but there were no spent cartridge shells to be found. Whoever had fired at him had used a revolver, not an automatic.

He walked back up to the old cemetery and flashed the light between the rows of headstones. Most of the graves dated from before the war, and the most recent headstone bore an inscription dated twenty years before; he guessed that the cemetery was a private one and had belonged to the cloister. There was no evidence of any freshly dug soil, and none of the graves appeared to have been disturbed.

Volkmann drove back on the Augsburg road, stopping twice for coffee and to check to see if he was being followed, but no one was tailing him; at that hour on the autobahn, the traffic was thin and he would have noticed.

He wondered about the men in the car. Kesser's people? Who else could it be? He had checked his rearview mirror all the way down from Strasbourg to Augsburg, and he definitely hadn't been tailed. And he realized that Erica was the only one who knew he was driving down to Dachau.

He had been too preoccupied to check if he was being followed when he left there; he should have heeded Ivan Molke's advice.

It was almost three in the morning when he let himself into the apartment. The girl was asleep in his bed, her blond hair strewn about the pillow. He stood there for several moments looking down at her face, thinking about what had happened, wondering if he had been reckless in trusting her.

In the kitchen, he saw the note by the telephone: *"André rang. He said to phone him."*

He made the call to the duty office and the Frenchman answered sleepily.

"Any luck with the names?"

"Depends on what you mean by luck, Joseph. The three you gave me—Henkle, Trautman, Klee—didn't turn up on our computer. There was a Franz Henkle, but it seems he's Dutch, and wanted for narcotics smuggling. I tried every area I could, but nothing came up for any of them. So I passed it onto the German desk like you said.''

''And?''

''They came back pretty quick. They wanted to know if we had anything on the names and what the story was. I told them I didn't know, just that I got a list of names to check, and if we came up with anything, I'd get back to them.''

''So what did the German desk say?''

''That if they're the same people, they turned up as homicides in the past six months.''

''How did they die?''

''Henkle was a hit-and-run victim, but a suspected homicide. That happened six months ago. Klee was shot, Trautman the same. The Klee killing happened four months back; Trautman, five. In each case, the victims had no criminal background. Middle-aged, middle-class men with no records worth talking of. No witnesses, no suspects arrested or charged. That's why the Germans were so interested to know if we had anything.'' The Frenchman paused. ''What are you on to, Joe?''

''I don't know, André.'' He wrote down the details on the pad beside the phone. ''Anything else I ought to know?''

''I got just the bare details. Henkle and Trautman came from Essen, Klee from Rostock. Henkle was a career army officer, *Bundeswehr*, rank of major, fifty-two years of age, married, two grown children. Trautman was a businessman, a year older. Divorced. Klee was a senior civil servant who was posted to Eastern Germany after the Wall came down. Married, no kids. Forty-eight years of age. That's about it. If you want to see the homicide reports, you'll have to request them through the BP.''

''What about a connection, André?''

''I specified that when I asked the German desk. Apart from the homicide link, there's no connection that they know of between the three men, but they'd be very interested to know if there is. Does any of that help?''

''I don't know, André. But it's something. What about Hanah Richter?''

''The university is closed for the holidays. But I got the

home number for the dean of Stuttgart from the BP headquarters in Altstadt and called him. He remembered her.
She retired about ten years ago, went back to Nicolassee in
Berlin, where her family came from. He had an address in
an old diary but no number, so I had the operator check.
She's listed. I got the number and the address. You want
to take them down?"

Volkmann jotted them down on the pad. "Thanks for
your help, André."

"Any time. And send my love to the girl. She sounds
okay."

He sat on the couch sipping the scotch, thinking over the
information André had given him.

So, there was no doubt about Kesser now. He was definitely connected with the people in the Chaco, no question.
The list implicated him.

But why were the three men killed? he asked himself.
*The way to find out, obviously, is to pull Kesser in. Which
means I'll have to go through the German desk.*

He continued searching for a pattern to the puzzle, but
found none. All the men—Henkle, Trautman, Klee—were
middle-class, with professional or business backgrounds.
Like Rauscher and the woman, Hedda Pohl. The only connection Volkmann could see apart from their class backgrounds was that they would all have been born while the
Nazis were in power, but that told him little, if anything.

As he lay back on the couch, he thought again of the
shadowy figure in the monastery courtyard. The car could
have followed him on the main autobahn and then tracked
him at a distance down the Waldweg road with its lights
off, and he guessed that was what had happened.

He found the tape in his briefcase and slipped it into the
cassette player. He listened to it play through a half-dozen
times, listened to the voices in the darkness, knowing the
words before they came, knowing each inflection.

"The shipment . . . ?"

"The cargo will be picked up from Genoa as arranged."

"And the Italian?"

*"He will be eliminated, but I want to be certain we don't
arouse suspicion concerning the cargo. It would be prudent*

*to wait until Brandenburg becomes operational. Then he
will be dealt with along with the others."*

Pause.

*"Those who have pledged their loyalty . . . we must be
certain of them."*

"I have had their assurances confirmed. And their pedigree is without question."

"And the Turk?"

"I foresee no problems."

*"The girl in Berlin . . . you're absolutely certain we can
rely on her?"*

"She will not fail us, I assure you." Pause. *"There are
no changes to the names on the list?"*

"They will all be killed."

When tiredness finally overcame him, he turned off the
cassette player and removed the headphones.

It was warm in the front room and he decided to sleep
on the couch, too tired to move into the spare bedroom. He
didn't want to wake Erica and he didn't want to talk with
her just then, his mind too troubled and confused.

His head throbbed and as he lay back, he massaged his
temples, closed his eyes and tried to empty his mind, but
the voices on the tape came in on him again. What was the
shipment? Who was the Italian? The Turk? And who were
the people to be killed? The people on the lists in Kesser's
notebook?

And who was the girl in Berlin?

As he lay there on the edge of sleep, he thought of the
images on the *Blockhaus* walls at Dachau: the white bodies
lying out in rows under the sun, and the big, dark lifeless
eyes of the woman clutching her dead little girl to her
breast, the grinning face of the SS man looking down at
her.

He closed his eyes as if to erase the sight.

But the last thought on his mind as he lay on the edge
of sleep was a line on the tape.

It came like a click in the back of his head, so obvious
he wondered why it hadn't come to him before now.

Pedigree!

It was too late to do anything about it and he would have
to wait until morning to check with Berlin. But he wondered if it might be a glimmer of light in the darkness.

CHAPTER 39

Strasbourg. Thursday, December 22

The business hours of government agencies in Germany are normally eight to four, and when Volkmann made the telephone call to the Berlin Document Center, it was exactly 8:00 A.M.

He asked to speak with Maxwell, and the voice that finally came on the line was soft and American.

Volkmann explained that Ted Birken had told him to contact Maxwell personally if he needed any information from the Center. Maxwell seemed mildly put out when Volkmann gave him the list of names and requested the information he needed.

"What the hell's up with DSE that you're checking all these names? We've had a couple of requests from your people in Strasbourg, apart from the one you routed through Birken."

"I'm afraid it's classified right now, Mr. Maxwell, but you think you could check the areas I asked you about?"

Maxwell sighed. "Well, I guess . . . but it may take a little time."

"How long?"

"Maybe a day or two. We're pretty understaffed, you know. And it's Christmas. We're winding down. Can't it wait until after the holidays?"

"I realize I'm asking a lot, but it is important. I need the information today. You think it can be had?"

Maxwell sighed again. "It depends how lucky I get. It means a lot of checking. So what you're looking for is a connection in regard to these names, right? Where these people were stationed in the period you specified. And if they had any children, their names and dates of birth."

"That's it."

"It's going to mean going back through a whole bunch of files to find the right ones, if they exist. You realize that? All you've given me is names. No dates of birth, no rank."

"I realize that, Mr. Maxwell. But as I say, it's important."

Maxwell seemed to hesitate before he said, "Okay, you better leave it with me. I'll see what I can do. But I can't promise I'll get through them all."

Volkmann thanked the man and then punched in the number for Hanah Richter in Berlin's Nicolassee.

When a woman's voice answered, she told Volkmann that Frau Richter was not at home and wasn't expected to return until later that morning. Volkmann left his name and number and asked the woman to have Hanah Richter phone him back.

The return call came an hour later. A woman's voice, deep and commanding. She introduced herself as Hanah Richter.

"What's this about, Herr Volkmann?"

Volkmann explained that he was with DSE and how he had gotten her name. He had heard she had worked for the German government during the Nazi trials of the nineteen-sixties and was an expert on the period. He explained that he was working on a case and had a favor to ask; would she take a look at a photograph of a young woman taken during the nineteen-thirties? He explained about the Nazi armband in the picture. Perhaps she might be able to identify the woman, or might know someone who could help.

"Is this something official?"

"Yes."

"Are you trying to track some Nazi?"

"No, Frau Richter." He told her he couldn't explain any more than he had, but that he would appreciate her help.

"You're going back a long time, Herr Volkmann. A very long time indeed."

He asked if he could call on her in Berlin the next day, and the woman said that wasn't possible. "You've caught me at a very bad time. I'm going to Leipzig early tomorrow to stay with friends. I won't be returning until after the holidays. And besides, I stopped doing that kind of work a long time ago, Herr Volkmann."

"I realize this might be an inconvenience, Frau Richter, but what if I flew to Berlin this evening?"

"Is this really that important?"

"Yes. And I'd greatly appreciate your help."

"This young woman . . . you've no idea who she might be?"

"Perhaps the wife or girlfriend of a senior SS officer or Nazi official. But I'm only guessing. The photograph was taken in nineteen thirty-one."

He heard a deep sigh at the other end.

"Herr Volkmann, you may have been told I was an expert on the Nazi period, but my depth of knowledge does not extend to every friend of every Nazi. And you're talking about two years before the Nazis came to power, you realize that?"

"I appreciate that, Frau Richter," Volkmann persisted. "But if you could just take a look . . ."

There was a long silence at the other end of the line, and then finally the woman gave another deep sigh.

"Very well, Herr Volkmann. I had better give you directions to my home."

He organized a return ticket to Berlin with Facilities. The flights out of Frankfurt were full, but there were plenty of seats on the six-o'clock shuttle out of Stuttgart, over an hour's drive away. It was almost two when he got the return call from Maxwell.

He listened as the director of the Document Center gave him the information, jotting the details in his notebook, and when the American had finished, he said to Volkmann, "You still there?"

"Yes, I'm still here."

"Does the information help any?"

Volkmann smiled. "I think you could say that."

"Now would you care to tell me what this is about, or is it still classified?"

"I still need to do some checking with the WASt, but as soon as I know for certain myself, I'll let you know. One more thing, Mr. Maxwell . . ."

"What?"

"Happy Christmas."

Volkmann cradled the receiver, looked down at his notebook, and started to make the phone calls.

* * *

It took him less than a half-hour to get the information he needed and when he had finished making the calls, he could feel the sweat running down the back of his shirt.

He was aware of his heart pounding in his chest as he drove to the apartment. Erica wasn't there, but she had left a note to say she had gone for a walk in the park.

He drove down to the Orangerie and parked the car. He found her walking by the lake and they went to sit on one of the benches.

He told her everything that had happened the previous day and saw the look of surprise when he told her about Busch and what had happened at the monastery.

"Whoever shot at me, I don't think he meant to kill me. I was an easy target, but he fired wide. And there's something else that's strange."

"What?"

"I had a feeling about the place. As if I'd been there before. Not there exactly, but somewhere like it."

"What do you mean, Joe?"

"I can't explain it. Like a feeling of déjà vu."

She raised a hand to touch his face. "Tell me you'll be careful. It frightens me. What happened to Ivan Molke's men? You think the two things are connected? You think it's the same people?"

"Maybe."

He told her he was flying to Berlin that evening to see Hanah Richter, and explained who she was. "She may be able to help identify the woman in the photograph. Or if she can't, she may know someone who can."

"I keep thinking about what Busch said. Was he certain about Erhard Schmeltz . . . and about the child? Is he sure the child wasn't Schmeltz', or his sister's?"

"Busch was adamant. And the woman would have been too old to have had a child. The question is, who did the boy belong to if he wasn't the Schmeltzes' child?"

"And the Brandenburg Testament. Do you think that's significant . . . now?"

Volkmann looked at her. "Yes."

"But how can you be so certain, Joe?"

He looked into the blue eyes and at the pretty face. He had wondered whether to tell her, and now he decided to.

"Because, Erica, I had the Document Center in Berlin do some checking for me. Let's take Manfred Kesser first. The records say he was an SS general. Leibstandarte SS. He was stationed in Berlin at the time this Testament would have been pledged by the Leibstandarte SS. So what Lubsch heard Lothar Kesser boast about is in all probability true. I also asked for seven other names to be checked."

"What names?"

"The ones in Kesser's notebook. Trautman, Klee, Henkle. And the other names, the people Lubsch was asked to kill. Massow, Hedda Pohl, and Rauscher."

"But why ask the Document Center to check those names? You said that only Rauscher's father was a Nazi officer."

"There was a word on the tape. Lubsch used the same word when he spoke of Kesser. "Pedigree." That was the first thing. But what made it click into place was the Chaco photograph. The Nazi armband on the man's arm." Volkmann paused. "It was the only connection I could think of that was possible, apart from middle-aged, middle-class backgrounds. And the information they came up with at the Document Center, it makes a connection between all of the names. Massow, Rauscher, Pohl, Trautman, Klee, Henkle."

"What connection? None of these people were Nazis, Joe. They were too young to have served during the war."

"I'm not talking about them, I'm talking about their fathers. Each of their fathers was a Leibstandarte SS officer. And every one of them was stationed in Berlin before the war ended. The time the Testament was signed."

"But how do you know for certain?"

"The three people Kesser wanted killed, Massow, Rauscher and Pohl. There were three Leibstandarte officers with those names, Erica. Each of them with the rank of *Standartenführer*, major. The same applies to the three names found in Kesser's apartment: Trautman, Klee, Henkle. There were three Leibstandarte officers with those names also, each with the rank of major or above. And they were each stationed in or near Berlin at the time Busch spoke of. My guess is that they could have been signatories to the Testament. And the people who were killed were children of those officers."

"But there could have been hundreds of officers with those names. How can you be certain that these people are the same children?"

"Every SS officer's file stated whether he was married and had children. The names and dates of birth of the wife and children were recorded in his file. And the three people Kesser wanted killed—Massow, Rauscher, and Pohl—their births were recorded in their fathers' files. After I got the information, I telephoned Walter Massow in Berlin. His father was a Leibstandarte officer, prosecuted and imprisoned for war crimes. Maybe that's why he's a liberal politician and helping the people he's helping, trying to do penance for his father's sins. I also called the detective in Friedrichshafen. He confirmed that Hedda Pohl's father had been a Leibstandarte officer."

"And Herbert Rauscher?"

"The Document Center had a file on one Wilhelm Rauscher, a Leibstandarte major. When I checked his name with the WASt, the information they had was that he was captured by the Russians in the battle for Berlin in April of nineteen forty-five. He was sent to a German prisoner-of-war camp in Siberia. They believe he died there. It just has to be the same Rauscher. The family address was in Leipzig, where Herbert Rauscher was born."

Volkmann let the information sink in, saw her hesitate before she looked at him.

"I don't understand. Why would Kesser want these people killed? He is a fascist, a neo-Nazi. Why would he want to kill Massow, Rauscher, Pohl—and the others? Why would he want to kill the children of former SS officers?"

Volkmann shook his head. "I'm only certain of one thing. We're not only talking about the deaths of Rudi and the others. This is something that goes much deeper, and goes back a long time. To the last months of the war in Berlin, when these people swore their allegiance to Hitler. There's a reason these people were killed. Maybe they knew something they shouldn't. Maybe there's a secret someone still wants to hide. Something damaging enough to kill for. And we're not only talking about six people. There were other names in Kesser's notebook. For all I know, they could be dead. Or they're going to die. Maybe that's what the voice on the tape was talking about when it said the names on the list would all be killed. The question is, why? What was it the children of these officers were involved in or knew that made Kesser want them dead?''

"Massow wasn't killed. Did you question him, ask him if he knew the others?''

Volkmann nodded. "I told him everything I could. He seemed totally baffled by the whole thing. No one approached him, hardly anyone knew about his father's past, and that's the way he wanted to keep it. He knew none of the other people. He didn't know of any secrets his father was privy to. Anyway, his father died in prison over twenty years ago.''

"Are you going to talk with Ferguson about all this?''

"Not until I find out why these people were killed. Whatever's happening, it has to do with the Leibstandarte SS and their senior officers. With the pledge they made in the last months of the war. The people who were killed, the children of those officers, are somehow tied into it. That's how I see it. Maybe it has to do with the cargoes being smuggled.''

"You think Rodriguez was smuggling gold?''

"Maybe. But I've got a feeling there's another angle to it, not just a smuggling operation. We'll have to pull Kesser in and have a talk with him.''

The girl hesitated. "You said there were seven names you checked besides Lothar Kesser's. You mentioned only six. What was the other name?''

He had been waiting for the question and he looked at her, searched her eyes. "Your father's. He was stationed in Berlin at the same time as all the others, posted to an SS training school in the district of Lichterfelde in January of nineteen forty-five.''

There was a long silence and Erica looked away, toward the park, then back again.

He saw the expression on her face and heard the defensiveness in her voice. "Why did you check on my father?''

"Because he was an officer, the same as the others. Because he could have been one of the people Busch told me about.''

"That's not the truth completely, is it, Joe? It was be-

cause you didn't trust me and you wanted to see my reaction when you told me. And you still don't trust me, do
you? Even though you're telling me all this. You look into
my eyes and I know you're searching for answers. You're
searching to see if I'm telling the truth or lying."

"I want to believe you, Erica."

The girl said nothing for a long time, then she looked at
him. "If I was one of Kesser's people, why would I have
come to your people in the first place? Why would I have
wanted you to investigate Rudi's death? Why, Joe? Why
would I have done these things?"

He had no answer and he knew it.

"Joe, I hardly knew my father. I never believed in his
ideals. I'm not one of Kesser's right-wing extremists. You
must believe this. You must trust me. The fact that my
father was in Berlin at the same time as the others, that he
even could have signed this Testament—I never knew any
of this until you told me."

He looked at the blue eyes watching his and remembered
the warm body and the hands touching him in the darkness
and how close he had felt to her. Looking at her now, he
wondered how he could doubt her.

Her hand came up to his face, touched his cheek, and
her voice was soft, almost pleading. "Prove that you trust
me, Joe. Please."

"How?"

"Just believe me. And don't leave me on my own. I
think I'm going to go crazy cooped up in your apartment
all day. Take me to Berlin with you. After what happened
to you and Ivan Molke's men, I'd feel safer."

When he hesitated, Erica said, "When is your flight to
Berlin?"

"Six."

"Will you take me with you, Joe?"

He still hesitated, aware of her watching him. Finally he
said, "I'll have Facilities get another ticket."

"Do you have to go back to the office?"

"Why?"

"We won't have to leave for another hour. There's
something else I want you to do for me."

"What?"

"Take me to bed. I've missed you."

The blue eyes looked into his face, and as she smiled again, he stood up and took her hand in his.

She leaned into his shoulder as they strolled back through the park.

Neither of them noticed the two men sitting in the parked car in the distance, observing them through the bare winter trees.

CHAPTER 40

Meyer saw the lights of the small Tyrolean villages in the valley below as the big, blunt-nosed Mercedes growled up the steep mountain road to the Kaalberg.

There was a sprinkling of snow on the thickly forested slopes and as he came around the bend in the forest track, the road ahead leveled off, the headlights of the Mercedes picking out the thick cluster of evergreens that ran in a half-circle about the small plateau. The closed metal barrier gate was off to the right, a sign attached, the words "*Eintritt Verboten!*" in bold red lettering, and the narrow road beyond it ran through thick forest.

Meyer halted the car on the clearing and switched off the motor. He flashed the headlights three times before dousing them completely, then pressed the button to roll down the electric window.

The scent of pine gum wafted into the car on the crisp, cold air and he heard a sound off to the right, saw one of the guards come out from behind the pine trees where the small wooden guard hut was hidden from sight.

The man had a Heckler and Koch MP 5K machine pistol draped across his chest, and as he approached the car, the flashlight in his hand came on suddenly. He shone the light at Meyer and around the inside of the Mercedes, and after several moments, nodded for Meyer to proceed.

As the guard moved back toward the trees, Meyer flicked on the car's headlights. Another man appeared, unlocked the barrier gate and waved Meyer toward him.

Meyer started the Mercedes and the car slowly moved forward.

Kesser and Meyer crossed the gravel driveway together to the flat concrete building. Kesser opened the double dead bolts on the the gray-painted steel door with a key from the bunch in his pocket. Once inside, he flicked the switch and the room was flooded with light.

The interior of the building was icy-cold, but the contrast

with the bland, functional exterior was stunning.

The wedge-shaped steel gantry stood in the center of the room. A metal launch pad cradled in the gantry held the oblong gray-painted warhead at a forty-five-degree angle. Below the gantry was a concrete pit measuring three meters by three meters, the bottom and sides of the concrete lined with matted asbestos sheeting, and Meyer knew it was to damp the launch burn-off.

Two metal sliding doors were set in the flat roof, and the building walls were painted military gray. To the right of the gantry stood the IBM mainframe, its chassis a meter wide and a meter deep. A console screen and a standard keyboard stood on top, two rotatable chairs set in front. A galvanized-alloy conduit ran from the base of the console to the bottom of the gantry, carrying the cables that would control the missile, gantry movement and launch.

There was a gray telephone on top of a wooden desk beside the mainframe, and Kesser's briefcase was open beside it, a screed of computer printout paper unfolded, notes scribbled on the paper where Kesser had written. A Thermos stood beside the briefcase, its plastic cup half filled with black coffee.

Kesser led the way past the gantry to the computer and sat in one of the chairs facing the screen. He flicked a switch on the fascia, and the screen flickered and turned blue, lights flashing on the panels.

Kesser said, "I ran the program. It's fine. No bugs."

"Is it safe?"

"Of course."

Meyer looked alarmed, but Kesser shook his head.

"The warhead hasn't been activated." He pointed to the computer. "The program's simply loading up. It takes about a minute."

Meyer saw the computer screen blank, then become blue again as a series of unintelligible figures and characters began scrolling rapidly across it. Finally the scrolling stopped and a white cursor blinked on the top left corner.

"Now the program's loaded," said Kesser. He pointed to the screen. "Watch."

He tapped in a series of commands and the screen blanked again, then showed a graphic, white against blue.

Meyer saw the grid outline-map of Germany, gray lines crisscrossing the blue screen.

When Kesser hit another key, Meyer heard a sound like muted thunder overhead. The metal doors set in the concrete roof began to roll open on their steel runners. An icy blast of air gusted into the building; Meyer shivered as the night sky came into view, stars glittering in the cold heavens.

When Kesser tapped the keyboard once more, the electric whirr of the stepping motor filled the room. Meyer saw the gray-painted missile twitch in the gantry until it assumed its programmed angle, and then the whirr of the stepping motor died and there was silence again.

Kesser said, "Now look at the screen."

Meyer saw a white image in the shape of a tiny circle appear on the grid in the area around Berlin. The white circle winked for several seconds, then stopped, but it remained on the blue screen.

Kesser said, "Locked on target. The middle of the circle is the epicenter. I can expand the scale if you want to see the exact point in Berlin, but you know how it works. Right now the target center is between the Brandenburg Gate and the southern side of the Reichstag building."

Meyer took a deep breath. The air in the dark concrete building had become incredibly chilled; the metal doors above were still wide open. As he pulled up the collar of his loden coat, he felt a shiver run through him again. Cold, or fear? He couldn't tell which.

Kesser said, "Of course it will never come to a confrontation. They will all back off—the Americans, the British, the others—once we tell them of our intentions, won't they?"

Meyer did not reply, but moved away toward the gray-metal gantry.

There was a long silence, and then suddenly the telephone by the console buzzed, the shrill noise echoing throughout the hangar. Kesser leaned across and lifted the receiver, listened, spoke briefly, then turned to Meyer.

"There's a call for you. Priority."

*   *   *

The flight to Berlin that evening was delayed, and it was just after eight when they landed at Tegel.

They took a taxi from the airport, and Volkmann told the driver to wait while they checked into the small hotel off the Kurfurstendamm. The reception clerk gave them a room facing the Wilhelmskirche, and it was half an hour later when they pulled up outside the lakeshore house.

It was one of the old, prewar wooden properties that ring the Nicolassee shore, painted brown and white, the clap-boarded windows shut to keep out the freezing blasts of Baltic wind that race across the lake in winter. Dark clouds drifted across the moonlit sky.

It was bitterly cold as they stepped from the taxi, and Volkmann again asked the driver to wait. They saw the porch light come on and a middle-aged woman appear behind the glass ante-door. She looked to be in her late sixties but very sprightly, and she wore a blue, heavy-quilted coat. She rubbed her hands to combat the cold and when they came up the path, she waited until the last moment before opening the door.

"It's kind of you to see us so late, Frau Richter."

The woman smiled at them both. "Please, come in, Herr Volkmann."

The house was warm and she led them into a study that Volkmann guessed overlooked the lake. Pleasant in summer, but in winter, the shutters were firmly closed. The study walls were lined with shelves of books, and Volkmann noticed that most of them were on the subject of the Third Reich. There was a framed, signed, black-and-white picture of Konrad Adenauer, the first president of the post-war German state, on the wall by the window.

He introduced Erica, and the woman shook their hands and told them to sit down.

Hanah Richter was tall, with a face that was more hand-some than pretty, her graying hair tied back, emphasizing her high forehead. But her eyes were bright Nordic blue and they sparkled, giving her the appearance of someone who lived life with much enthusiasm.

Moments later, a very old woman came into the room carrying a tray with three steaming cups.

"Some hot chocolate," Hanah Richter explained. "It's

my nightly ritual. I thought it might warm you both before your journey back.''

They thanked the old woman and she smiled, bade them goodnight and left.

Hanah Richter sipped her chocolate and looked at both of them, her keen eyes searching their faces. ''So what's so special about this photograph, Herr Volkmann?''

''It's of a young woman, taken on July eleventh, nineteen thirty-one . . .''

Hanah Richter interrupted gently, ''Perhaps you can show it to me?''

Volkmann removed his wallet and handed the picture across: the photograph of the blond young woman smiling out at the camera, the mountains behind her, the sun in her eyes, the unseen hand linking hers. Hanah Richter put down her cup and took the picture, held it in both hands. She stared down at the image and after a brief moment, she looked up.

''You said it was taken on July eleventh, nineteen thirty-one?''

''That's what was written on the back of the original. But I'm afraid we've no way of knowing for certain if the date is correct.'' Volkmann paused. ''Why?''

Hanah Richter shook her head as if dismissively, then squinted down at the image once more as she reached into her pocket and removed a pair of reading glasses, placed them carefully on her nose.

There was a blank expression on her face as she stared intently at the photograph for a long time. The wind gusted and whistled outside, lightly shook the clapboarded windows, but the historian didn't look up.

Volkmann said finally, ''Do you recognize the girl in the photograph?''

When she looked up, Hanah Richter said, ''Yes.''

PART FIVE

CHAPTER 41

"Her name was Angela Raubal."

Hanah Richter looked down at the photograph again as a gust of wind rattled the clapboarded window. The fire crackled and flickered in the hearth, casting dark shadows about the room.

"She was Adolf Hitler's niece. The daughter of Hitler's half sister, also named Angela Raubal. But the young girl was called Geli, to distinguish her from her mother."

Volkmann stared at the historian. "And there's no doubt in your mind that it's the same person?"

Hanah Richter shook her head. "Absolutely none whatsoever. During my academic career, I wrote several papers on the period from nineteen twenty-nine to nineteen thirty-one, describing how it influenced Hitler's personal life. The girl—Geli Raubal—figured largely in that period. I researched her background as thoroughly as possible. It was a very difficult time for Hitler. He was beset by all sorts of problems, personal and otherwise. And this young woman was one of them." Hanah Richter pointed at the photograph, then put it down. She looked at Volkmann. "May I ask where you got this? I've never seen it before."

"From South America."

She raised her eyebrows for a moment. He thought she was going to question him further, but then she seemed to change her mind.

"You don't look very convinced, Herr Volkmann. About the identity of the young woman, I mean."

Volkmann glanced at Erica. She said nothing, but she looked at him silently, then over at the photograph. Volkmann turned back to Hanah Richter.

"It's a question of certainty. We need to be absolutely sure."

"If you won't take my word for it, I can show you several other photographs of the same girl. Then you can compare them and come to your own conclusion. Would that help?"

"That would help greatly, Frau Richter."

"Please, call me Hanah."

She stood up and crossed to a bookcase, where she searched along a shelf and finally selected two books, then came back to where Volkmann and Erica sat.

She laid the books side by side, then moved one under the reading lamp. Slips of yellow paper, reference markers, stuck out between the covers.

"These are fairly standard books dealing with the period. This first is Toland's biography of Adolf Hitler. The man's an absolute expert on the subject. I met him at a Harvard lecture once. Fascinating person. This second book I wrote myself." She smiled. "My one brief moment of literary glory."

Volkmann looked down at the blue-bound cover she had placed a hand on, and she smiled and said, "I'm sure you'll find copies in the secondhand book stores if you care to look. I'm afraid the book had a rather limited academic interest."

She opened the first volume, leafed through the plates of black-and-white photographs inside and finally found what she was looking for.

Her finger pointed to a snapshot of a young, dark-haired girl standing against a black Daimler. Behind her sloped a blurred forest. From the look of the car, Volkmann guessed it was a mid-1920s model. The girl stood with one foot on the running board, one hand on her hip. She wore a pale, sleeveless summer blouse and a darker skirt to knee length.

"This particular photograph was taken sometime in the summer of nineteen-thirty."

Volkmann and Erica examined the image closely. The girl was dark-haired and pretty, her face square-jawed but attractive. A light-hearted girl trying to look serious for the camera. There was a faint likeness to her in Volkmann's photograph, but not a very noticeable one.

Volkmann looked at Hanah Richter and said, "She's not blond?"

The elderly woman smiled and glanced briefly at Erica before looking back at Volkmann.

"It was common practice then as much as now for girls to dye their hair. Peroxide may change appearances, but the facial structure remains the same. She often changed her hair color. In some photographs, she's blond, in others, dark-haired. But if you look closely, you'll see it's definitely the same girl.''

Hanah Richter opened a drawer in the desk and took out a magnifying glass, handed it to Volkmann. ''Please, be my guest.''

Volkmann held the glass over the image and focused. The basic facial structure of the girl in Hanah Richter's photograph was without doubt the same: square-faced, high cheekbones, pensive eyes, thin, wide mouth.

''You see a resemblance?''

When Volkmann nodded, Hanah Richter said, ''But you're still not convinced, are you? Perhaps it's the color of the girl's hair?''

''That, and her figure.''

The historian smiled. ''True. In this photograph, she looks much thinner. In yours, she appears quite plump. Let me show you another, taken in the spring of nineteen thirty-one.''

Hanah Richter opened the second book. Midway through was a collection of photographs, and again she leafed through and found the one she was looking for and pointed to it.

The scene was a Bavarian restaurant. Four people sat at a table: two men, two women. Both women were blond, one young, one middle-aged. The younger of the two women definitely resembled the young woman in Volkmann's photograph. Her features were fuller and remarkably similar, her hair blond and done in plaits in the style of young German girls. She wore a traditional Bavarian costume with lace collar. She smiled out at the camera, as if someone had just made a joke.

Two of the people seated with her around the table Volkmann recognized at once. To her left, Adolf Hitler, his arms folded, a trace of a smile on his thin lips. Opposite sat the diminutive, grinning Joseph Goebbels, the Nazi propaganda minister. The older blond woman seated next to him had her arm linked through his.

Hanah Richter said, ''The girl with Hitler is Geli Raubal. This time with blond hair. The woman with Goebbels is his wife, Gerda. And in this photograph there's something much more interesting. A clue that relates to your photograph. Pass me the magnifier, if you would be so kind.''

Volkmann did so and Hanah Richter placed Volkmann's photograph beside the photograph in the book.

''Now look closely, please.''

She positioned the glass over the new photograph and Volkmann held it. The focus swam and settled. Erica leaned in closer and Hanah Richter said, ''If you look at her right wrist, I think you'll see something interesting.''

A faintly glinting bracelet. Hanah Richter shifted the glass to Volkmann's photograph. Again, clearly visible, was a metal bracelet on the girl's right wrist.

Hanah Richter said, ''The bracelet was a gift from Hitler to his niece, in October of nineteen twenty-nine, when he took her to a Nazi Party rally in Nuremberg. It was made of solid white gold, with rubies and sapphires. Hitler mentioned it in a letter he wrote to a close friend. A white-gold bracelet that Geli Raubal later always wore on her right wrist.'' Hanah Richter looked up at them over her glasses. ''Even besides all that, the facial features of the girl in your photograph are unmistakable, I assure you. It's definitely the same person.''

Volkmann took the magnifying glass again, held it over the photograph as Erica stood beside him, comparing the two photographs. The same wide, thin lips. The same cheekbones. The same eyes. The same-shaped face. He looked at Erica, but she said nothing. She stared at him blankly before she looked back at Hanah Richter.

''I realize the hour, Hanah, but can you tell us about her background? You said she was one of Hitler's problems. How was she a problem?''

''Because she committed suicide.''

''When?''

''Almost two months after your photograph was taken. After a blazing row with Hitler in his Munich apartment, the girl shot herself through the heart. You see, the two had been lovers for a long time.''

When Volkmann and Erica stared at her in disbelief, Hanah Richter looked at them both and said, ''I'm afraid you've aroused my curiosity. Is this very important?''

Volkmann said, "It may be."

"Would you care to tell me why?"

Volkmann hesitated. "It has to do with a criminal investigation, Hanah. I'm afraid I can't tell you more than that."

There was a puzzled look on the historian's face, and then she said, "When you say 'a criminal investigation,' what do you mean? To do with the girl?"

Volkmann said, "Not her. Someone else."

"But what has she got to do with it? Her death happened such a long time ago."

"I'm sorry, Hanah. I can't tell you any more than that."

Hanah Richter frowned slightly at Volkmann, her disappointment evident. Then she sat back and said, "Very well, what is it you wish to know about Geli Raubal?"

Volkmann said, "Everything you can tell us."

Hanah Richter offered them cigarettes from a silver box, took one herself, then lit each of them in turn.

Volkmann sat forward. "You said she and Hitler were lovers. Can you tell us about that?"

The elderly historian drew on her cigarette and sat back in her chair. "Certainly there was a relationship between them. One that went far deeper than a normal uncle-niece relationship. You see, she lived in the same house as Hitler for a time, and they had become very close. In nineteen twenty-seven, when Hitler moved to his *Berghaus* in the mountains at Berchtesgaden, his step-sister moved in with him to act as his housekeeper. Hitler distrusted many of those around him, so his half-sister was an obvious choice. She tended to his housekeeping needs, organized his meals, his clothes. And with her came her daughters, Friedl and Geli."

Volkmann said, "What about their father?"

"He had died when Geli was quite young. Perhaps that was part of the girl's attraction to Hitler. Very early on, he became a kind of father figure. She was a high-spirited girl. Flighty, if one is to believe the history books." Hanah Richter smiled. "She was born in Vienna, so perhaps it was her Viennese charm. Of course, Eva Braun took center stage as far as Hitler's private life is concerned. She was the mistress all the history books record. But before her came Geli Raubal. She was Adolf Hitler's first real romantic attachment——I won't say love because the man was incapable of human love. But let us say it was a romantic attachment that was reciprocated. She adored her uncle, and he her.

"For a time they went everywhere together, and when Hitler moved from Berchtesgaden to an apartment in Munich, Geli Raubal joined him. She was studying medicine at Munich University at the time, so the move was convenient, but close friends knew that the arrangement was more than simple convenience, that it was an excuse for them to remain together."

"What do you mean?"

The historian half smiled as she looked at Volkmann and Erica. "Think about it. It was rather a strange relationship. Just the two of them, uncle and niece, living in the same apartment together. And Geli was only twenty-three when she died. Naturally, tongues wagged in the Nazi Party about the arrangement. Hitler had always had a preference for young, fresh-faced girls——the younger, the better——because he couldn't relate to women of his own age. And besides, young girls were more easily manipulated, and fell easily under his spell. Of the seven women with whom we can be reasonably sure he had intimate relationships, most of them were young. And of the seven, six committed suicide or made a serious attempt to do so. So Geli Raubal wasn't alone in that regard.

"Hitler seemed to have had a mesmeric effect on women. The ones he was successful with intimately as well as the mass of German women he was to appeal to when he became Führer.

"And like a lot of women in Germany at the time, Geli Raubal found his personality magnetic. She would have done anything for him. She most certainly wanted to marry him despite the circumstance of their being related. And for a time, Hitler plainly acted like a suitor. He hinted to some of his close party friends that he might actually marry the girl."

Hanah Richter looked at Volkmann and Erica. "Repugnant as that might seem, one must remember that this was before Hitler's true brutality began to show. His career was on the rise and he had started to make a name for himself politically. He seemed to many destined to lead Germany. Geli Raubal would have gladly married her uncle, despite their age difference of nineteen years and despite the near-incestuous connotations it would imply. So she flirted wildly with him, seduced him, if you like.''

The wind rattled at the clapboards again and the fire embers flickered. Volkmann stared at the flaring coals for a moment, then looked back at Hanah Richter as the woman started to speak again.

''It was an absurd situation of course, and it couldn't last. The people close to Hitler in the Nazi Party who knew what was going on were horrified: middle-aged uncle who intended marrying his very young niece. In their public lives, most Nazis were outwardly moral, but we know that privately they were vipers. And they were against it all the more because Hitler was preparing to take part in the presidential campaign. It was a decisive time. A Nazi victory was absolutely vital. It was everything the party had struggled for. Geli Raubal was Hitler's niece and half his age. So marriage or the hint of scandal would have been disastrous for the party. One must remember the morals of the period. Such a thing certainly wouldn't have helped Hitler's image in his public life. But I think that in the end he just led the poor girl a pretty dance until he got tired of her and moved onto Eva Braun.''

Volkmann glanced over at the photograph lying on the table. ''So why did Geli Raubal kill herself?''

Hanah Richter looked away for a moment, then back again. ''If we're to believe the history books, she was going through some kind of emotional disturbance. Probably because she realized Hitler was slowly but surely withdrawing from their relationship. On the seventeenth of September, nineteen thirty-one, the two had a heated argument in Hitler's Munich apartment on the Prinzregentenplatz. When Hitler was leaving, Geli Raubal calmly said good-bye to him, then went up to her room and locked herself in. The next morning she was found dead, shot through the heart at close range. There was a small-caliber pistol on the bedroom floor next to her. The Bavarian police determined that she had died sometime in the early hours of the eighteenth.

"Hitler was in Nuremberg when he heard the news of her death.

"Outwardly, he appeared devastated, but some of those close to him in the party thought he was actually relieved that the girl was out of his life. And of course there were the rumors. The press at the time went wild and printed all kinds of stories."

"What kind of rumors?"

Hanah Richter smiled at Volkmann. "They ranged from the slightly believable to the utterly ridiculous."

"Tell me."

"That Hitler had the girl killed in a fit of jealousy because she was seeing someone else. Certainly he was prone to violent fits of jealousy. It was said that on one occasion he broke her nose during a row. It's possible he *had* her killed, of course. He would have been quite capable of that, and just as possible that his associates in the Nazi Party killed her because they saw the relationship with the girl as a threat of scandal that might ruin their hopes of power. But it's more likely she killed herself out of some sort of desperation. If you want my opinion, I'd have to say a combination of accident and desperation—the fact that she realized Hitler was never going to marry her and wanted to end their relationship, and some kind of depression. But then, we shall never really know the true story."

"What else did the newspapers say?"

Hanah Richter smiled. "There were so many rumors, not all of them credible. The most scandalous suggested that Hitler had his niece killed because the affair had gotten out of hand and threatened his public image. The police were called in to investigate because of the suicide and the very same rumor, but nothing came of it and no charges were brought. There were allegations that the minister for justice at the time, Herr Gürtner, had the file of evidence destroyed. Certainly it disappeared, and whatever evidence there was against Hitler was never found.

"After Hitler came to power, Herr Gürtner rose very quickly within the ranks of the Nazi Party, so perhaps that speaks for itself and deepens the mystery. Perhaps he did help Hitler in some way to hide the real truth, whatever it may be." Hanah Richter shrugged. "Certainly there was some mystery about the death, but most people close to her thought the suicide was simply a dramatic accident that happened when she was at a low ebb emotionally. That she was playing theater with the gun when it went off. And I'm inclined to agree."

Volkmann stared down at the girl's image in the Chaco photograph, the mountains in the background, the unseen hand linking hers and the Nazi swastika emblazoned on the armband.

He asked quietly, "Who do you think the other person in the photograph might be?"

"Possibly Hitler. They were still seeing each other at that time, though for a period before that, Hitler tried to extricate himself from the relationship because of pressure from the party. Geli decided to make him jealous and started seeing Hitler's chauffeur, Emil Maurice. She even became secretly engaged to Maurice. When Hitler found out, he flew into a rage and dismissed his chauffeur. Then Hitler started seeing her again secretly, until her death."

Volkmann hesitated, then said, "The eleventh of July, nineteen thirty-one. Can you recall anything special happening on that date?"

"You mean special for Geli Raubal?"

"Yes."

Hanah Richter thought for a moment. "She died on September eighteenth, so your photograph would have been taken over seven weeks before her death. She had been in the hospital for a minor problem a week before your date, during her semester from medical school. And about two weeks later, I believe, she stayed with some friends in Freiburg. In between, she saw Hitler a number of times, but he was busy with the presidential campaign and didn't have much time for her." Hanah Richter thought again, her brow furrowed in concentration, then finally said, "No, I'm sorry. The date you mention is not one that sticks in my mind. Believe me, if it were, I'd remember."

"One more question. Did Geli ever visit South America?"

The elderly woman shook her head. "No, definitely not. She only traveled in Germany and Austria." She looked from Erica to Volkmann. "Has your question got something to do with how you came to have the photograph?"

Volkmann nodded and said, "Does the name Erhard Schmeltz mean anything to you?"

"In what connection?"

"In connection with Geli Raubal."

The historian frowned. "Who was Erhard Schmeltz?"

"A Nazi Party member. Someone Hitler knew when he served in the First War."

The historian shook her head slowly. "Well, whoever he was, he mustn't have been very important. I don't recall having heard the name in connection with either Hitler or Geli. Not ever."

"Have you any idea, Hanah, how a photograph such as this could have ended up in South America?"

"You're absolutely certain it was an original and not a copy?"

"Yes."

"So many Germans emigrated to South America at the end of the war. The photograph could have been taken there by someone close to Hitler or the girl." Hanah Richter shrugged. "As to who, I haven't the faintest idea. People like Eichmann and Mengele never knew her. And Bormann, well, he would have known her, certainly have met her often socially, but the possibility of him having survived the war and escaping to South America has been well and truly eliminated. Possibly a close friend, or a high-ranking Nazi official or trusted SS. But who, I'm afraid, I couldn't possibly suggest." She glanced pointedly at her watch and said, "Does that answer all your questions?"

Volkmann stared down at the photograph in his hand, then looked up at the woman and nodded. "Thank you for your time, Hanah. Our apologies for keeping you up so late."

"That's quite all right." The woman smiled and stood up.

As Volkmann replaced the photograph in his wallet, Hanah Richter said, "I would appreciate a copy of that for my files, if you could send me one?"

"Of course."

Hanah Richter shook their hands and led them to the

door. The taxi was still outside, and as they stood in the open porch, Volkmann turned to the woman.

"Do you know where Geli Raubal was buried?"

"In Vienna. The old Central Cemetery."

"Is the grave still there?"

Hanah Richter shook her head. "I'm afraid the Nazi authorities in Vienna had that part of the cemetery destroyed in nineteen forty-one. The grave and all the others around it were completely razed."

"Why?"

"Heaven knows. It seems most strange. No one I ever spoke to about the matter knew who issued the order. I suppose it only added to the whole mystery of Geli's death."

"Do you think the Nazis wanted to cover something up?"

"You mean about her death? It's possible, considering that the circumstances were never fully explained. But then, we've no way of ever knowing."

Volkmann hesitated. "There is one last thing, Hanah."

"Yes?"

"You said that Geli Raubal was a hospital patient. When?"

"In late June of nineteen thirty-one. She spent a few days in a private nursing home in Garmisch-Partenkirchen."

"What was she being treated for?"

"Some said depression, because Hitler had spurned her and was secretly seeing his new mistress, Eva Braun. Others said she went in for minor surgery. I have no way of knowing. And certainly you won't find any hospital records. They would have been long ago lost or destroyed, I'm sure. Why do you ask?"

Volkmann felt the biting wind coming in across the lake waters, glimpsed the waiting taxi driver in his cab, drumming his fingers impatiently against the steering wheel as he stared at them through the glass.

Volkmann turned back, saw Erica pull up her coat collar against the icy wind. Hanah Richter waited, shivering, for the question to be answered.

For a long time Volkmann seemed to hesitate, then he

said, "This proposition may seem absurd, Hanah. But could Geli Raubal have been pregnant?"

Hanah Richter raised her eyebrows and looked at him. "Actually, that supposition was suggested as one of the reasons she might have been murdered by Hitler or his people. But it was never proven. A journalist at the time, a man named Fritz Gerlich, claimed the girl was pregnant and Hitler had her killed for that reason. But the story was never published."

"What happened to Gerlich?"

"He was arrested and later murdered in Dachau. But really his information was never proven. And there were other reasons the Nazis would have wanted Gerlich dead, besides that story."

"What reasons, Hanah?"

"Gerlich owned the newspaper he wrote for. The paper was strongly anti-Nazi. Many of its articles and editorials had condemned Hitler before he came to power." Hanah Richter paused. "But why do you ask?"

Volkmann hesitated. "What if Geli Raubal already had a child?"

"You mean by Hitler?"

"Yes."

Volkmann saw the woman's expression change. She stood in the doorway, open-mouthed, the question totally unexpected, a look of utter amazement on her face. Erica looked at him too, a white, stricken look that for a moment made her look ill.

Then Hanah Richter stared at Volkmann and said incredulously, "Really, Herr Volkmann, something like that would *never* have escaped the history books."

He saw the woman's expression of amazement become disbelief. Then suddenly the disbelief turned to irritation as she hunched her shoulders against the biting cold and shivered.

"You can't *possibly* be serious?"

Volkmann said quietly. "No, of course not, Hanah. You've been most kind. Thank you for your help."

CHAPTER 42

Berlin. Thursday, December 22

They hadn't spoken during the entire journey in the taxi back from the lakeshore house. Volkmann stared out at the lights of Berlin from the cab window, but said nothing.

When they pulled up outside the hotel off the Kurfürstendamm, Erica had looked at him, her face troubled, the aftershock of the question he had posed the historian half an hour before still evident on her face.

As soon as they had stepped into their room, Volkmann went to pour each of them a drink. He saw Erica stare palely at him as he handed her a half-tumbler of scotch.

"What you said to Hanah Richter . . . you really meant it, didn't you, Joe? That the girl could have been pregnant? That she could have had a child by Adolf Hitler?"

"Yes."

"But Joe, that's absurd."

There was tension in Volkmann's voice as he put down the glass and said, "Erica, it fits the jigsaw. It fits everything we know and don't know about the identity of Karl Schmeltz. And you heard what Hanah Richter said. The girl could have been pregnant. It was also a likely reason she might have been killed or committed suicide. Everything Hanah Richter told us tonight explains the puzzle about Karl Schmeltz. Surely you see that?"

Erica Kranz stared back at him. "I can accept that the girl could have been pregnant. But that she actually had a child? Joe, how could it be possible? As Hanah Richter said, such a thing could *never* have escaped the history books. If Hitler had fathered a child, it could *never* have been kept a secret all these years."

Volkmann heard the strain of incredulity in her voice. She ignored her drink, but Volkmann quickly swallowed his scotch and put down the glass.

"It sounds crazy, Erica, I know, but it also makes some kind of sense. Just *think* about it. Erhard Schmeltz and his sister emigrate to South America from Germany under mysterious circumstances in late nineteen thirty-one, two

months after Geli Raubal's death. They take with them a
boy who's obviously not their son. Remember what Wilhelm Busch said about Schmeltz? He didn't have any children and had never married. As for Schmeltz's sister, she
was older than her brother, most likely too old to have a
child that young. So that discounts either of them.''

The girl looked at him. ''But the child *could* have belonged to one of them, Joe. It's not impossible to imagine.
Either of them could still have been the child's natural par-
ent.''

''If the child belonged to one of them, why did they
leave Germany so mysteriously? Why suddenly disappear?
And I told you what Busch said about the rumors that went
around when Schmeltz and his sister vanished. One of them
was that Schmeltz had been sent away secretly. The circumstances suggest that the boy most likely wasn't theirs.
So who did he belong to?''

There was a mounting excitement in Volkmann's voice
as he looked at her. ''Erhard Schmeltz was a loyal and close
friend of Adolf Hitler's. And his party membership application was recommended by Himmler, which suggests he
was on good terms with those at the top of the party. People
he had served with in the First War. People he knew as
friends and who accepted his loyalty. Now consider what
Hanah Richter said: Hitler had been having an affair with
Geli Raubal, an affair that was well-known among Hitler's
friends and close acquaintances.''

Volkmann crossed to the window, turned back to look
at Erica. ''According to Hanah Richter, two months before
Geli Raubal was found dead in her uncle's apartment, she
was a patient in a private nursing home. When she comes
out, she's under stress, something troubling her. It must
have been something significant, because two months later,
the girl supposedly kills herself. Whether Hitler had her
killed or she committed suicide isn't relevant.

''But what *is* relevant is what could have been troubling
her. The girl's in love with Hitler. She wants to marry him.
So why did she kill herself? Hanah Richter said Hitler had
spurned the girl. That he was preparing for the presidential
elections and it was vital for him to win or at least gain
ground for the Nazi Party. The last thing he needed at that

time was the kind of scandal his relationship with Geli might have caused.''

"But Joe, that the girl could have had a child? It's just not possible.''

"Why isn't it possible? You admitted she could have been pregnant. What if she *was* expecting a child by Hitler? What if the reason she went into the hospital in Garmisch-Partenkirchen was because she was expecting a child by her uncle? Hitler knows or learns about it, realizes the whole affair could ruin his career. *Think* about it. If the girl *had* been pregnant, if that kind of news had gotten out, Hitler would have been ruined, politically and every other way. Just like Hanah Richter said, he may have dragged the Nazi Party down with him because of the scandal. So he, or those closest to him, come up with a plan. Send the child away, somewhere a long way from Germany. And with someone Hitler could trust. A couple like the Schmeltzes would have been ideal. And the place they emigrated to with the child couldn't have been more remote, a jungle region in Paraguay, so the secret is safe.''

He saw Erica look at him unbelievingly, and he stared down at her. "That scenario would explain three things, Erica. Three very important things. One, the amount of money Schmeltz had when he arrived in Paraguay. Two, the fact of his sudden emigration just before Hitler prepares for the presidential election. Three, the drafts from the Nazi Reichsbank sent to Paraguay right up until nineteen forty-five. Someone high up had to sanction such large sums of money. And only someone high up would have the authority to keep it secret and unrecorded.''

"If we're to believe what Wilhelm Busch said, Erhard Schmeltz wasn't a rich man. And a man who had fallen out of favor with the Nazi Party doesn't receive money from the Reichsbank. Nor does he keep his party membership in absentia. And blackmail's out because if that was the case, then Schmeltz wouldn't have had the child *with* him.'' Volkmann looked intently at Erica. "That still leaves the question of whether Schmeltz was hoarding the money for someone else. I don't believe he was. The money he received was sent through the Reichsbank, and no Nazi would have done that. They would have used some anony-

mous Swiss bank. Only Hitler or a very high-ranking Nazi
would have had the kind of authority to use the Reichsbank.
So that suggests only one remaining possibility. The money
was sent to Schmeltz to support him and his sister and the
boy. Geli Raubal's and Hitler's son.

"The very fact that we found the girl's photograph at
the house in the Chaco confirms the link between Erhard
Schmeltz and Geli Raubal. And you heard what Hanah
Richter said about the girl's relationship with Hitler. If she
had an affair with him, why couldn't it be possible that she
had a child by him?"

He saw Erica shake her head. "But if what you're saying
is true, why didn't Hitler have her abort the pregnancy?"

"Maybe the girl didn't tell him until it was too late.
Maybe she wanted the child and didn't want to tell him
until abortion wasn't possible. And even if she *did* commit
suicide, she must have been desperate over something.
Something very emotional was hanging over her. She also
could have been depressed after the birth. And if Hitler had
refused to marry her or acknowledge the child and wanted
the whole affair covered up by sending the boy away, it
might have been enough to send her over the edge."

"But there must have been people who knew. People
who would have talked about such a thing. It couldn't have
been kept secret after all these years. It just *couldn't.*"

"Geli Raubal was a medical student, Erica. She could
have had help from friends or contacts in the profession,
people who would have helped her keep her secret. Medical
people who could have helped her with the birth. Isn't that
possible? And you heard what Hanah Richter said about
the journalist who was sent to Dachau. What if he had heard
the truth? What if *that* was the reason he was killed?"

Erica hesitated, then shook her head. "Joe, there are too
many ifs. Believe me, part of me wants to accept what
you're saying, because it does make some kind of sense.
But another part of me is saying it's crazy."

Volkmann looked at her intently. "Then consider this.
Why did the Nazis destroy the part of the cemetery in Vienna where Geli was buried? Why did they want to destroy
her grave? There could only be one reason. There was a
secret someone wanted to hide. Geli Raubal's secret. A post

mortem could have determined if the girl had given birth. Destroying the grave meant destroying the evidence.''

He saw the look on Erica's face. She was pale, and her eyes looked away vacantly. He heard his own labored breathing, the thought of what he had said dizzying.

''Then answer me this, Joe. Why didn't whoever wanted to keep the secret simply get rid of the girl's body? Why didn't they destroy the evidence that way?''

''Maybe they did.''

''I don't understand.''

''By removing the girl's body and destroying the graves around it, it would have made it impossible for anyone to know whether the girl's corpse had been removed from the grave or not. All that remained would have been a tangle of unidentifiable bones. That way any subsequent forensic examination could never have determined identities.''

There were beads of perspiration on his brow as he looked at Erica. ''Consider everything I've said and how it connects to the present, to everything that's been happening. To Rudi's death, to the other deaths. Why sanitize a house in a remote jungle? Why destroy all traces of occupation in the Chaco property? Why be so obsessive about secrecy? What had those people in the Chaco *really* got to hide, Erica? Not a simple smuggling operation. Not simply a connection to Rudi's death and the others. But something that goes far deeper. Not only about the present, but the past. You sensed something at the Chaco house, remember? We all did.''

''Joe . . .'' Erica opened her mouth to speak, but she broke off.

He saw the tension in her, her mouth set grimly, before the blue eyes looked away. There was a hopeless look on her face that said it all, as if she had tried hard to convince him he was wrong and failed.

He knew that what he was suggesting was unreal, but it had a strange kind of truth and the thought made him shiver violently as he looked at her, his voice thick with emotion.

''There's only one possible answer that can explain Karl Schmeltz's identity, Erica. *Karl Schmeltz is Adolf Hitler's son.*''

For a long time neither of them spoke, as if the awesome

possibility that had joined them in the stillness of the room lingered like a living thing.

"What are you going to do, Joe?" There was no emotion in her voice, and he looked back at her. "Tell Ferguson and Peters, and just hope they believe everything I've said."

"You think they will?"

"When they hear the evidence, yes, I think they will." The girl said flatly. "And then?"

"Find Karl Schmeltz. Because he's part of what's happening, Erica. He's part of everything that's happened and is about to happen."

He looked at her, held her stare. He spoke quietly, and for the first time, he heard real fear in his own voice.

"The voices on the tape Rudi recorded. The voices on the tape, and what Busch said was promised in Hitler's bunker. They're talking about the same thing, Erica. The voices on the tape are talking about the same Brandenburg. What happened over sixty years ago in Germany when the Nazis came to power." Volkmann paused, looked into her face. "I think it's going to happen all over again."

Friday, December 23

They managed to get seats on the 7:00 A.M. shuttle from Berlin, and they landed in Frankfurt just after eight. They reached the DSE office by eleven-thirty.

He had telephoned Peters' secretary on the way from the airport, requesting an urgent meeting with Peters and Ferguson. He parked the Ford in the underground garage and when they went up, he left Erica waiting in his office while he went in search of Peters.

He found him in his office, talking with Ferguson's secretary, and as Volkmann entered, Peters came toward him.

"Joe, I'm glad you made it back, something's come up . . ."

"We need to talk, Tom. *Urgently*. Didn't you get my message?"

"I got it." Peters saw the look on Volkmann's face and said, "Is everything okay?"

"Where's Ferguson?"

"Gone to an early lunch with the section heads."

Peters saw the look of frustration on Volkmann's face and turned to the secretary behind him and smiled as he said, "Can you leave us, Marion?"

When the secretary had gone, Peters said, "What's this about, Joe?"

"I'd rather wait until Ferguson's here, Tom. I'd like to discuss it with both of you present."

Peters recognized the urgency in Volkmann's voice but said, "I'm afraid it'll have to wait. Something's come up, something important maybe. And Ferguson won't be back until the afternoon."

"What's come up?"

"You're going to love this. I got a call from the Carabinieri headquarters in Genoa. They think their people have found something that fits in with our request to the Italian desk. They want us to take a look at a container that came in on a ship called the *Maria Escobar* on the ninth of this month."

"Where from?"

Peters smiled. "Montevideo. I told them you'd be on the next available plane."

"How long have I got?"

"There's an Al Italia flight from Frankfurt in under two hours. A return flight tonight at nine. You're booked both ways, pick up the tickets at the airport. You ought to just make it back unless something develops. I've already arranged a private charter from Strasbourg to Frankfurt-Main. It's waiting at the airport now."

"What about our meeting?"

"I'll set it up for this evening at Ferguson's place. Phone me the minute you get back."

Volkmann said, "Do me a favor, Tom. While I'm gone, stay with Erica."

Peters frowned. "Any particular reason?"

"This thing I'm working on is beginning to make sense, and it's looking more dangerous and crazier by the second. It's very possible she's at risk. I want someone I can trust to watch over her."

*   *   *

He spoke with Erica before he left for the airport. He told her not to talk with anyone about the case until he returned.

A few moments later, Peters came into the office and he introduced them.

Peters said charmingly, "How about I take the young lady to lunch, Joe? Then I can drive her back to your place." He smiled. "Pretty much everyone's finishing early for the holidays. I'll leave a note on Ferguson's desk about the meeting, tell him it's imperative we talk."

Five minutes later, Volkmann left them.

As he drove to the airport, there was a knot of tension in his stomach like a ball of steel.

CHAPTER 43

Chancellor Franz Dollman grimaced as he sat in the back of the black Mercedes. Beyond the bulletproof windows of the stretch limousine, a police escort guided the car through the streets of Bonn.

As the car passed the Münster Platz, Dollman looked up from his paperwork. The lights of a Christmas tree winked on the Platz. The thought of Christmas approaching normally depressed him, but this time he looked forward to a few relaxing days away from his grueling state duties. Already his Cabinet was a week behind the scheduled holiday recess, so many problems still remained to be dealt with.

Dollman sighed as he sat back. He had flown in from Munich that morning, after a late-night meeting with the Bavarian prime minister, had been up since six assembling his paperwork, then breakfast, followed by a quick glass of schnapps to help brace himself for the day ahead and the emergency Cabinet meeting.

The Wednesday-morning meetings in Bonn's Villa Schaumburg were always the same of late, had been for the last year—an utter shambles. Dollman expected the same of this one, wondered how the country had managed to survive, put it down to the resolute, hardworking nature of the German people. They had seen adversity before and were certainly seeing it now.

As the car sped past the Markt Platz, Dollman glimpsed the broken shop windows, the littered glass, the paint daubed on walls. All the hallmarks of another riot. He turned to Ritter, his personal bodyguard, sitting beside him. The man was disrespectfully chewing gum.

Dollman nodded gravely toward the scene beyond the glass. "What happened?"

Ritter's jaws moved slowly as he chewed. "It started off as a protest march about unemployment. Then the right-wing groups joined in. Before long, it was a riot."

Dollman sighed. "Anyone killed?"

Ritter shook his head. "Not this time. The riot squad

moved in after midnight and cracked a few skulls, that's all. But I hear there's another scheduled to start tonight from the Rathaus. A protest march by immigrants.'' Ritter's jaw tightened. ''If you ask me, these demonstrators ought to be locked up.''

It was getting out of control, Dollman reflected as the Mercedes turned toward the Hofgarten and headed south toward the Rhine and the Villa Schaumberg. There were more shattered windows along the route. Pavement slabs had been torn up, shopfronts vandalized.

Dollman didn't bother replying to Ritter's remark. The man was an excellent bodyguard, tough and discreet and reliable, but had a limited intelligence and so Dollman always kept their conversations to a minimum. If Ritter had his way, half the world would be behind bars.

It was the same everywhere these days. Riots. Marches. Protests. The immigrant problem. The French interior minister had complained of the same to him only last week.

''Lock the lot up and throw away the keys. That's the answer,'' Ritter added.

If only it were possible, Dollman reflected. He personally would start with half of his bickering Cabinet.

The Mercedes had turned slowly into the courtyard of the Villa Schaumburg and come quietly to a halt outside the imposing entrance. His wife would be in their residence on the grounds. There would just be time to see her after the Cabinet meeting before he left for the Charlottenburg Palace in Berlin. Another boring function to attend, before Weber's special security meeting the next morning. Still, Weber's meeting suited him perfectly. He would spend the night in Wannsee, and that at least Dollman looked forward to. The thought briefly lifted his spirits as the chauffeur stepped out smartly and opened the rear door. Dollman gathered up his papers, closed his briefcase and handed it to Ritter.

As he climbed out, he saw Eckart, the finance minister, waiting in the doorway to greet him. The man looked as glum and depressing as the dark, brooding sky over Bonn. No doubt there was more bad financial news even before the Cabinet meeting began.

Dollman sighed and strode grimly toward the villa entrance.

The meeting had gone on for almost two hours.

It was no different this morning as Dollman observed the drawn faces of the men seated at the large oval table.

There had been riots the previous night in Berlin, Munich, Bonn and Frankfurt, and even in Dollman's own beloved Mannheim. The latest financial news was depressing. Eckart had wrung his hands in despair when he imparted the details.

Dollman removed a fresh white handkerchief from his pocket and dabbed his brow; the Cabinet room was hot, the heating turned up to counter the chill outside. Beyond the bulletproof windows, he glimpsed a harsh wind whipping the trees.

A tall, distinguished-looking man in his early sixties, Dollman had thinning gray hair that was swept back off his fleshy face. He had been chancellor for eighteen months. Eighteen hard, difficult, trying months. He would gladly have resigned—indeed, had considered such a course of action on two occasions at least—but knew that he was the only one in the room capable of a semblance of leadership in these pressing times.

He looked up now from the reports lying in front of him on the polished oval table and replaced the handkerchief in his breast pocket. All of the ministers were present except for Weber, the vice-chancellor, who was expected later. A fresh outbreak of rioting in Leipzig had demanded his presence. He didn't envy the man. Weber had requested the position, his temperament suited it because he brooked no nonsense, but a security job was just asking for nothing short of a permanent blinding headache. Still, that was Weber's problem.

Eighteen men at the big table, including himself.

Dollman heard a cough and turned his head to see Eckart trying to catch his attention.

"The economics reports, Chancellor. Do you wish me to start?"

Dollman glanced at his watch. "What's remaining?"

"Just the economics reports, and of course the report on

federal security. But we're still waiting for Vice-Chancellor
Weber to arrive. If he is further delayed, I fear we shall
have to reconvene after lunch.''

Dollman sighed. ''Very well, Eckart, you may begin.''

Dollman sat back. He knew what was coming as Eckart's
dry, monotonous voice called the ministers to attention before he launched into the report proper.

Dollman's mind was elsewhere. On the house in Wannsee. There would be time to call on the way to Charlottenburg, then come back after the civic function. He had
telephoned the night before, said he would stay over. Even
the thought of the voice and the voluptuous body sent him
into spasms of anticipation. Lisl was a politician's dream.
Discreet, beautiful, undemanding, lustful and willing in
bed. He always found her company invigorating.

Dollman suppressed the smile of contentment that threatened to cross his lips as Eckart's depressing monologue
droned on. He saw the assembled ministers stare ahead or
look toward the windows. He should have read the report
himself if only to avoid Eckart's tedious delivery.

He had gone past trying to make sense of the chaos. At
that moment, all he hoped was that he could make it to
Berlin by evening. He looked up as at last Eckart's boring
monotone was coming to an end.

''. . . And that concludes the economics reports. Thank
you, Ministers, for your attention.''

What attention? thought Dollman. Half of them were
sleeping, or trying to, or bored to death. There was a sudden
eruption of coughing, and then a hushed silence. Dollman
looked at the faces around the table. Minister Franks raised
his hand.

''Yes, Franks?''

''What does the chancellor propose to do about the situation in Hesse and Bavaria?''

''I'm glad you asked that question, Franks. I'm sure that
Minister Eckart will have some proposals for discussion at
our next scheduled meeting. Until then, I ask you to be
patient.''

A politician's answer. Dollman avoided Franks's stare,
saw the look on Eckart's drawn face.

''Any further questions?''

There was a murmur from some of the ministers at the back. He saw Streicher raise his hand, no doubt to probe Dollman's glib reply. But that was how he felt this morning. Glib and depressed. Dollman deflected any further questions by looking pointedly at his watch.

"Gentlemen, I suggest we reconvene after lunch to hear the vice-chancellor's report. As interior minister, I believe he has some important points to discuss."

As Dollman finished speaking, he heard the door to the Cabinet room open and saw Konrad Weber step into the room. He carried a thick folder in one hand, his briefcase in the other. He was a tall, grim-looking man; his drawn, pallid face looked serious, as always. But a good vice-chancellor. One who took his responsibilities seriously. Dollman was glad to have him on his side, but from the strained look on his thin, Prussian face, Konrad Weber looked as if he were about to impart doom.

"Chancellor, gentlemen, my apologies for being late . . ."

"Take a seat, Weber. You are ready to read your special report?"

Dollman looked up at him, glad of the interruption, but dreading Weber's report. At least it saved him from further questions. Now Weber could take some of the flak.

The vice-chancellor nodded to Dollman as he moved to his place at the table but remained standing. He placed his briefcase on the floor beside him and opened the folder. As he placed his papers in front of him, Dollman saw that several of them bore official red BfV stamps. *Highly Confidential*.

Dollman sat back and sighed quietly; the meeting had gone badly enough without further depressing news. Weber had already informed him privately on the phone the night before that the news would be serious, and the vice-chancellor's stance and demeanor looked grave. From the look on Weber's and the Cabinet's faces, his security reports would send them all rushing toward the windows.

Dollman tried hard to relax, wondered where it would all end. He thought of Lisl, lying naked in bed in the house at Wannsee.

If it wasn't for the girl, he felt certain he would have rushed toward the windows himself long ago.

CHAPTER 44

It had started to snow as Peters drove up outside the apartment on the Quai Ernest.

He parked in the courtyard and he and Erica went up. She had been subdued during their lunch in Petite France, and Peters had guessed that something was troubling her, but he hadn't pressed her to talk.

When they stepped into Volkmann's apartment, he could see that she had made herself at home and had tidied the rooms, here and there small items rearranged since he had last visited. *Very interesting*, he thought. *So Volkmann and the girl have something going.*

A little later he excused himself as she made coffee, and he went to the bathroom. On the way back, he paused in the hallway and stepped into Volkmann's bedroom. The bed was made but he could smell the lingering scent of her perfume. Her clothes were in Volkmann's open wardrobe and her makeup bag lay by the bed.

He stepped outside into the hallway again and opened the door to the second bedroom. The bed was made, but the air in the room was odorless, the room tidy but unused.

As he stepped back into the living room, she came out of the kitchen. "I never asked if you take sugar and cream?"

Peters smiled. "Both. Two spoonfuls."

She went back into the kitchen and Peters lit a cigarette and went to stand at the window. Flakes of snow drifted against the glass and he stood there reflecting on the relationship between Volkmann and this German girl. On the one hand, this wasn't surprising. Erica was quite beautiful and intelligent. On the other hand, she was a German, and her father had been a Nazi in the SS . . . which ordinarily would have been disqualifying marks where Volkmann was concerned. She certainly must be something special, he concluded, to have broken through Volkmann's walls.

As he moved away from the window and went to flick on the remote control for the television, Erica came back in holding two mugs of steaming coffee. Peters took his and sat down, flicking a mote of cigarette ash from his white shirt.

As he leaned forward to pick up his coffee again, he saw her stare at his waist. He looked down. The holstered Beretta was visible, clipped to his belt. He looked up and saw her stare briefly at him before turning away. Without another word, he stood and unclipped the weapon and placed it on his overcoat, then sat back down again.

The Mercedes drove up and down the Quai four times and then halted outside the apartment building. Snow brushed against the car's windows, and the wipers were on.

The passenger checked the address again and then nodded to the driver before he pulled up the collar of his raincoat and stepped out into the snow.

As the man disappeared into the courtyard, the driver sat there, tapping his hand on the steering wheel, the motor still running, his eyes scanning the Quai. The traffic was thin as occasional amber headlights swished past in the growing darkness, and besides, the man knew that in poor weather, people took less notice of what was happening around them, concentrating on the road ahead.

Three minutes later, the passenger returned and climbed back into the car, his hair and raincoat flecked with snow. The driver turned the heater up further and the passenger wiped his wet face with a big hand.

The passenger said in German, "It's the right apartment. Volkmann's name's on the doorbell. There's a window at the back. Two people inside. A man and a woman."

The driver checked his watch. "Okay. Once more around the block, then we come back."

As the Mercedes pulled away, the passenger reached under his seat and took out the two silenced pistols.

Genoa. 3:15 P.M.

A tall Italian detective with a bushy mustache introduced himself to Volkmann at a warehouse by the river. His name was Orsati, and he seemed confident that he had broken the case: the container on the *Maria Escobar* had a hidden compartment.

"There's an official of the Italian customs service—his name's Paulo Bonefacio—who found it." He pointed out the man, who was standing off to the side. "By the way, the container is back in Genoa."

Volkmann gave a nod to that.

"So Bonefacio did some checking, and it turned out that the container has been back and forth to Montevideo several times over the past year, and he figured that an inside man must have taken the contents of the hidden compartment. He did some further checking and found that the container has been handled exclusively by a clerk named Franco Scali. He's a senior clearance clerk here."

"He's the inside man?" Volkmann asked.

"It seems so. Though we haven't finished interviewing him yet, I'm sure he'll have a great deal more to tell us."

"Let's hope so," Volkmann said.

"So anyhow, let me introduce you to Scali." Orsati made an over-here motion with his hand to another detective. And a moment later, the detective led a very frightened-looking clearance clerk to Orsati and Volkmann.

"Signore Volkmann, meet Franco Scali."

Scali nodded a greeting, "Ciao," he said.

"Scali," Volkmann said quietly.

Orsati said, "Let's start with the container."

Scali forced a smile. "Sure."

The detective led the way.

The Fiat carrying Beck and Kleins drove into the dockyard and came to a halt a hundred meters from the warehouse. There had been so many police cars on the apron that no one had bothered to stop them.

As Beck switched off the engine, Kleins glanced at his watch, then looked back up at the cars parked outside the warehouse. A hundred meters away, a knot of men stood gathered around the big blue container.

Kleins reached behind him for the powerful Zeiss binoculars and focused on the men.

*   *   *

Volkmann stood on the docking apron, a soft breeze blowing in off the sea beyond the harbor. The klieg lights were on overhead, the powerful light flooding the area, and the carabinieri had sealed off part of the apron with rolls of yellow plastic ribbon.

Then Paulo Bonefacio led them across the apron to a blue container with three gray-striped markings.

Volkmann saw that a plate had been removed from the side and it lay on the ground, perfectly matching the gaping, quarter-meter-wide hole it had covered. The customs official beamed over at them.

Volkmann said to the detective, "How did he find it?"

"He has a little metal hammer. He uses it to tap containers. Hollow spaces sound hollow. On this one, there was a slight difference in the metal sound toward the right-end wall. But he knows of this container. Last time it was on the docks, he suspected it, but didn't have time to do a thorough check."

Orsati knelt beside the container, stared in at the small chamber within the gaping hole. Then he looked up at Volkmann and said, "You want to take a look?"

Volkmann nodded and Orsati handed across a slim pencil light. Volkmann knelt down and flicked it on, probed inside the empty chamber. He saw the twin brackets welded onto the inner metal frame, left and right sides, maybe one quarter of a meter apart. The chamber smelled of paint and rust. He stood and turned to glance at Scali. The clerk looked at him uncertainly.

Volkmann asked Orsati, "Does Scali speak English?"

The detective turned to the clerk and asked him a question. Scali shrugged, said something in reply.

Orsati said, "He says he doesn't speak English."

"Then I won't be very useful when you interview him," Volkmann answered. He looked at Scali for a time, thinking. "How do you plan to get him to talk?" he asked, turning again toward Orsati.

"The evidence against him is circumstantial, but solid. Like I said, no one else had access to the container. That's leverage enough, I think."

Volkmann nodded and glanced back at the clerk. The man looked anxious, no question about it.

"There's an office in the warehouse," the detective said. "I'll talk to him there. When I'm finished, believe me, I'll know everything Franco Scali knows." He paused, thinking, then smiled. "Why don't you wait outside? Grab a cigarette, get some fresh air. After Scali's made his speech, I'll call you in."

"Fine," said Volkmann. "That sounds good to me."

Kleins saw the knot of people around the container move away toward the warehouse. He picked out Scali with the Zeiss. He nodded to Beck, who reached behind on the seat for the two briefcases.

It took less than a minute to assemble the two Heckler and Koch MP 5K machine pistols and slam home the magazines. When they looked up, they saw the group reach the warehouse.

Kleins pulled back the hammer of his weapon, flicked his safety catch to off, and Beck did likewise.

Strasbourg. 3:55 P.M.

Ferguson sat in the office, snow falling outside. He had arrived back late from lunch with the section heads and seen the note from Peters about the meeting with Volkmann, Peters stressing it was urgent. There was a postscript to the note saying that Peters was at Volkmann's apartment with the girl. He wondered what it was about, guessed it had something to do with Volkmann's investigation, and was about to telephone Volkmann's apartment when the telephone rang and he picked up the receiver.

Jan De Vries came on the line and told him that a classified communication had arrived from Asunción for his attention, marked "Urgent," and he was delivering it to him personally.

Three minutes later, De Vries arrived. He appeared to be subdued, and Ferguson had waited until the man left the office before breaking the waxed seal and opening the envelope.

Inside he found the signal and he read it slowly, then put it down, stood and crossed to the window, ashen-faced. He stood there for a full minute in silence, in disbelief, oblivious to the snow brushing against the glass; then he crossed back to the desk and picked up the signal and read it again.

When he had finished this time, he hesitated, but only briefly, before picking up the telephone and quickly punching in the numbers. When he got no reply, he clicked the cradle with his free hand and thought for a moment, his brow furrowed in concentration; then he hit the receiver cradle smartly again and began to punch in numbers once more.

Had he stayed at the window, he would have seen the black Mercedes draw up in front of the building and the two raincoated men climb out, one of them carrying a briefcase.

They entered the building ten seconds later, showed their identity cards at the security desk, then crossed the lobby and moved toward the elevator.

A kilometer away on the Quai Ernest, another two men stepped out of their parked Mercedes into falling snow.

They walked purposefully across the white courtyard and climbed the steps. When they halted outside Volkmann's apartment, the driver of the car nodded to his partner. Each man opened his raincoat and withdrew a silenced pistol.

While the driver scanned the courtyard below, the second man took a heavy bunch of keys from his pocket.

He selected one and tried it in the lock.

CHAPTER 45

A cold breeze swept in from the sea, and it washed Volk-mann's face. As he stepped out onto the apron from the warehouse entrance, he searched in his pockets for a ciga-rette. Finding none, he realized he must have left them in his overcoat in the unmarked police car.

As he reached the parked car ten meters away, he looked up, saw the figure of a man move toward the warehouse from the harbor side in the growing darkness, caught for a moment in the sweep of silver light from the lighthouse out in the bay. The man was fifty meters away, maybe less, a dark Fiat obscured behind him.

Volkmann saw the machine pistol in his hands, and for a brief moment he thought the man was one of the cara-binieri, but the man moved at a trot and he wore no uni-form.

Volkmann froze. Something was wrong. The man's stride was too purposeful, too determined, the weapon in his hands held across his chest at the ready.

For a second or two, Volkmann turned and glanced back at the warehouse. Lights on in the tiny office where the Italian detectives and the customs man had taken Scali—looking like characters in some drama beyond the lit glass, Scali's lips moving, the others listening. Easy targets.

Volkmann looked back again toward the man. Forty me-ters from the warehouse now, moving fast. As he passed under a klieg light on the apron, Volkmann saw the bur-nished glint of the Heckler and Koch in his hands.

Volkmann started to reach for his Beretta, then suddenly realized he hadn't taken the weapon with him on the flight to Genoa.

He swore, moved rapidly back toward the police car, yanked open the driver's door and searched frantically in the glove compartment for a weapon. He realized that the man with the machine pistol had a clear line of fire toward the warehouse, realized that Scali was the target, the voices

on the tape echoing like an alarm bell in his head as he
tried to find a weapon.

"And the Italian?"

"He will be eliminated."

Apart from papers, the glove compartment was empty.
He tried to think. Detectives always carried weapons in an
unmarked car; Italian cops were no different. But where?
Sometimes in the trunk; sometimes overhead in a zipped
compartment. Volkmann felt along the coarse vinyl. No zip.
No weapons compartment. He felt under the seats.

Nothing.

He checked for the keys in the ignition.

None.

Volkmann swore again as his right hand shot down to
the side of the driver's seat, felt for a trunk release, found
one, pulled it hard. Then he looked back out through the
rear window, seeing the man twenty meters away now as
the trunk yawned open and up.

As Kleins moved at a trot across the apron, he could see
the knot of men standing in the lighted office window, see
the faces plainly beyond glass, two men standing, two sitting, one of them looking like he was talking while the
others listened.

Scali.

Fifteen meters to go now, and still the men in the office
hadn't seen him.

He had left Beck sitting in the parked Fiat, watching his
back, ready for the getaway; the second car parked in a side
street four blocks from the harbor entrance, ready for their
escape to the safe house.

But a difficult hit. Not impossible, but too many people,
too many things to go wrong, but the kill imperative, according to Meyer.

Twelve meters from the warehouse window and still the
men beyond the glass hadn't noticed him. His finger slid
around the trigger as he ducked under the line of yellow
tape.

Ten meters from where the apron ended and the parking
area in front of the warehouse began, Kleins hesitated, animal instinct telling him something was wrong. He saw a

movement out of the corner of his right eye. As he looked
to the right, the trunk of the unmarked police car yawned
open. Kleins glimpsed the figure of a man, crouching as he
moved quickly toward the rear, his hand reaching inside
searching frantically. Kleins couldn't see the man's face,
but in those split seconds, he knew the man was marked
for death.

He swung the Heckler and Koch around and fired in one
swift motion. The apron erupted with a thunderous volley
of sound as the man darted back for cover, lead ripping
into the police car, shattering glass, puncturing metal.

Kleins swung the weapon back toward the warehouse
window, saw the men behind the glass react to the sound
of gunfire, mouths open as they froze in disbelief and stared
out at him.

He squeezed the trigger.

The office window shattered, glass fragmenting, lead hitting concrete and wood and flesh as the Heckler and Koch's
deadly chatter sprayed the tiny room, the figures beyond
the window dancing like crazed puppets as Kleins kept the
pressure hard on the trigger and discharged one long, sustained burst.

Click.

The magazine emptied. Kleins tore it out, slammed home
a fresh one from his pocket, cocked the Heckler again.

Suddenly he glimpsed the figure move out again from
behind the car, his hand coming around to pull something
from the trunk.

Kleins swung the Heckler and Koch, leveled it and
squeezed the trigger again.

Volkmann had crouched helplessly behind the car, eyes
flicking from the man to the open car trunk, to the shattering office window and the figures caught in the deadly burst
of fire from the Heckler and Koch.

As the man concentrated on the targets beyond the window, Volkmann had seen the opportunity, crouching low
again as he moved forward once more toward the trunk,
hand reaching frantically inside, fingers probing, feeling for
metal, for the hard form of a shotgun, a machine pistol.

Nothing.

Then the cold metal of a wheel jack.

Then . . .

Something hard in his fingers, an L clamp, then another, then the outline of a weapon, fingers touching the hilt of an Uzi, grasping the comfort of cold, hard metal.

Volkmann heard the chatter of the Heckler and Koch suddenly stop, saw the man tear out the magazine, slam in a new one.

Volkmann swung around and up, saw the Uzi held in the L clamps with two rubber stays, tore them off, wrenched out the weapon, praying it was loaded.

The volley of gunfire that came just as he grasped the Uzi sent him reeling back behind the car and he hit the ground, hearing the jackhammer crack of bullets as they ripped into metal. As he fell back and rolled along the side of the car, the fingers of one hand fumbled wildly for the safety catch, found it, then the hammer.

He flicked the Uzi onto automatic fire with his thumb, bullets cracking into the ground around him.

The man with the Heckler and Koch moved forward, firing wildly; Volkmann rolled to the right on the asphalt, and on the third roll he aimed and squeezed the trigger.

The Uzi exploded in his hands.

Bullets ripped into the man's chest, his body lurching, hammered back onto the ground as Volkmann kept the pressure on the trigger.

Click.

The magazine emptied.

Silence.

Volkmann dropped the Uzi, stood and looked back toward the warehouse window. He saw no movement beyond the shattered glass, but he heard the moans of pain and the cries for help.

At that moment, he heard the roar of a motor and saw the headlights of a car flash onto his left.

Beck saw everything happen from where he sat in the parked car.

He swore. He saw Kleins fall under the hail of fire, saw the man drop his weapon, stand and move out from behind the shattered police car.

Beck gunned the Fiat's engine and flicked on the headlights.

As he reached for the Heckler and Koch on the seat
beside him, he hit the accelerator hard and the Fiat lurched
forward.

Volkmann heard the screech of tires and saw the blinding
beams of light race toward him out of the twilight.

Eighty meters.

Seventy.

Sixty.

He crouched as a burst of fire suddenly raked the ground
to his left, chips of stone flying as lead cracked into asphalt.

Fifty meters.

Forty.

The Fiat growling toward him out of the fading gray
light, headlights like the glaring eyes of some crazed wild
animal, blinding him.

The empty Uzi lay five meters away.

He raised his hand to shield his eyes from the piercing
lights, glimpsed the Heckler and Koch beside the man's
pulped body, raced toward it, flung himself down and rolled
the last five meters, his hands scrabbling wildly for the
weapon as another burst of fire raked the ground to his left.

Thirty meters.

Twenty.

Volkmann grasped the Heckler and Koch, rolled to the
right, aimed, squeezed the trigger just as the Fiat appeared
under the wash of the apron's klieg lights.

The burst from the Heckler and Koch shattered the left
headlight and the left side of the windshield, turned it white
under the klieg lights, but the car kept coming, weaving
crazily. Volkmann glimpsing the face of the driver beyond
the half-shattered glass, the barrel of his weapon spitting
flame.

At the last moment, Volkmann released the pressure on
the trigger, rolled to the right again, squeezed the trigger
hard, felt the weapon chatter madly in his hands as the
bullets ripped in through the shattered windshield.

The second burst decapitated the driver, sent his severed
head flying back hard against the headrest as the Fiat veered

to the left, wildly out of control, screaming past Volkmann with a rush of air. There was a grinding screech of metal hitting metal as it smashed into the unmarked police car, and then came a sharp crack as the gas tank exploded and a geyser of orange flame erupted into the gray twilight.

Volkmann shielded his eyes as a wave of intense heat rolled toward him. He pushed himself up and raced back toward the warehouse, the tangled metal behind him engulfed in a pall of flame and acrid smoke.

The light was still on in the tiny shattered office, but there was no sign of life.

And then he saw a figure stand up shakily. Orsati—blood streaming down his face, his hand covering a head wound as he tried to steady himself against a wall.

Suddenly the harbor came alive. A siren screamed, and seconds later a ghostly blue light swirled in the gray twilight as a police car raced out of nowhere and screeched to a halt.

Two carabinieri stepped warily from the car, pistols at the ready. As they crouched and aimed their weapons at Volkmann, they cast disbelieving looks at the shattered warehouse office, then at the tangle of blazing metal.

As the men rushed forward, unsure of their enemy, Volkmann slowly raised his hands over his head.

And then another police car wailed into view and halted, and then another. More cops jumping from cars, unholstering guns, until finally all the sirens died and were replaced by babbling and screaming voices, the gray twilight streaked by the corona of revolving blue lights and the shadows of cops everywhere.

Strasbourg. 4:03 P.M.

The two men stepped out of the elevator into the empty corridor.

The one carrying the briefcase led the way. It took them less than twenty seconds to find the office, the name on the plaque on the door.

Ferguson was on the telephone and clutching a sheet of paper when the door burst in. He saw the men and the

silenced pistols in their hands and started to open his mouth
to speak.

Four times he was hit in the chest, twice in the head, the
force of the bullets sending him flying backward and up,
dragging the telephone and papers with him, his body
hurled against the wall.

The receiver was still clutched in his hands when the
man with the briefcase stepped forward and coldly fired
another two shots into his head.

The two men remained in the office no more than another
twenty seconds, one of them searching through the unlocked cabinets and desk drawers, the other opening the
briefcase he carried, setting the timer on the bomb, then
closing the briefcase again and placing it under Ferguson's
desk.

Neither man noticed the classified report from Asunción
lying on the floor, the page streaked with blood.

They checked the hallway, saw that it was clear and
stepped outside, closing the door after them.

Erica sat alone in the bedroom.

When Peters had started probing her with a few gentle
questions, she had excused herself, saying she was tired.

A gust of wind rattled the glass, and a flurry of snow
brushed against it. She started. As she went to draw the
curtains, she heard the noise. It came from the hallway: a
sudden rush of heavy footsteps.

She moved quickly across the room. As she opened the
bedroom door, she heard the television, saw Peters rising
quickly from his chair, staring at some point toward the
hallway, saw the color drain from his face.

Peters said, "Who the hell are you . . . ?"

And as he went to reach for the pistol lying on his coat,
Erica saw the two men with guns in their hands rush forward toward him, saw the backs of their pale raincoats.

As Peters reached for his pistol, there was a strange whistling sound, and then another and another as both men fired
rapidly into Peters' body, blossoms of red erupting on his
chest and face as he was flung back against the chair.

Erica screamed.

*   *   *

The Mercedes halted on the Quai Aperge and the man in the passenger seat checked his watch.

Fifteen seconds later, both men heard the blast in the distance as the air ruptured with the sound of the explosion. The man nodded and the driver pulled out from the curb.

Minutes later they heard the wail of sirens behind them in the distance, but neither man looked back.

And neither saw the dark-colored sedan that pulled out quietly twenty meters behind them.

CHAPTER 46

Genoa. 5:30 P.M.

Volkmann waited his turn to speak as he sat in the commissioner's office on the Plaza di Fortunesca.

The tension in the room was as thick as the cigarette smoke that rose like a gray cloud to the white ceiling. Orsati sat in the center of the brightly lit office; a broad strip of flesh-colored plaster ran from just below his left eye to the middle of his cheek. Around his head was a white bandage where a bullet had nicked and rutted flesh.

He had smiled at Volkmann nervously after the doctor and nurse had attended him on the dock apron, but he had brushed aside their request to come with them in the ambulance.

"A flesh wound. Nothing to worry about," he had said to Volkmann, white teeth flashing behind his mustache, but the man looked badly shaken.

Apart from Volkmann and Orsati, there were two other men present in the room. One was the Genoese police commissioner. A bespectacled, handsome man wearing civilian clothes, a smart gray business suit with a pale blue tie and white handkerchief. A touch of flamboyance but the man totally in control, professional brown eyes peering sharply from behind metal-rimmed glasses.

The fourth man present was the chief of detectives, tall, parchment-white skin, an aquiline nose and flecked, steel-gray hair. He wore casual clothes as well.

Orsati had explained that Scali had talked before he was shot. One small box, the last consignment. A heavy box, concealed in the false side of the container. There had been several other consignments over the past year. Weapons, Scali had guessed, or maybe even gold. But the little man had not been sure, the contents of all the consignments a mystery.

Orsati had explained that the forensic people were still conducting tests. The commissioner sat behind the desk, chewing an unlit cigar.

The only one talking now was the chief of detectives.

Volkmann watched him, listening but understanding only a word here and there, and waiting for the man to finish talking to his commissioner, waiting for the man to translate. He spoke good English, the commissioner only a little.

The man had been speaking for almost five minutes now, uninterrupted. Volkmann had told his story in English, corroborated by the detective.

As far as the commissioner was concerned, it came down to four bodies and two badly wounded men on life supports in Santo Giorgio Hospital. His own two men had escaped with minor flesh wounds. One of the dead was an official of the Italian customs service, Paulo Bonefacio, the others were Scali and the two armed men on the apron.

The assassin's clothing was of German manufacture. But he carried no identification papers of any sort.

"Like a suicide squad," Orsati had remarked of the men's action. "Crazy."

Now Volkmann looked up as the chief of detectives stopped talking. He turned to Volkmann and said, "I have explained everything to the commissioner as you and Detective Orsati told it to me. However, there are some things that need clarification. Do you have any idea of why the two men wanted to kill Franco Scali?"

Volkmann looked away, toward the window, darkness outside, black sky, no stars. He looked back again and said, "I can only tell you what you know already. We received information about a cargo from South America, with Genoa as the possible destination. We passed that onto your people in DSE. We requested that a thorough check be made on all cargoes from South America, in particular from Montevideo and São Paulo." Volkmann stared at the man. "I gave you the name and telephone number in Strasbourg. I suggest the commissioner contact Ferguson urgently and tell him what's happened."

The man sighed. "Signore Volkmann, we are trying to make contact with your superior. But in the meantime, your help in this matter would be greatly appreciated. I must point out that cooperation is vital. You understand?"

The man paused, stared at Volkmann. "There is nothing else you can tell us?"

"Nothing."

The man sighed again, impatiently. "You must understand our predicament." He glanced over at Orsati, then back at Volkmann. "I think we have been more than cooperative. Now it is your turn. Four men are dead and we don't know why. I want to know why."

Volkmann recognized the frustration in the man's tone. But he would need permission from Ferguson before going further. It wasn't a question of noncooperation, merely approval from Ferguson. He or Peters would have to be the arbiters of how much he could tell the Italians.

Volkmann said, "I need clearance."

The man's face showed his frustration. "Then what has happened goes much deeper?"

Volkmann nodded.

The chief of detectives looked at him. "We've tried to contact your headquarters, but have been unable to get through. The operator thought there was a faulty line, but the exchange knew nothing."

There was a knock on the door and a detective entered. He looked at the chief of detectives and asked to speak in private. Both men stepped outside for a moment into the hallway, their heads bowed in whispered conversation. Moments later, the chief came back into the room, his face pale. He looked at Orsati, then at the commissioner, went to speak, but hesitated and looked at Volkmann instead.

"We contacted one of our liaison officers in Strasbourg at his home number . . ." The man paused. "He said there has been an explosion at your headquarters. Our officer knows nothing concerning casualties, only that all his own people are accounted for."

The man hesitated again, flicked a glance at the others before he looked back, saw Volkmann's face drain to white.

"There is something else, Signore Volkmann. Something important, I believe. Our forensic people at the harbor, one of the tests they carried out on the container . . . they used a Geiger counter. It registered a high reading." The man paused. "It suggests that the cargo Scali removed contained radioactive material."

Wannsee, Berlin. December 23

The stretch black Mercedes turned into the large private grounds of the house in Wannsee just after six.

Set twenty meters back off the lakeshore road and surrounded by high poplar trees, the property was not overlooked front or rear by any of the big old prewar houses that ringed the lake.

Ritter stepped from the car and led Dollman to the front door, the two other bodyguards in front of the Mercedes remaining in their seats.

The beautiful young woman who opened the door greeted Dollman with a smile but ignored Ritter. Once the two men were inside, Ritter was consigned as usual to the comfortable front study on the ground floor, while Dollman and the young woman waited a respectful five minutes in the sitting room at the back of the house before they went upstairs.

Fifteen minutes later, Chancellor Franz Dollman lay naked on pink satin sheets in the master bedroom. The girl had slid the disc into the stereo, the sounds of Mozart filling the room. His favorite music to relax by. He held a glass of champagne in one hand as he stared up at the reflection in the mirrored ceiling.

There was an expression of pure pleasure on his face as he watched the image of the girl's naked body, sending pleasure shocks through his flesh.

Her blond hair lay strewn across his stomach, her long nails stroking the insides of his thighs, sending exquisite waves between his loins. She was a rare specimen indeed, his Lisl; she helped him dissipate all those tensions that came with high office. And there had been many of those of late.

Until he had met her almost a year before, there had been a physical void in his life: he and his wife hardly ever made love together. There were public expressions of endearment, for the television cameras, for the newspapers, but his Karin was not a sexual woman, a trifle dowdy, yet an ideal chancellor's wife: loyal, moral, conservative.

But Lisl.

Twenty-three and a body made for pleasure.

She ran two pink-nailed fingers slowly across his chest and pouted her perfect lips. Moments later, her hand went down to stroke him in an unhurried rhythm.

"Good?"

"Exquisite."

A tiny, sensual sigh, and then Lisl asked, "Would you like me to dress up for you?"

Dollman said, "Something nice."

"What if you're late for the palace?"

"To hell with them."

The girl smiled and stopped stroking him, raised herself gently from the bed onto all fours, displaying her well-rounded buttocks.

Dollman watched as she stepped slowly from the bed, swaying her hips and bottom as she crossed to the dresser. She opened the top drawer, removed a pair of coral-pink silk stockings, ran the sheer material sensually through her hands.

Next came the garter belt, pink and flimsy. She clasped it around her hips and Dollman watched as she dressed slowly, seductively, sliding the sheer stockings onto her long, shapely legs. He suppressed the urge to reach out and take her there and then, prolonging the torturous but delectable pleasure.

When she had stepped into a pair of coral-pink stiletto high heels, she turned to face him.

Dollman said urgently, "Come to me . . ."

"No, I want to tease you first."

She was playing with him, something she liked to do now and then, the feline in her, and Dollman tried hard to control his urgency. She came and lay next to him on the bed. Pink fingernails scraped along his legs, sending tiny, sensuous shivers up his spine.

The thought of spending Christmas in a boring house, with a boring family, when he could have this woman.

Another woman would have bitched about the important times when a family came first. Lisl, as ever, hadn't complained. "I understand, *Liebchen*. That's where you should be at Christmas."

She was purring now, and as she began stroking him again, Dollman relaxed and enjoyed the erotic pleasure.

He had managed to keep her out of the limelight with no great effort. Besides, it was a tacit understanding among Cabinet members: one's private life was just that, private. Unless the press got hold of it. In which case, you swam with denials or sank ignominiously. Much depended on the woman in question and her tacit understanding. In Lisl's case, her desire for secrecy had been on a par with his own. It was the answer to a prayer.

"Tell me about your meeting."

The fingers that gripped his hard flesh suddenly slowed. *Keep going*, he wanted to scream. *Don't stop*. The throbbing in his loins was unbearable now.

"As usual, Weber sees extremists under every bed. He's scheduled an emergency security meeting for tomorrow morning."

"In Bonn?"

Dollman smiled and shook his head. "The Reichstag."

The girl frowned. "Is it serious?"

"Weber seems to think so."

Dollman didn't elaborate. Federal security was not a subject to be discussed with a mistress. Besides, the girl would hardly be interested. He didn't tell her that Weber was putting the finishing touches to an emergency decree that very night, to resolve finally the extremist problem, and wanted full Cabinet approval. Weber's plans for the internment of all extremists would put the final nail in the coffin.

The meeting in the Reichstag was to be held in room 4-North, the secret room. The place always intrigued Dollman; a few Germans knew about it. Specially designed to counter any possibility of bugging or electronic eavesdropping, suspended in midair on eight steel wires from each corner so that no part of it touched walls or floors.

He felt her fingers on his thighs and saw her smile.

"That means you've no excuse not to stay tonight."

Dollman smiled. The function at the palace would be finished by midnight, no later. Then he could spend the night with Lisl before the Christmas holiday and family beckoned.

She turned her magnificent breasts toward him and purred. He cupped one in his hand as she spoke.

"I'll cook supper. Just the two of us, alone."

Dollman glanced toward the curtained window. Even as they spoke, he knew there were three armed men stationed strategically in the two cars outside in the driveway, another three positioned along the cold street in an unmarked car. Ritter, as always, in the study below. In the brains department, the man might be lacking, but his loyalty and discretion were beyond question.

The tiny transmitter Dollman himself carried everywhere was on the bedside table. The nine-millimeter pistol he was supposed to carry he had left in the Mercedes. The thing troubled him, made him think of violent death. A necessary precaution, but one he often disregarded.

She continued stroking him, her plump breasts swaying. *My God, what a body!* It was like a pain in him, wanting her.

She smiled. "You're going to be late for the palace."

Dollman smiled back, "Lisl, come here . . ."

She stopped stroking him. Dollman reached across and gently kneaded a breast.

Lisl said, "What time will you be back?"

"A little after midnight. No later."

"You promise?"

Dollman let his eyes wander over her magnificent body, the triangle of golden hair between her legs. At that moment, he would have promised her the vice-chancellorship.

"I promise."

In the darkened study below, Ritter relaxed on the couch with his feet up. The portable phone was in his pocket and he had turned down the volume on the walkie-talkie that lay on the coffee table in front of him; his holstered nine-millimeter Sig and Sauer P6 pistol draped over the end of the couch.

He heard the moans of sexual pleasure coming from the bedroom overhead, rising above the faint sounds of Mozart, and he smiled to himself.

CHAPTER 47

Strasbourg.

It was after seven when the Lear jet touched down.

Volkmann telephoned his apartment from a call box in the terminal and let the number ring for a long time. No answer. When he tried the office numbers, the same happened. He guessed that the lines had been damaged, and he wondered if Peters had heard the news and had taken the girl with him to the building.

He picked up the Ford from the airport parking lot, and twenty minutes later he was standing at the corner of the Orangerie. Lights blazed from the emergency units in the winter darkness. In the lobby, temporary lighting had been rigged up, and he heard the whine of a mobile electric generator, but most of the building was still in darkness.

The snow had stopped and the streets were covered in gray slush. A half-dozen police cars stood outside, their blue lights flashing. Two fire-trucks were parked nearby, the firemen talking among themselves and smoking, others reeling in hoses. A couple of forensic men in dark overalls were still sifting through the debris that lay littered about the Platz.

On the third floor, shadows moved in and out of the rigged lights, and Volkmann guessed they were more forensic people. The third floor appeared to have taken most of the damage, and Ferguson's window was blown out, revealing a black cavity where the office had been. Where windows had been shattered, black traces of soot from the blast and the flames had stained the external walls.

As he stood in the shadows, he saw several faces he recognized in the crowd, but he saw no sign of Erica or Peters. His heart raced and his mind was in turmoil. One of the German officers, tieless and wearing casual clothes, stood chatting with one of the policemen, smoking a cigarette, and Volkmann thought of approaching him, but some instinct made him hesitate.

He stood there for five minutes before he turned and walked back along the street, wondering what to do next.

He decided to try calling the duty officer once more. He walked to a phone box at the end of the street and this time he got through on a crackling line.

He heard the voice of the young French officer, Delon, answer, and Volkmann gave his name.

Delon asked urgently, "Where the hell are you, Joe?"

Volkmann ignored the question and said quickly, "Tell me what happened."

There was a deep sigh at the other end, and then Delon said, "Ferguson is dead, Joe. A bomb went off in his office two hours ago. I was on duty in the basement. As soon as the blaze was out, we found him. What's left of him is in the police morgue. Jan De Vries is in the Civil Hospital with a severe concussion. He was in one of the offices on the second floor when the bomb went off. I've taken over as duty officer."

"How did it happen?"

"The guy on the front desk admitted two men fifteen minutes before the blast. They had Belgian Section IDs that looked bona fide. They took the lift up to the third floor but never came down. We found a fire-escape door on the first floor open. They must have left that way." Delon paused and then Volkmann heard the panic in the young man's voice. "All hell's broken loose, Joe. No one knows what's going on."

"Are you the only one on duty?"

"No, Reauld from the Belgian section's with me. He's duty officer on the next shift. He's in the next room talking to his people in Brussels about the IDs. But no names so far."

"Who was on the front desk when it happened?"

"One of our guys from the French desk. He's been with us only three months. I'm going to recommend he's transferred back to where he came from. The dumb son of a bitch never even got them to sign in."

"Did Lamont get descriptions of the men?"

"I questioned him earlier. It was snowing outside and the men wore overcoats with their collars up. Both tall, fair-haired, mid-thirties, but that's about it. They didn't speak, just showed their IDs. According to Lamont, they seemed familiar with the layout of the building and knew where they were going.''

''What time does Reauld take over?''

''Half an hour from now. He heard the blast from his apartment and came in early to see if there was anything he could do.'' Delon paused. ''I've been trying to contact Peters, but there's no reply from his number. The same with yours. There was a security signal for Ferguson. It came in just before the blast.''

''From where?''

''South America. De Vries delivered it to Ferguson just before the place went up.'' Delon paused again. ''I think that either Peters or you should see it, Joe. It's important. Not something I want to discuss over the phone. I've got a copy in the basement safe.''

''Is there anyone from the German desk in the building?''

''One or two.'' Delon paused. ''Why?''

''You don't show the signal to anyone, André. Not until I've seen it. Do you understand?''

''Of course.''

''My place is on the Quai Ernest. Meet me there as soon as you come off duty. Come alone, and tell no one where you're going. And bring the signal copy.''

''What the hell's up, Joe?''

''Just do as I tell you, André.'' He gave Delon the address, then said, ''When did you last see Peters?''

''This afternoon. He left early with some girl. Why?'' Volkmann heard the pause and then the young Frenchman said, ''Is everything okay?''

''For now, just do as I say. I'll talk to you later.''

It took Volkmann two minutes to drive to the Quai Ernest. Peters's Volvo was parked in the courtyard, caked in snow, and as he went up the steps, he saw the smudged footprints in the slush leading down to the courtyard.

At the top of the balcony, he hesitated. The front door to the apartment was closed and there were faint noises coming from inside. The light in the small bedroom was on beyond the curtained window, and he rang the bell before he went to insert the key. When no one came to the door, he hesitated, then retraced his steps down to the Ford.

He found the Beretta under the driver's seat, closed the door again, flicked off the safety catch and cocked the weapon. He walked around the side of the courtyard to the small garden at the rear of the building and looked up at the windows. The light was on in the front room, but he saw no movement, just the blue flicker beyond the curtained glass that told him the TV was on. The bedroom window next to it was lit by the sulfur-colored light from the bedside lamp. His heart was pounding as he walked back around and climbed the courtyard steps once more.

He unlocked the front door warily and stepped inside, the Beretta at arm's length, aware immediately of the stench of lingering cordite as he went through the rooms, his heart pounding wildly in his chest.

He saw Peters's body lying across the settee, and the room in disarray. He felt a jolt of fear, then caution, replaced by anger as his eyes flicked from the bloodied corpse to take in the rest of the room. The air smelled of cordite and there was blood on the carpet, blood clotted and caked on Peters's face and neck and clothes. There was a bullet wound above Peters's right eye and two more in his chest cavity. A trickle of dried blood had congealed in the eye socket, and the other eye stared open in death. He touched Peters's left wrist. Rigor was beginning to set in; the man's flesh was ice-cold.

It took him ten seconds more to check the apartment. He saw the splintered wood of the bedroom door, the telephone off its cradle, and one of Erica's shoes by the door. When he didn't find her body, he felt relief, and then fear, and then a terrible anger took over.

For a long time he simply stood in the center of the living room, staring at the bloody scene. He thought of what might have happened to the girl and felt his hands tremble with rage, and he was aware of an overwhelming need to act, knowing Kesser's people had been responsible for what had happened, knowing they had taken Erica.

And then for a moment, he felt his insides wrench and fall, as though he was being torn through a hole in space. *What if Erica is one of them?* he asked himself. *She fits the profile. She has the pedigree. What if she brought them here?*

For a time, that thought burned within him. But then another came to him. *No,* he told himself, *she doesn't fit the profile, even though she has the pedigree. Betraying me, deceiving me? No, that doesn't make sense. It just doesn't fit my experience of her.*

It took several minutes before his self-control returned.

He flicked on the safety catch of the Beretta, found a towel in the bathroom, placed it over Peters's face, and went to sit in the chair by the door.

He waited for Delon to arrive.

Volkmann removed the bloodied towel briefly and then replaced it.

The Frenchman's face had turned pale and his fists were clenched tight by his sides as he stared at Peters's body with disbelief.

"Jesus!"

As Delon shook his head from side to side and looked about the room, Volkmann said, "He's been dead for maybe a couple of hours."

"Who did this, Joe?"

"The same people who killed Ferguson."

The young Frenchman looked badly shaken. Then suddenly the sharp blue eyes regarded him with detachment and his professionalism took over.

"Joe, I think you had better tell me what is happening here."

Volkmann ignored the question and said, "You brought the signal copy with you?"

Delon hesitated, then slowly took an envelope from inside his overcoat pocket, opened it and handed it across.

"You think this information has something to do with what happened tonight?" he asked. "Because if you do, you had better tell me what's going on. I was the acting duty officer. This is my concern also."

Volkmann glanced at Delon before he took the signal copy and read it slowly.

TO: Head, British DSE.
FROM: Chief, Seguridad Paraguaya, Asunción.
The following information is classified and urgent:

(1) Regret to inform the deaths of Captain Vellares Sanchez and officer Eduardo Cavales in Mexico City, approx 20:00 hours local time, Dec. 20. Deaths occurred in the course of police raid on residential property in suburb of Chapultepec, during attempted arrest of one Franz Lieber, traveling on alias passport of Julius Monck, from Asunción. Lieber—alias Monck—also confirmed dead. Lieber known acquaintance of Nicolas Tsarkin. In course of raid, two occupants thought to have escaped. Both male Caucasian. One believed named Karl Schmeltz. Second escapee believed named Hans Kruger. Chief Inspector Gonzales in charge of case in Mexico City. Gonzales mounted immediate search but suggests that the two may have already fled Mexico. The Chapultepec property owned by one Josef Halder, naturalized Mexican citizen, but formerly wanted for war crimes. Halder also died in course of raid. Investigation proceeding. Will contact if further information from Gonzales, Mexico City.

(2) Priority and highly classified: Confirmed to us by Gonzales, Mexico City, that one of the men arrested at above residence identified as Ernesto Brandt, Brazilian passport holder. Subject refuses to cooperate, but it has been confirmed by First Secretary, Brazilian Embassy, that Brandt is employed by Brazilian government civil nuclear research establishment and suspected of involvement in disappearance of 12 kilos— REPEAT: 12 KILOS—weapons-grade PLUTONIUM. Investigation proceeding. ENDS.

Another nail in the coffin, Volkmann thought as he finished reading. *So the radioactive material in the container was plutonium. Christ! They're always ahead of us. And they get farther ahead by the second.*

For a moment, sickeningly, he felt very alone, and very exposed.

He hesitated before he looked up, and as Delon saw the look on his face, he said, "This has something to do with what happened?"

"Yes," Volkmann answered.

"I'm going to have to bring my superiors in on this thing," Delon said.

"Has anyone else seen the signal, apart from you and me?"

"Only De Vries."

"Then before you contact anyone, I want you to listen to me. The people who did this to Peters—the people who killed Ferguson—they've taken someone else."

"Who?"

"A German girl. The one you saw Peters leave the building with. She was staying here and Peters was playing guardian."

Delon frowned and said, "Who is she?"

"A journalist. She put us onto this." Volkmann held up the signal. "That's why she was taken tonight. Whoever's behind it, they want to find out what she knows, who she told her story to. And it's probably why Ferguson and Peters were killed. The two men who were killed in Mexico City, Sanchez and Cavales, were involved in the case."

The Frenchman saw the look of anger on Volkmann's face, then shook his head and said, "Joe, you're telling me very little." He glanced uncomfortably at Peters's body. "Who are the people who did this?"

"They're neo-Nazis, André." Volkmann saw the look of confusion on Delon's face. "The German names I had you check. The same people who took the girl were responsible for their deaths. Why they were killed, I don't know, but it's tied in somehow with what's happening."

Delon said hoarsely, "What are you saying? The people who killed Peters have this plutonium?"

"They've been taking it into Germany in small consignments from South America over the past year. The last one came through Genoa a couple of weeks ago." Volkmann told Delon what had happened in Genoa, saw the man turn paler still.

When Volkmann explained about the tape, Delon said angrily, "Why weren't we informed?"

"Because until I went to Genoa today, I didn't know there was radioactive material involved. And until you showed me that signal, I didn't know the material was plutonium. Until now, the pieces of the puzzle didn't fit together.''

The Frenchman shook his head. "Then this isn't something that solely concerns the British desk. I will have to inform my superiors.''

"André, I need time before the alarm bells start ringing. If these people learn that we know about the material, then God knows what they might do.''

Delon looked at Peters's body, then back again. "What do you mean? How could they know?''

"Because they're planning a coup. A *putsch*.''

The Frenchman's face was ghostly pale. His head shook slowly, as if not daring to believe what he had heard. His eyes stared into Volkmann's face as he spoke, his voice almost a hoarse whisper.

"How do you know this?''

"Trust me, André. It's going to happen. The signal confirms it. And the people behind it have sympathizers and supporters in the German police. In the German Army. At the German desk of the DSE too, I wouldn't be surprised. They must, if they intend to succeed.''

Delon looked at him doubtfully. "I don't understand. Why the plutonium?''

"To stop others from interfering. It's the only answer that makes sense.''

Delon moved slowly across the room and let his body slump onto the couch. It was an act of indecision and it showed on his face; his brow furrowed in deep concentration and his big hands clenched and unclenched. A hand went up to his face and cupped his brow.

Volkmann watched him. Telling him about Schmeltz would totally bewilder him, and Volkmann decided not to. For a long time Delon just sat there. When he looked up and saw the grim look on Volkmann's face, he seemed to finally realize he was being told the truth. He sat forward suddenly and shook his head.

"What you ask, I can't do it, Joe. I can't take the chance. It's too much to ask.''. The Frenchman's blue eyes regarded Volkmann keenly. "You're close to the girl?''

"Yes.''

"Then emotion is clouding your judgment. You must realize that?"

Volkmann shook his head. "You're wrong, André. Believe me."

"Then I have a question. How much support do these people have?"

"I don't know, André, but with the material they've got, they don't need it. They simply hold the country to ransom."

Delon thought for a moment. "You say you need time, but what do you propose to do?"

"There's one of their people in Munich named Kesser. He may know where they have the material. You give me eight hours. If I can find out, I'll call you. In the meantime, you contact your people. You contact every section head personally. But stay clear of the German desk. Tell the others what I told you. There are people in Berlin I'd trust, but I'd want to talk with them personally. The first thing to do is to locate the material. Point our people to it. You have the signal from Asunción. Show your people, and the others. Tell them what I intend doing."

"And when is this *putsch* going to happen?"

"My guess is soon. It's Christmas, every army in Europe will have most of its personnel on leave. No one would be expecting something like this."

Delon looked at Volkmann anxiously. "And what if I don't hear from you within eight hours?"

"Then it's up to our governments. If it means crossing German borders to stop these people, I hope they're capable of making that decision."

Delon sighed deeply and wiped his brow, and Volkmann knew the Frenchman had given in.

Volkmann said, "Can I keep the signal copy?"

"Yes. The original's still in the basement safe."

"Give me a number where I can contact you, André."

The Frenchman wrote a number on a piece of paper and handed it to Volkmann. "You know the security-desk number and the others. I'll stay at headquarters. But that's my own private line, in case you can't get through. The lines were damaged by the blast, but we patched up the emergency ones just before you rang. I'll call the section heads on a secure line as soon as I get back. I just hope they believe me.'' The young man looked at him. ''You're sure you don't want any backup?''

Volkmann shook his head. ''There isn't time, André.'' He saw the beads of sweat on the young Frenchman's face as he looked at him.

''You think this is the right thing, doing it this way, Joe?''

''It's the only way, André, believe me.''

''Then good luck, my friend.''

Volkmann took the road to Kehl. He estimated that it would take over three hours to drive to Munich, sticking to the main autobahn and avoiding the road through the Black Forest to Herrenberg.

As he turned onto the autobahn to Ulm, it started to snow and by the time he reached Augsburg almost two hours later, it was coming down heavy, the fields of Württemberg already ghostly white.

The traffic was thin and as he passed Augsburg, a column of twelve German Army personnel carriers and six supply trucks lumbered in single file in the slow lane, heading toward Munich.

Volkmann's heart pounded as he overtook the army trucks slowly, trying to glimpse the stenciled divisional markings, but the vehicles were caked with snow and mud. Fifteen minutes later, he pulled into the next filling station and made a call from a phone booth. The conversation lasted less than a minute.

As he climbed quickly back into the car, he checked his watch before he turned back onto the Munich road. It read ten-fifteen.

CHAPTER 48

The Turk stepped out of the crowded S-Bahn Station at Wannsee.

Kefir Ozalid carried the briefcase and wore his overcoat, scarf and woolen gloves. He walked across the street toward the lake and stepped into the shadows between two street lights. From where he stood, he could see the dark jetties and the tourist boats tied up for the winter. The wind coming in off the choppy water was biting cold but he scarcely noticed the icy blasts. Other, more important things were on his mind. During the past six years, the Turkish assassin had been hired to kill fourteen men and women. All fourteen were now dead. Tonight he had a contract to kill his fifteenth.

He had hesitated at the station exit to make sure he hadn't been followed and now he checked again, pausing for several moments to light a cigarette, his breath fogging in the chilled air as he looked across at the darkened lake, then back over his shoulder.

He saw no one following him, only workers and Christmas shoppers coming out of the station, returning late from the city, but no one remotely interested in him. He waited for a few moments, then turned toward the narrow road that led down to the lakeshore. It took him ten minutes to reach the house.

There were lights on downstairs, and a Christmas tree stood in the window. As he walked past, he saw that the porch light was off, as it should be. He took the narrow footpath that led around the back and found the gate he had seen earlier, when he had checked out the house and the neighborhood. He was a careful man.

Now he flicked up the wooden latch and let himself in, eyes alert and watchful. The houses nearby were bordered with high evergreens, and their privacy ensured that no one could see him.

There were no lights on at the rear of the house, but he could see the open basement window and he walked

smartly across the lawn and knelt down. There was enough
room for him to squeeze through, and moments later, he
was standing in the basement.

He closed the window and made sure the latch was
firmly locked before he removed the pencil light from his
pocket and shone the beam around the room.

The walls were painted lime-green, and there were five
wooden boxes stacked against the wall farthest from the
window. He saw the bare wooden stairs that led up. He
placed the briefcase on the floor, crossed the room and
climbed the stairs carefully, keeping to the side so the
boards didn't creak.

When he reached the top, he gripped the door handle.
As he opened the door a crack, faint music came from
somewhere in the house. He felt a pleasant wave of heat
against his face, and he saw the stairs leading up to the
bedrooms. He couldn't hear the girl, but he knew she was
somewhere in the house, a faint scent of perfume lingering
in the hallway.

He closed the door and descended the basement stairs,
then crossed over to the ottoman. He lifted the lid and
played the light inside, smelled the musty odor and saw the
jumble of discarded women's clothes. He picked up the
briefcase and flicked open the locks. When he had removed
the Beretta pistol, the silencer and the two loaded magazines, he closed the briefcase again and placed it beside
him.

It took him less than twenty seconds to screw on the
French-made Unique silencer and slide a magazine into the
pistol butt. When he felt it gently click home, he slipped
the second magazine into his left pocket. He left the Beretta's safety catch on, but held the weapon lightly on his
lap.

That morning, after checking into the small hotel off the
Witzleben, he had taken the S-Bahn out to Wannsee, had
walked by the house twice before taking the narrow side
path that came out at the rear of the property, quickly examining the layout of the house and grounds, relating the
reality of his surroundings to the map and the photographs
the German had given him at the safe house in Stockholm.
He had spent an hour walking through the narrow streets

and footpaths that bordered the lake, getting his bearings. He rode back on the train to the S-Bahn station on Witzleben, and an hour later, as he sat in his hotel room, the knock came on the door.

The blond young man who stood there had looked him over silently before handing him the brown-wrapped parcel. Ozalid had waited until the man had gone before he unwrapped it and removed its contents.

He had checked the action of the blue-metal weapon, examined the silencer and magazines, and then placed them carefully in the cut-out foam in the briefcase. Five minutes later, he had locked the room after him and stepped down into the street and walked toward the S-Bahn station.

Now, sitting in the cold basement, he checked his watch: 8:45 P.M.

Four more hours.

Four more hours and Dollman would be dead.

He flicked off the light and sat waiting patiently in the darkness, aware only of the faint sounds of his own breathing and the distant music coming from above.

Munich.

It was 10:45 P.M. exactly when Volkmann pulled up outside the house in the Starnberg district.

Ivan Molke came out to stand under the porch light in the lightly falling snow as the Ford halted in the driveway. The older man didn't waste any time but quickly led Volkmann into a paneled study where a fire blazed in the grate.

When they were seated, Molke said seriously, "Your phone call was very brief, Joe. Has this got something to do with what happened in Strasbourg? I heard it on the news."

For a long time Volkmann looked at Molke, saying nothing. When Volkmann finally spoke, his voice was thick with emotion. It took him almost five minutes to explain all that had happened, and he saw the reaction on Molke's face as he spoke, disbelief mixed with fear, and when he had finished, Molke stared at him with incredulous eyes.

"*Jesus . . .*" he breathed. "You're certain about the girl in the photograph?"

"Hanah Richter identified her, no question. The other part's guesswork, Ivan, but it makes some kind of sense. All the pieces of the puzzle fit together when you consider everything that's happened."

"Karl Schmeltz is Adolf Hitler's son?" Molke shook his head and as he stood up, he said, "It sounds crazy, Joe." His face was pale. "A neo-Nazi *putsch* I can imagine as possible, yes. But not another Hitler, Joe. Never that. No way."

As Molke continued to shake his head, Volkmann took out the signal copy from Asunción and placed it on the desk. Molke read the paper. After a time, he looked up as if in a daze, walked back across the room and stared into the fire, then turned and looked at Volkmann.

"Do you think the people who trailed my men belonged to the same group?"

"I don't know, Ivan. But it's possible. Has anyone been watching your house or tailing you since we last spoke?"

Molke shook his head grimly. "Not that I'm aware of. And I've been careful, Joe, believe me. After what happened with my guys, I've been extra vigilant." He slipped his right hand into his pocket and removed a slim automatic Browning, weighed it in his palm. "I haven't been taking any chances. I keep this with me." He swallowed hard as he placed the pistol on the desk. "Do you have any idea of where Erica Kranz is now?"

"Assuming she's still alive, Kesser's people probably have her."

"Where's Schmeltz, do you know?"

Volkmann shook his head. "After what happened in Mexico City, my guess is that he's already in Germany. If not, he will be soon."

For a long time Molke looked at Volkmann blankly; then he said, "What do you want me to do?"

"Do you know someone with authority in the State Ministry? Someone you'd trust your life with."

Molke said palely, "I don't know if I'd go that far with those guys. They're career types. But there's a politician in the Upper House named Grinzing I'm on first-name terms with. He's the only one I can think of right now who might listen to me."

"Then I want you to deliver a letter to him by hand, tonight. See that he reads it. In the letter will be everything that I've told you, everything I suspect, except what I told you about Karl Schmeltz. Because no doubt Grinzing will want to ask you a few questions about me." Volkmann paused. "Like if I'm crazy. If the letter is some kind of joke. The contents he'll have to judge for himself. Regarding me, I want you to be honest. Just tell him my background. Make him know that he can trust me." He looked directly at Molke. "We worked together in Berlin for four years, Ivan. You know my character. You know I can be trusted. Simply tell him that when he asks. But above all, tell him it's vital that he act on the letter. Tell him the signal from Asunción can be verified by Strasbourg. His own state security people can make contact there directly."

"Why don't you want me to tell him about Schmeltz?"

Volkmann shook his head. "He'd never believe it, Ivan. You must know that. And explanations will only waste time. I don't know how long we've got before these people start to move, but I can guess from what's happened that it's going to be soon."

"And if Grinzing doesn't believe me, what then?"

"You still know people in Berlin. Contact them. The same with the Landesamt here. Tell them what's going to happen, everything you're going to tell Grinzing."

"You honestly think they'll believe me?"

Volkmann shook his head. "I don't know. But you're the only hope I have, Ivan."

"What are you going to do?"

"Drive over to Kesser's place. If he's not at the apartment, his girlfriend may be. One of them's got to know something. If neither of them are there, I'll drive up to the place at Kaalberg."

"And do what?"

"Find Kesser. He'll know what's going to happen and who's supporting them."

Molke shook his head vigorously. "Joe, you saw the armed guards up there. It's too dangerous. Let me call a couple of my people in as backup."

"There's no time to lose, Ivan, and it would complicate things further. Just deliver the letter."

Molke sighed. For a while, he said nothing, simply looked at Volkmann solemnly. Finally he shook his head.

"You know, I never thought this would happen again in Germany. Not in my lifetime. Sure, there've always been the crazy, extremist groups like the ones who burn down immigrant hostels or cause unrest. The shaven heads with swastikas who march and give the Nazi salute at the Brandenburg Gate every anniversary of Hitler's birth." Molke shook his head again and crushed his cigarette fiercely into the ashtray. "But not this. *Never this.*"

He tried not to think of Erica, but her face kept coming into his mind, and she was still in his thoughts when he reached Kesser's apartment off the Leopoldstrasse twenty minutes later. The snow had stopped falling and he tried to check his anger as he stepped out of the car, forcing himself to figure out how to handle Kesser or his girlfriend.

There were Christmas candles burning in the windows of the apartments and nearby houses, and here and there the lights of a Christmas tree winked on and off. The lights were off in Kesser's apartment, and as he walked toward the entrance, he saw no sign of the gray Volkswagen in the parking lot. His heart skipped a beat when he thought Kesser or his girlfriend might not be at home.

He had the Beretta in his pocket. This time he used the copy keys Ivan Molke had given him, and he let himself in the front entrance and went up to the second floor.

He hesitated before knocking on the apartment door, but when he knocked three times and there was no reply, he let himself in, the key offering a little resistance before it turned in the lock.

The apartment was in complete darkness and as he flicked on the light, nothing happened; then suddenly he was caught in the glare of a powerful beam of light. As he wrenched the Beretta frantically from his pocket, he felt the hard, stinging blow on the back of his neck. Then there was only a blinding pain and whiteness as he heard the muffled voices and felt strong hands and arms immobilize him, and then something sharp jab his left arm.

He was barely conscious as he was carried back down the stairs and out into the cold air; then there were only the distant far-off sounds of car doors opening as he was bundled into a narrow space.

After that, the blinding whiteness took over and it seemed to smother him.

When Volkmann came awake, he saw the snow falling beyond the windshield wipers as the car's headlights probed the way ahead. He was faintly aware of the lights of the city far below him and beyond the falling snow, and he heard the engine whine as the car moved up a steep hill. As he strained to look again, a stab of pain arced across his forehead.

The last thing he saw before he started to go under once more was the pistol in the hand of the man seated beside him.

CHAPTER 49

Munich.

It was almost 11:40 P.M. when Ivan Molke saw the black BMW pull into the driveway of the house in Bogenhausen, the exclusive inner suburb across the Isar.

He had telephoned only to be told that Johann Grinzing was unavailable and had gone to a ministry Christmas party at the Steigenberger Hotel on the Hofplatz.

Molke had telephoned the hotel and had Grinzing paged. After several checks, a colleague had come to the telephone and said that Grinzing was not taking calls.

Molke had driven back across the Isar and parked outside Grinzing's residence. There was a uniformed policeman on duty in the hut that stood inside the gates. Molke showed his ID and the man phoned through. Molke had told the policeman that he would wait. The man had regarded him warily, and twice afterward he had appeared at the gate, walking down from the house to observe Molke's car, until a plainclothesman had come out from the gatehouse to join them and, recognizing Molke, walked over to the car.

"What's this all about, Ivan?"

"I'm waiting for Grinzing. Private business."

"You've no appointment?"

"No."

"I can't let you wait inside, Ivan. Grinzing will have to give me clearance first."

When Molke saw the lights sweep up the snowy, tree-lined avenue sometime later, he waited until the car had entered the driveway. Then the BP bodyguard telephoned through and one minute later, Molke found himself in Grinzing's study. The paneled room was cold, and the walls were lined with expensive, leather-bound tomes.

Johann Grinzing was forty-two, tall, with blond, thinning hair. An ambitious man who exuded an air of confidence, he wore his expensively tailored suits well. His face was rugged and his slim hands were perfectly manicured.

Grinzing lit a cigarette and sat down behind his desk, gesturing for Molke to be seated opposite.

He glanced at his watch and regarded Molke with questioning eyes. "So, what brings you here, Ivan? Is there a problem?"

Molke nodded. "I need your help, Johann."

Grinzing said simply, "Tell me."

Molke reached inside his overcoat pocket and took out the buff-colored envelope. He saw Grinzing stare at it, and before Molke handed it across, he said, "I want you to do two things for me, Johann. First, I want you to listen to what I have to say, then I want you to read the contents of this envelope."

"What's this, Ivan?"

"A friend asked me to give it to someone I trusted in the State Ministry. Someone with influence. Once he had told me what it was about, I chose you."

"I'm flattered, but go on."

"The man's name is Volkmann. Joseph Volkmann. He works for the DSE in Strasbourg."

Grinzing raised his eyebrows perceptibly. "This has something to do with security?"

"Yes."

"Bavarian or national?"

"Both. I could have gone to the state interior minister, Kaindel, or even contacted Weber myself, but I don't know either personally."

Grinzing hesitated, then lifted the cigarette to his mouth, drew on it slowly as if considering something, before he blew out smoke.

"So, how can I help you?"

"Before you read what's in the envelope, I want you to know two things. One, there was a bomb planted at the DSE offices this afternoon."

Grinzing nodded solemnly. "I heard it on the news in the car. Has this got something to do with it?"

Molke nodded. "Then you may also have heard that the head of the British DSE was killed. Plus another man. Also British."

"I thought it was two missing. That's what the last report said."

"That's Volkmann. He hasn't contacted his people in London."

Grinzing raised his eyes again and said, "Go on, please."

"Number two, Volkmann is totally trustworthy. I worked with him in Berlin. He's one of the few people I'd trust with my life."

"Why are you telling me all this?"

"Because after you read the signal here, probably the first question you're going to ask me is, do I trust him? I want that clear from the start. I do! Absolutely."

Grinzing averted his eyes for a time, thinking. Then he said, "May I see it?"

Ivan Molke handed the envelope across. Grinzing opened and plucked out the contents, unfolded the pages promptly and read.

Molke watched Grinzing's tanned face become waxen, and then the politician looked up.

"And you really trust him?" There was a tone of incredulity in the question.

"I told you already, Johann. Please believe what you read."

Grinzing shook his head slowly, his voice only a whisper. "It's almost beyond comprehension." He looked down at the pages again and then up at Molke. "You really expect me to go to the state prime minister with this? Tell him that a group of neo-Nazis is planning to take over the country? That it may have a nuclear weapon?"

"If you don't, then I will. There isn't much time. A matter of hours perhaps."

"And where's Volkmann now?"

"In Munich."

Grinzing put down the pages. "I'd be laughed at. You must realize this."

Molke said grimly, "And you must realize that if these people carry out what they intend, this entire country is in danger of stepping back over fifty years."

"I find that difficult to believe. And even if what you said were true, a democracy like Germany cannot be dismantled overnight. It's absurd."

Molke looked pointedly at his watch, then back at Grinzing determinedly.

"They'll have supporters. In Parliament. In the armed

forces. In the police. They have to have because it's the only way they can stand a chance of succeeding. And it only takes a small number to lend their support to this act of madness for the whole country to be plunged into the nightmare again.''

Grinzing shook his head, but his face was pale and his voice hoarse. "I really can't believe that, Ivan. It's not possible.''

Molke sighed deeply. "Very well. May I have the letter back? I'll take it to the minister myself, even if I have to kick down his bedroom door.''

Grinzing hesitated. For a long time he looked at the papers in his hand and then he looked up at Molke slowly, as if reconsidering.

Grinzing said, "What if the minister believes you? What do you expect him to do?''

"Alert Berlin and Bonn. The BfV federal office in Cologne will have a list of loyal army and police officers the country can rely on. Every sensible democracy takes that precaution to counter such a situation as this. A coup that threatens its existence.''

"And if the minister doesn't believe you?''

"I think he will. But if he doesn't, I still have friends in Berlin who might listen.'' Molke's voice became strained. "My God, Grinzing, we have to do *something*.''

There was an uncharacteristic anger in Molke's voice, and Grinzing hesitated, looking as if a great weight were pressing down on him. Finally he stared directly at Molke.

"I want you to do something for me.''

"What?''

"Give me five minutes alone to think this through. You must understand my position. Such a decision cannot be taken lightly.''

Molke looked at his watch, saw the anxiety on Grinzing's face.

He nodded. "Okay.''

Grinzing stood, clutching the pages. "I'll leave you here alone. You'll have my answer within five minutes.''

As the door closed softly after Grinzing, Ivan Molke let out a deep sigh.

At least the man was beginning to take him seriously.

*   *   *

Johann Grinzing stepped out into the hallway, past the guard sitting in the chair reading a newspaper under the portrait of Grinzing's father.

The guard went to rise out of respect, but Grinzing gestured for him to remain seated. He crossed out through the kitchen and stepped toward the back door, opened it softly and moved outside.

The gardens were white and the air crisp and cold, the branches of the bare apple and pear trees at the end of the garden covered in fingers of snow and the house behind him eerily quiet. His wife had gone to her mother's in Bodensee with their two daughters for the holidays, and even the servants were on leave. He hesitated briefly before he lit another cigarette.

For eighteen years, he had been a public servant. For all those years, he had never been faced with a decision as grave as this one. He stared down at the pages in his hand, legible in the harsh wash of light from the security floodlight on the back wall of the house. What Molke had said was true. There *was* a list of people loyal to the government. They could be activated quickly, if necessary. Cover all the major cities and ports, air and sea.

He thought of making a call first to seek advice but reconsidered. He was on his own. It was his decision to expedite the matter if he chose. Any delay would be on his shoulders.

He would have to inform his superiors, and urgently. But he would extract the most from it, of course. If he came out of it well, there was opportunity here.

But how to approach it? How to resolve it?

Three minutes later, he had figured out what to do. He stepped back inside, went through the kitchen and out into the hallway again. This time the BP man didn't rise but simply gave a respectful nod and went back to reading his paper. Late-night visitors were common in Grinzing's household.

For a few brief seconds, Grinzing glanced up at the painting of his father. The blue-suited man stood erect, behind him in the portrait the distant image of the Munich Rathaus, the state and federal flags flying above the clock tower. A loyal Bavarian to the core. It was strangely appropriate, Grinzing reflected. The man had been dead some twenty-five years. The portrait's blue eyes stared down and seemed to warn him. What he was about to do could ruin him if it went wrong. Already there were doubts in his mind. Yet he knew he had to go through with it. His future could hang on this. And the future of the Fatherland.

His father's eyes looked on just as he remembered them. Blue. Honest. True. A loyal servant to his Fatherland and state. Only the blue business suit looked out of place.

All that was missing, Grinzing reflected—recalling the old photographs he had kept since childhood—was the black uniform of the Leibstandarte SS.

Molke turned as Grinzing stepped back into the study and closed the door after him. When the man had crossed the room and sat down behind the desk again, Molke said, "You've reached a decision?"

"Yes."

"Which is it?"

"There are a few matters I wish to discuss first."

Molke saw Grinzing's hand reach over slowly behind the desk. In an instant the drawer was opened, the Walther cocked and pointing at Molke's chest.

Molke stared over and went to speak, but no words came.

Grinzing said, "I want you to listen to me very carefully, Ivan. What I have to say and how you react may determine whether you live or die in the next few minutes."

Molke still said nothing, simply stared at the man and then at the Walther again, his mouth open in disbelief.

Grinzing said calmly, "You're surprised, I can see that. I have a confession to make, but one which by now you've undoubtedly guessed. The people you fear, I belong to that group. I and many, many others."

Molke said simply, "Why?"

There was a grim, nervous smile on Grinzing's thin lips. "Because for the first time in years, this country has a chance to be truly strong again. To reinstill the old virtues we once prided ourselves on. To stop apologizing for our past. To cleanse our country of all the filthy, stupid imported breeds our politicians had the mendacity to invite here. To reawaken a sense of pride in being German. And I wish to be part of that change that is about to take place. It offers a great future for someone like me, I think you'll agree.''

"You're a fool, Grinzing. It can't succeed."

"On the contrary, it can. Too much planning has gone into it for it not to succeed. It can't fail and it won't.''

"Dollman and the Cabinet would never sit back and allow this country to be dragged into the gutter again.''

"Dollman won't be alive to obstruct us. As for the Cabinet . . ." Grinzing hesitated and smiled. "I think I've said enough already. Suffice it to say that they won't stand in our way.''

"And you think the German people would support any of this?''

"But they will, Ivan. It has all been worked out. Our strategy will ensure that the people will rally behind us. And once they see that we are capable of elevating this country to its former greatness, building a new and prosperous and powerful Reich that will stand tall and proud and strong again, they will thank us. It can and will be done, I assure you, and that's all you need to know. Doesn't the prospect excite you just a little?''

Molke ignored the question. "A nice speech, Grinzing. Did it take you long to rehearse it?''

Grinzing's thin smile widened. "If you're trying to anger me, Ivan, trying to deflect me in an attempt to make a run for it, forget it. You'd have a bullet in you before you'd gone one pace. And believe me, I'm a capable marksman. But you can take your chances if you wish. It would be my word against the word of a dead man. A dead man who had already waited anxiously outside my home for my return. Rather suspicious, don't you think? One of the guards even asked me if I wanted him to be present. He said you looked troubled. And troubled men are capable of strange behavior. Like attempting to murder a state politician.'' Grinzing smiled again nervously. "I'm certain I could come up with a plausible reason as to why you tried to kill me and how I was forced to defend myself.''

Molke said grimly, "I want to hear your reasons.''

Grinzing raised his eyebrows before he spoke. "You just heard them."

"And the nuclear material? Tell me why."

"I would have thought that was obvious. There is a war-head. It will give us the leverage to seize NATO nuclear missiles on German soil and foil any attempt by outside powers to interfere. If any of the world powers attempt to stop our progress, they face the possibility of a holocaust. And Germany still has the largest army in Western Europe, don't forget that." Grinzing paused. "There's nothing more to say, except that after the *putsch*, there will be a reck-oning. Those with us, those against us. Those against will be dealt with harshly, I assure you."

"No doubt, Grinzing, you're going to start building con-centration camps once more."

Grinzing smiled again. "I'm sure that will be on the agenda if these imported breeds refuse to leave our country. A necessary evil, I'm afraid, to rid us of unacceptable el-ements." He paused. "You're a sensible fellow, Ivan. I've always thought you so. You have an option now. There's a door off to my right. It leads eventually to the garage. I can phone through to the guard and tell him we're leaving. You come with me quietly and sensibly. If you make no fuss, I promise that by noon tomorrow, I shall make those who will be in power aware of your . . . shall we say, silent compliance. You'll be a free man."

Molke glanced toward the door, then looked back. "I'm a free man now."

Grinzing smiled. "Of course you are. Except that I have a gun pointed at your chest and won't hesitate to use it if you try to call the guards or attempt to escape."

For a long time Molke hesitated as he looked blankly toward the far wall; then he turned back to stare at Grinz-ing.

"I want to tell you something, Grinzing. And to ask your advice."

Molke stared across at the man seated opposite. "It con-cerns my father." He saw the frown on Grinzing's forehead and then went on: "I'm sure you understand father-son relationships, don't you? The portrait on the wall outside. Is it of your father?"

"Yes."

Molke nodded. "I thought as much. So you were close. He influenced you."

"Of course."

"If you told me he was a Nazi Party member, I doubt if it would surprise me."

"Both Nazi and SS. Leibstandarte SS."

Molke saw the look of pride on Grinzing's face. "Do you know anything about that organization, Molke?"

"They were murderers."

"On the contrary. They were the best, most loyal soldiers this country ever had. The cream of Germany. The chosen few. And their officers were the élite of the SS. The most dedicated, unswerving men the Reich had. Let me tell you something, Molke. My father and many others like him took an oath to Adolf Hitler and the Reich. To perpetuate the ideals they fought for and made sacrifices for. To serve their Fatherland with every atom of their being. And the only people who have the given right to lead this country to greatness again are their children and their children's children. I am one of them. We've waited a long time for the right moment, and now it's come. Look at what's happening in this country, Ivan. Not only on the streets. Even, ordinary Germans are saying the Reich had its merits. Why? Because they know it's time to clean this country up. Time to wake up and be Germans again. Time to shake off that stupid mantle of pious remorse for the past. To purify this country and clean up its mess. And yes, you were right, there are people, many in positions of power, people like me, men and women who have waited a long time for this moment. They are bound in blood to fulfill their fathers' pledges. And believe me, when the time comes, and it will come within the next hours, they will do their duty."

Molke looked at Grinzing palely. "I can't believe you think that every German thinks like that, Grinzing. If you do, you ought to be certified. Or that every son and daughter of every SS officer will support this madness."

Grinzing half smiled. "Those who don't will be dealt with. Some already have been. They disgraced their fathers' testimony by refusing to help us plan for the days ahead.

But those with us will help mold the future, will help create an even greater Germany. I'm talking about a formidable force, Ivan, not some half-baked group of anarchists.''

Molke said nothing for several moments. There was an almost maniacal look on Grinzing's face. Finally Molke said, ''Then I think you're going to appreciate what I have to say.''

Ivan Molke hesitated. When he spoke, his voice was calm, almost without emotion. ''In nineteen thirty-five my father was a young man with a young wife and a baby. He was a socialist and lived in Berlin. After the Nazis came to power, they began to purge the socialists and communists, but doubtless you know that . . .'' Molke paused for a second, saw Grinzing stare at him quizzically. ''My father was called on one night by the Gestapo. They took him to Spandau and beat him to within a breath of his life. Why? Because he was a socialist. Because he had dared to join a party other than the Nazi Party. Because, in the words of the Nazi propaganda writers, he was ''an antisocial element.'' For that privilege, he spent twelve years in concentration camps. At Flossenberg he broke and carried rocks and was treated worse than a pack mule. He was beaten, humiliated, starved. He was treated as less than human. He was whipped on the whipping block until he couldn't walk, and that for simply losing a button on his camp uniform. All these things, the endless beatings, the humiliations, the erosion of his privilege as a human being, they affected him deeply. He saw men being killed on the whim of a guard. Men being killed for no reason other than the sadistic pleasure of a camp commandant. He saw boys of no more than fourteen being hung from gibbets because the SS guards wanted some fun to liven up their dull afternoons; place a bet on who would squirm the longest before death.'' He paused for a moment. ''Please bear with me,'' he said then. ''I'm nearly finished.

''My father survived the camps. But he wasn't my father anymore. He was dead.'' Molke raised a finger, put it to his head. ''Up here he was dead. A ghost walking in our house. A father we could never get close to because his pain was like a wall around him.'' He looked intently at Grinzing. ''There are no Jews worth talking of in Germany,

Grinzing. Not anymore. But there are Turks and Serbs and Poles and others who no doubt your neo-Nazi comrades would class as racially inferior. Scapegoats to blame. Impurities to cleanse. Will they be the new Jews? Will they go to the ovens too?''

There were tears in Molke's eyes, and very slowly he leaned a little forward toward Grinzing. He saw Grinzing move back slightly in his chair and raise the Walther.

''So I have a question for you, Grinzing. What would you do in my situation? If your father had been an inmate at Flossenberg, would you keep your mouth shut and believe in someone like you? Or even in this man Schmeltz? This man you believe to be Hitler's son. Would you, Grinzing? Or would you take your chances?''

There was a brief, quizzical smile on Grinzing's lips and then Molke shifted his hand quickly to his right pocket and shifted left just as the Walther in Grinzing's hand exploded.

The first shot clipped Molke's right shoulder blade, shattered bone, the force of the nine-millimeter bullet jacking his body backward, the second bullet nicking the aorta above his heart.

But the third shot was from Molke's own Browning automatic that he carried in his right pocket. One shot before the weapon jammed on the reciprocating load.

The bullet hit Johann Grinzing square in the face, striking him just above his right eye. As the impact drove the other man backward, Molke slid off the chair and slumped on the floor.

As his head thudded against the carpet, there were screams and shouts from outside, and then the door burst in and he heard cries and the sound of rushing feet. Hands gripped Molke, shook him, wrenched his hand from his pocket.

As consciousness went from him, he heard voices swearing, saw hands moving about Grinzing. The politician's body had been flung back against the wall; then it slid down and listed to the right before collapsing on the floor behind the desk, his shattered face lying directly across from Molke's dimming sigh.

The last thing Ivan Molke saw was the look of utter surprise on Grinzing's dead face.

CHAPTER 50

As the car jerked to a halt, Volkmann became conscious again.

The headlights were extinguished and the car doors opened. He saw the secluded house directly in front of the driveway. There was a garage off to the left, and the front door of the house was open.

A row of pine trees ran up along the sloped driveway, and he could see the lights of the city beyond the trees and the thinly falling snow. He thought he saw the lights of other houses through the pines, and he guessed they were somewhere in the mountains near Munich. When he looked back, he saw the figure of Wolfgang Lubsch step out of a lighted doorway and into the falling snow. The man wore a heavy parka and his glasses glinted under the light.

There was an arc light on overhead somewhere, and as the terrorist stood watching, Volkmann was dragged from the car. Moments later they were in a warm, comfortable living room. Glass doors led to a balcony and all the lights were on. On a table were a half-bottle of schnapps and some glasses.

Lubsch kicked forward a chair. "Sit down, Volkmann."

When Volkmann ignored the command, the terrorist said, "Under normal circumstances, I'd have no hesitation in putting a bullet in your head. You're not a journalist, are you, Volkmann?"

Volkmann stared back at Lubsch. The icy blasts of air that hit him as he was dragged from the car had brought him quickly awake, but he was still fighting to regain his senses.

Lubsch lit a cigarette and looked at him. "It wasn't difficult to discover who you are. People like you and me scent each other like cat and dog. After our talk at the lake, you worried me. Who were you? Why were you so interested in Winter's death? So interested that you'd risk coming after me."

Volkmann spoke slowly as he stared at the young man's face. "Those were your people at the airport in Zurich?"

Lubsch blew smoke out into the air. "And at the monastery. We've been watching every move you and the girl have made since the day at the lake.''

"How?''

Lubsch sat down. "How did we follow you? The girl was easy. But you . . .'' He reached into his pocket, removed a small electronic device with a pinlike aerial, held it between two fingers. "A simple transmitter attached to your car. That way, we couldn't lose you. The same with your friend Molke and his men. You see, you confounded us, Volkmann. Everything about this business confounded us. Until now.''

"You're not with Kesser and his people?''

"Give me some credit, Volkmann. We accepted his help. But that was necessary.''

"Where are we?''

"Someplace where we won't be disturbed.''

Volkmann looked around the room. Two men stood in front of the door that led out. One held a Walther in his hand. Volkmann recognized them both. One was Hartig; the other was the scar-faced man with the truncheon. Both looked over at him, their faces expressionless. Volkmann turned back to face Lubsch.

"Why have you brought me here? To settle old scores?''

"Hardly. We have matters to discuss.''

"What have we got to discuss?''

"Something important to both of us.'' Lubsch paused. "You must forgive the behavior of my friends, Volkmann. But you see, we thought Kesser's people would turn up looking for their missing friend. Instead, you showed. It was quite a surprise.''

Volkmann looked at the terrorist's face. "Where's Kesser, do you have him?''

Lubsch ignored the question and stood. He crossed to the window and turned back to face Volkmann.

"We Germans, we have a dramatic flair. We can be loud, aggressive, unfeeling. But we are not all beasts, Volkmann. And we don't all want another Reich.''

"You know what Kesser's people intend?''

"Yes, Volkmann, I know.''

"Did Kesser tell you?''

"Hardly. He's dead.''

Volkmann began to speak, but Lubsch interrupted. "Two of my men were waiting for him outside his apartment. My instructions were to take Kesser alive. I had hoped he would tell us what we needed to know. Kesser came out and drove to the mountain. Halfway there, my men overtook his car and blocked the road. When Kesser realized what was happening, he pulled a gun and shot one of my men. They fired back. One of them hit Kesser in the head. He was still alive when they took him to one of our safe houses. But by the time I got there, he was dead."

Volkmann took a deep breath in anger, let it out. "Do you know what you've done, Lubsch?"

"The world's a better place without him, believe me, Volkmann."

"Did you kill Winter too?"

"That was Kesser's own people."

"Why?"

"I told you at the lake, Volkmann. Winter was a braggart. Especially when he was drunk. He liked to talk about the new order he and his friends were going to create. The new Germany. The closer it got, the more Winter talked. So Kesser used him less and less. Until Kesser gets a call from one of their people in Berlin to say Winter's in a bar and drunk and shooting his mouth off about things he shouldn't. For that, Kesser had him hit. And they hit him near the Zoo Station so maybe the cops will think there's a drug connection and Winter's been killed because of that."

Volkmann looked away, toward the lights of the city beyond the glass doors, then back again.

"Why did you want to take Kesser?"

"The same reason as you. To find out what his people intend. Two of my men were watching your apartment in Strasbourg. They saw the girl being taken by two men in a black Mercedes. They heard an explosion and decided to keep tailing the Mercedes. They managed to follow the car as far as Augsburg, but lost it in the bad weather. We guessed that Kesser's people were behind what happened, so we decided it was time to pay him a visit."

Volkmann stared at Lubsch.

"Do you know where Erica Kranz is?"

"At the Kaalberg."

"She's alive?"

"I've no idea, Volkmann."

"How do you know she's at the mountain?"

"The same way I learned about Winter. After what happened to Kesser, we went back for his girl. Once we showed her Kesser's body, the rest was easy. She's involved, only her loyalty didn't extend to losing her own life. Taking the girl in Strasbourg was part of a plan Kesser's people had. To find out how much she and your people knew."

"What else did Kesser's girlfriend tell you?"

Lubsch looked steadily at Volkmann. "The people behind it. What they intend. Everything she knew."

"Tell me."

Lubsch hesitated, reached for the bottle of schnapps and one of the glasses. He filled the glass quickly and handed it to Volkmann.

Volkmann pushed it away. "I don't want a drink, Lubsch. I want to know what the girl told you."

"Take it, Volkmann. You're going to need it when I tell you. And then, my friend, I'll tell you what we're going to do."

Snow flew against the windows. Volkmann had emptied the glass and replaced it on the table. Lubsch poured himself a drink and went to stand by the fire.

"They've got a missile sited at the Kaalberg. The nuke variety, not a conventional warhead. They've got neo-Nazi cells in the army and police, and politicians who are supporting them. The man you asked me about at the lake, Schmeltz. He's there, at the mountain; he's the one who's pulling the strings. They're trying to repeat history with a *putsch*, just like the Nazis tried in nineteen twenty-three. Only this time there's a missile as a lever. If any outside power tries to march over German borders and interfere, it risks a calamity."

Lubsch swallowed the liquid in one gulp. "The girl wasn't privileged enough to know everything. But she knew enough. To start with, they're going to kill Dollman and his Cabinet.'' Lubsch saw the look on Volkmann's face.

"How?"

"There's a house in Berlin's Wannsee where Dollman keeps his mistress. Her name's Lisl Henning. She's one of Kesser's people. Dollman's due there sometime after midnight. There's a Turk named Kefir Ozalid waiting to put a bullet in his head. Ozalid is an assassin, he's killed over ten people. He knows what he's doing.''

"And the Cabinet?''

"The girl didn't know. Only that it happens after Dollman gets hit. They'll all be killed.''

Volkmann hesitated, the voices on the tape suddenly clear. There were beads of sweat on his face as he spoke. "Why Ozalid, why not one of Kesser's own people?''

"Because they've been very clever, Volkmann. As soon as Ozalid pulls the trigger and the Cabinet get hit, the streets are going to be full of righteous Germans baying for immigrant blood. Kesser's friends have set it up perfectly. They blame the deaths of Dollman and the Cabinet on immigrant extremists. They pit German against immigrant and in the chaos, make their *putsch* a walkover.'' Lubsch put down his glass. "They've got everything worked out down to the last detail. The monastery you went to see. You know what it's for? It's to be a detention center . . . for undesirables. Immigrants and others. Another Dachau, no doubt. And it's not the only one. Kesser had a long list of such places to fill once their people take over. And they'll have most of the country on their side after Dollman and his Cabinet are killed.''

For a long time Volkmann looked toward the windows, saying nothing, then he looked back at Lubsch.

"Tell me what you intend doing.''

"The only thing we can do. We can't reach Berlin, but the Kaalberg is half an hour from here. My men and I are going to try to take out the missile. Neutralize it.''

"You're making a mistake, Lubsch. There's no way you'll succeed on your own. Let me call Berlin. They'll send in their people . . .''

Lubsch shook his head. "How long's it going to take

you to convince them, Volkmann? And by then, it may be too late.''

''What makes you think you and your men can succeed?''

''Volkmann, in this weather, we'll be lucky just to make it up the mountain. But if we do, we stand some chance. By simply informing Berlin, we have none. The girl didn't know how Kesser's friends are going to hit the Cabinet, but someone up there will know. If Dollman's killed, this country can still pull together and stop what's happening. Without a government, there isn't a chance in hell and Kesser's friends can do what they want.''

''According to the girl, there's never more than a dozen armed guards on the property. There are four of us, including me. You make five. With care, and with the help of surprise, the odds should not go against us.''

''You'll need weapons.''

''We have them. Machine pistols, grenades.'' Lubsch half smiled. ''Most of them supplied by Kesser's people. Ironic, don't you think?'' He hesitated. ''So what do you say, Volkmann?''

Volkmann looked out beyond the window, at the lights discernible beyond the mist of slanting white. He turned back to Lubsch. His eyes searched the terrorist's face. ''Why are you doing this, Lubsch? Why are you helping me?''

''For the reason I told you, Volkmann. I don't want another Reich or anything like it. I'm a freedom fighter. I believe in a better future for the ordinary people of Germany. That future may not be to your liking, and to you, I may seem to be a foolish idealist. But I'm certain of one thing: Men like Kessler don't belong in my country . . . in my world. I don't want the mistakes of the past repeated. Because if that happens, there would never be another Germany. Not ever.'' Lubsch smiled grimly. ''Absurd, I know, you and I joining forces, but there you have it.'' He stared at Volkmann. ''So are you with us?''

Volkmann hesitated. ''There are two things I want to make clear.''

''What?''

''I make my call to Berlin.''

Lubsch considered for a moment, then said, "And the second?"

"If we make it up the mountain, Schmeltz is mine."

Lubsch said nothing for several moments. "It's not only because of the girl, is it, Volkmann? Not only because of Erica Kranz?"

"There's something the girl didn't tell you about Schmeltz."

The terrorist grimaced and his voice was suddenly strained.

"She told us, Volkmann. I didn't mention it because I thought you'd think I'd lost my reason." Lubsch shook his head as if in disbelief. "Part of me wants to believe what she said, and yet another part of me is questioning my sanity. Still, I know she didn't lie. They say that history repeats itself. Only, in this case, who would have believed it?" He paused. "What do you want, Volkmann? A chance to speak for the dead?"

CHAPTER 51

The Mercedes braked to a halt on the gravel driveway.

The porch light was on outside the house and as Ritter opened the car door for Dollman, the chancellor slid out of the warm limousine.

The girl was waiting in the hallway and she hesitated while Ritter disappeared as usual into the study before she closed the front door and led Dollman inside.

On the dining-room table supper was laid. A bottle of Dom Perignon stood in a silver bucket of crushed ice. There were fresh flowers and two lit candles. The girl had drawn the curtains to stop the prying eyes of the bodyguards, and as Dollman crumpled into a leather armchair by the fire, the girl smiled and went to stand behind him.

She massaged his shoulders and Dollman moaned with pleasure. Moments later she felt his hand grasp her arm, and he pulled her around. She saw the look of impatience on his face and said, "Let's eat first."

Dollman's hand started to slide along her thigh, but she smiled, took his hand and led him to the table.

Dollman wolfed down his food and drank three glasses of champagne. When it came to dessert, the girl stood and came around to serve him chocolate mousse. He looked longingly at her and let his hand slide down the curve of her thigh.

The girl smiled down at him. "What about dessert?"

The chancellor grinned. "I'd much rather have you."

She smiled back, and Dollman stood, took her by the hand and led her upstairs to the bedroom.

Five minutes later, as Dollman undressed, he watched as Lisl slid a disc into the stereo and listened as the strains of Mozart filled the room.

The girl undressed slowly and came to lie beside him on the pink silk sheets. For several moments, Dollman's eyes feasted on the perfect body, and then he took her hungrily.

Five minutes later, his body shuddered as he spent his frustration.

He kissed her shoulder, the scent of her perfume mingling with the musky smell of sex, but when his hand moved to satisfy her minutes later, she gently pushed it away.

"Sleep, *Liebchen*. You're tired."

Dollman murmured gratefully and turned over.

The girl waited for several minutes before she slid off the bed, crossed to the window and peered out through a parting in the curtain. She could see the three cars parked below: one in the street, the others in the driveway, though there was no movement. But Ritter's men were out there. And Ritter himself was downstairs in the study, as usual.

As the curtain fell back into place, she heard Dollman begin to snore, his big naked body rumbling under the covers. She checked her watch before she crossed to the stereo again. She lowered the volume to near silence, waiting for the second hand to sweep past for one minute exactly, aware of her heart beating furiously; then she raised the volume again gradually until the music resumed its former pitch. She pulled on her silk nightgown and went to sit at the dressing table, her hands trembling as she stared down at her watch again.

1:10 A.M.

In another ten minutes, it would all be over.

In the basement room, Ozalid tensed as he heard the sounds of Mozart die and flicked on the pencil light. He watched the second hand sweep around; one minute and then the volume of the music rose again.

He had heard the cars pulling into the driveway, heard the sounds of footsteps on the stairs as the man and the woman moved up to the bedroom. But nothing this last half-hour. Until now.

He tensed again. His watch read 1:10. He flicked off the light and stood in the darkness, a knot of expectancy in his stomach, but every sense alert.

He would wait five minutes, just to be certain.

Then he would move.

12:46 A.M.

Christian Bauer was director of the Berlin Landesamt, a tall, lean man in his mid-fifties with gray sleeked hair and a handsome face. He wore a dressing gown over blue crumpled cotton pajamas, but even so, the man had the well-groomed look of the diplomat about him.

He had made coffee, but Werner Bargel ignored the steaming black liquid. Bargel had telephoned him five minutes before to say he was coming over. That it was urgent.

It was strictly business, and Bauer saw that his assistant's face was deathly pale, but Bauer spoke calmly, as if he were used to emergency calls to his home in the early hours.

"Tell me what's so urgent, Werner."

Bargel took a deep breath before he spoke. "I got two telephone calls just before I rang you, sir. Both from Munich. The first was from a man named Volkmann. He's with DSE, but he worked here in Berlin with British SIS."

"Go on."

Bargel said quickly, "According to Volkmann, a man named Kefir Ozalid was going to assassinate Chancellor Dollman." Bargel paused briefly, saw the look of alarm on Bauer's face. "He also said the entire Cabinet is going to be killed . . ."

Bauer's mouth was open. "When?"

"Tonight. Now. How the Cabinet is going to be assassinated, he didn't know, only that it's going to happen after the attempt on Dollman's life." Bargel swallowed. "All the Cabinet are staying in Berlin, sir, for Weber's security meeting in the Reichstag this morning."

Bauer put down his cup and raised his eyebrows, his face draining of color.

His assistant director flicked a glance at his watch, as if for emphasis. "Before I came here, I asked the security desk to run Ozalid's name through the computer. We're also trying to locate the chancellor."

Bauer hesitated despite his alarm, not a man to rush into things, the cautious eyes searching Bargel's face. "What did the computer say?"

"There's a Kefir Ozalid listed under security-risk category two. He's Turkish. Twenty-seven years old. A professional assassin. We know for sure that he's responsible for six killings. There are certainly more. He's very smart, and very efficient."

"In other words, if he sets his sights on the chancellor, there's a high likelihood he'll kill him."

"Absolutely."

Bauer thought for a moment. "Do you trust Volkmann?"

"Yes."

"Where is he in Munich? Can we speak with him?"

Bargel shook his head. "He just made the call to my home number, pressed on me the absolute urgency of the situation and gave me the information. Then he hung up." Bargel paused. "But there's something else, sir, tied in with Volkmann's information. Something very disturbing."

Bauer's sharp blue eyes stared piercingly at his assistant's face.

"What?"

Bargel took a deep breath. "According to Volkmann, the threats to Dollman and the Cabinet are only part of it. There's going to be an attempted *putsch*."

Christian Bauer looked at Bargel disbelievingly. "By whom?"

When Bargel told him, Bauer shook his head slowly and said, "Jesus Christ!"

Bargel did not stop; he told Bauer about the missile and its location, then caught his breath nervously, drew in a deep lungful of air, saw Bauer's face white as a sheet.

The director of the Landesamt asked quickly, "Where's Dollman now?"

"With Lisl Henning." Bargel swallowed. "Volkmann said she was involved."

"He mentioned her by name?"

"Yes, sir. I ordered security to contact Dollman's personal bodyguard Ritter as a precaution and inform him what's happening. However, because of the complexity of the situation and the protocol involved, the other orders I gave await your confirmation."

"What orders are those?"

"I gave the duty officer a list of senior military officers

and security personnel to contact. On your command, they're to come here immediately. There's a twenty-man team assembled and already on its way to the girl's house in Wannsee—I took the precautionary liberty of issuing the order as soon as I heard from Volkmann." Bargel quickly checked his watch. "They should be arriving within the next few minutes. Another team is making ready in Munich to move to the Kaalberg. We can do the coordinating from here over a secure line." Bargel paused. "You may, of course, countermand my orders, sir."

"What about the Cabinet?"

"I've already ordered that their personal security be trebled and put on alert."

Bargel looked at his superior expectantly. Bauer's face was tense. He nodded quickly.

"Okay. We act on this. Confirm your orders, with my approval."

"What about the interior minister, sir? He'll have to be informed."

There was a strict hierarchy in German federal security, and Bauer couldn't neglect his duty. The interior minister and vice-chancellor were the top of the pyramid.

Bauer was under pressure and he spewed out his words. "I'll contact Weber myself. But for God's sake, get onto Ritter."

At that moment the portable buzzed in Bargel's hand. He listened for several moments and then spoke sharply into the receiver. *"Keep trying! For God's sake, keep trying!"*

Bargel covered the mouthpiece and looked up.

Bauer said urgently, "What is it?"

Bargel shook his head. "It's Ritter, sir. We're getting no reply from his phone."

Karl Schmeltz stepped out onto the snow-swept balcony and buttoned up the green loden coat to the collar. He crossed to the end of the low wall and stared out at the snowy darkness.

Ghosts.

Ghosts everywhere.

An icy wind gusted up the valley, eddying the snowflakes. He looked down again at the obscured view, snow falling thinly in the valley below.

He had been in these mountains before, listening to the *Föhn*, knew it with certainty. Osmosis. Absorbed in his bone jelly. The memory ached there now like a soft, pleasant pain.

Flakes of icy snow brushed against his cold cheeks. Chilled, invigorating.

Bone-cracking coldness.

He sucked in a deep breath, felt the chilled air probe his lungs like icy fingers.

Good.

Twice, in youth, he had been taken here, to the south, remembering faces and names before his journey began: *Bormann, Mengele, Eichmann.* Secret trips and safe houses and furtive meetings. *Yes, here's the boy. Take a good look at him. Someday, not in your lifetime perhaps, but someday . . . when the time is right, when the opportunity presents itself.*

The Prussian snapping of heels, the firm shaking of hands, the pledges of allegiance. Old faces and new faces, faces that kept the torch burning.

Who would have thought it would have taken so long?

An icy blast blew across the balcony. He sucked in another deep breath of the chilled air through gritted teeth.

So close, so very close.

He heard a noise and turned toward the French windows. He saw Meyer step out onto the balcony, his footsteps crunching on snow as he came to join him.

Schmeltz looked at him expectantly. Meyer said, "The girl's here." Schmeltz nodded, and both men strode back into the house.

Ozalid flicked on the pencil light.

1:14 P.M.

Four minutes had passed. He flicked off the light.

In the darkness, he took a quiet, deep breath. Impatience was setting in.

Do it.

He began to climb the steps very slowly. When he reached the top, he flicked off the Beretta's safety, switched off the light and slid it into his left pocket, then gripped the door handle lightly.

He opened the door a crack. The table lamp was on in the hallway, the study door closed, and he could see no light under the door where the guard would be resting.

He stepped out quickly into the hallway.

Above him, the landing was in darkness, but he could hear the music coming softly from the bedroom. He crossed toward the stairs.

When he reached the landing, he hesitated, the music louder now. The bedroom door was open a crack, a thin shaft of light breaking through the gap.

Ozalid took a deep breath, let it out quietly as he raised the silenced Beretta.

He stepped toward the light.

In the study darkness, Ritter heard the buzz of the portable and came awake with a start.

He had lain back on the couch and flicked off the table lamp, tired after a hectic schedule with Dollman, resting his eyes but falling asleep in the process.

Now he fumbled for the portable in the darkness, found it, said sleepily, "Ritter."

"Ritter, this is Werner Bargel. Where the hell have you been? Are you with the chancellor?"

Ritter found the lamp and switched it on, almost knocking it over as the voice crackled with urgency.

"Why? What's up?"

"There's no time to explain, just listen, Ritter. There's going to be an attempt on the chancellor's life. Stay close by him. Do you hear? Stay close! Don't let him out of your sight. There's a support team on its way. They'll be with you in minutes. *But stay with Dollman!*"

Ritter dropped the portable, swung his legs around and stood up, every sense alert. He grasped the walkie-talkie on the table and spoke into it rapidly, not waiting for a reply from the men in the cars outside.

"*Watch units . . . Alert Red! . . . Repeat, Alert Red! Watch units . . . !*" Ritter shouted into the mouthpiece, his voice strained. "*Cover entrances and exits, now!*"

He turned and reached the door in one big stride, stepped

frantically out into the hallway, the Sig and Sauer P6 nine-millimeter already out and raised in his free hand, eyes scanning the ground floor, left and right. Music, but other sounds too, doors opening outside in the driveway, the other men responding to his call.

As Ritter moved toward the stairs, he glimpsed the open door leading down to the basement, his every sense signaling danger. He hesitated, but only for a split second. The door hadn't been open earlier, he was certain, and if it was open now, then someone must have . . .

Jesus!

He could hear the men moving frantically about outside, but he ignored the sounds now as he turned and raced up the stairs. Pistol at the ready and taking three steps at a time, he bounded up toward the landing.

As Ozalid stepped into the bedroom, he saw the man sleeping in the pink-covered bed, the beautiful young woman wearing the nightgown sitting by the dressing table.

She stared over at him silently, not making a sound, but with fear in her eyes.

There was something surreal about the scene, the music playing on, and for an instant Ozalid hesitated as he stared back at the young woman.

He recognized the beautiful face he had seen in the photographs. Their eyes met and her stare shifted nervously to the figure lying on the bed, as if pointing out the target.

Ozalid saw Dollman's body half covered by the pink bedclothes, his white shoulders, his back and part of his torso visible, the gray chest hair and his belly rising and falling as he breathed.

As Ozalid stepped forward, lowered the Beretta and went to aim, he heard the noise coming from the stairs.

Racing footsteps.

Then other sounds from below the landing, wood splintering, a door crashing in . . .

Ozalid turned instantly as the bedroom door burst in and the bodyguard appeared, a pistol in his hand.

The bodyguard saw the gun in Ozalid's hand swing around, his face registering his shock and his disadvantage.

As Ritter rolled suddenly to the right, Ozalid fired two

quick shots, one of them clipping Ritter's left shoulder. The bodyguard screamed as the bullet cracked into bone. Then the Turk turned back to face his target.

He aimed sharply as Dollman came suddenly awake, a startled look on his face, the big body rising from the covers.

Ozalid fired twice before the chancellor could speak.

He saw the red blossom on Dollman's left cheek just below the eye socket as the first bullet hit him in the face; then Dollman was flung back in the bed as the second shot punctured his chest.

As Ozalid started to fire a third time, out of the corner of his eye he saw the bodyguard raise his pistol.

Before Ozalid could turn back to aim at Dollman again, he heard the explosion and felt the piercing hot lead enter his right side. And then he was punched sideways by a quick series of shots, lead tearing into his flesh as the bodyguard emptied the P6.

Ozalid reeled back, glimpsing the woman in the pink nightgown, hearing her screams.

As he was spun around by the force of another bullet, the gun went off in his hand. The shot tore into the woman's throat, and she was flung back against the wall, her hands flailing as she gasped for breath, her pretty face contorted, eyes wide open in pain.

As the last burst of lead hammered into Ozalid's body, he pitched forward violently onto the soft pink covers on top of Dollman, not aware of the rush of feet on the stairs or the sounds of the men bursting into the room, or of the harsh voices screaming frantically, but dimly conscious of the hands tearing at his body, pulling him off the chancellor.

It was only forty seconds later that Konrad Weber got the call in his suite on the sixth floor of the Kempinski Hotel on Berlin's Kurfurstendamm. He had received the message from the Berlin Landesamt on his portable phone, requesting him to stand by for an urgent call.

Despite the hour, Weber was still dressed and reading through his papers, and he sat up expectantly and placed his leather briefcase on the bed beside him. When the call was patched through ten seconds later, Weber listened intently as Christian Bauer described the events in Wannsee. And then, after Bauer had answered Weber's few questions, Bauer outlined for him the details Bargel had given him about the impending *putsch*.

When Bauer had finished, there was a brief silence and then Weber said, "Oh, my God."

The two men spoke for another six minutes exactly.

As is customary in German politics, on the death or incapacitation of a chancellor due to ill health, the vice-chancellor assumes the position of head of the German government until a new chancellor is nominated and elected.

Konrad Weber, a pragmatic and precise man who normally responded calmly under pressure, was clear about his responsibilities and duties as vice-chancellor despite the shocking news of Dollman's death, and he left Christian Bauer in no doubt as to what had to be done to protect the security and integrity of the German Federal State. Weber would assume the position of chancellor immediately and convene an emergency Cabinet meeting within the next hour.

The threat to the lives of the Cabinet was a grave and real one, and Weber agreed with Bauer's extra security measures. Reichstag security officers were already contacting ministers staying at hotels throughout the city; the Intercontinental, the Schweizerhof, the Steigenberger. Security at the Reichstag was to be stepped up in case of an attack on the building itself during the coming hours.

A state of emergency would be declared by Weber and enacted at once. Those in the army and police whose loyalty was without question would be contacted immediately and both forces put on instant alert and borders sealed.

Weber ordered Christian Bauer to confirm the location of the site in Bavaria but to hold off any confrontation or any attempt to seize the missile until Weber had informed the Cabinet and considered a course of action. He was quite adamant about that, and despite Bauer's protests, Konrad Weber said he wasn't going to risk the decimation of Germany and its people until he had all the facts concerning the *putsch* and who the plotters were. He ordered Bauer to stand by until he had consulted with the Cabinet, and to keep him informed of any further news.

The next minutes and hours were of grave importance, and Bauer was to answer only to him and no one else, no matter what their position or authority. Weber would assume control of the armed forces and police, and all significant requests for their use were to be routed through him.

When he finally terminated the phone conversation in his suite at the Kempinski, Konrad Weber looked over at his brown leather briefcase on the bed beside him, certain he had everything he needed for the emergency Cabinet meeting he was about to convene at the Reichstag Parliament building.

CHAPTER 52

The driver had pulled in under a clump of trees on the mountain road. Switching off the engine, he doused the headlights and five men climbed out of the cramped Opel. There was a sudden burst of activity, the car's trunk opening, weapons being dispensed in the snowy darkness.

One of the terrorists thrust a Kalashnikov into Volkmann's hands. He took the weapon and checked that the safety was on, made sure the magazine was loaded. Lubsch had returned his Beretta and he slipped the automatic into his pocket.

He looked up toward the mountain. The weather had turned worse, snow coming down heavily now. A thick clump of pine trees faded into a mist of snowy whiteness, the visibility down to no more than ten meters, the mountain invisible beyond a curtain of snow. The snow was an ally, Volkmann knew. It was worth a dozen men. They had made it up the steep road with difficulty, the engines straining up the sharp incline before they halted on the main road, fifty meters from the private track that led up to the Kaalberg. The driver had kept the engine revs low for the last two hundred meters to mute the noise of their approach.

Volkmann tried not to think about Erica, tried not to worry about her. He had to concentrate on the climb ahead. Flakes of snow stung his face. As his eyes became accustomed to the poor light, he looked over at Lubsch. He was talking to Hartig, who gave his head a nod as Lubsch tapped him on the shoulder. Hartig then disappeared into the swirl of snow, a Kalashnikov draped across his chest.

Lubsch came to stand beside Volkmann. "The two of us will go up through the trees. As soon as we get close enough, I use this." Lubsch held up a CEL transceiver. "When the men below get the order, they start firing on the men on the plateau. If they can't eliminate them, they'll try to keep them pinned down. Hartig has gone to try and find the telephone and power-line junction boxes. If he can do that, he'll cut them. That way, Kesser's friends will be cut off from the outside world. If we need to use the telephone line, Hartig can reconnect us. If the worst happens, there's a call box a kilometer from the main road.''

"Why the power lines? They may have an emergency generator.''

"No doubt they will. But Hartig's the expert and he says to cut them. If an emergency generator kicks in, Hartig says the supply will only be connected to the lighting circuits and power sockets. But nothing heavy-duty, like electric motors, because the emergency circuit wouldn't take a heavy load. That way, the missile will be out of operation.'' Lubsch smiled. "But let's not count on it, Volkmann.''

Lubsch took a deep breath and exhaled, the air around him fogging in the icy coldness. "We'll have to play the cards as they fall. But we have the advantage of surprise, so let's just hope the bastards on the plateau barrier don't hear my men coming.'' He glanced up toward the trees and the blanket of white, then checked his watch and called the rest of the men together. Two minutes later, he had gone over the plan again and had the others synchronize their watches.

The Reichstag Parliament building on the Platz der Republik was as busy as an anthill, inside and out, and lit up like a Christmas tree.

Werner Bargel had never seen so much activity. Not since the Wall had come down and the crowds had swarmed over toward the Reichstag building from the Brandenburg Gate, two hundred meters away. That was a night to remember.

So was this.

Bargel stood on the steps outside the double glass doors at the southern entrance on the Scheidemannstrasse, his breath fogging in the December air as he paced the concrete nervously, the shock of Dollman's death still on his mind.

On everybody's mind.

The massive, imposing granite building had witnessed much history. The Reichstag fire. The storming of Berlin by the Russians. The Berlin Wall going up and coming down. And it was witnessing history in the making again right now.

It seemed like half the cops in Berlin were swarming around the Reichstag.

At least sixty green-and-white Volks, the same number of police Mercedes vans, green-and-whites with riot-squad police inside and out, dressed in full riot gear, some with leashed Alsatians, white helmets and Perspex shields and tear-gas guns, at least four helicopters hovering overhead, their noisy rotors throbbing in the darkness swept by the blue lights on top of the police cars.

Green-uniformed cops milled around in nervous clusters, talking, worried looks on their faces; other groups raced off into the trees in the small park opposite, flashlights flaring and sweeping in the dark, dogs barking, voices calling out, walkie-talkies and car mobiles crackling. Everywhere, frantic activity.

Jesus!

The threat to the Cabinet's lives was daunting enough without having the threat of the missile to worry about too.

Bargel checked his watch.

2:10 A.M.

Three of the ministers had already arrived without incident. Grim-faced, all of them as they nervously climbed the stone steps on Scheidemannstrasse, flanked by a deep wall of antiterrorist police as they entered the Reichstag. Dollman's death had shattered them. No doubt the threat to their own lives wasn't helping their nerves. Streicher looked like a corpse already, Eckart like someone had a gun at his back.

Bargel looked out toward the waves of green uniforms and plainclothes. All of them wore yellow discs on their lapels, marking them out as part of the security teams. But a yellow disc meant nothing. Anyone out there in the street could be waiting for the right moment, including someone in uniform. Bargel scanned the faces of the cops, chatting nervously in groups, some of them watching the entrance.

Any one of them, or more.

Who to trust?

Jesus!

But Bargel doubted that anyone in his right mind would risk an assault on the Cabinet now. If he did, it would be suicide. Security at the Reichstag was tight as a duck's ass.

No one allowed in or out without the personal permission of the Berlin chief of police, except Cabinet ministers and the Reichstag security force, and Bargel himself on Bauer's instructions. The chief of police stood outside on the cold street, ten meters away—his face looking like someone had cut his arteries and he was slowly bleeding to death—as he talked with a beefy, dark-haired young man in his early thirties, Axel Wiglinski, the head of Reichstag Security, both men's eyes darting nervously every now and then to survey the crowds.

No one looked sure of anything, despite the precautions. Wiglinski's teams had already scoured the Reichstag building three times with specially trained dogs in tow, checking all the rooms and every cranny, the basement, every floor, every wing of the building, north, south, east, west.

Nothing.

No one there who shouldn't be, no bombs or explosives.

Bargel had talked with the chief of police, discussed what would happen next. As the Cabinet arrived, they were to be led to an elevator that would take them to the third floor and the north wing of the building, to the room designated 4-North. The route was two minutes' walking distance from the Scheidemannstrasse entrance. When Weber arrived, accompanied by his bodyguards, Bargel and Axel Wiglinski would lead him there personally.

The room called 4-North had another name in the Reichstag. The Wire Room, they called it. Used only in emergencies and for high-security meetings.

Not so much a room as a big sound-proofed box with one double-door entrance, the room was suspended on eight thick steel wires above the floors of the Reichstag. There was no way to bug it because the walls, ceiling, and floor touched nothing. No telephones. No communication. Only one way in and out, sealed by oak doors with bullet- and bomb-proof sheathing. And that entrance would be heavily guarded, even with the Reichstag police and antiterrorist squad in the hallway outside the room.

Bargel glanced over at faces in the swarms of cops, picking out several in the crowds, thinking again about Volkmann's warning. Any one of them could be an assassin, waiting for the moment to strike.

But that was too risky, too unlikely.

It had to be a bomb, Bargel thought. But the building had been thoroughly checked, even Room 4-North, even the security staff's own personal lockers. Nothing. Clean. Not a trace of explosive. Unless Wiglinksi's men had missed something. He doubted that, too. The man was thorough in the extreme, and the bomb-squad boys had used three teams, going over the same ground, one after the other, working fast, efficiently.

So if not a bomb, how?

There was a sudden scream of sirens, and Bargel's heart jumped. A cavalcade of Mercedes and motorcycle cops swept around onto the Scheidemannstrasse. More ministers arriving, worried men stepping out of black limos, fogging breaths, cops surrounding the cars, helicopters hovering lower overhead, radios crackling.

Three members of the Cabinet climbed the steps smartly in single file. Axel Wiglinski greeted them at the door, eighteen of his armed men waiting inside, ready to guide each minister to Room 4-North, along with one of his bodyguards.

More wailing sirens, blue lights. Four more ministerial Mercs, then another two.

The next car was Konrad Weber's.

There was a buzz of activity as faces strained to see Weber arrive, a rush of men from the antiterrorist squads as they surrounded the car to protect him.

Bargel prayed that none of the A-T squad were there to kill Weber.

They jostled four deep, and as Weber approached the steps, Bargel deftly unbuttoned the jacket under his raincoat where the Sig and Sauer P6 pistol was clipped to his belt, ready just in case, but somehow knowing that nothing would happen here. He waited at the double glass doors until Weber had climbed the steps, the man's long, dark winter overcoat flapping about his legs, a grim look on his white face, the two bodyguards flanking him trusting nobody, not even the Berlin chief of police leading the way.

Once inside the glass doors, Weber nodded solemnly to Bargel.

Bargel gestured at the long hallway that led toward the elevator and Room 4-North. He let out a quiet sigh. With Weber inside the Reichstag, he felt safer.

For a moment, Bargel hesitated. What did he call Weber

now? Vice-Chancellor, or Chancellor? Stick with the safe one.

"This way, sir," he said gravely.

Bargel led the way across the polished hall, and Weber, his bodyguards and Axel Wiglinski followed.

Meyer had left the house and walked across the lit snowy driveway to the concrete building.

As he stepped in, he hit a switch and light flooded the cold room. He closed the door after him and crossed to the console and telephone, his eyes flicking to the gray gantry standing in the center of the building as he picked up the receiver, aware of his heightened anxiety.

He had tried calling Brenner, the head of security, from the house, but the line had gone dead. The same from the phone upstairs.

Brenner had called twenty minutes before, relaying the news from Berlin. Not only Dollman was dead. Meyer had heard the alarm in Brenner's voice and as he listened, his face drained.

Grinzing dead too.

Kesser and his girlfriend gone, the apartment in disarray.

Brenner had said he would call back within ten minutes; his men were searching Kesser's apartment, hoping to find some clue, trying to get further news on Grinzing.

But still no call.

The lines dead.

Meyer swore as he tried the only other line, aware of the beads of sweat on his face, of the others waiting in the house for him to return before Kruger went down to the barrier to find out if anything was wrong.

Dead.

He tapped the cradle a half-dozen times just to be certain, but still nothing. He slammed down the receiver just as he heard the far-off sound, a welter of crackling gunfire . . .

For several seconds he paused to listen, hardly breathing, like an animal scenting the wind. The crackling gunfire raged in the distance; he pulled himself together and hurried toward the door.

*   *   *

Snow fell incessantly as Volkmann and Lubsch came out of the bank of trees to the right of the driveway.

There were floodlights on overhead, white light washing across the snowed-under driveway, tire marks on the white carpet, empty except for two Mercedes, their bodies caked in snow. Off to the right, the roof of the flat concrete building was covered in white. They moved quietly toward it and crouched low behind the rear of one of the Mercedes.

Volkmann looked over at the house through the falling snow. There were lights on, but beyond the veil of white, they saw no movement in the windows. He turned to Lubsch. The terrorist nodded and flicked on the CEL, spoke quickly, then turned to Volkmann.

"Hartig cut the telephone. Let's hope he can find the power lines. You ready?"

Volkmann nodded.

Lubsch barked a command into the CEL.

Seconds later came the distant chatter of small explosions as the woods and valley below filled with gunfire.

Volkmann moved forward across the snow-covered gravel toward the *Berghaus*, Lubsch after him, just as they heard the door open behind them.

As he stepped out into the falling snow, Meyer saw the two men standing there, a surprised look on their faces. Each pointed a Kalashnikov at him.

Meyer froze in shock, icy flakes brushing against his cheeks.

The dark-haired man put a finger to his lips, said quietly, "Not a word, not a whisper. Keep your hands by your side." He took a step toward Meyer. "Where's Erica Kranz? And where's Schmeltz?"

For a moment, Meyer hesitated. The man pointed the barrel of the weapon directly at his head.

Meyer's legs began to buckle as he swallowed. The man stepped closer, grazed the cold tip of the Kalashnikov against his forehead.

"Answer!"

"Inside the house."

"Your name?"

"Meyer."

The man with the Kalashnikov flicked a glance back toward the gray concrete building, light spilling out from the open steel door. "Move back inside."

Meyer hesitated, his mind in turmoil. He glanced at the second man; young, in his twenties, the light from the floodlamps overhead reflecting off his glasses. The noise of gunfire grew louder, and Meyer wondered why the others hadn't heard it and come out of the house.

The cold tip of the Kalashnikov's barrel pushed painfully hard into his head and Meyer faltered.

"Move or I blow your head off."

Anger in the man's eyes, a kind of madness, but controlled; he would squeeze the trigger, no question.

Meyer began to move into the building.

There was a faint noise from behind, and a split second later, Kruger came running out of the house, the Walther in his hand, a look of alarm on his face.

There was the briefest second of indecision as Kruger took in the scene before he raised the Walther in one swift movement.

Before Volkmann could swing the Kalashnikov around, the man fired wildly.

Meyer's body was punched back, and the Kalashnikov was wrenched from Volkmann's grasp as a bullet pierced his hand.

Bullets ripped through the frozen air, a scream from behind as Lubsch took the brunt of Kruger's fire, bullets cracking into concrete and flesh.

As Volkmann crouched and rolled to the right in the snow, he felt another round hammer into his right arm, glimpsed Kruger moving back frantically toward the house, still firing wildly.

Volkmann gripped the Kalashnikov in his left hand, brought it up and fired in one fluid movement just as Kruger reached the door.

As the Kalashnikov bucked wildly, the hail of bullets tore into Kruger's left side and he spun violently.

Volkmann squeezed the trigger again.

The second burst caught Kruger in the neck, almost decapitating him, and his body arched and fell.

The gunfire echoed and died.

Volkmann stood, suddenly aware of a numbing sensation in his arm as he stared down at his wounds. A bullet had pierced his right hand, exiting through the palm, and blood oozed from the gaping wound; a second bone-shattering wound just below the elbow, thick rivulets of warm, dark red trickling down under his sleeve. No pain, not yet, just a dull sensation, but terrible pain would come soon enough.

The bodies of Lubsch and Meyer lay on the snow. Meyer's eyes were open in death, and there was a gaping hole in Lubsch's face, his glasses lying in the white snow-powder.

From far below, Volkmann could hear the faint, drifting sounds of sustained gunfire—Lubsch's men, meeting stiff resistance by the sound of it, but it seemed far away, as if happening in another time, another place.

There was a timelessness to everything, but he was aware of the ticking seconds, aware of the pain now flooding into his arm and hand.

Suddenly he was plunged into darkness, every light extinguished. Volkmann stood there in the dark, feeling cold snow on his face, his heart pounding.

Seconds later, the area flooded with intense white light, blazing through the falling snow as the floodlamps came on again.

Hartig had cut the powerlines; the emergency generator was kicking in now.

The porch light of the house and the floodlights overhead flickered a couple of times, then came bright again as the generator settled.

Volkmann turned, looked back at the concrete building. The door was still open, but the inside was in darkness.

If Hartig was wrong . . .

The sound of gunfire rose, raging, eddying, dying, rising again.

Then suddenly, awesome silence seemed to fill the snowy darkness like a force as the firing died abruptly.

He turned back toward the house, light spilling out from the hallway, dropped the heavy Kalashnikov, fumbled as he wrenched the Beretta from his pocket with bloodied fingers, felt a sudden weakness engulf him, his mind fogging.

He closed his eyes as unspeakable pain began to flood into his wounds.

He opened his eyes again, inhaled a deep lungful of chilled air, tried desperately to remain conscious.

Volkmann crossed quickly to the door, past Kruger's body, and stepped into the house.

CHAPTER 53

A log fire blazing, French windows leading to a balcony. Salt-and-pepper darkness beyond, white flakes dashing against glass.

The man stood by the fire, a surprised look on his face, but no fear. Erica stood beside him. As Volkmann came into the room, she saw the Beretta, went to speak.

Volkmann said, "Nobody move."

He held the weapon at arm's length, took a deep breath, tried to take in the scene. Erica and the man, standing close together. The girl looked at him palely, shock on her face, and Volkmann felt the confusion. Blood draining from his shattered arm, senses blurring.

He stared over at the man. Fit-looking. Tanned skin, fine wrinkles around the soft eyes. Handsome. Silver hair. Schmeltz, no question.

Volkmann watched as the man's eyes flicked to the Beretta, then back at him.

Erica started to move toward him, and the man made no move to stop her.

"Joe . . ."

Volkmann swung the Beretta to point at her, said hoarsely, "I said nobody move. Just do as I say."

Erica froze, her face white.

Volkmann aimed at the man's head, gestured toward the table.

"Move away from the girl. Slowly."

Schmeltz hesitated, then did as he was told. The lights suddenly flickered overhead, then settled. Schmeltz glanced up for a moment.

Volkmann said, "Sit down. At the table. Keep your hands on top."

The man hesitated, then moved slowly to the table, placed his slim hands on the polished wood as he looked over at Volkmann impassively.

Schmeltz said calmly, "Who are you?"

"My name is Volkmann."

For several seconds Schmeltz stared at him. "Yes, Joseph. I know of you." The blue eyes becoming hard; then he looked toward the floor between Volkmann's feet.

Volkmann glanced down. Blood trickled onto the carpet. Red spots. His face burned.

He looked back up as the girl said, "Joe, listen to me, please."

Concern in her voice. Or was it his imagination? Volkmann felt his senses slipping away, his vision going. An unreality about the scene.

He blinked, tried to focus. Erica moved toward him again, slowly this time. He swung the Beretta around sharply. She hesitated, then stood still, stared at him in astonishment.

"I told you. Don't move. Don't speak."

Schmeltz said suddenly, "If you came here to stop us, you can't." He shook his head, the knowing eyes watching Volkmann. "You really can't stop us."

"Why not?"

"Our action has gone too far. If you kill me this moment, it would make no difference. Do you intend killing me, Joseph?"

Volkmann ignored the question, tried to keep his eyes focused, to fight the darkness threatening to engulf him as he stared down at the man.

"I've talked to people in Berlin. They are already moving to stop you."

Schmeltz looked toward the French windows. Snow dashing against glass. A look on his face as if nothing mattered. When he turned back, he shook his head slowly.

"It hardly matters. Dollman is already dead, believe me, Joseph."

"And the others?"

Schmeltz's eyes opened wide as he reacted to the words. His face turned pale as he glanced over at Erica, then back at Volkmann. When he spoke, his voice was almost a whisper.

"How did you know?"

"Just answer the question. What's going to happen to the Cabinet?"

"That doesn't matter now. It's too late to stop it, believe me."

Volkmann's finger tightened on the trigger. "It matters if you want to stay alive."

Schmeltz paused, as if considering. "You didn't come alone, did you?" He looked over at the telephone. "Your people cut the lines?"

Volkmann nodded faintly.

Schmeltz looked back. "That was stupid. The telephone would have been your only chance of warning Berlin."

Volkmann moved closer. The tip of the barrel touched Schmeltz's forehead. The man's head jerked back in alarm and his eyes opened wide in fear, but Volkmann kept up the pressure, pushing the Beretta hard into his flesh.

"Tell me, and tell me quickly. Or so help me, I'll squeeze the trigger."

Konrad Weber looked at the faces seated around the table in room 4-North.

In the harsh neon lights, every face looked like death.

The doors were locked and the meeting had begun. Weber was on his feet. He had spoken for almost a full two minutes uninterrupted, outlining the situation to the Cabinet of ministers. Now he paused for breath, saw the stunned looks on the faces around the table.

He carried on, addressing the seventeen men.

"Gentlemen, I have several proposals to counter this unprecedented emergency. Very firm action must be taken." Weber's voice was resolute.

"I hope to have your full cooperation in each and every one of these proposals. The president has been informed of the situation. Those senior officers in the army and police force whose loyalty we can absolutely depend on are already at their posts. All the forces at the disposal of the Republic are ready to act. Those responsible for these outrages must be swiftly dealt with. I need hardly remind you that all our lives may be in danger, not only the lives of the Republic's citizens."

Weber cleared his throat, saw heads nod in solemn agreement.

"First, a state of emergency will be immediately declared. Second, a decree for the protection of the people and the federal state will be enacted. It will dispense with all civic and constitutional rights until the state has been purged of those elements that threaten democracy. Third, I want every known neo-Nazi and every extremist, irrespective of political leanings, rounded up and interned at once. This will be coordinated with the Landesamt offices and the BfV.''

Weber paused, wiped the sweat from his brow with a handkerchief from his pocket. ''The problem of the missile is a grave and alarming one. As soon as Bauer and the BfV have more information on the organizers behind this outrage, we shall act immediately.''

Weber saw the deathly faces and frightened nods. He knew that the pressure and apprehension were telling on his face. In the silence that followed, he heard a faint ticking noise and looked down, alarmed. The sound grew louder. Weber looked up, realized the noise came from the electric clock on the wall, the second hand ticking away. He let out a small sigh, recognized his paranoia, looked at the faces at the table.

''Gentlemen,'' he said firmly, ''I must telephone the president out of protocol before we enact these proposals and any others we deem necessary. So let us proceed. Are we all agreed on these measures?''

Weber looked at the sober faces around the room and quickly asked each minister by name in turn, as protocol demanded.

Every one of them agreed.

Snow dashed in flurries against the French windows and the log fire crackled.

Volkmann kept the Beretta pointed at Schmeltz's head. He felt the faintness begin to sweep in again, the butt of the weapon sticky with red, blood dripping onto the floor. Eyes losing focus, images fading. He blinked, sucked air deep into his lungs, tried to clear his head. He heard Erica, panic in her voice, but she seemed to speak from far away.

''Joe . . . let me help you.''

If she came closer, she could distract him, allow Schmeltz to make a move. He forced himself to ignore the voice.

Suddenly a surge of pain flooded his entire body and he

faltered, slumped back in the chair. He snapped open his eyes, kept the pistol pointed at Schmeltz as she spoke again.

"Joe, please."

Volkmann said, without looking at her, "Stay where you are, Erica."

He saw Schmeltz lean forward in his chair, heard him speak softly.

"You'll bleed to death, Joseph. Listen to what she says."

"Just tell me what's going to happen."

"You're a remarkable man, do you know that?"

"Tell me."

"To have unraveled what is happening. To have found me. I admire your ability, your tenacity. Your courage." Schmeltz paused. "Your name is German, but you are not German, are you, Joseph? You're British."

"Tell me, Schmeltz. Whoever the hell you are."

"You know who I am, Joseph. Just as I know who you are. Just as I know about your father."

There was a flash of anger in Volkmann's face. He looked at Erica as she said, "Joe, he made me tell him everything."

He saw what looked like pain in her face.

Schmeltz leaned closer. "Forgive me. But I wanted to explain. The mistakes of the past won't be repeated. What happened to your father won't happen again, Joseph. Not ever."

"I don't believe that, Schmeltz. And neither do you. It may not happen to Jews, but it will happen to others. Your time's up. No more talk. Tell me what's going to happen in Berlin, or I kill you right now."

Schmeltz hesitated, looked toward the telephone, sat back in the chair, the soft blue eyes more confident.

"You have no way of stopping what is about to happen. No way of informing Berlin or the Cabinet."

"Tell me, *quickly*." Volkmann's finger tightened, went to squeeze. "TELL ME!"

Volkmann's scream rang around the room. Schmeltz's eyes dilated as he swallowed.

"The Cabinet is meeting in the Reichstag. Weber has assumed Dollman's position. He is proposing measures to stop what is happening. But the meeting is a charade."

"Why?"

"Because once Weber has made his proposals, he will excuse himself. Leave the room. Go to his office."

Schmeltz hesitated. Volkmann looked at his face, tightened his finger on the trigger again.

"Keep talking."

"Weber will have left his briefcase behind. When he reaches his office, he will detonate a device in the briefcase. A bomb will explode, killing only those inside the room where the Cabinet is meeting. The structure of the room makes it impossible for anyone to survive. The Cabinet will all be killed. Weber will have assumed complete control."

Schmeltz paused. There was a long silence, and Volkmann looked away, toward Erica.

There was a pleading look on her face, tears at the corners of her eyes.

His mind began to fog again, pain rolling in. He looked back at Schmeltz.

"And where do you figure in this?"

"Weber's position will be temporary." Schmeltz looked directly at the Beretta. "But my part is not important. Not now." His eyes shifted back to Volkmann. "Even if you kill me, it would make no difference. The seeds have been sown. There is no going back once the Cabinet members are dead. Only Weber can hold Germany together. Weber and others like him. Men and women who will uphold their fathers' testimony." Schmeltz leaned forward. "And they will do it, Joseph. Believe me, they will."

There was a hint of excitement in Schmeltz's voice. Volkmann stood up, Schmeltz's face clouding in front of him.

He looked away, tried to focus, couldn't. When he looked back, Schmeltz's features were a blur.

Volkmann flicked a look at Erica, her features hazy too, like seeing her through frosted glass. He filled his lungs with air, short deep bursts, blinked hard, cleared the fog. He tried to concentrate on Schmeltz's face.

"Not all Germans are Nazi supporters. Not all of them will support you."

"Enough will. You think we haven't planned this to the last detail?"

"How?"

"Weber will denounce the murders as a treasonable act by immigrant extremists to destabilize the Fatherland. There will be a surge of nationalist fervor that has not been seen in fifty years." Schmeltz paused, looked at him. "Listen to me, Joseph. Do as I say and you won't be harmed. You can walk away from here. You have my word. The Austrian border is—"

"Stand up."

Schmeltz stood up slowly, his tall frame towering above Volkmann, his eyes cautious. "What are you going to do?"

"It's what you're going to do. You and the girl are going to walk to the car outside. If any of your people are left to try and stop us, I'll put one in your head."

Schmeltz licked his lips nervously. "If you're trying to reach a telephone, you're wasting your time. And others will come here because they cannot get through on the line. You won't get far."

"Move."

As Volkmann flicked the Beretta, blood dripped onto the carpet from his wounds. He started to feel himself go under, gripped the back of the chair.

"Joe, for God's sake . . . you'll bleed to death."

Volkmann stared at Erica, saw the tears brimming over.

He didn't see Schmeltz's hand move until the last moment. It came up smartly and gripped the Beretta, twisted, pointed the weapon toward Volkmann.

Erica screamed.

As Schmeltz grasped the Beretta, Volkmann gripped the man's arm blindly with his good hand, clung to it, oblivious to pain. Schmeltz tried to wrench himself free. Volkmann pulled down hard, heard the sharp crack as the bone broke, heard Schmeltz scream in agony as he squeezed the trigger.

The weapon exploded.

The bullet tore into Erica's side and Volkmann watched with horror as she was slammed back against the wall.

As Schmeltz struggled to release himself, Volkmann pushed with all his weight into the man's body, both men tumbling back, shattering glass and wood as they crashed out through the French windows, the weapon flung from Schmeltz's grasp as they rolled across the breadth of the balcony, snow and shattered glass crunching under their entangled bodies.

Volkmann struck the concrete rail, the force knocking him breathless, Schmeltz's weight crushing into him a fraction of a second later.

Icy blasts of wind, flurrying snow.

Pain. Piercing cold.

As he struggled to move, Volkmann felt Schmeltz's weight come off him. He closed his eyes, opened them again; the image of Schmeltz swam before him, crawling back across the balcony, scrabbling wildly in the snow, breath rising in hot, panting bursts like an animal's.

Volkmann forced himself to stand, saw Schmeltz's hand reach out for something.

Volkmann lunged.

He landed on Schmeltz's back, and the man exhaled air like a bellows.

Volkmann clambered over him, fingers groping in the snow, eyes searching frantically for the weapon.

And then Schmeltz's arm came out of nowhere and his weight landed on Volkmann's back, knocking him breathless, arms locking around Volkmann's throat, strangling him, knuckles digging into his windpipe, crushing throat muscles.

Volkmann felt himself go under as he fought for breath, tried to grasp Schmeltz's arm, the effort painful, impossible.

Someone else was there. Volkmann turned his head and saw Erica, her side drenched with blood, her hands on Schmeltz, dragging him. Volkmann twisted his body, and with Erica's help, wrenched the other man up and off.

Schmeltz's body tumbled into snow.

Volkmann glimpsed the dark metal against white, a meter away, turned toward where the pistol lay, fingers scrabbling in the snow, cold, so cold, difficult to discern metal, difficult to move.

Please, God.

Something hard, still warm.

He found the handle of the weapon, gripped it in his left hand.

He turned, saw Schmeltz crawling back toward the balcony.

Volkmann held the pistol at arm's length, aimed at the back of Schmeltz's head, trying to judge distance, two meters, less.

"Stop." The words painful.

Schmeltz ignored the command, stood up, chest heaving as he fought for breath, blood streaming down his face from the shattered bridge of his nose, eyes wide and staring.

"I said stop."

Snow swirling. Silence except for the labored breathing of the three people on the balcony and the gusting flurries of snow.

"Listen to me, Joseph—"

Volkmann stood panting, looking into Schmeltz's face, fought the nausea sweeping over him.

He glanced at Erica. She was huddled against the rail, her face clenched with pain. The left side of her sweater and skirt were covered with blood. And a surge of anger gripped him.

And then there was a sudden throbbing of helicopter blades from somewhere in the swirl of snow above. Volkmann heard it and glanced up. The sound coming closer, coming in fast. More than one craft. Swishing of blades as they cut the icy air.

Bargel's people.

Or Schmeltz's.

Volkmann aimed the pistol at the center of Schmeltz's forehead.

Schmeltz's eyes opened wide.

Volkmann thought of the pictures hanging on white walls. A dead woman clutching the lifeless body of her child. The grinning SS man standing over her.

His father's pain.

Schmeltz's voice, coming to him faintly now.

"Joseph, listen."

Schmeltz moving closer.

Volkmann felt himself start to go under again, his eyes beginning to cloud. His body winding down, a terrible, excruciating wave of pain almost suffocating him. He grit his teeth, fought the pain. A chill went through him, making him shiver. He took a deep breath.

Let it out.

Slowly.

Schmeltz moved closer.

"Don't fucking move."

Schmeltz stopped.

Volkmann aimed between Schmeltz's eyes.

The dull, chopping noise of blades coming closer. Schmeltz's eyes flicked up to the swirling heavens, then came back to Volkmann.

Volkmann wanting to scream the words aloud, but instead, said them softly.

"They say every sin has its own avenging angel. Do you believe that?"

Volkmann looked at Schmeltz's face.

He didn't wait for the reply.

The Beretta exploded.

When he came to, he was lying on a stretcher.

He was aware of the ghostly swirl of flashing red and blue lights in the thinly falling snow; he heard the wailing sirens, and there was a harsh, metallic clatter of blades somewhere overhead. A babble of loud and desperate voices faded in and out, guttural orders being shouted and carried on the icy wind.

When he tried to look around, he saw ghostly figures in white Arctic fatigues appear out of nowhere, weapons at the ready, but then they began to blur and he lay back again.

A rugged-faced man in white fatigues and with a Heckler and Koch machine pistol draped around his neck loomed over him suddenly, looked down into his face.

He smiled briefly, and his hand touched Volkmann's shoulder as if to reassure him. Volkmann tried to speak, tried to tell him about Weber, tried to tell him to contact Berlin, tried to tell him about Erica, but the words would not come.

The man looked away. There was a voice, telling him something, then a burst of gunfire from somewhere out in the whiteness and the man turned away grimly, barked an order, and there was a rush of feet crunching on snow and he was gone.

And then all life seemed to go from Volkmann again. He saw only a hazy nimbus above, a feeling of lightness in his head, washing in on him, as moments later he felt the stretcher lifted, or so it seemed, and he was suspended in midair.

And then a wave of intense pain washed in and smothered him.

It took Konrad Weber three minutes to walk to his private office on the third floor of the Reichstag.

Werner Bargel and Axel Wiglinski accompanied him and his two bodyguards.

When they reached the vice-chancellor's office, Weber unlocked the door and stepped inside, then locked it again, leaving the four men outside in the hallway.

In the oak-paneled room, he crossed to his desk and sat down.

His hands were shaking as he opened the drawer and removed the remote-control transmitter, placed it in the palm of his left hand.

As he clenched the fingers of his free hand, he took a deep breath.

The portable buzzed in Werner Bargel's hand.

Bauer's voice, frantic. *"Where are you, Bargel?"*

"Outside the vice-chancellor's office."

"Jesus, Bargel, listen to me, for God's sake . . ."

Konrad Weber heard the frantic voices in the hallway, heard the crash of splintering wood as the door burst in, saw the Sig and Sauer pistol in Bargel's hand.

As Bargel raised the pistol to aim, Weber touched the button.

The distant explosion, when it came a split second later, cracked through the Reichstag like a clap of thunder.

EPILOGUE

Volkmann came awake in the private ward in Munich General Hospital a little after 10:00 A.M. two days later.

He heard a radio on somewhere, music beyond the closed door. "Tannenbaum." The carol that had always made his father cry, and he wanted to cry too, not because of the music, but because he was breathing, alive.

He was connected to tubes, and there were probes wired to his arms and chest and linked to a machine, his heart beating in tandem with white blips on a green screen. He touched the cotton dressing on his numbed right hand, the hard bond of white plaster around his right arm.

Werner Bargel was seated at the end of the bed. A nurse appeared out of nowhere and then there was a sudden rush of activity.

He heard Bargel's voice.

"How do you feel?"

His lips stuck together; it was an effort to part them.

"Lousy."

It was another twenty minutes before Bargel spoke again, not until after the doctors had been called and examined him, after the nurse had attended him, proffering sips of cold water to wet his cracked, parched lips. A couple of yellow pills to swallow. A damp cotton cloth dabbed on his face and neck. Refreshing. Cool.

He saw Bargel talk with the doctors out of hearing range, and then the room emptied, the door closed, and he and Bargel were alone.

Bargel sat in the chair beside the bed.

"The doctors assure me you'll make a speedy recovery. But for a while there, it was touch and go. You'd lost a lot of blood. You put more stress on your body than it was designed to take."

Volkmann raised himself, then slumped back in pain. The throbbing in his right temple became a blinding ache.

"Take it easy, Joe. They've given you something to ease the pain, so it should take effect soon."

Volkmann said, "Erica . . . ?"

Bargel sat forward. "She's in a private room a floor below us. The medical team got to her in time. Don't worry, Joe, she's going to be all right.''

He saw Bargel smile faintly and he turned his head, tried to take in the room, but there was a fuzzy quality to everything. He looked back slowly.

Bargel said, ''God knows all she thought when you staggered into the room up on the mountain, but I suspect she was glad to see you.'' He smiled. ''And she was worried sick for you . . . you were a bloody mess. It was a miracle that you stayed conscious. And then when you waved her off when she tried to help, she thought you must have gone out of your mind.''

''I wasn't thinking clearly,'' Volkmann admitted.

''As for her,'' Bargel continued, ''the poor girl went through an ordeal of her own. They'd pumped her full of that truth drug, scopolamine, to make her talk . . .'' He leaned closer to Volkmann. ''A terrific lady, Joe. But I suppose you know that.''

Volkmann nodded. ''Did she tell you that she saved my life?''

''No, she didn't.''

Volkmann explained.

''As I said, a terrific lady,'' Bargel said.

''She told you about Schmeltz?'' Volkmann asked then, changing the subject.

Bargel nodded, his face pale and serious. ''She told us everything she knew. The rest we were able to piece together.''

''How long have I been unconscious?''

''Two days.''

''Tell me what happened.''

It took ten minutes to explain. Dollman and the Cabinet were dead, except for Weber, who was in a high-security cell in Moabit Prison. During the confusion in Berlin, Bargel explained, Weber ordered Bauer not to take action against the Kaalberg. But fortunately, when he gave the order, Bargel had already set the action in motion. The president had taken over the duties of chancellor and a caretaker government had been formed. They had found a list of conspirators in the safe in Grinzing's study. These people were now keeping Weber company in Moabit. All known extremist neo-Nazis and their supporters had been arrested. In addition to Lubsch himself, one of the men with him had been killed in the assault; the others had escaped into the mountains before the all-weather choppers had landed.

When he mentioned Ivan Molke, Bargel saw the look of pain on Volkmann's face.

"Ivan was a good man, Joe. And a good German."

Volkmann looked away, toward the white wall. Bargel's voice brought him back.

"And so was Lubsch," he went on, "in his way. What he and his friends did for you—for all of us—was heroic. It was splendid. It gives me some faith in the future of this country."

Bargel leaned forward. "When the girl told me about Schmeltz, at first I didn't believe her. It sounded so damned crazy. I thought she had cracked after her ordeal. It sounded so impossible."

"What made you believe her?"

"One of the people on Grinzing's list talked. An army officer named Braun. Everything you deduced, everything Erica told us, it's true. Geli Raubal had a son. The Schmeltz couple took him to South America in nineteen thirty-one. He lived with them as their child until *Die Spinne* took over as his protector."

"What about the body?"

"It's been disposed of, secretly."

"Where?"

Bargel shook his head. "Even I can't tell you that, Joe." Bargel paused. "The army's on the streets, restoring order. Most people don't know what the hell's happened. There's been a newspaper blackout until things are completely under control. This country came close to stepping back over fifty years. The measures we've taken are extreme, but we want to make certain there's no chance that the past will be repeated."

Volkmann looked away toward the window, then back at Bargel. "There's something I don't understand. Erica's father was Leibstandarte SS. Why wasn't she contacted like the others?"

Bargel nodded. "She was on their list all right. But it

was quite a list and she was only one of many. From what we can gather, Winter himself was responsible for making an approach to her not long before he was murdered. But he didn't make her a priority. Maybe he thought she wasn't important enough. Or because he had known her personally at Heidelberg, he knew she wouldn't be the kind to help. Besides, Winter himself had become disaffected long before his own people decided to get rid of him. He'd have known that Erica would have been killed if she had refused to cooperate.'' Bargel shrugged. ''Whatever reason Winter had, it probably saved her life.''

Bargel saw the strain on Volkmann's face and stood. ''We'll talk again, Joe. For now, get some rest. I owe you a great debt of gratitude. Not only me, but the country. I just want you to know that.''

Bargel crossed to the door and smiled over at Volkmann. ''I'll tell her you're awake. She's anxious to talk with you.''

The snow had started to fall as they traveled in the taxi from Heathrow, but by the time they had reached the neat square of Victorian houses, it had stopped.

Everywhere white, deserted. New Year's Eve.

The flight from Frankfurt had been delayed and he had telephoned from the airport, told his mother he was coming, heard the surprise in her voice, saying how good it was to hear from him.

When he told her about the girl staying for a few days, he recognized the excitement in her voice, like the young woman on the beach in Cornwall he always remembered, with her hair tied back, the smile on her lips, and the aura of happiness that made him know why his father had married her.

It was four o'clock in the afternoon when the taxi pulled up at the top of the square. Darkness was falling, the gates of the tiny park were open, branches heavy with snow, here and there erratic footprints where a child had strayed and an adult followed. But no one there now. Empty.

He led Erica in through the park gates, placed the two overnight bags beside the bench, brushed away snow. As she sat beside him, across the white wasteland and through the trees he could see the house, lights on already, a plume of gray smoke rising faintly from the chimney.

There were lights on in other houses too. Candles burning, Christmas trees winking in the twilight through fogged windows, the vestige of Christmas. Another eight hours and a new year.

A pigeon cooed in the branches above. A fir tree rustled. The sound of beating wings.

Erica asked, "Which house is yours? You never told me which one."

Volkmann pointed to the red-bricked house, and she studied it for a long time.

"It suits you."

"How?"

She smiled. "Solid. A little old-fashioned. But dependable."

He smiled back and Erica looked about the park.

"This is where you played when you were a boy?"

"Yes."

She closed her eyes and said, "I can picture you, you know. From the photograph I saw in your apartment."

"Tell me what you picture."

"A boy who is quiet and very serious. A loner, but curious. And a boy who loved his father and mother very much."

"You see all that?"

She smiled again. "It's what I picture." She opened her eyes, brushed a strand of blond hair from her face, looked across at him. At the handsome face she wanted to touch as he looked silently about the snowy landscape.

She said, as if reading his thoughts, "This place is special for you, isn't it, Joe?"

"I used to come here with my father."

He felt the touch of her hand, the silky warmth of her fingers twining through his. Comforting. He wondered how he had ever doubted her.

She said, "His pain has been repaid now. And the pain of all the others who suffered."

"You believe that?"

"Yes, I believe it. Because you stopped it from happening all over again. And now you can bury your father's pain.''

Volkmann looked at her face. He took her hand in his, brought it to his lips, kissed the cold fingertips. Then he stood up slowly, looked about the park.

"I'd like to believe that," he said.

Through the trees, he could see the house. His mother would be waiting.

He looked down at the blue eyes watching him.

"Come. She's expecting us. And I'd very much like you to meet her."

Volkmann picked up the overnight bags and they started to walk back across the park toward the row of red-bricked houses.

The suite on the top floor of the Hilton Hotel had a clear view to the mountains beyond the city. It was a cold, clear New Year's Day in Madrid and both men sat by the window. There were no buildings overlooking this side of the hotel and the men had taken all the necessary precautions before their arrival.

The younger of the two was in his early thirties, lean and fit looking. His briefcase was open and a sheaf of papers lay on the coffee table in front of him.

The second man was in his early fifties. His tanned face looked haggard and tired after almost two days without sleep. The hotel computer recorded his name as Federico Ramirez but the man had changed passports and tickets twice in the last twenty-four hours during his connections from Asunción.

He wasted no time on small-talk nor did he offer his young visitor a drink.

"The number of arrests and detentions, you have the latest figures?"

The younger man glanced briefly at his notes before speaking. "We estimate twenty-three thousand, as of midnight last night."

The face of the older man betrayed no emotion at the figures and his visitor carried on talking.

"But the situation is still fluid and the figures may increase. By how much we don't know. Apart from those on the list, the authorities are simply pulling in those with a strong past record of support, so it's likely they'll be released if charges can't be pressed.''

The gray-haired man said impatiently, "And the cells, how are they holding up?''

"In the eastern region, they remain pretty much intact. The other three points of the compass are the ones really affected. But the damage isn't that great. We've been relatively lucky.''

The gray-haired man stood up and said sharply, "Lucky? What happened, Raul? How the hell did it go wrong? We were that close.'' The older man held up two fingers, the tips close together.

The younger man sighed and looked at his superior. "You got the preliminary report in Asunción. I'm afraid it's the best we can do for now. Over the next few days we ought to have a clearer picture. Certainly the man and the woman, Volkmann and Kranz, were largely responsible.''

The young man paused, then leaned forward. "But something positive has actually come out of this. Something that wasn't in the report you got. I wanted to tell you personally.''

"What, for God's sake?''

"Many of the rank supporters didn't really believe we would attempt what we did. Now that they've seen it can happen, they're more determined than ever to carry on.'' The young man leaned forward more eagerly. "We were unsuccessful this time, but when it happens next time we'll be even more prepared. We'll have learned from our mistakes. You know the Western democracies can't sustain their problems. Immigration. Unemployment. Recession. They're already crumbling. It's only a question of time before we try again.''

"What's the estimate?''

The young man shook his head. "I can't give you a definite answer on that. Not just now. But in the meantime we continue to try and strengthen our position.''

"I can confirm that to Asunción?''

"Absolutely. You know we have the resources. It's really only a question of time.''

The gray-haired man sat down and lit a cigarette. "Do we know what's happened to Schmeltz's body . . . ?"

"Five days ago it was cremated. And buried in a forest near the Polish border."

The gray-haired man sighed and shook his head. "The man and the girl, Volkmann and Kranz, how did they find out?"

"A photograph they found at the Chaco house of Geli Raubal. That was the clue they worked from. That and the journalist's death." The young man looked across at his superior. "You want us to take care of them?"

The gray-haired man thought a moment, then shook his head. "Not right now, Raul. But later, I promise you, they'll pay the price."

The gray-haired man looked at his watch and then his visitor. "You're flying back to Germany this afternoon?"

The young man shook his head. "I have a meeting with our friends in Paris first. Their immigrant problem's getting worse. They're interested to hear our damage reports and our future intentions for co-operation. The same with our contacts in Rome. Hass is already on his way there. And you?"

"London tonight. Then Asunción, via Rio."

The young man looked at him. "They've got the preliminary report, but impress on them we still go ahead with our plans. Assure them of our determination, sir."

"The older man placed a hand on his visitor's shoulder. "I'll let them know, don't worry, Raul. And thanks for coming."

The young man picked up his briefcase and replaced his papers and clicked shut the security lock and thumbed the numbers. He picked up his overcoat and the gray-haired man led him to the door.

They shook hands firmly and the young man checked the corridor before stepping out.

He had pressed the button for the lift and the doors had already opened when he heard the gray-haired man call after him.

"And Raul. . . "

"Yes?"

"I almost forgot. Happy New Year."

"The same to you, sir."

AFTERWORD

In the winter of 1941, ten years after Geli Raubal was found dead in her uncle's Munich apartment, the Nazi authorities in Vienna issued a secret instruction that the girl's grave and those around it in the Vienna Central Cemetery were to be completely destroyed. No reasons were given and the order was carried out.

To this day, Plot 23e is an unused expanse of green in the midst of a cluttered maze of family vaults and graves in the old cemetery. Whether the remains of Geli Raubal are still buried there is a mystery. There have been numerous and recent attempts to have the remains found and exhumed, but the Viennese authorities have consistently delayed granting permission, thus prolonging the mystery.

In the months and years after the girl's ''suicide,'' several people claimed to know the truth behind her death, a ''secret'' that had ultimately led to her murder.

All died violent deaths, including the journalist, Fritz Gerlich, mentioned briefly in this book.

But what was the ''secret''?

There are clues.

In late 1931, one month after Geli Raubal's death, Erhard Johann Sebastian Schmeltz, a fervent Nazi and a close friend of Adolf Hitler's, disappeared mysteriously from his home in Munich, along with his sister. The couple was never seen again in Germany.

Seventeen years later, and over two years after the war had ended, a former Waffen SS officer, wanted by the then American CIC for his involvement in the disappearance of a quantity of Nazi gold bullion and for secretly transporting it to South America, wrote to a friend in Munich from his new home in Asunción, Paraguay. In his letter he said that he had been shocked to come across the sister of an old friend from before the war; the woman was now living in a remote town in a region north of the Paraguayan capital.

The friend's name was given as Erhard Schmeltz.

Accompanying Schmeltz's elderly unmarried sister, the writer noted with some surprise, was a pensive, dark-haired youth no more than seventeen.

It is 1953. Joseph Stalin, the world's most tyrannical dictator, is teetering on the edge of insanity, and about to plunge the world into nuclear chaos. Only one man and one woman can penetrate the Iron Curtain and stop this madman, before it's too late.

But someone inside the Kremlin knows. And as the KGB's deadliest manhunter pursues these two CIA-hired assassins, another duel unfolds, between secret warriors of the West and East, with a U.S. agent caught in between. Now that agent must do the unthinkable: find his way to the heart of the Soviet Union and stop the mission he himself set in motion—before it ignites World War III.

SNOW WOLF

The International Bestseller from

Glenn Meade

"A riveting thriller in the tradition of <u>The Day of the Jackal</u>... A white knuckler!"——<u>Washington Post Book World</u>